Praise for the novels of
#1 *New York Times* bestselling author
Debbie Macomber

"Macomber is a skilled storyteller."

—*Publishers Weekly*

"It's easy to see why Macomber is a perennial favorite: she writes great books."

—*RomanceJunkies.com*

"Debbie Macomber writes characters who are as warm and funny as your best friends."

—*New York Times* bestselling author Susan Wiggs

"Macomber's storytelling sometimes yields a tear, at other times a smile."

—*Daily Press*, Newport News, VA

"[Debbie Macomber] demonstrates her impressive skills with characterization and her flair for humor."

—*RT Book Reviews*

"When God created Eve, he must have asked Debbie Macomber for advice because no one does female characters any better than this author."

—*Bookbrowser Reviews*

"Debbie Macomber is one of the most reliable, versatile romance authors around. Whether she's writing lighthearted romps or more serious relationship books, her novels are always engaging stories that accurately capture the foibles of real-life men and women with warmth and humor."

—*Milwaukee Journal Sentinel*

"Popular romance author Debbie Macomber has a gift for evoking the emotions that are at the heart of the genre's popularity."

—*Publishers Weekly*

March 2015

Dear Friends,

As a kid, one of my favorite pastimes was playing make-believe. I'd line up my dolls and tell them stories that generally started with "Once upon a time..." Later, paper dolls played a large role in forging my romantic imagination. I've always loved fairy tales and in my own make-believe world, there was usually a prince involved. Fast forward...and the game of make-believe transitioned into the written word. And why *not* a prince?

The Bachelor Prince and *Yesterday's Hero* are among my favorite early stories, written as they were in 1994 and 1986 respectively. They're filled with romance, adventure and (of course) make-believe. In reading them over and tweaking a little here and there to update them, I was pleased at what fun reads they turned out to be. My sincere wish is that you feel the same way.

And so, my friends, join the bachelor prince as his search for a wife—which he undertakes to meet family obligations—clashes with true love. And in *Yesterday's Hero*, two professionals are forced into a marriage of convenience that becomes something much deeper and richer when they discover...oops, I'm getting ahead of myself. I tend to do that. I always want to give away the best parts of the book in my letter to the reader. Difficult as it is, I'll resist and let you discover the fun and the make-believe on your own.

My readers have been the guiding force of my career. I consider your feedback invaluable. You can reach me at DebbieMacomber.com or on Facebook. Or you can write me at PO Box 1458, Port Orchard, WA 98366.

Warmest regards,

Debbie Macomber

DEBBIE MACOMBER

A Real Prince

MIRA

MIRA®

Recycling programs for this product may not exist in your area.

ISBN-13: 978-0-7783-1551-3

A Real Prince

Copyright © 2015 by Harlequin Books S.A.

The publisher acknowledges the copyright holder of the individual works as follows:

The Bachelor Prince
Copyright © 1994 by Debbie Macomber

Yesterday's Hero
Copyright © 1986 by Debbie Macomber

For questions and comments about the quality of this book, please contact us at CustomerService@Harlequin.com.

www.MIRABooks.com

Printed in U.S.A.

Also by Debbie Macomber

Blossom Street Books

The Shop on Blossom Street
A Good Yarn
Susannah's Garden
Back on Blossom Street
Twenty Wishes
Summer on Blossom Street
Hannah's List
The Knitting Diaries
  "The Twenty-First Wish"
A Turn in the Road

Cedar Cove Books

16 Lighthouse Road
204 Rosewood Lane
311 Pelican Court
44 Cranberry Point
50 Harbor Street
6 Rainier Drive
74 Seaside Avenue
8 Sandpiper Way
92 Pacific Boulevard
1022 Evergreen Place
Christmas in Cedar Cove
  (*5-B Poppy Lane* and
  A Cedar Cove Christmas)
1105 Yakima Street
1225 Christmas Tree Lane

Dakota Series

Dakota Born
Dakota Home
Always Dakota
Buffalo Valley

The Manning Family

The Manning Sisters
The Manning Brides
The Manning Grooms

Christmas Books

A Gift to Last
On a Snowy Night
Home for the Holidays
Glad Tidings
Christmas Wishes
Small Town Christmas
When Christmas Comes
  (now retitled *Trading*
  Christmas)
There's Something About
  Christmas
Christmas Letters
Where Angels Go
The Perfect Christmas
Call Me Mrs. Miracle
Choir of Angels
  (*Shirley, Goodness and Mercy,*
  Those Christmas Angels and
  Where Angels Go)
5-B Poppy Lane in
  Together for Christmas (with
  Brenda Novak, Sheila Roberts
  and RaeAnne Thayne)

Heart of Texas Series

VOLUME 1
  (*Lonesome Cowboy* and
  Texas Two-Step)
VOLUME 2
  (*Caroline's Child* and
  Dr. Texas)
VOLUME 3
  (*Nell's Cowboy* and
  Lone Star Baby)
Promise, Texas
Return to Promise

Midnight Sons

VOLUME 1
(*Brides for Brothers* and
  The Marriage Risk)
VOLUME 2
(*Daddy's Little Helper* and
  Because of the Baby)
VOLUME 3
(*Falling for Him,*
  Ending in Marriage and
  Midnight Sons and Daughters)

This Matter of Marriage
Montana
Thursdays at Eight
Between Friends
Changing Habits
Married in Seattle
  (*First Comes Marriage* and
  Wanted: Perfect Partner)
Right Next Door
  (*Father's Day* and
  The Courtship of Carol Sommars)
Wyoming Brides
  (*Denim and Diamonds* and
  The Wyoming Kid)
Fairy Tale Weddings
  (*Cindy and the Prince* and
  Some Kind of Wonderful)
The Man You'll Marry
  (*The First Man You Meet* and
  The Man You'll Marry)
Orchard Valley Grooms
  (*Valerie* and *Stephanie*)
Orchard Valley Brides
  (*Norah* and *Lone Star Lovin'*)
The Sooner the Better
An Engagement in Seattle
  (*Groom Wanted* and
  Bride Wanted)
Out of the Rain
  (*Marriage Wanted* and
  Laughter in the Rain)

Learning to Love
  (*Sugar and Spice* and
  Love by Degree)
You...Again
  (*Baby Blessed* and
  Yesterday Once More)
Three Brides, No Groom
The Unexpected Husband
  (*Jury of His Peers* and
  Any Sunday)
Love in Plain Sight
  (*Love 'n' Marriage* and
  Almost an Angel)
I Left My Heart
  (*A Friend or Two* and
  No Competition)
Marriage Between Friends
  (*White Lace and Promises* and
  Friends—And Then Some)
A Man's Heart
  (*The Way to a Man's Heart*
  and *Hasty Wedding*)
North to Alaska
  (*That Wintry Feeling* and
  Borrowed Dreams)
On a Clear Day
  (*Starlight* and
  Promise Me Forever)
To Love and Protect
  (*Shadow Chasing* and
  For All My Tomorrows)
Home in Seattle
  (*The Playboy and the Widow*
  and *Fallen Angel*)
Together Again
  (*The Trouble with Caasi* and
  Reflections of Yesterday)
The Reluctant Groom (*All Things
  Considered* and *Almost Paradise*)

Debbie Macomber's
  Cedar Cove Cookbook
Debbie Macomber's
  Christmas Cookbook

CONTENTS

To Lillian Shauer, quilter, wine connoisseur and dear friend.

THE BACHELOR PRINCE

Prologue

Prince Stefano Giorgio Paolo needed a wife. A very rich one. And soon.

He couldn't put off the inevitability of marriage any longer, not if he planned to save his country from the international embarrassment of bankruptcy.

Tightly clenching the Minister of Finance's latest report, he paced the royal office, his mind racing as he trod past the series of six-foot sandstone windows adorned with heavy red draperies.

The view of the courtyard with the huge stone fountain, which dated from the seventeenth century, escaped his attention. At one time the scene below would have given him great joy. But no longer. Now it brought a heaviness to his chest. All because the courtyard was empty of tourists.

San Lorenzo, a tiny European principality, had once thrived as a fairy-tale kingdom, and drawn hordes of sightseers from all across the globe. But with the civil unrest in the Balkan states so close to its borders, the tourists stayed away.

It didn't help that San Lorenzo had no international airport of its own and the closest one was now closed to commercial traffic because of the fighting.

A knock against the heavy oak door distracted him. "Yes," Stefano blurted out impatiently. He'd left word he wasn't to be disturbed. Only a fool would dare interrupt him.

His personal secretary and traveling companion, Pietro, stepped inside the room. Stefano amended his earlier thought. Only a fool *or a friend* would dare intrude on him now.

"I thought you might need this," Pietro said, carrying in an elaborate silver tray with two glasses and a cut-crystal decanter.

"You know I don't drink during the day," Stefano chastised, but without any real censure.

"Generally that's true," Pietro agreed, "but I also know you're thinking about marriage, and the subject, as always, depresses you."

"Once again you're right, my friend." His shoulders sagging, Stefano rubbed a hand over his face and stared out the window at his small kingdom.

"Have you made your decision?" Pietro asked, lifting the stopper from the decanter and splashing two fingers into the glasses. He handed the first to Stefano, who gratefully accepted it.

"Do I have any choice, but to marry?" He felt as if he were sentencing himself to the gallows. He savored his life as a bachelor, and the freedom it offered him to sample the favors of some of the world's most beautiful women.

Frankly, he enjoyed the title of the Bachelor Prince that the tabloids had bestowed on him. The papers, if they were to be believed, claimed he was the perfect romantic prince. They touted him as tall, dark and handsome, with enough charm to sink a flotilla.

It was true he was tall—six foot two—and his skin was tanned a healthy shade of bronze from the many hours he spent out-of-doors. The handsome part, he took with a grain of salt. His features were aristocratic, he supposed. His forehead was high and his chin stately, but then his family had reigned over San Lorenzo for nearly seven hundred years.

"Have you decided upon the lucky lady?" Pietro asked in that casual way of his that made Stefano's most troublesome worries appear minimal.

Frowning, Stefano thought for a moment, one hand clenched behind his back. "No." He gestured with his drink toward his friend. "I prefer to marry an American," he decided suddenly.

"Having attended Duke University, you're well acquainted with their ways. American women can be most charming."

Stefano slapped his drink down on the desk. "I don't need charm, I need money."

"Trust me, Stefano, I know that." Pietro reached inside his perfectly tailored black suit and withdrew a piece of paper. "I've taken the liberty of listing several eligible American women for your consideration."

Stefano paused and steadily regarded his friend. Oftentimes he wondered if Pietro could read his mind. "How well you know me."

Pietro bowed slightly. "It was a lucky guess."

Stefano laughed, doubting that. Pietro was much too thorough to leave anything to guesswork. In some ways his secretary knew him better than he did himself.

Like a spoiled child, Stefano had put off dealing with the unpleasantness of his situation. He sat down and rested against the back of the plush velvet chair. "Tell me what you've learned."

"There are a number of excellent young women from whom to choose," Pietro began.

For the next half hour, his secretary provided him with a list of names and the information he'd collected on each woman. There wasn't one who even mildly captured Stefano's curiosity. Perhaps Stefano was just old-fashioned enough to believe in marrying for love. When it came to choosing a wife, he would have preferred to cherish his bride with all his heart and soul, without an eye on her purse strings. But courtly ideals weren't going to save San Lorenzo.

"Well?" Pietro asked, when he'd finished.

Stefano gestured weakly with his hand. "You choose."

Pietro's eyebrows arched. "As you wish."

His companion ran his index finger down the list, pausing at one name and then another. His frown grew darker. Gauging from his reaction, Pietro was having as difficult time choosing as Stefano.

"Priscilla Rutherford," Pietro announced thoughtfully.

"Priscilla," Stefano repeated, attempting to remember what he could about the woman. "The shipping magnate's daughter?"

"She's the one." Having made his decision, Pietro relaxed and sampled the first taste of his drink.

"Why her?"

Pietro shrugged. "I'm not sure. I've seen her picture."

"She's beautiful?"

It took Pietro a moment to respond. "Yes."

"You don't sound convinced."

One side of Pietro's mouth quirked upward. "She's not a flawless beauty, if that's what you want, but she's a gentle, kind woman all San Lorenzo will love."

"Do you have as much faith she'll fall in love with me?" Stefano asked.

"But, of course." Pietro crossed to the other side of the room and pulled open a drawer. "I've even come up with a way for the two of you to meet."

Stefano slowly shook his head. "You never cease to amaze me, my friend."

"Do you remember the letter we received last week from Ms. Marshall from Seattle?"

"Marshall, Marshall," Stefano repeated, running the name through his memory. "Wasn't she the one who wrote to invite me as her guest of honor to some kind of conference? Some group, something nonsensical… I don't recall what—only that I'd rather be shot than attend."

"She's the one, and it was a Romance Lovers' Convention."

"I sincerely hope you declined," Stefano said with an elongated sigh. "For the love of heaven, I have no time for such nonsense." Romance had no place in the life of a man who was forced to marry for money.

"Fortunately, I haven't responded one way or the other."

"Fortunately?" Stefano eyed his companion wearily.

"I have it on good authority that Priscilla Rutherford will be attending the convention. It would be the ideal way of casually meeting her."

Stefano resumed his pacing, circling his desk a number of times, his hands clasped behind his back. "You can't be serious? The Marshall woman had come up with some ridiculous idea of raffling off a date with me. Dear sweet heaven, Pietro, has it come to this?"

"This conference can help you achieve your goal."

Stefano's gaze narrowed. Surely his friend wasn't serious. He had no desire to stand on the auction block and be awarded to the highest bidder.

"The Romance Lovers' get-together offers you the

perfect opportunity to meet Priscilla Rutherford," Pietro reiterated.

"You're serious?"

"Yes, Your Highness, I am."

It was the reference to his title that told him exactly how sincere Pietro was. "See to the arrangements, then," Stefano murmured. This had to be the low point of his life. He was about to become a sideshow at the circus, but if that was what it took to save his country, then Stefano would gladly sacrifice his considerable pride.

Chapter 1

"The phone's for you."

Hope Jordan glanced irritably toward the wall of her minute coffee shop on Seattle's Fifth Avenue and dragged her wet hands across the white butcher's apron tied about her waist. She hurried toward the phone and reached for the receiver.

"Hello, Mom," she said, not waiting for her mother to announce herself.

"How'd you know it was me?" Doris Jordan asked, her voice revealing her surprise.

"Because no one else phones me when I'm this busy."

"I'm sorry, sweetheart," her mother said, not sounding the least bit contrite, "but you work too hard as it is."

"Mom, unless this is really important, I have to get

off the phone. I've got three runners waiting for orders."
Hope smiled apologetically toward the trio.

"You'll phone me back?"

"Yes…I promise. But sometime this afternoon, all right?"

"Sure. It's important, Hope. I'll give you the details later, but I want you to know that I've invested twenty-five dollars in tickets to win a date with Prince Stefano Giorgio Paolo of San Lorenzo."

Hope's head bobbed with each one of his names. She'd recently read a lengthy article about Prince Stefano, and his beautiful country. "You want to date someone young enough to be your son?"

"No," Doris said with an impatient sigh. "I bought the tickets for *you*."

"Mom…"

The line went abruptly dead. Hope stared at the phone for several seconds before replacing the receiver. Her mother was bound and determined to see her married, but buying her raffle tickets for a date was "one step over the line" of what Hope found acceptable.

Not that it would do her any good to argue. Her mother wanted her married. The wedding itself wasn't the important point. Grandchildren were. Her mother's three closest friends were all grandmothers. It had become a matter of social status for Doris to see Hope married and pregnant. In that order, of course. And if Hope needed a bit of encouragement along the way, well, Doris was more than happy to supply it. Unfortunately, her means of nudging Hope toward marital bliss bordered on meddling into her already-complicated life.

"We're ready anytime you are," Jimmy, the lovable nineteen-year-old college student, said with a mildly sarcastic smile.

"All right, all right," Hope muttered, lifting the thick paper cups holding a variety of coffees and carrying them from the counter to the waiting trays.

"The idea is to deliver them while they're hot," Jimmy reminded her.

Hope poked his ribs with the sharp end of her elbow.

"Hey," Jimmy protested, "what was that for?"

"Just a little incentive to get you to move faster," she said, grinning broadly.

"I'm outta here."

"That's the idea, Jimmy, my boy." She laughed as he rushed out the back door toward the Federal Building, where the majority of his thirsty clients waited.

When this last batch of runners was out the door, Hope brewed herself a latte and slumped into a chair. The morning rush was a killer.

Coffee Break, Incorporated, had been an idea whose time had come, if sales these past few months were any indication. Hope had started the business with a staff of three who made daily exotic coffee and latte deliveries to the office buildings around Seattle's thriving downtown area.

Soon she'd added a variety of low-fat muffins and other products to the menu and expanded to fifteen runners, who serviced a number of businesses each morning and midafternoon.

"What's wrong?" Lindy, the woman who baked the world's greatest muffins, asked as she pulled out a chair and plopped herself down next to Hope.

Hope flip-flopped her hand, too tired to complain. "My mother's up to her old tricks."

"Has she found another matchmaker?"

Hope was tempted to smile at the memory. Unfortunately, the woman at the matchmaking service hadn't completely understood that the men Doris wanted were meant for her daughter. Consequently Hope had been matched with a man sixty-three years old. Doris had been outraged and demanded her money back. But in the end, it had worked out for the best. The gentleman had taken a fancy to Doris and the two had dined together several times over the winter months.

"That was the last time," Hope said.

"Did she arrange another date for you with her doctor's nephew?"

Despite her fatigue, Hope was tempted to laugh outright this time. "That mistake isn't likely to be repeated, either." Her dear, sweet, matchmaking mother had learned a lesson with that fiasco. Doris had insisted Hope meet Arnold Something-or-other. A doctor's nephew was sure to be a real catch, the perfect husband for her stubborn daughter.

Fool that she was, Hope had agreed to the blind date because her mother had been so excited. Doris had made it sound as if she'd miraculously stumbled upon the perfect man for Hope. If she agreed to just one date, then Hope would realize it herself.

Unfortunately, Arnold was a kleptomaniac and was wanted by the authorities for questioning in three different states. The date had been a nightmare from beginning to end. The moment they sat down in the restaurant, Arnold started lining his pockets with pink packages of artificial sweetener. Hope could see this man was no prince.

"Mom's on a different kick this time," Hope said, musing that her mother was determined to find her a prince, only this time it was for real.

Lindy handed her a fresh applesauce-and-raisin muffin still warm from the oven. "What's she up to now?"

"I'm not entirely sure," Hope said, lifting her tired feet from the floor and securing them on the seat of the chair across from her. "It was something ridiculous about buying raffle tickets for a date with a prince."

"Hey," Lindy said, taking notice, "I read about that. It's part of the Madeline Marshall Romance Lovers' Convention that's going on at the Convention Center next week."

"The what?" Hope brushed a stray strand of blond hair from her forehead.

"Come on, Hope, you must have heard about the conference. The newspeople have been having a heyday with this all week. It starts Thursday evening with a fancy cocktail party. Romance writers from all over the world are flying in to meet their fans. Why, it's the biggest thing to hit Seattle since the World's Fair."

"You've got to be joking."

"I'm not. Romance novels are big business. Bigger than the man on the street realizes."

"Are you telling me that you read romances?" Hope asked. Lindy? Her down-to-earth baker? It didn't gel.

"Of course I do. You mean you don't?"

"Heavens, no," Hope said, shaking her head. "I don't have time to read anything right now." The demands of her business left little time for leisure activities.

"Then you're missing out, girl. Everyone needs to kick off their shoes and escape from the harsh realities of the world every now and again."

"But romance novels?" Her mother had been hooked on the books for years, reading them for therapy after Hope's father had passed away. Although Doris had brought several of her favorite novels to her daughter, Hope had never taken the time to read one. Most of her reading material consisted of magazine articles and nonfiction.

"Do you have something against romance novels?" the talented baker asked, standing. In her defense of the reading material, Lindy dug her fist into her hip and glared down at her employer.

It was all Hope could do not to laugh. Lindy's tall white baker's hat was askew, and her eyes flashed with righteous zeal. Apparently her friend took the subject seriously.

"I didn't mean to offend you," Hope offered as a means of keeping the peace.

"You didn't," Lindy was quick to assure her, "but

having someone trash romance novels without ever having read them is a pet peeve of mine."

"I'll give one a try someday," Hope promised, but doubted that it would be anytime soon. Romance didn't interest her. Perhaps later, when Coffee Break, Incorporated, was firmly on its feet, she'd consider searching for a husband.

"I bought a raffle ticket myself," Lindy announced sheepishly. "I don't know what I'd do if I won. I swear Prince Stefano is the handsomest man alive."

Hope had seen his picture often enough in the tabloids to agree with her friend's assessment. The prince was said to be the world's most eligible bachelor. "But if you won the date with him, what would you have to talk about?"

Lindy wiggled her eyebrows suggestively. "Talk? Are you nuts? If I won the date with Prince Stefano, I wouldn't waste precious time talking."

Hope laughed, then shook her head. "Of course you'd talk. That's the point of the evening, isn't it?"

A dreamy look came over Hope's friend. "Even if we did nothing but sit across the table and stare at one another all evening, I'd be thrilled."

Not Hope. If she was going to date a prince, she'd make sure the time was well spent. Oh, good grief, she was actually contemplating what it would be like. Clearly she'd been breathing too many fumes from the espresso machine.

"You won't need to call your mother back," Lindy announced all at once.

"Why not?"

"Because I just saw her crossing the street."

Hope walked over to the picture window in front of her shop. Sure enough, her dear, sweet mother was heading straight for Coffee Break, Incorporated.

"Mom," Hope breathed when the front door opened, "what are you doing here?"

"I thought I'd come see my only child who never visits her mother anymore."

The hint of guilt hung in the air like a low-lying cloud. Hope didn't think now was the time to mention that each visit had been turned into another match-making opportunity. The last two trips home had been enough to keep Hope away for life.

"Mom, you know how busy I've been this summer. Besides, I talked to you no more than twenty minutes ago. Didn't you trust me to call you back?"

"I didn't want to chance it. Besides I was in the neighborhood."

Her mother avoided trips downtown like the plague. "What are you doing here?"

"Hazel and I came down to that fancy hotel on Fourth Street to make reservations for next week. Gladys and Betty, Hazel and I decided to spring for the big bucks and stay in the hotel for the conference."

"You're actually going to stay at a hotel in Seattle? We *live* in Seattle."

"We want to network. Who knows all the fun we'd miss if we had to catch the five o'clock bus back to Lake City? We decided not to chance it."

"I see," Hope said, but she wasn't entirely sure she did.

"By dividing the price of the room four ways, it costs hardly anything. You can't blame us for wanting to be where the action is, now can you?"

"Where's Hazel?"

"I left her at the hotel. She's checking out the room they're giving us. Rumor has it Prince Stefano's suite is on the nineteenth floor." She paused and Hope swore her eyes sparked with mischief. "Hazel made up a story about her blood pressure and the medication she's taking. She insisted the higher the room, the better it is for her heart." A smile dimpled each of Doris's tanned cheeks. "It worked. Our room's on the eighteenth floor."

Hope could see it all now. Four retired schoolteachers lurking in corridors waiting for a glimpse of Prince Stefano. "So you're going to be rubbing shoulders with royalty."

"Just think of it, Hope. We might run in to the prince on the elevator."

"Indeed you might." Her mother sounded like a star-crazed teenager waiting for a glimpse of her favorite rock star.

"It's all for fun, Hope." She glanced at her daughter as if she feared Hope would say she was acting like an old lady.

"I think it's great, Mom," she said, resisting the urge to laugh. "You and your friends will have the time of your lives."

"You don't think we're a bunch of old biddies, do you?"

"Of course not."

"We're so excited."

"About meeting the prince?"

"That, too, but the opportunity to see all our favorite romance writers, and get their autographs. It's like a dream come true."

"You're going to have the time of your life."

Her mother didn't seem to hear her. All at once her face grew somber. "I always said someday your prince would come, didn't I, Hope? Now the time has come. He's going to fall head over heels in love with you, sweetheart."

Already Hope could see the wheels turning in her mother's fevered brain. It'd be best if she could root Doris in a bit of reality. "Mother, my winning the date with Prince Stefano is a long shot. I imagine they've sold a thousand chances."

"More," Doris said confidently. "It doesn't matter. You're going to win."

It wouldn't do any good to point out the mathematical odds of that happening were astronomical. Letting her mother dream wasn't going to hurt anything, Hope supposed. The whole thing was harmless. Hope had as much a chance of winning as the man in the moon.

"You'll be there for the drawing, won't you?"

"When?" Hope had no intention of attending, but she didn't want to tell her mother that.

"The lucky winner will be announced Thursday night at the cocktail party."

"I can't," she said automatically. "I'm meeting with

my accountant to go over this quarter's taxes. You'll stand in for me, won't you?"

"If I must." Doris looked a bit disappointed, but Hope could see that the more her mother thought about it, the better she liked the idea. "Naturally, Hazel and the others would want to meet him."

"Naturally," Hope concurred. "I'll tell you what, Mom. If I win the date with Prince Stefano, I'll be sure that the four of you have a chance to chat with the prince, and it won't be in any elevator." It was easy to be generous when it cost her nothing.

Doris's face broke into a smile as wide as the Grand Canyon. "Wouldn't that be a kick."

Hope was convinced it would.

Prince Stefano looked out over the crowded ballroom floor and felt a cold chill race down his spine. Glasses clinked, champagne bubbled. Lights glowed and warmed the room from the huge crystal chandeliers. Stefano swore the eyes of a thousand women followed his every move.

He wasn't a man who frightened easily, but this situation was enough to try any man's soul. Stefano didn't doubt that if he were to stumble from the security of the stage, he would be stripped bare of his clothes within seconds. The crowd resembled a hungry school of piranhas.

For the first time in his lengthy history with Pietro, Stefano questioned if his secretary was friend or foe.

After all, his agreeing to stand upon the auction block like a slab of fresh meat had been Pietro's doing.

Stefano's gaze scanned the crowd until he found his secretary. His companion was standing against the wall with a short young woman, wearing a revealing dress that clearly made her uncomfortable. Each time Stefano glanced her way, she was nervously smoothing the full skirt, or adjusting the spaghetti-thin straps.

So this was Priscilla Rutherford. Stefano had learned everything he could about the young woman in the past several weeks. She was the only daughter of one of America's wealthiest men. As Pietro had assured him, she was a lovely creature, comely and pleasant to the eye. Priscilla Rutherford was a gentle soul who loved animals and children. She lived with her parents in their Lake Washington estate, and volunteered her time to a number of worthy charities.

The only drawback that Stefano could see was her domineering, manipulating mother who would like nothing better than to see her daughter marry well. It was unlikely that Elizabeth Rutherford would find fault with Stefano, but he wasn't looking forward to having a barracuda for a mother-in-law. A woman such as this could wreak havoc in his peaceful kingdom.

"I sincerely hope you're enjoying yourself, Your Highness," Madeline Marshall said as she curtsied deeply before him. She offered him her hand and Stefano bent forward at the waist and kissed her fingers.

"How can I not enjoy myself when I am with you?" he murmured. Madeline Marshall was another of life's small surprises. The woman was an eccentric, true, but she was a cagey businesswoman who knew her product. And her product was romance. Madeline had earned his grudging respect with her organizational expertise and her leverage with the media.

Pietro had reported to Stefano earlier in the day that the autographing that was scheduled for Saturday afternoon had the potential for drawing in nearly eight thousand ardent romance readers. Stefano had been amazed, and had suggested to Madeline earlier in that evening that San Lorenzo would be the perfect location for a future conference. The tourist bureau would appreciate the plug.

"We've sold over thirteen thousand tickets," Madeline whispered to him, her eyes twinkling.

"I am honored that so many beautiful women are eager to spend an evening in my company," Stefano said with a graciousness that had been drilled into him from his youth.

"From what I understand, Priscilla Rutherford bought a thousand tickets. I don't mind telling you, I purchased a fair share of them myself," Madeline said with a short, nervous laugh.

"I would be most happy if I were to draw your name, Ms. Marshall," Stefano said, inclining his head toward her.

The businesswoman broke out in a sigh and pressed her hand over her heart. "If only I were ten years younger," she whispered. "I'd give you a run for your money."

Stefano didn't doubt the truth of that.

Sighing once more, Madeline asked, "Are you ready for the drawing?"

"Of course." As ready as any man could be who was about to face a firing squad.

Madeline Marshall stepped toward the podium. An excited hush fell over the crowd as a huge plastic barrel containing the entrants' names was wheeled onto the stage. Two muscular hotel employees stood guard at each side of the barrel.

"Ladies and gentlemen," Madeline said, commanding their attention. Not that the hungry crowd needed encouragement. "The time we've all been waiting for has finally arrived. Romance lovers have snatched up over thirteen thousand tickets, all seeking the once-in-a-lifetime chance to date Prince Stefano Giorgio Paolo, the Crown Prince of San Lorenzo—the world's most eligible bachelor."

An enthusiastic chatter circled the room. It seemed to Stefano that the group was pressing closer and closer to the stage.

"As I explained earlier," Madeline Marshall continued, "the winning ticket entitles the winner to an all-expense-paid evening with Prince Stefano at the restaurant of her choice. The monies collected for this evening's event have been donated to the Literacy Councils of King, Pierce and Kitsap Counties."

Applause followed. The two burly men edged closer to the barrel and energetically stirred the hopes and dreams of thirteen thousand women. The white entries tumbled one on top of the other.

When they'd finished, Madeline Marshall opened the trapdoor and motioned for him. "Prince Stefano, would you kindly do us the honor?" she asked.

Stefano nodded, stepped toward the plastic barrel and with a sigh, inserted his gloved hand. He burrowed his fingers through the entries, grabbed several and shook his hand until only one remained. He pulled that one out.

Stepping up to the podium, he looked out over the expectant faces of the women staring up at him. Priscilla Rutherford held her arms close to her breasts, her eyes closed and her fingers crossed. He wouldn't dare to hope he would draw the name of the woman he planned to make his wife. The Fates would never make it that easy.

He swore he could have heard a pin drop in the silence. He unfolded the slip, and mentally he reviewed the name.

"Hope Jordan." He spoke into the microphone.

A scream came from the back of the room as an older, gray-haired woman raised both hands. Stefano's gaze found her and he felt his heart drop to his knees.

He was about to go out on a date with a woman old enough to be his mother.

Chapter 2

"You won!" The nearly incoherent voice shouted into Hope's ear.

Hope propped open one eye and stared at the digital dial on her clock radio. It was nearly eleven. One arm dangled over the side of the bed and the other held the telephone receiver to her ear. The side of her face was flattened against the pillow.

"Who is this?"

"It's Lindy."

"For the love of heaven, why are you calling me in the middle of the night?"

"To tell you Prince Stefano drew your name."

Both Hope's eyes flew open. Scrambling into a sitting position, she brushed the hair from her face, pressing her hand against her forehead. "Why are you calling me instead of my mother?"

"Because when your name was announced, your mother screamed, threw her arms into the air and promptly fainted."

"Oh, my goodness—" Hope bounded to her feet and paced across the top of her mattress "—is Mom all right?"

"I think so. She keeps saying something about fate and Providence and the stars all being in the right place. The paramedics don't have a clue what she's talking about."

"The paramedics?"

"That's the other reason I phoned," Lindy announced. "They need you to answer a few questions."

"I'll be there as soon as I can," Hope said, and in her rush nearly fell headfirst off her bed, forgetting where she was standing. She swore she never dressed so fast in her life, pulling on jeans and a sweatshirt. She hopped around the room on one foot like a jackrabbit in an effort to get on her tennis shoes.

Driving into town, she happened to catch a glimpse of her reflection in the rearview mirror. And cringed. She must have been sleeping hard because the mattress had creased her cheek and the hair on one side of her head resembled a ski slope. Her deep blue eyes seemed to have trouble focusing.

Hope left her car with the hotel valet and rushed around the ambulance parked by the entrance and hurried inside the lobby where Lindy was waiting for her.

Hope's appearance must have taken her friend aback because Lindy reached inside her purse and handed Hope her comb.

"The prince is with your mother," she explained when Hope regarded the comb.

Hope had to stop and think what Lindy was telling her. "So?"

"I...I thought you might want to freshen up a little."

"Lindy, my mother fainted, the paramedics don't know what's wrong. I think Prince Stefano isn't going to care if I brushed my teeth."

"All right, all right. I wasn't thinking."

If meeting Prince Stefano was enough to cause her mother to require smelling salts, frankly Hope wasn't all that keen on being introduced.

Lindy led the way to the elevator, and they rode up to the eighteenth floor. Her mother's friends, Hazel, Gladys and Betty all rushed toward Hope when she stepped off the elevator. The three were all talking at once, telling her their version of what had happened after Prince Stefano read Hope's name.

"Your mother went terribly pale," Hazel said.

"I told you she wasn't getting enough carrot juice," Betty insisted. "She isn't juicing properly."

Gladys agreed. "This is the kind of thing that happens when you let yourself get irregular."

"She asked for you," Hazel said, ignoring the others, as she gripped Hope's arm. She opened the door to the room, and with an indignant sigh, said, "Those firemen wouldn't let us in. You tell your mother we're out here waiting for her." Hope started inside the room, when Hazel stopped her. "Tell Doris she can have the Hide-A-Bed if she wants."

"I will," Hope promised.

Hope found her mother sprawled across a davenport, the back of one hand pressed against her forehead. The other hand was being held by the most incredibly good-looking man she'd ever seen. If this was Prince Stefano, then no wonder her mother had fainted.

He was dressed in some kind of deep blue uniform with gold epaulets at the shoulders. A bright red banner crossed his chest, which was adorned with three rows of medals.

All at once Hope wished she'd heeded Lindy's suggestion about combing her hair. She looked a fright. Well, that couldn't be helped. It was too late to worry about it now.

Her mother moaned softly, and noticing Hope for the first time, Prince Stefano stood.

"Is that you, Hope?" Her mother's voice sounded as if it were coming from the bottom of a dry well. The question was followed by another low, breathy sigh-moan.

"Mom," Hope said, falling to her knees beside the sofa. "What happened?"

"I...I think I must have fainted."

"I'm wondering if you could answer a few questions?" a paramedic with a clipboard asked her.

"Of course." Hope reluctantly left her mother's side.

"There are just a few things we need to know," he said matter-of-factly.

Hope responded to a series of predictable questions, such as her mother's address, phone number, age. "As far as we can determine," the medic said when she'd finished supplying the information, "the fainting spell was caused by a sudden drop in blood pressure. Your mother seems to be doing fine for now, but she should check in with the family physician within the next week or two."

"I'll see that she does," Hope said.

The medic had her sign at the bottom of his report. "Do you have any questions?"

For one crazy moment, Hope toyed with the idea of asking if this fainting spell could be linked to a lack of carrot juice and irregularity. Fortunately, she stopped herself in the nick of time.

"Nothing, thank you," she said.

The medic tore the sheet from the top of the clipboard and handed it to her. Hope folded it in half and stuck it in the pocket of her acid-washed jeans. "Thank you for your trouble," she said, as the two paramedics gathered their equipment.

"Mom, let me take you home," Hope suggested gently, kneeling down at her mother's side.

Doris ignored the suggestion. Instead she tilted her head back so that she could get a better look at Prince Stefano. "Hope, this is Prince Stefano," Doris said, gazing at the prince as if he were a Roman god. Actually that assessment wasn't far off.

"I'm very pleased to make your acquaintance," Prince Stefano said politely.

"Me, too." She held out her hand, and then, thinking this might be considered unladylike, quickly withdrew it.

The prince offered her his own hand just as she dropped hers. He dropped his, and she raised hers. Their eyes met and Hope saw a flash of amusement dance in his deep brown eyes.

"Prince…" Doris whispered, "please excuse how my daughter's dressed. She doesn't normally look… this bad."

Hope's face filled with color hot enough to fry eggs.

"Your daughter is as beautiful as her mother."

Doris released a languished sigh.

"I understand you and I will be dining together tomorrow evening," Prince Stefano said, smiling toward Hope. He was the picture of propriety and as stiff as cardboard.

"Do you like Chinese food?" Hope asked.

"Chinese food?" Her mother propelled herself off the davenport as if she were bounding off a trampoline. "You're dining with Prince Stefano Giorgio Paolo, not Gomer Pyle. We'll start off with cocktails at Matchabelles, followed by dinner at the Space Needle…. No," Doris corrected. "You won't have a moment's privacy there. The tourists will gawk at you every moment you're there."

Hope and Prince Stefano were left speechless by her mother's miraculous recovery.

"We must plan every detail," Doris said, her voice high and enthusiastic as she started pacing. "I'll need

Hazel and the others to help me with this. You two leave everything to us, understand?"

"Ah…" Hope had yet to find her tongue.

"As you wish," Prince Stefano said, ever gracious. "I'm sure you and your friends will plan a lovely evening for your daughter and me."

Doris blushed with pleasure. "I promise you Hope won't look a thing like she does now."

"Mother!"

Prince Stefano's gaze briefly skirted past Hope's, and she caught a glimmer of amusement. He reached for her mother's hand, pressed his lips to it and said, "I'm pleased to see you're feeling better, Mrs. Jordan. If you need anything further, please don't hesitate to call either me or my assistant." He reached inside his pocket and handed her a small card.

"It was a pleasure to meet you," Hope mumbled, after finding her voice.

The prince smiled warmly. "The pleasure was all mine. I'll look forward to our evening together, Miss Jordan."

"I…I will, too."

It wasn't until after he'd left the room that Hope realized it was true.

Priscilla Rutherford stood, hiding out on the balcony, sipping from a champagne glass, and feeling mildly sorry for herself. She'd counted on winning the date with Prince Stefano. It would have been a dream come true to meet His Royal Highness. Priscilla was half in love with the handsome prince. The opportunity to meet him was the reason she'd signed up for the Romance Lovers' Convention. Now that didn't seem likely, although she wasn't sure what she'd say if they did meet. She'd probably embarrass them both by staring at him, too tongue-tied to speak.

The night was lovely with stars scattered like diamond dust across a black velvet sky. The honey-colored moon was full and seemed to be smiling down on her, or so she'd like to think.

Most people assumed Priscilla lived the perfect life. She was well educated, had traveled extensively and was heir to a vast fortune. But what she sought most seemed out of reach. She longed to be a wife and mother to a man who loved her for herself and not for her father's money.

She hungered for a simple life with a husband who hurried home at night to the meals she'd cooked herself. Mostly, Priscilla longed to be a mother. How different she was from her own ambitious one. It often puzzled her that she, who was so homey, could have been born to two highly motivated, sophisticated people.

The cocktail party was winding down, but Priscilla lingered, grateful for these few moments apart from the crowd. She enjoyed people, but often felt awkward and gauche when she was in a group of strangers.

Drinking the last of the champagne, she gazed out over the midnight-dark waters of Puget Sound. A foghorn from one of the ferries sounded in the distance.

"May I join you?"

Priscilla turned around to find a tall, dignified-looking man silhouetted against the bright light spilling from the doorway. She thought he might be part of the group traveling with the prince, but she wasn't sure. During the course of the evening, she'd seen him several times. Almost always he was in close proximity to her.

He was formidable in stature, muscular and nearly as good-looking as the prince himself.

"I...I was just leaving," Priscilla said shyly.

"Please don't," he said, joining her at the railing. Resting his forearms against the wrought iron, he gazed out over the city. "It's a lovely evening, isn't it?"

Priscilla detected a hint of an accent; otherwise his English was flawless.

"Very," she whispered. It would have been far more lovely if her name had been the one drawn by Prince Stefano.

"Are you terribly disappointed?" he turned and asked her unexpectedly.

She thought for a moment to pretend she didn't know what he was talking about, then decided against it. Her disappointment was obvious. "A little."

He straightened. "Perhaps I should introduce myself. My name is Pietro. I'm the personal secretary to Prince Stefano."

"Pietro," she said, testing the name on her tongue. "You have just one name?"

He hesitated before answering. "Yes. The prince has six, and I've decided one is less confusing."

Priscilla smiled into the balmy night. "It certainly hasn't hurt Madonna any."

"No," he agreed amiably, "it hasn't."

Their silence was a companionable one. "Do you mind if I ask you a few questions about Prince Stefano?" She hoped she wasn't being impertinent.

"It would be my pleasure."

Self-conscious, Priscilla dropped her gaze. "Is the prince as charming as you are?"

"Much more so, I believe."

Priscilla turned and braced her back against the railing in an effort to better see this handsome, mysterious man. The moonlight beamed over his shoulder, illuminating his strong facial features. Prince Stefano was world-class handsome, but Pietro was no slouch in the looks department. "What's it like working with royalty? I mean, is it continual pomp and ceremony?"

"Not at all," Pietro assured her. "Naturally, there are a number of customary obligations the prince is required to attend, but I make sure his schedule is balanced with plenty of free time. The prince loves to ride. He's an excellent swordsman, and…"

"Swordsman? But who would dare to challenge the prince?"

Once again Pietro hesitated, and Priscilla could sense his amusement. "No one challenges the prince, Ms. Rutherford. Most often he's the one who offers the challenges."

"But whom does he fight?"

Pietro chuckled. "I'm afraid I'm his favorite opponent."

"Have you ever bested him?" Priscilla wasn't sure why she was so curious about Pietro's relationship with the prince, but the man fascinated her.

"We're evenly matched," Pietro explained.

"Then you've won?"

"On occasion."

Although everything she knew about Prince Stefano had come from gossip publications, Priscilla didn't think he'd take kindly to losing at anything. She'd only just met Pietro, but she had the unshakable impression that he wasn't a man who enjoyed losing, either.

"Have you ever *let* him win?"

"Never." His quick response assured her he was telling the truth.

"What's the prince like as a person?"

Pietro mulled over his response. "He's a gentleman. Generous to a fault. Sympathetic and sincere. He cares deeply for his country and his people."

"You make him sound like a saint."

Pietro cocked one eyebrow. "I hadn't finished yet."

"Sorry," she mumbled.

"He's not quick-tempered, but when he does become angry, it's best to find someplace to hide until he's worked out whatever is troubling him."

"My father's like that," Priscilla added thoughtfully, "but he's never angry for very long."

"Neither is Stefano."

"You're his friend, aren't you?" And just about everything else, Priscilla speculated.

Pietro didn't answer. Instead he surprised her with a question of his own. "Would you care to meet him?"

Her hands flew to her chest. "Is that possible? I mean, I understand he's only going to be in the area a few days and I wouldn't want to take up his time."

"Prince Stefano would deeply enjoy making your acquaintance." Pietro's voice was almost a monotone, crisp and businesslike, as if he were performing a necessary duty.

"I'd love to meet the prince. Every woman here would give their right arm for the opportunity." That she would actually have the chance was more than she could believe.

"He'd enjoy meeting you, as well."

"Me?"

"Why do you sound so surprised?" Pietro asked. "You're a lovely young woman."

It did her ego a world of good to hear Prince Stefano's personal secretary say such things to her. If only she weren't so clumsy and awkward.

"Tomorrow around ten for tea," Pietro suggested.

"So soon? I...I mean sure, anytime would be great."

Pietro removed a small card from inside his suit jacket along with a pen and scribbled the information down on the back. "I'll have the footman meet you in the lobby at ten. If you'll be kind enough to give him this card, he'll escort you to the prince's suites."

"Will you be there?"

It took Pietro a long time to answer. "I don't believe I will be."

"Oh," she whispered, unable to hold back her disappointment. He was about to leave when she stopped him.

"Pietro, after I show the footman the card, would it be all right if I asked for it back? I'd like to keep it as a souvenir."

"That would be fine."

"Good night, and thank you."

He squared his shoulders and bowed slightly before turning and walking back into the ballroom.

"You met her?" Stefano asked when Pietro joined him in the suite.

"Yes. Priscilla Rutherford's agreed to meet you tomorrow morning at ten for tea."

Stefano waited, and when his friend wasn't immediately forthcoming, he raised his hands imploringly. "Well, are you going to tell me about her, or keep me in suspense?"

"Her picture doesn't do her justice. She's beautiful."

Briefly Stefano wondered if they were discussing the same woman. The Priscilla Rutherford he'd seen from the stage was short and self-conscious. She looked like a timid soul who would run for cover the moment someone raised their voice at her. Not that it mattered. It wasn't her he was forced to marry, but her father's money. A bad taste filled his mouth at the thought.

"I could use a drink," he murmured.

"So could I." Pietro walked over to the wet bar, brought down two glasses, filled them with ice and poured them each a strong drink.

"How's the woman who fainted? What was her name…Charity, or something along those lines?" Pietro inquired. Stefano had the impression his friend didn't want to talk about the heiress, but then he was just as reluctant to mention Hope.

Stefano lowered his gaze to his drink, watching the ice cubes melt. "Her name's Hope. Hope Jordan. Actually the woman who screamed and then fainted is the mother of the young lady I'll be having dinner with tomorrow evening."

"You met her?"

"Yes. Briefly."

"And the mother?"

"She's fine…a little excited, but otherwise I'd say she made a complete recovery."

"And the daughter?"

"The daughter," Stefano repeated, mentally reviewing his encounter with Hope. A smile tempted him. She had blue eyes that snapped like fire, and a look that could shuck oysters. Besides being completely incapable of disguising her feelings, the woman was downright impudent. Suggesting Chinese food… Damn, but he wished that was exactly what they could do. He'd like nothing better than to order out, then sit on the floor and use chopsticks while he learned about her life. Hope Jordan, despite her original hairstyle, interested him.

Of course getting to know her beyond this one evening was impossible.

Even deep in thought Stefano could feel his secretary's scrutiny. "I'm sorry, Pietro. What was your question?" he asked.

"I asked about Hope Jordan."

"Ah, yes. We met."

"So I understand. What time's your dinner date?"

"I'm not sure," Stefano said. "Hope's mother and her friends are making the arrangements. By the way, be sure and send flowers to Doris Jordan, Hope's mother. I believe she's staying at the hotel." He paused and thought about what he wanted to say on the card. "Tell her it isn't often a beautiful woman faints at my feet."

Pietro laughed, but grew serious once more. "Could you set a time that you'll return from your dinner date?"

"Why?"

"I was just thinking you might want to make arrangements to meet Priscilla for a drink afterward."

"No," he said adamantly, surprised by his own vehemence. "Ms. Jordan won a dinner date with me, and I don't want to cheat her by abruptly ending the evening in order to meet another woman."

"You're being unnecessarily generous with your time, aren't you?"

"Perhaps," Stefano agreed, but he didn't think so. He had the feeling he was going to enjoy Hope Jordan. It might be selfish of him to want to spend time with her, but frankly, he didn't care. A lifetime of getting to know Priscilla Rutherford stretched before him like a giant vacuum.

"Tell me more about the Rutherford woman."

Pietro's hesitation captured Stefano's attention. It wasn't often his friend was at a loss for words. "You don't like her?"

"Quite the contrary. She's delightful."

"But will she make me a good wife?"

"Yes," he answered stiffly. "She'll make you an excellent bride, an asset to the royal family. The people of San Lorenzo will be crazy about her."

"Excellent."

Pietro took a long, stiff taste of his drink, and then stood. "Is that all for this evening, or do you need me for anything more?"

Stefano was disappointed. He would have preferred it if Pietro had stayed. Stefano was in the mood to talk, but he was unwilling to ask it of him.

"Go on to bed," Stefano advised.

"Will you be up much longer?"

"No," Stefano said, but he wondered exactly how long it would take him to fall asleep.

"Don't quit on me now, ladies," Doris pleaded, sitting Indian-style at the foot of the mattress. Her hair was confined to a cap and she wore a thick cotton bathrobe. "I told Hope and the prince that the four of us would make all the arrangements for their dinner date."

"Can't we do this in the morning?" Hazel asked, sounding like a whiny first grader. That was understandable, seeing that Hazel had taught first grade for nearly thirty years.

"I don't know about the rest of you, but I'm exhausted."

A chorus of agreement followed Gladys's announcement.

"I thought we were here for the Romance Lovers' Convention?" Betty muttered, her eyelids at half-mast.

Gladys lifted her head from beneath the pillow. "Just how much longer is that light going to be on anyway?"

Doris braced her hand against her ample hip. "What's wrong with the three of you?"

"I'm exhausted," Gladys repeated.

"It's barely midnight," Doris said, shocked by her friends. "How could you possibly be tired?"

Her question was answered with a chime of reasons that included a big dinner, cocktails and the excitement of meeting the prince.

"What was all this talk about renting a hotel room and being party animals?" Doris couldn't believe she was rooming with such deadbeats. "Wasn't it you, Betty, who claimed you wanted to call your son at three in the morning and tell him he had to come bail you out of jail?"

"Yes, but…I wasn't serious."

"Gladys," Doris said, eyeing her friend whose face was buried beneath a hotel pillow. "I thought you were going to stick your head out the window and serenade the prince."

The pillow elevated three inches in the direction of the ceiling. "The windows are sealed shut."

"Ladies, ladies," Doris tried once more. "We have work to do."

"We'll never agree…it's *hope*less," Hazel said. And thinking herself clever, she added, "No pun intended."

After debating for the better part of an hour, they hadn't gotten any further in planning Hope's evening with the prince than predinner drinks. From that point on, everyone had an opinion on where the couple should dine.

Hazel was partial to the restaurant where she and Hank had celebrated their fiftieth wedding anniversary. But Betty seemed to think the prince might frown upon a steak house.

Gladys was sure Hope would be the one to object. "Would a woman who sells low-fat muffins eat red meat?"

"Can't we please decide this in the morning?"

"Oh, all right," Doris said. Her friends were a bitter disappointment to her. She reached over and turned out the light.

"Wouldn't it be something if Hope married the prince?" Betty asked with a romantic sigh into the stillness.

"It won't happen."

"Why won't it?" Doris insisted, chucking back the sheets.

"First off, men like Prince Stefano marry princesses and the like."

"Prince Rainier married Grace Kelly."

"That was in the fifties."

Silence fell over the room.

"Did Hope say anything when they met?" The question came from Betty.

"Not with words," Doris answered, "but a look came over her, like none I've ever seen. I tell you, ladies, it was like magic. I felt it. The prince felt it. It was like a bolt of electricity arced between them."

"You're not making this up, are you?"

"Either that or she's been reading too many romance novels again," Hazel inserted.

"I swear I'm not making this up," Doris insisted. "Prince Stefano didn't know what hit him."

Silence once more. Doris's eyes drifted closed. Someone sighed. Two more sighed collectively, and then…

"What about McCormick's?"

"We already decided against a steak house," Betty muttered.

"Yes, but they serve seafood, too, and I know someone there who owes me big-time. They can make sure this is an evening Prince Stefano and Hope will never forget."

The light switch was turned on, and Doris squinted.

"McCormick's," Hazel mused aloud. "Now there's a possibility."

Chapter 3

The following morning Priscilla waited in the hotel lobby. Her fingers repeatedly ran over the business card Pietro had given her the night before. The tall and stately footman arrived and read over the card without emotion when she handed it to him.

"Would it be all right if I kept it?" she asked. "I want it for my scrapbook."

He nodded briefly and returned it. Nervous, Priscilla held her breath as they approached the elevators. She'd dressed carefully for this meeting with the prince. Her mother had insisted on a white linen suit with a soft pink blouse, and a diamond brooch. It was something Elizabeth would have chosen to wear herself. If Priscilla could have had her own way, she would have picked a flower-speckled summer dress with a broad-brimmed white hat, but it would have been useless to argue. Besides, her mother paid far more attention to fashion trends than she ever did.

Both her parents were thrilled that Priscilla had been granted an audience with Prince Stefano. Although she was quick to assure them the invitation had come from a staff member, not the prince himself.

Priscilla feared they were putting far too much emphasis on a simple invitation to tea. Apparently they expected her to bowl the prince over with her wit and charm, and that just wasn't possible. She so hated to disappoint them.

"Could you do something for me?" Priscilla asked the footman as he inserted the special key into the elevator lock that would permit them entry onto the nineteenth floor.

"If I can," he said, looking mildly surprised.

"I need to talk to Pietro after my meeting with the prince. Would you tell him it's important? I promise I'll only take a few minutes of his time. I wouldn't disturb him if it wasn't necessary. Tell him that for me, if you would."

"I'll see to it right away."

"Thank you."

The elevator made a soft mechanical noise as it ascended. Priscilla's heart was close to blocking her air passage, and she worried about being able to speak normally when introduced to the prince. Her hands felt cold and clammy, and her knees seemed to be losing their starch. She couldn't remember being more nervous about anything.

The elevator doors smoothly glided open and Priscilla was escorted into a plush suite that overlooked downtown Seattle and majestic Puget Sound. As always her gaze was captured by the beauty of the scenery.

"Your city is beautiful," the deep, male voice said from behind her.

As if caught doing something she shouldn't, Priscilla whirled around. Finding Prince Stefano standing there, she curtsied so low, her knee touched the thick wool carpet. The prince stepped forward, gripped her hand with his own and helped her upright.

The prince was even more dashing close up, Priscilla noted, and not nearly as frightening as she'd expected. She tried to remember the things Pietro had told her about His Highness. She tamed her fear by remembering he was a gallant gentleman who deeply loved his country. If she concentrated on the things she'd learned from Pietro, she might not worry so much about making a fool of herself.

"I'm pleased to make your acquaintance, Miss Rutherford," Prince Stefano said. "Pietro spoke fondly of you."

"I am very honored and pleased to meet you, Your Highness," Priscilla said through the constriction in her throat. "I appreciate your taking the time from your busy schedule to see me. I promise not to take up much of your morning."

"Nonsense. There's always time in my schedule to

meet a beautiful and charming woman, such as your-self."

Priscilla blushed.

"Please sit down." The prince gestured to the pair of white leather wing-back chairs.

"Thank you," Priscilla murmured, wondering just how long she'd be required to stay before she could speak with Pietro. "I have something for you," she said, taking the handwritten invitation from her mother and giving it to the prince.

He opened it, read the message and smiled. "I'd be honored to meet your family. Tell your parents they can expect me around three."

The prince engaged Priscilla in mundane conversation, and when there seemed to be nothing more to say, he carried the dialogue himself. He told her about the beauty of San Lorenzo, and invited her to visit his country at her earliest convenience, promising to show her the sights himself.

Forty-five minutes later, when it was time to leave, Priscilla stood gratefully and thanked him for his generous hospitality and the invitation to visit San Lorenzo.

The same footman who'd come for her earlier escorted her from the room. The minute they were out of earshot, Priscilla stopped. "Did you speak with Pietro?"

"Yes. He asked me to take you to his office."

"I hope I'm not interrupting anything important."

"He didn't say, miss." With that he led her down a wide hallway to a compact office.

"Please have a seat," he said. "Pietro will be with

you momentarily." He closed the door when he left her alone. Priscilla sank into the cushioned chair, her knees giving out on her. She pressed her hand over her heart, closed her eyes and drew in a deep breath.

"Was it so terrifying meeting Prince Stefano?" Pietro asked from behind her, amusement woven through his words.

"Not exactly terrifying," she answered, straightening. "But I don't think I took a complete breath the entire time I was with him."

"What did you think?" Pietro walked around and sat down at a brightly polished desk across from her.

"Of the prince?" She hadn't had time to properly form an opinion, frightened as she was of making a mistake, or spilling her tea. "He's…a gentleman, just the way you said. He told me about San Lorenzo and invited me to visit, but I think he was just being polite."

"I'm sure he was sincere," Pietro countered.

"I've visited San Lorenzo twice before, but that was years and years ago. I didn't tell the prince that because I was far more comfortable letting him do the talking."

"You asked to see me?" Pietro asked.

"Yes." She noted that the prince's secretary was more reserved and aloof than he had been the night before. "I don't mean to make a nuisance of myself, but I thought I should explain about the invitation my parents sent." For forty-five minutes she'd sat with Prince Stefano and spoken no more than few words. Now, she couldn't seem to stop talking.

"My parents invited the prince to meet them tomorrow afternoon. I tried to explain to Mom and Dad that none of this would have happened if it hadn't been for you, but they wouldn't listen." They seemed to be under the delusion that she'd charmed the invitation from him herself.

"I'm sure Prince Stefano would enjoy meeting your family."

Dejected, Priscilla's shoulders drooped. This was exactly what she didn't want to hear.

Pietro hesitated. "Are you saying you'd prefer for the prince to decline?"

She nodded, feeling wretched.

"Is there any particular reason? Has Prince Stefano offended you?"

Her chin flew up. "Oh, no, he's wonderful. It's just that…well, if the prince comes, my parents might think he's romantically interested in me."

"If ticket sales for the date with the prince were any indication, this is what several thousand American women profess to want."

Priscilla didn't express her feelings for the prince one way or the other. She couldn't.

"If he meets my family, I'm afraid the prince might mention inviting me to San Lorenzo. You can bet my parents will jump on that."

"You don't wish to visit my country?"

"I love San Lorenzo. Who wouldn't?" This was going poorly. Every time she opened her mouth, she made matters worse.

"Then I don't understand the problem."

"No," she whispered, "you wouldn't."

"Tell me, Priscilla."

It was the first time she could remember him saying her name. Although his English was flawless, he said "Priscilla" in such a way that it sounded exotic and special. As if she were, herself.

"Are you free this afternoon?" she found herself asking all at once, the words rushing together. "It would be a shame for you to be in Seattle and not see some of the city. I could show you Pike Place Market and we could ride the monorail over to Seattle Center." Priscilla had never been so forward with a man. She couldn't believe she was doing so now.

The expensive gold pen Pietro rolled between his palms slipped from his hand and dropped to the floor. Looking flustered, he bent down and retrieved it.

When he didn't answer her right away, she knew she'd committed a terrible faux pas. A man like Pietro, Prince Stefano's personal secretary and companion, didn't have time to spend with her. By blurting out the invitation she'd placed him in an impossible position. He couldn't refuse without offending her, and he couldn't accept, either. A man in his position didn't go sightseeing, and if he did, he wouldn't necessarily want to do so with her.

"Of course you can't.... Forgive me for asking. I wasn't thinking." She was far too embarrassed to meet his gaze. She stood abruptly, gripping her purse against her stomach. "If you'll excuse me, I'll..."

"Priscilla," he said in that gentle way of his, "sit down."

She was too miserable to do anything but comply. "I'm sorry," she whispered, hanging her head in shame.

"There's no reason to apologize."

She didn't contradict him, although she didn't agree.

"First tell me why you don't wish to accept the prince's invitation to visit our country."

She swallowed tightly. "It's because of my parents. They think there's a chance Prince Stefano will become enamored with me. They don't understand that he was just being polite."

"Your parents are the reason you'd prefer the prince refused their invitation for tomorrow afternoon, as well?"

She nodded. "I shouldn't have said anything, I know. It was tactless and rude of me. I was hoping…"

"Yes," Pietro urged, when she hesitated.

"He would decline."

Pietro sighed heavily. "I'm afraid that's impossible. Prince Stefano has already asked me to accept on his behalf."

"I see." So much for that.

"I don't think you should so readily discount yourself, Priscilla. The prince was quite taken with you. He told me himself what a beautiful woman he found you to be."

Priscilla blinked several times, uncertain if what she heard could possibly be true. "He told you that?"

"Yes. Why are you so surprised?"

"I just am."

"You shouldn't be. You're a beautiful person, Priscilla Rutherford." Pietro's smile was warm and gentle, and Priscilla felt mesmerized by it.

"Thank…you," she whispered.

Pietro's gaze abruptly left her, breaking the magical spell between them. "Prince Stefano will see you tomorrow at three," he said, becoming businesslike all at once.

"Will you be joining him?" She'd feel worlds better knowing Pietro would accompany the prince.

"No."

She signed heavily, and nodded. It would have been too much to hope for.

"Now…about your invitation."

Her gaze went expectantly to his. Their eyes met and held for a long moment. Priscilla didn't bother to disguise her wishes.

Pietro reluctantly dragged his eyes from hers, and it seemed to Priscilla that he found it difficult to speak. "I must decline, but having you ask is one of the greatest compliments of my life."

She managed a wobbly smile, hoping that he understood that if he'd accepted it would have been one of the greatest compliments of her life, as well.

Hope had never had anyone fuss over her more. Her mother and her mother's three softhearted friends had driven her crazy, going over every minute detail of her hair, her nails, makeup and outfit. The dress was made of black crepe that clung to her hips and looped down her spine, revealing nearly her entire flawless back. She'd never have chosen the dress on her own, but Betty knew somebody who knew somebody who owned the perfect dress.

The high heels were leftovers from her high school prom days. A bit snug, but doable for one short evening.

She dripped diamonds—not real, of course—from her wrists, neck and ears. Between the four women, they'd come up with enough rhinestones to sink a gunboat.

The phone had been ringing since eight o'clock that morning. The *Seattle Times* asked for an exclusive interview following her date. Hope declined, but that didn't stop five other area newspapers from making a pitch.

How the media found out about her was beyond Hope. The last she'd heard, *Entertainment Tonight* had flown in a camera crew. On learning that, Hope appointed her mother as her official contact person, which kept Doris occupied most of the afternoon. It also gave her a feeling of importance to be the mother of the woman dating Prince Stefano. Doris ate up the attention.

"The limousine will be here any minute," Hazel said, checking her watch. "Are you ready?"

Hope didn't think she could be any readier. One thing was for certain, she'd never have agreed to all this primping if she hadn't personally met the prince the night before.

It wouldn't take much to improve on his first impression of her, that was sure. If the truth be known, she wanted to razzle-dazzle the man. This evening was a means of proving she didn't generally look like an escaped mental patient.

"The limo's here," Gladys shouted excitedly. She sounded like a sailor lost at sea sighting land.

Doris and the two other women rushed toward the window. Hope heard them collectively sigh. One would think Prince Stefano had come for Hope in a coach led by six perfectly matched white horses.

"Oh, my heavens," Betty breathed, gazing longingly out the window. "He's so handsome."

"I'll get the door," Doris announced, as if being Hope's mother entitled her to that honor.

"You can't be out here," Hazel insisted, taking Hope by the hand and leading her down the hallway to one of the bedrooms. "The prince might see you."

"He's taking me to dinner, Hazel. That's the reason he's coming to the house."

"I know. We just don't want him to see you right away. It wouldn't be proper."

"You're confused," Hope said, holding in a smile. "The bride is hidden from her groom until the last moment, not on the first date."

"I know that, dear, but this is a special first date, don't you think? We want to make an impression."

Since Hope was aiming for that goal herself, she allowed herself to be ushered from the room.

The doorbell chimed and she could hear a flurry of activity taking place. What her mother and Doris's three friends were up to now, Hope could only speculate.

Hope heard the prince and was amazed at his patience with the older women. They engaged him in a lengthy conversation while they reviewed the itinerary they'd so carefully planned for the evening.

"Hope," her mother called, as if she were wondering what was taking her daughter so long.

Hearing her cue, Hope stepped into the living room where Prince Stefano stood waiting. Once more, her attention was captured by the mere presence of the man. He seemed to fill every inch of space in the room.

Holding her breath, Hope's searching gaze met his.

She wanted to impress him, wanted to be sure he didn't regret that she'd won this night with him. But she was the one who felt as if someone had knocked her alongside of the head. Her lungs froze, and it was impossible to breathe. He was the most dynamic man she'd ever encountered.

Hope didn't believe in love at first sight. That was something reserved for romantics, for women with time on their hands, not hardworking coffee-shop owners.

This whole thing with winning a date with a prince had originally amused her. She found it incredulous that a woman would actually pay for the opportunity to date any man. Personally, she couldn't understand why someone would even want to date royalty.

All at once the answers were crystal clear, and she felt as if she were the most incredibly fortunate female alive. It was as though this evening would be the most important of her life. That this time, with this man, would forever change her.

Prince Stefano's eyes met hers and it felt as if every bit of oxygen from the vicinity had been sucked away. The prince was a man of the world, sophisticated and suave. He'd dated the most prominent, wealthy women on the continent, and yet when he gazed at her, he made her feel like a princess. His princess. She, in her borrowed dress and rhinestone jewels.

"Miss Jordan, your beauty takes my breath away."

Hope's mother and her devoted friends each folded their hands as if they were praying and sighed audibly.

"Thank you," Hope murmured. It seemed such a mundane thing to say in light of the way seeing him affected her, but she suspected that her reaction wasn't unlike a thousand others.

"My car is waiting, if you're ready."

She reached for her evening bag, a bejeweled purse that had once belonged to Hazel's grandmother, kissed each of her fairy godmothers on the cheek and turned toward her prince.

Prince Stefano led her to the limousine. On the walkway, Hope heard the click of cameras, although she didn't see anyone taking pictures.

"The press has gotten inventive over the years," Stefano explained. "It wouldn't surprise me to find several hiding out in the trees. The press is something I've learned to live with over the years. Everything I say and do appears to interest them. I apologize if they trouble you, but I have little or no control over what they print."

"I understand."

"They're a nuisance, but unfortunately, necessary."

"I'm not concerned," Hope assured him. "I deal with all kinds of people every day at my coffee shop. People are people. It doesn't matter if they wear a camera around their neck. There's no need to be rude or unpleasant. The press has a job to do, and so do we."

"A job?" He cocked one thick eyebrow in question.

"You and I, Prince Stefano, are about to have a most enjoyable evening."

He smiled, and Hope had the impression it had been a good long while since he'd relaxed and enjoyed himself. A good long time since he'd last thrown back his head and laughed. Really laughed. Hope wanted to see that, if only so he'd remember her. And she definitely wanted him to fondly recall their time together.

The chauffeur opened the door, and Hope and the prince climbed into the backseat. The first thing Hope noticed was a bottle of champagne on ice, and two crystal flutes.

The prince's gaze followed hers. "The champagne is compliments of Madeline Marshall."

"The conference organizer… How thoughtful of her."

"The flowers are from me," he said, handing her a bouquet of a dozen long-stemmed red roses, tied with a white ribbon.

Hope cradled the flowers in her arms and buried her nose in their fragrance. It was the first time a man had given her a dozen roses, and she was deeply touched. "They're lovely."

"So are you." The words were whispered and it

seemed to Hope that it surprised Prince Stefano to realize he'd said them aloud.

"From what I understand we'll be dining at McCormick's," Prince Stefano said next, recovering quickly.

"Yes. Hazel was the one who insisted we eat there. From what I understand, the food is delicious, but I think Mom and her friends were more interested in atmosphere." The four romantics were determined to do whatever was necessary to motivate the prince to fall in love with her, as if such a thing were possible. Hope had gone along with them because...well, because she'd met the prince by that time and was already half in love with him herself.

Once they arrived at the restaurant, the hostess greeted them warmly. Hope heard murmurs and whispers as they walked the full length of the restaurant to a private booth, separated from the other diners on three sides.

"Enjoy your dinner," the hostess said, handing them each oblong menus.

Prince Stefano set his aside. "From what I understand, our dinner has all been prearranged."

"You mean to say Mom ordered for us, as well."

"So it seems." No sooner had he spoken when a basket of warm bread was delivered to the table. The wine steward followed, bringing a bottle of chilled white wine for the prince to inspect.

Prince Stefano read over the label and approved the choice. The steward peeled off the seal and skillfully removed the cork. He filled the two wineglasses after

Prince Stefano had sampled the wine and given his consent.

"I didn't dare to hope such a beautiful woman would hold the winning ticket," he said, saluting her with his glass. "To what shall we toast?"

"Romance," she said automatically.

Her choice appeared to trouble him because he frowned. Recovering, he nodded once and said, "To romance."

They touched the rims of their glasses and then Hope brought hers back to her lips. A feeling of sadness came over her all at once. She didn't understand how it was possible. Not when she was dining with the most eligible bachelor in the world, in an exclusive restaurant.

The newspapers had touted how fortunate she was, how lucky to have won a date with the prince. It dawned on her then that this sadness, this melancholy feeling came from Stefano.

She was about to ask him about it when the sound of a violin playing a hauntingly beautiful song caught her ear. A strolling musician came into view. He nodded as he played and lingered at their table. The music was poignant and bittersweet and swirled around them like an early-morning London fog.

"That was so beautiful," Hope whispered when the minstrel drifted away. Unexplained tears gathered at the edges of her eyes. She'd never heard the tune before, but it was compellingly sorrowful.

"You know the song?" Prince Stefano asked.

"No," Hope admitted.

"It is from my country. It's a story of a princess who fell deeply in love with a merchant's son. Her family has arranged for her to marry a nobleman and refuses to listen to her pleas. They forbid her to see the man she loves, insisting she follow through with the marriage contract."

"Don't tell me she kills herself," Hope pleaded. "I couldn't bear it."

"No," Stefano assured her softly. "The merchant's son knows that his love has only hurt his princess and so he leaves her, and travels to another country, never to return."

"What happens to the princess? Does she go through with the marriage? Oh, how could she make herself do it?"

"No, she never marries. Against her family's wishes she enters a convent and becomes the bride of the Church, forever treasuring the love she shared with the merchant's son in her heart."

"Oh, how sad."

"It is said their love for each other, however brief, was enough to carry them each through the rest of their lives."

"I...don't understand stories like that," Hope said suddenly. "They're so sad and so unnecessary. When two people love each other, truly love each other, there are no real obstacles."

The prince smiled sadly. "How naive you are, my beautiful Hope."

It seemed he was about to say something more when

a plate of crab-stuffed mushrooms arrived. "I gather this is our appetizer," Stefano said, sounding grateful for the interruption.

They were enjoying their meal, a decadent assortment of meat and vegetables, when Hope first heard the rustle of voices outside their booth. She thought, for an instant, that she recognized her mother, but quickly discounted that. Doris had been adamant that Hope and the prince not be interrupted.

No sooner had the memory surfaced than Hope heard a pitch like the one used by the church choir director.

"What was that?" Prince Stefano asked.

"I'm afraid to ask."

Sure enough it was her darling mother and company, who'd come to serenade the happy couple with a rendition of Henry Mancini love songs.

Hope grimaced and gritted her back teeth as they hit a discordant note in "Moon River." Listening to them was almost painful. Hope just happened to catch the prince's eye and they both just missed breaking into hysterical laughter.

When they'd finished the song, the prince had composed himself enough to slip out of the booth and politely applaud their efforts. He personally thanked each one. Doris grinned broadly and blew Hope a kiss on her way out of the restaurant.

"I'm so sorry," Hope said when the prince rejoined her.

"Your mother and her friends are…" He struggled for the right word.

"Hopeless romantics," Hope supplied.

"And you, Hope Jordan? Are you a romantic, as well?"

She wasn't sure how to answer him. Only a few days before she would have unconditionally declared herself a realist. Romance was for…those interested in such matters. She wasn't. She hadn't the time or the inclination.

Until now.

What a fool she was. If she was going to be this strongly attracted to a man, why, oh why, couldn't it be someone other than a prince? The likelihood of her ever seeing him beyond this lone night was improbable. This was Prince Stefano Giorgio Paolo of San Lorenzo, after all.

They left the restaurant and discovered the limousine had been replaced by a horse-drawn carriage. Hope laughed out loud. "I swear they thought of everything," she said, looking to Prince Stefano. "Do you mind?"

"How could I object?" he asked.

With her slinky style of dress, Hope found it to be something of a task to climb onto the carriage. Prince Stefano gripped her waist and hoisted her upward, until her shoe found the footing.

His touch was gentle, and it seemed his hands lingered several seconds longer than actually necessary. Hope's heart rate accelerated substantially as he climbed into the carriage and settled next to her, instead of across from her as she'd suspected he would.

His arm circled her shoulders and he smiled down

on her. "I think it's only fair that we live up to your mother's expectations for us this evening, don't you?"

"Of course," she agreed.

Seeing that they were settled, the driver urged the horse forward. The carriage wheels clanked against the cobble road that stretched along the side streets leading to Seattle's waterfront.

The night couldn't have been more perfect.

Hope thought of a hundred things she wanted to say, and didn't voice any of them. The silence held a message of its own. For this one night, for this moment, words were unnecessary. It was as if she and the prince had known each other all their lives, as if they'd been intimate friends who knew each other's deepest secrets.

The prince brought her closer into his embrace and without her remembering exactly when or how, she found her head pressed against his shoulder.

Hope had never experienced anything like this. She closed her eyes, yearning to savor each moment, knowing they must last her a lifetime.

"How is it possible that I should find you now?" the prince breathed at the ragged end of a sigh.

Hope didn't understand his question and twisted her head back in order to meet his eyes. They were filled with a bitter kind of sadness, the same bittersweet melancholy she'd sensed in him earlier that evening.

"I don't understand," Hope answered.

"You couldn't," he said, and breathed heavily. She brought her head back to his shoulder and felt his kiss against her crown.

Hope held her palm against his heart and heard the strong, even beat. His hand folded over hers as they left the waterfront and headed toward the hotel where the limousine awaited them.

Their night would soon be over, and Hope wanted it never to end.

By the time they arrived at the hotel, a small crowd had gathered. Prince Stefano climbed down from the carriage, and then expertly aided her. The lights were bright and there seemed to be a dozen cameras trained on them.

Whereas Prince Stefano had been tolerant and patient earlier, he was no longer. He shielded Hope as best he could from the glaring lights and hurried her toward the waiting limousine.

The car sped away at the earliest possible moment. The driver, without her having to give him her address, drove directly to her small rental house.

Prince Stefano reached for Hope's hand. "I shall remember and treasure this evening always."

"So will I," she told him, forcing herself to smile.

She didn't expect him to kiss her, but when he reached for her and brought his mouth to hers, it seemed natural and perfect.

Over the years, Hope had been kissed many times, but no man's touch had affected her as profoundly as the prince's. Hope's heart seemed to swell within her chest at the surge of emotion that overtook her.

She parted her lips to him and groaned when he deepened the contact. He couldn't seem to get enough of her, or her of him. By the time he broke away, they were both panting and breathless, clinging to each other as the only solid object in a world that had suddenly been knocked off its axis.

Stefano kissed her again and again with a growing urgency and then stopped abruptly, his shoulders heaving. His hands framed her face and his large, infinitely sad eyes delved into hers.

"I apologize."

"Don't, please." She clasped her hand around his wrist and brought his palm to her lips, kissing him there.

"I had to be sure…."

"Sure?" she questioned.

Stefano shook his head, and briefly closed his eyes. "Thank you for the most beautiful evening of my life." He paused, and she watched as his facial features tightened as if he were bracing himself for something. "Please understand and forgive me when I tell you I can never see you again."

Chapter 4

"Are you ready?"

Pietro's question interrupted Stefano's thoughts as he stood gazing out the huge picture window of the hotel suite. "Ready?" he turned and asked. He'd never felt less so.

"You're meeting with the Rutherfords in less than thirty minutes."

"Ah, yes." Dredging up some enthusiasm for this get-together with the heiress and her family was beyond him just then.

"The car is waiting."

Stefano turned away from the window. "Pietro, have you ever met someone…a woman, and known from the very moment your eyes met hers that you were going to love her?"

"Your Highness," Pietro replied with ill patience. "If you don't leave now, you'll be late for your appointment."

Frankly, Stefano couldn't dredge up the energy to care. "Apparently you haven't experienced this phenomenon or you wouldn't be so quick to dismiss my question." Reluctantly, Stefano reached for his jacket and fastened the buttons with a decided lack of haste.

"What are the Rutherford names again?" he asked. Pietro must have told him a dozen times as it was. Stefano couldn't explain why they slipped from his memory, and then again he could.

Hope.

He hadn't been able to stop thinking about her from the moment they'd parted. In the beginning, realizing how fruitless it all was, he'd resisted, but as the night wore on and morning approached, his ability to fight his feelings for her weakened considerably.

By early afternoon, he felt as though he'd been walking around in a cloud. Certainly that was where his head was. His heart, too. Dreaming impossible dreams. Seeking what he knew could never be. And yet…and yet, he couldn't make himself stop.

"James and Elizabeth Rutherford," his secretary replied.

"Ah, yes," Stefano said, silently repeating the two names several times over in an effort to remember them once and for all.

"As I understand, they're both anxious to make your acquaintance," Pietro added, following Stefano into the next room. "Speaking of Priscilla," he added, as though in afterthought, "have you given any consideration to your next meeting with the heiress?"

"No," Stefano stated honestly. "Should I?"

"Yes." The lone word flirted dangerously with insolence. "As I understand it, marrying her is the purpose of this entire journey," he added.

Stefano turned and his eyes searched those of his friend, wondering at the other man's strange mood. "As I recall she was the bride you chose for me."

"Yes," Pietro said with what sounded like regret. "I was the one who believed Priscilla would make you an excellent princess."

Try as he might, Stefano couldn't picture Priscilla Rutherford as his wife. It seemed a hundred years had passed in the past twenty-four hours since he'd first met the heiress. Stefano vaguely recalled the gist of his conversation with her, although as he remembered it, he'd done the majority of the talking. Every word she'd spoken, he'd been forced to coax out of her.

Stefano found Priscilla to be a gentle and likable soul. She'd been as nervous as a rabbit, fidgeting and discreetly glancing at her watch when she didn't think he'd notice. Once they knew each other better, and she learned to relax around him, Stefano was confident they'd make a compatible couple.

"I assume you plan to ask Priscilla to accompany you to the banquet this evening," Pietro said crisply.

"Ah, yes, the banquet." The Romance Lovers' Convention was ending the festivities with a lavish dinner affair—or so the brochures promised. Stefano was scheduled to speak briefly, but he hadn't given a thought to bringing a date.

"It would be a nice touch to invite Priscilla," Pietro suggested, "don't you think?"

Stefano nodded, making a mental note to remember to ask the heiress when he was with her later. He'd ask, because it was part and parcel of what needed to be done in order to save his country from financial ruin, but it was Hope he wanted at his side. He forced his thoughts away from Hope and made himself concentrate on Priscilla.

"Miss Rutherford's quite lovely, isn't she?" Stefano murmured more to himself than his friend.

Although a response wasn't required of his secretary, Stefano was surprised when Pietro didn't give one. He studied his companion, wondering at his friend's strange behavior of late. He might have said something, but his own conduct had been questionable.

Pietro crisply stepped across the carpet and held open the door for him. "As I explained earlier, the car's waiting."

"I want you to come with me," Stefano said, deciding all at once.

"Come with you?" Pietro repeated, as if he wasn't sure he'd heard correctly.

"Yes." Having said it, Stefano realized this was what he'd wanted from the first. "You can answer any questions Priscilla's parents might have while I talk with the young lady. I'll do as you suggest and invite her to the banquet. It might be awkward doing so in front of her family."

"I'd prefer not to go."

Stefano dismissed his companion's reluctance. "I want you with me, and be quick about it. We're going to be late."

Priscilla deeply loved her parents. She'd never understood how it happened that her gregarious parents had spawned a timid soul such as her. Personally, Priscilla would rather leap off a skyscraper than speak in public, yet her parents thrived on being the center of attention.

Priscilla also knew her parents deeply loved her, but she was realistic enough to know she was a painful disappointment to them both.

As a young girl, she'd striven to gain their approval, but as she matured, she realized she couldn't be anyone but herself. In theory it sounded quite simple, but often she felt like a salmon, fighting to swim upstream, battling the desire for their approval while struggling to be herself.

"Let me look at you, sweetheart," Elizabeth Rutherford insisted for the third time in fifteen minutes. "Now remember to square your shoulders. You don't want the prince to see you slouch."

"I'll remember." After three semesters in an exclusive charm school, Priscilla was intimately acquainted with all the ins and outs of etiquette.

"And please, Priscilla, you must smile. This is a joyous occasion." Her mother poked a finger in each of her cheeks, cocked her head to one side and grinned grotesquely. "The prince of San Lorenzo is coming to call on you."

"Mother, please. Prince Stefano is accepting your invitation. His visit has little or nothing to do with me." Priscilla didn't know why she argued. Just as she'd feared, her parents had her all but married to the prince. Little did that dear man realize what he'd done by agreeing to meet her family.

She'd tried to warn Pietro, but he hadn't listened. He didn't understand that her family viewed her meeting with the prince as something of a social coup. Nothing she said could make them believe that her time with Prince Stefano had come as a result of her meeting his secretary. Pietro had been the one who made all the arrangements.

Her parents had discounted that information from the very beginning. The prince, they told her, had sent Pietro to issue the invitation. A secretary did not make appointments without first conferring with his employer.

Their assertion seemed all but confirmed when Prince Stefano promptly accepted her family's invitation. The entire house had been in a flurry of activity ever since. The housekeeper had polished every piece of silver on the huge estate. Mrs. Daily, the cook, had been concocting delicacies for two days.

The staff had been with the family for years and this meeting with the prince gave them the opportunity to shine. And if their efforts prompted the prince to fall in love with Priscilla, then all the better. Everyone in the household glowed with pride that Priscilla had captured the attention of Prince Stefano.

At last everything was ready for the prince's arrival. Fresh flowers from the huge garden, Priscilla's first love, were beautifully arranged and graced nearly every room of the house.

Priscilla and her parents gathered in the formal living room, which was tastefully decorated in mauve and gray, and impatiently awaited the prince's arrival.

Priscilla couldn't remember ever seeing her mother this nervous. Even her unflappable father had seemed unusually tense. Every now and again, he'd smile at Priscilla and tell her how beautiful she was. In all her life, Priscilla couldn't remember her father saying such things. It seemed she'd waited all her life for a compliment from him and now that he'd given her one, she felt sick to her stomach with trepidation.

The doorbell chimed and Priscilla's parents exchanged looks as if they'd both been taken by complete surprise, and hadn't a clue as to who the visitor might be.

"I'm sure that's the prince," Priscilla said unnecessarily.

Her father cleared his throat and stood, his shoulders and back ramrod straight.

Silently Priscilla prayed that she wouldn't do anything to embarrass herself or her family. More than anything, she pleaded with the powers on high that once her parents met and talked to the prince, they'd understand that he wasn't romantically interested in her.

When she looked up, the first person she saw wasn't Prince Stefano as she suspected, but Pietro. His gaze briefly locked with hers and she knew within the space of a single breath that he didn't want to be there. She didn't share his sentiments. The moment she saw him, the room lit up with sunshine and her heart gladdened.

It would do her no good to explain to her parents that the prince's personal companion sent her pulse racing ten times faster than Prince Stefano.

Pietro diverted his attention away from her long enough for her to introduce him and the prince to her parents. After the pleasantries were exchanged, the five sat in the living room and sipped coffee and sampled a variety of delicate pastries.

Priscilla noticed that Prince Stefano and her father seemed to find a number of topics to discuss. They were deeply involved in conversation while her mother engaged Pietro in small talk. Although respectful, Pietro was clearly displeased to be thrust into this setting.

After a while, as she'd been instructed, Priscilla asked her guest if he'd enjoy seeing her garden. This was her mother's blatant effort to have the prince spend time alone with her.

To Priscilla's surprise and delight, Prince Stefano motioned toward his secretary. "Pietro's the one who appreciates gardens. I'm sure he'd be more than happy to see yours."

Priscilla cast her mother a plaintive look, when in

reality it was all she could do not to leap to her feet and shout for joy.

She stood and watched as Pietro fiercely glared at the prince. Nevertheless he obediently followed her through the French doors. Once outside they walked down the winding brick walkway that curved its way through the lush, blooming flower beds.

Knowing he wasn't the least bit interested in viewing the garden, Priscilla led Pietro to the huge white gazebo that overlooked Lake Washington. A light, cool breeze came off the waters, ruffling her hair. Rainbow-colored spinnakers glided their way across the water, cutting a swatch of bright paint across the blue skyline.

"You can sit here and wait, if you prefer," she said politely.

"Wait?" he asked.

"I know you aren't interested in the garden. Why the prince insisted you come out with me, when it's so plain you had no desire to do so, I can only guess." It hurt to say it, but she braced herself and added, "I know you'd rather not spend time with me."

He was silent for a moment as though carefully weighing his words. "That's not necessarily true, Priscilla."

She loved the way he said her name, as if it were as pleasing to the tongue as the pastries they'd feasted on earlier. She closed her eyes wanting to savor the feeling.

"If you prefer, I can leave."

"Don't go," he said.

Priscilla swore those were the two most beautiful

words she'd ever heard. Sitting inside the sun-dappled gazebo with Pietro at her side was a simple pleasure she hadn't anticipated in the events of this afternoon.

"I don't understand you," she said, studying Pietro. "Either you find me completely objectionable and deplore every minute you're forced to spend in my company, or…"

Pietro burst out laughing.

"Or," she said, smiling up at him, "you like me far more than you care to admit."

His laughter died as abruptly as it had erupted.

"Would you mind kissing me?" she asked him.

Pietro leapt off the bench and backed away from her as if she'd asked him to commit a heinous crime.

She laughed softly and shook her head. "Maybe kissing me would help you decide how you feel."

He paced the area in front of her like an escaped panther. His hands were buried deep inside his pockets, and he refused to look at her. "That won't be necessary."

Slowly Priscilla stood and planted herself directly in front of him. He was much taller than she was, at least six inches and she was forced to stand on the tips of her toes in order to meet his gaze. In an effort to maintain her balance, she braced her hands against his chest.

"Your pulse's pounding as hard as a freight train."

Pietro didn't comment, nor did he move away from her. His heart thudded hard and evenly beneath her palm. She watched a play of emotions work their way across his face as if he were involved in some great battle of will.

Encouraged by his lack of resistance, she closed her eyes and slid her arms upward until they were linked behind his neck. Then, with great care, she moved her lips over his.

The kiss was gentle, more of a meeting of the lips than anything deeply passionate.

When she'd finished, Priscilla blinked, lowered her arms and flattened her feet on the floor. It was then that Pietro eased her back into his arms. Holding herself perfectly still, the same way he had, she allowed him to kiss her. Only it didn't stop with a mere brushing of their lips as it had when she'd instigated the contact. Pietro's kiss intensified until a slow heat began to build in the pit of her stomach and her legs felt as if they would no longer support her.

"Does that answer your question?" Pietro whispered against her temple.

She nodded, because speaking just then was beyond her. What he didn't seem to understand was that she wasn't the one with the questions. The answers had been clear to her from that first night on the balcony.

Pietro braced his forehead against hers. Several moments passed before he spoke. "I shouldn't have kissed you."

"But why? Oh, Pietro, don't you realize it's what I've wanted from the moment we met?"

He laughed softly, but he wasn't being sarcastic.

"I like it when you kiss me." She wrapped her arms about his torso and burrowed as deep into his embrace as possible, seeking a haven for the complex emotions brewing inside her.

"Priscilla, this is all very sweet, but unfortunately, you don't seem to understand. I don't mean to hurt you, but I don't share your feelings." The change in him came on as fast as an August squall. His hands gripped her upper arms.

Hurt and stunned, Priscilla voluntarily backed away. Her cheeks flared with color so hot, it felt as if her face were on fire. She'd misread him and the situation, and embarrassed them both by throwing herself at him.

The constriction in her throat moved up and down several times before she managed to speak. "I'm...terribly sorry." Pressing her hands to her fevered face, she added in a thin, pain-filled voice, "Please...accept my apology." With that she turned and ran to the house.

By the time she arrived at the patio just outside the garden, Priscilla's heart was pounding hard and fast and she was breathless. Taking a moment to compose herself, she was standing on the other side of the French doors when her mother unexpectedly appeared.

"I was about to come and search for you. Where's Pietro?"

For the life of her, Priscilla couldn't answer. Gratefully, she wasn't required to speak because the prince's secretary rounded the corner of the garden, his steps filled with purpose. He paused when he found Priscilla with her mother.

"I hope you enjoyed your tour of our garden," Elizabeth Rutherford said.

"It's delightful," Priscilla heard him answer.

She trained her eyes away from him and called upon a reserve of composure stored deep within her. Pride wouldn't allow her to reveal how his words had crushed her. In all her life, Priscilla had never been so brazen with a man. What he must think of her didn't bear considering.

With her pulse thundering in her ears, Priscilla walked back into the living room to find her father and the prince chatting as if they were longtime friends.

Priscilla sat back down and neatly folded her hands on her lap. Her father looked approvingly at her and smiled.

It was her mother who noticed something was wrong. "Are you feeling all right, Priscilla?" Elizabeth asked. "You look flushed."

"I'm fine." It amazed her she could lie so smoothly.

"I think it must be the excitement of having the prince visit," her father supplied eagerly.

For the first time since his arrival, Prince Stefano turned his attention to Priscilla. "Did Pietro enjoy the garden?" he asked.

She opened her mouth to answer and discovered her throat had frozen shut. For an awkward moment there was silence.

"I found the gardens to be most pleasant," Pietro supplied for her. "Miss Rutherford is an engaging tour guide."

The heat in her face intensified tenfold.

"I realize this is short notice, Priscilla," the prince

said, "but I'd consider it a great honor if you'd consent to accompany me to the Romance Lovers' banquet this evening."

Once again, Priscilla found herself struck dumb. The invitation couldn't have surprised her more.

"She'd be delighted," her mother supplied, glaring at her.

"I'd be...delighted," she echoed, her heart sinking all the way to her ankles. This was exactly the thing her parents had been hoping to happen.

Priscilla found herself contemplating the prince. From the moment he'd arrived, he hadn't paid her as much as a whit of attention, and yet he sought her company. She could have sworn he was no more interested in her than the man in the moon.

Her gaze drifted involuntarily toward Pietro, and her heart clenched with an unexpected stab of regret. From the first she'd experienced an awkward fascination with the prince's companion. She'd believed he'd shared her feelings. Now she knew that not to be true.

Pietro wanted nothing to do with her.

"I can't stand this," Lindy cried after the last runner had left the coffee shop for his appointed rounds. She slumped into a chair and reached for a sugar-coated doughnut.

"Can't stand what?" Hope pried, although she was fairly certain she knew the answer.

"You've hardly said a word about your date with Prince Stefano. I asked you how it went, and you said great. Do you have a clue of how much that leaves to the imagination?"

"'Great' is a perfectly adequate description of our time together," Hope argued.

"See what I mean," Lindy cried. "You somehow manage to cleverly sidestep every other question. It just isn't fair."

"I had a fairy-tale date with a fairy-tale prince."

"Did he kiss you?"

"Lindy!" Hope flared, making busywork at the counter.

Lindy grinned from ear to ear, and wiggled her eyebrows several times. "He must have, otherwise you wouldn't look so outraged."

"It isn't any of your business."

"Did you get to talk to John Tesh from *Entertainment Tonight*?"

"Yes, briefly." This interest the media gave her had been a nuisance.

"I bet you told them more than you did me."

Hope hadn't, but she doubted Lindy would believe her.

"Are you going to see the prince again?" That appeared to be the key question on everyone's mind.

A sadness melted over Hope's heart, and she shook her head. "No."

"Why not?" Lindy was indignant. "Aren't you good enough for him? It makes me downright angry to think that after all the trouble your mother and her friends went through to make you beautiful..."

Hope couldn't help it; she laughed outright.

Her friend frowned, not understanding what Hope had found so amusing. True, getting beautiful had indeed been a chore, but Hope would have willingly gone through ten times the effort if it meant she could be with Stefano again.

But that was impossible. He'd said so himself.

"It wasn't just your mother and her friends, either," Lindy continued. "You put a good deal of effort into the evening yourself. Aren't you the least bit upset?"

"The ticket entitled the lucky winner to one date with Prince Stefano. Nothing less and nothing more. I had my one date, and it was the most beautiful night of my life. Demanding more would be greedy."

"Is he everything the tabloids claim he is?"

Hope had read the articles herself. Prince Stefano was touted as being suave, gracious and gorgeous.

"He's much more." Hope couldn't make herself regret a single minute of her time with the prince. The memory of their one night together would last her a lifetime. Someday she would hold her grandchildren on her knee and tell them the story of her one magical date with a fairy-tale prince from a kingdom far away. What she would hold a secret for the rest of her life was how the prince had managed to steal her heart away.

"How's your mother taking the news you won't be seeing Prince Stefano again?"

Hope closed her eyes, knowing this would be difficult. "She doesn't know yet." Her mother and company had waited up half the night for a report. The four were so exhausted from all the planning and arranging that Hope could only guess that they were still asleep.

"Mom will understand," Hope said, and knew she was being unrealistically optimistic.

"When is Prince Stefano leaving Seattle?" Lindy asked next.

"I don't know. Soon, I suspect." But not too soon, her heart pleaded.

"What are you doing this evening?" Lindy asked, between bites. She dunked her doughnut into her coffee and then carried it to her mouth, leaving a trail of coffee en route. "I don't know why I'm eating this. I think it's because I'm so jealous."

"Of what?"

"You and Prince Stefano."

"Your prince will come," Hope assured her.

"Only mine will be disguised as a frog. Life isn't fair. I would have given my eyeteeth to have bought the winning ticket, and you didn't even care. Maybe that's my problem. I've got to stop caring."

Hope realized her friend was only half-serious. She saw the irony of the situation herself. Winning the date with Prince Stefano had been a fluke, but even so, it had forever marked her life. She couldn't shake the feeling that they'd been destined to meet, destined to fall in love and destined to never have more than a single night together.

"I'm going to read a romance novel," Hope announced with a good deal of ceremony. "You asked me what I planned to do this evening, and that's it."

True, it was something of a comedown after the romantic night she'd spent with the prince. But it was a way of holding on to the memories of what she'd so recently experienced.

"At last," Lindy cried triumphantly. "To think it took a date with a prince to get you interested."

They talked for several minutes more and then the phone rang. The two women looked at each other and both knew it had to be Doris.

"At least she waited until the runners were gone this time," Lindy said, as Hope reached for the receiver.

Although her mother had heard nearly every detail of Hope's evening with the prince the night before, Hope was forced to repeat them. Naturally, there were a number of places where she skipped the more private details.

"It's all so romantic," Doris whispered.

"Yes, Mother, it was."

"You like him, don't you, Hope?"

It took Hope a moment to answer, as if she were admitting to a wrong. "Yes, Mom, I do, but then I don't know anyone who could possibly dislike him. Stefano is a…prince."

Satisfied, her mother sighed.

It had taken nearly twenty minutes for Hope to extract herself from the conversation, and afterward, she found an excuse to work in the kitchen. Her thoughts and her heart were heavy.

No matter how hard she focused on the positive, it felt as if there were a giant hole inside her. It would take a very long time to fill. A very long time to forget. That was what made it all so difficult because she wanted to remember, but remembering produced pain.

She was standing in front of the automatic dishwasher, loading cups onto the tray before sliding it inside the washer for sterilization, when Lindy joined her.

"There's a man out front who wants to talk to you."

"I'm not in the mood to deal with any salesman. Talk to him for me, would you?"

"Nope." Lindy was wearing that Cheshire cat look of hers, grinning from ear to ear. "This person insists on speaking to you himself."

"I'm busy." Stopping the washer now was a hassle she wanted to avoid. It was bad enough to be indulging in this pity party without having to deal with some slick salesman who was keen on selling her coffee filters.

"Are you coming or not?" Lindy demanded.

"Not. If someone finds it so all important to speak to me, right this instant, when I'm in the middle of this mess, then you can tell them to come back here."

Lindy frowned, and then shook her head. "I don't think that's wise, my friend." There was a singsong quality to her voice as if she were just barely able to keep herself from breaking into peals of laughter.

"Being prudent has never been my trademark," Hope muttered.

"Do you want me to get his business card for you?"

Grumbling under her breath, Hope nodded. "If you insist."

"Oh, I most certainly do."

Lindy disappeared around the kitchen door and despite her melancholy mood, Hope's gaze followed her. From the way her friend was acting, one would think… Her thoughts came to a slow, grinding halt. Prince Stefano. Was it possible?

No. It couldn't be. Stefano had told her himself anything between them was futile. She'd viewed his regret, experienced her own.

Slowly, removing one yellow rubber glove at a time, she walked out from the kitchen, her eyes trained on the front of the coffee shop.

Her breath caught when she saw him, standing as stiff as a marble statue just inside the door.

Chapter 5

"What are you doing here?" The question was barely above a whisper. Hope was rooted to the spot, unable to do anything but gaze upon the prince in all his glory. He was even more devastatingly handsome and debonair than she remembered. Regal and noble all the way to his toes.

Prince Stefano smiled demurely and moved toward the counter. "I had an urge to sample your coffee," he said as he slipped onto a stool.

She didn't believe him for a moment, but had no choice but to pretend otherwise. "Would you like a latte?" It was difficult to keep the trembling out of her voice.

"That's the drink that's so popular in Seattle?"

Hope nodded. They'd briefly discussed her business, but she'd assumed his questions had only been polite inquiries. She hadn't realized he'd been paying such close attention.

Hope felt the sharp point of her friend's elbow in her ribs and assumed Lindy was waiting for an introduction. Hope didn't have the heart to tell her friend that she was meeting royalty with powdered sugar coating her lips.

"It sounds very much like café au lait."

"They're similar," Hope said and, looking to Lindy with her white lips, swallowed a smile. "This is Lindy Powell. She does all the baking."

"I'm pleased to meet you, Lindy."

"I'll get you one of my muffins," Lindy offered. "It's on the house."

The minute her friend was out of earshot, Hope leaned close to the counter. "I thought you said…"

His hand covered hers. "I know." He closed his eyes, and when he opened them again she saw a flicker of pain move in and out of his expression. "I came because I couldn't stay away. Last night…I couldn't sleep for thinking of you. I shouldn't be here. I'm afraid my self-ishness will only hurt you."

"Having you stay away hurts me more," she whispered.

His hand tightened over hers. "Did you sleep?"

"No," she admitted reluctantly.

Her answer appeared to please him, because he broke into a wide grin. "Then you felt it, too?"

She nodded, unable to lie.

The door to the shop opened and Hope glanced up to find the windows crowded with several curious faces. Apparently the throng was hoping to catch a glimpse of Prince Stefano. Looking flustered, his bodyguard stepped inside the shop, safeguarding the door against intruders.

"We must leave, Your Highness," the beefy man said, looking concerned.

Stefano's mouth thinned, and he reluctantly nodded.

"So soon?" If anything was cruel, it would be Stefano reentering her life so briefly. All that held back the urge to beg him to stay was her pride.

"Meet me tonight," he whispered. "On the waterfront, inside the ferry terminal. You will be safe there?"

"Yes. But what time?"

"Ten...perhaps ten-thirty. I will come as soon as it is possible for me to get away."

Once more Hope's gaze was drawn to the growing multitude of onlookers, pressing against her shop window. She doubted that they'd have a moment's peace that evening once the prince was recognized.

"You'll be there?"

The wisdom of it was doubtful. She was setting herself up for a fall, but even knowing that, Hope found, she couldn't refuse him. "I'll be there," she promised.

He smiled then and it seemed the whole room brightened. He reached for her hand and gently kissed it, then abruptly turned away. The prince's bodyguard opened the door and with the aid of two footmen cleared a path to the waiting limousine. A commotion broke out once the prince appeared, and Hope heard several requests for autographs.

Within seconds Stefano was gone.

"He didn't wait for his muffin," Lindy complained, wandering to Hope's side.

"I know." Both of them stood immobilized, staring out the window as if they expected him to magically reappear. In a way that was exactly what Hope prayed would happen.

From the way Priscilla's family had reacted to the prince's dinner invitation, one would think he'd asked for her hand in marriage. The minute the prince was out the door, her parents clapped their hands with glee and hugged Priscilla.

"Mom…Dad, it's only a dinner date. Don't make more of it than there is," she pleaded on deaf ears. Her parents, however, were much too excited to listen to her protests.

"There's so much that needs to be done," her mother cried. "He'll be back to pick you up in—" she studied her diamond watch "—oh, my heavens, in less than three hours. Priscilla, come, we have a million things to do." On the way to the door, Elizabeth Rutherford barked orders to Mrs. Daily. When she realized Priscilla wasn't directly behind her, she returned to the living room and grabbed hold of Priscilla's arm.

Given no time to dissent, Priscilla was whisked off to an exclusive dress shop and forced to endure two hours of intense shopping. Her mother insisted her evening gown must be perfect, and after being subjected to at least fifty different ones, she hadn't the strength to object to the billowing chiffon creation her mother chose.

Personally, Priscilla thought she resembled Scarlett O'Hara without the nineteen-inch waist. She wasn't oblivious to her mother's choice. It was the dress that made her most resemble a princess, direct from the pages of a Grimm fairy tale.

Nothing was left to chance. By the time Prince Stefano arrived, she'd been pushed, prodded, pampered and prepared. Priscilla felt more like a French poodle than a grown woman.

The real problem was that her heart wasn't in this dinner date. If she'd had her way, she would have escaped to her room and curled up with a good novel. Burying herself in fantasy was the only means Priscilla knew would ease the ache left in her heart after her confrontation with Pietro.

Remembering what had happened inside the gazebo was enough to turn her cheeks to a brilliant shade of red. She prayed with all her being that somehow she would escape seeing Pietro that evening. Since he was almost always with the prince, she doubted that was possible.

The prince arrived promptly at seven, dressed in full military splendor. It amused her because other than the palace guards, she was fairly certain San Lorenzo didn't have an army.

His eyes brightened when he saw her. "I didn't think it was possible to improve on perfection," he said, taking her hand, and tucking it into the curve of his elbow. "My car is outside if you're ready."

"Have a good time," Priscilla's mother crowed.

The prince seemed preoccupied on the drive into downtown Seattle. She wondered at his silence, but didn't question it since she wasn't in a talkative mood herself. All she wanted was for this evening to be over with so she could go back to her own life.

This entire business had taught her a valuable lesson: to be careful what you wish for. She'd wanted so desperately to win the date with Prince Stefano. It had seemed like such a fanciful thing to meet a prince. Now that she had, everything had gone wrong.

By the time the limousine delivered them to the hotel, the banquet was about to get under way. The prince escorted Priscilla to a table at the front of the ballroom, which put him in easy reach of the stage where he'd be making his speech.

They were soon joined by Madeline Marshall, her husband, another couple—and as Priscilla had known and dreaded, Pietro. Brief introductions were made, and the necessary small talk exchanged.

To her dismay, Priscilla was positioned between the prince and Pietro.

"Good evening, Priscilla," Pietro said softly, once they were seated.

"Good evening," she said, not looking at him.

What little appetite she possessed vanished. She picked at her salad, skipped the rolls and partook in polite conversation, all the while painfully conscious of Pietro's presence.

She felt the warmth of his body so close to her own. She smelled the scent of his aftershave, a spicy rum concoction that flirted with her senses. She struggled against the memory of his arms holding her close, of his breath against her face and the whisper of his kiss over her lips.

But the beauty of that moment had been forever destroyed. She wanted to erase his words, bury them under a romantic heart and pretend. But she couldn't.

In an effort to save her from making a bigger fool of herself, Pietro had been brutally honest, brutally clear. He didn't share her feelings. Nor did he welcome her attention. The embarrassment she'd suffered then felt more acute now as she sat next to him at the banquet, wishing she could be anyplace else in the world.

"There's something wrong with your dinner?" the prince asked, when she did little more than taste the prime rib. Others were raving over the meal, while she couldn't force down another bite.

"Oh, no, it's very good," she hurried to assure him. "I guess I'm not hungry."

Stefano studied her briefly. "Are you unwell?"

"I have a bit of a headache."

"Do you wish to return home?"

"Oh, no. Please, that won't be necessary. I'll be fine."

"An aspirin perhaps? I'll send Pietro for some." He glanced in his secretary's direction and she stopped him by placing her hand on his forearm.

"Thank you, but I have some in my purse."

The prince's attention flustered her. As for his offer to take her home, it had been more than tempting, but she didn't want to explain to her parents why she was back so early in the evening. They'd never believe she had a headache. And they were right. It wasn't her head that was troubling.

It was her heart.

When the program started, the others at the table relaxed and turned their chairs around in order to get a better view of the stage.

When the prince stepped forward to speak, Priscilla stiffened, not realizing how much she counted on him as a barrier between her and Pietro.

"You're not feeling well?" Pietro asked as the prince stepped onto the stage.

"I'm fine," she whispered, focusing her attention on the prince, not daring to meet Pietro's gaze.

The silence between them was as power-packed as a minefield. Every glance his way held the potential of exploding in her face. Conversation was unthinkable; she'd never be able to manage it without revealing her pain.

The prince's speech was short and effective. He spoke of romance and love, and claimed its strength transformed lives. Love had the power to change the world. His message seemed to come straight from his heart as if he were deeply in love himself.

Priscilla noticed that she had become the focus of attention, especially when the prince joined her once more. She was momentarily blinded by the flash of cameras. Apparently the press assumed she was the woman who had captured Prince Stefano's heart. She considered that almost ludicrous, but knew her parents would be ecstatic to have the speculation printed on the society page of the *Seattle Times*.

Following the programs and the award ceremony, Prince Stefano was surrounded by a handful of admirers, seeking an autograph or a moment of his attention. Priscilla stepped aside and patiently waited.

The prince looked apologetically her way, but she assured him with a smile that she didn't mind. Indeed if circumstances had been any different she might have been one of the throng herself.

"We need to talk." It was Pietro's voice that came to her, low and sullen.

Risking everything, she forced herself to turn and meet his eyes. Pain constricted at her heart. "It isn't necessary, Pietro. I understand. Really I do. If anything needs to be said, it's that I'm so terribly sorry for placing you in such an uncomfortable situation."

"You understand nothing," he said. His jaw was clenched and a muscle leapt in the side of his face.

"Perhaps not," she agreed, "but what does it matter? You and the prince will be gone in a few days, and it's unlikely we'll meet again."

"It matters."

Priscilla was saved the necessity of an answer when the prince motioned for his friend. Pietro immediately left her side, and returned a few minutes later, frowning.

"The prince has asked me to escort you home. It seems he's going to be tied up here for some time and he doesn't wish to detain you, seeing that you're not feeling well."

Priscilla's stomach knotted with relief that this evening was finally over. And with regret that the last portion of this night was to be spent with Pietro. "That won't be necessary," she said quickly in an effort to escape. "Really...I can catch a taxi."

"Nonsense. Neither the prince nor I would hear of such a thing. You'll come with me."

His tone brooked no argument, and knowing it would be a losing battle to argue further, she obediently followed him. He guided her out of the ballroom through a back entrance. She traipsed behind him as he wove his way around the kitchen staff. Several seemed to think Pietro was the prince, and stopped and whispered in awe.

To her surprise he didn't call for the limousine, but had the valet bring a compact sports car to a side entrance.

"What's this?" she asked. She was unwilling to sit in such close proximity to Pietro. At least she could put some space between the two of them in the limousine.

"A car," Pietro answered simply, while holding open the passenger door. Only moments earlier Pietro had sought her out, and now it seemed as if he would have given anything to avoid her company. Her pride had been badly wounded by this man once already. She didn't know if her heart was up to a second round.

"I appreciate the ride, but I'd prefer a cab." She ignored his protest, and raised her hand, hoping to attract the attention of a cabdriver on the street. Naturally, when she was desperate for one, the streets were bare.

"Priscilla, don't be ridiculous."

Standing on her tiptoes, she frantically waved her arm and called out, "Taxi!"

"Prince Stefano has asked me to personally escort you home," Pietro argued.

"Do you always do as the prince asks?" she challenged, walking into the middle of the street.

"Yes," he said bitterly. "Please allow me to take you home."

The gently coaxing quality of his words was what persuaded her to do as he asked. As the prince's right-hand man, Pietro was a man accustomed to issuing orders and having them obeyed without question. Yet he was willing to plead with her.

"Please," he said again.

Defeated, Priscilla lowered her arm and walked back to the curb. "All right," she breathed in an exercise in frustration.

"Thank you," Pietro murmured.

She walked back to the sports car and climbed into the front seat. The billowing skirt of her dress obliterated the view out the front window and she was forced to push it down. She felt like a jack-in-the-box who would spring out the minute her lid was opened.

Pietro joined her and had trouble locating the gearshift between the folds of chiffon. Priscilla pushed the fabric out of his way as best she could.

Pietro started the engine and when they stopped at a first light, he glanced at her. Priscilla felt his gaze, but couldn't see much of him because of her skirt.

She wasn't sure who started it, but soon they were both consumed with laughter. For safety's sake, Pietro pulled over to the curb. Soon their merriment died down, and there was silence.

"You are a beautiful woman," Pietro said with all sincerity, "but this dress is wrong for you."

Priscilla had known it the moment she'd tried it on. Her mother had attempted to dress her in a way that would prove to the prince she would make him an ideal wife.

"I've offended you?" he asked.

"No," she assured him.

He waited a moment and Priscilla assumed he was going to say something more, but she was wrong. When traffic cleared, he eased the car back into the flow.

More at ease with him now, Priscilla relaxed. "You... you said you wanted to talk to me," she reminded him. Now was as good a time as any.

Once again he hesitated. "Not now."

She hated that imperious way he spoke, as if everything were on his terms, on his time. "Why not?" she demanded.

"Because I'm angry."

"With me?"

"No…no." His tone gentled considerably. "Never with you, Priscilla. Never with you."

She wouldn't be so easily appeased this time. This man confused and frustrated her. "Then who?"

He waited for several seconds, then said, "Prince Stefano."

His answer surprised her. "But why?"

"You wouldn't understand."

"I might."

"No, my love. It's complicated and best left unsaid."

His love. Only that afternoon he'd pushed her out of his arms and left her reeling with shock and embarrassment. Now he was speaking to her in the tenderest of endearments.

Unwilling to be hurt again, Priscilla gathered her pride about her like a shawl and slowly drew inside herself.

Other than the hum of the engine, there was no sound. The void seemed to stretch and expand, like yeast in bread dough. She felt Pietro's gaze studying her in the dark.

"Don't be angry with me," he implored. "I can't bear that."

"Then don't call me your love," she returned heatedly. Her voice quivered, making it sound as if she were close to breaking into tears.

Her words were met with stark silence, as if she'd shocked him. At the first opportunity, Pietro pulled off to the side of the road. He sat with his hands braced against the steering wheel, and after a moment a deep sigh rumbled through his chest.

"I'm going to kiss you, Priscilla."

She blinked, uncertain she'd heard him correctly. "Kiss me?" He made it sound as if this were the last thing he wanted. "But why…?"

"I don't think I can keep from kissing you."

"But you said earlier that…"

"Forget what I said for now." He turned off the engine and turned toward her. Their gazes met in the dim light and locked hungrily. "Forget everything I said this afternoon."

Slowly he lowered his mouth to hers.

Priscilla wanted to turn away from him, if for nothing more than to salvage her pride, but she couldn't summon even a token resistance. The moment his lips touched hers, she realized that being in Pietro's arms was more important than anything.

Hope sat with her hands buried deep in her windbreaker on the hard wooden bench inside the ferry terminal. She'd been waiting nearly twenty minutes and Stefano still hadn't shown. By all that was right she should be home and in bed asleep.

The sound of heavy footsteps echoed against the hard floor. Her heart leapt with anticipation and she looked up, and saw that it wasn't the prince. She couldn't quite believe it, but whoever it was, resembled Elvis.

Her shoulders sagged with disappointment, and she buried her chin against her chest. She was a fool. No one else would have waited this long. No one else would have gone on hoping he'd come when it was clear he wasn't going to show.

"Hope."

Her head shot up, and she frowned. The man standing before her was Elvis and yet...

"Stefano?"

He grinned and, breathing heavily, he sat down next to her. "I fooled you?"

"Yes." She couldn't keep the amusement out of her voice or her eyes. She'd looked directly at him and hadn't realized it was Stefano. He wore a pair of rhinestone-studded white bell-bottoms and matching top, and a white scarf was draped around his neck. "What have you done to yourself?"

"I needed to escape the hotel without being noticed."

"In that outfit?"

He laughed. "Don't scoff. I paid good money for this costume."

"Where in the name of heaven did you get it?"

"From the Elvis impersonator who's performing in the cocktail lounge." He was only now catching his breath. "I can't believe you're still here. I was afraid you'd left, but I found it impossible to slip away unnoticed."

"But why?" That was by far the more curious of her questions.

The laughter drained from his eyes. "So I could be alone with you. If I came as myself, we'd be interrupted constantly. I am being selfish, but I don't wish to share this time with anyone but you."

If that was being greedy, then she was guilty, as well.

"Come," he said, standing and reaching for her hand.

"Where are we going?"

The question seemed to catch him unaware. "I don't know yet. It is enough that we are together."

They walked down the ramp out of the ferry terminal and onto the sidewalk. Although it was almost eleven o'clock, the streets were filled with the continual flow of foot traffic.

Stefano slipped his arm around her waist and they strolled together. Stefano seemed unconcerned with the attention his disguise attracted. Every now and again someone would shout, "Hello, Elvis," and he'd give a friendly wave.

Finally Stefano turned off the sidewalk and led her down a long pier lined with tourist and art shops. They stopped at the end and looked out over the deep, dark waters.

The night was gorgeous and the lights from West Seattle and the smaller islands of Puget Sound glowed like rows of bright bulbs on a Christmas tree.

Stefano turned Hope into his embrace and locked his hands at the small of her back. Sighing softly, she found a peace, a serenity she couldn't explain.

Stefano kissed her cheek, her ear, her hair, before claiming her mouth. Hope experienced a deep, almost painful longing. The prince trembled and she knew he was as deeply affected by their kisses as she.

Hope pressed her head against his shoulder and closed her eyes as the warm sensations melted over her. Biting into her lower lip, she tried not to think of the impossibility of their situation.

"I was afraid of that," Stefano murmured against her hair.

"Of what?" she asked.

"Your kiss. It's even better than before." His words were sad, almost bitter, and she lifted her head, wanting to look into his eyes. He wouldn't let her.

"Please," he said gently, "let me hold you a little longer."

Hope hadn't the strength of will to resist him. Nestled in his arms, it seemed as if the world and all the troubles that plagued the universe were a million miles away.

"When I was a little girl, I used to dream of meeting a handsome prince," she told him, finding life ironic. "My mother would read me a story before I went to sleep and she'd kiss me good-night and then tell me that someday my prince would come."

"Ah, yes, your mother." Amusement laced his words. A moment passed and he chuckled softly.

Hope's head sprang upward. "What's she done now?"

"Nothing," he said, pressing her head back to his shoulder. "Don't be so concerned."

"Stefano, I know my mother. Please tell me what she's up to this time."

He chuckled softly and brushed his lips against hers. "I received a letter from her this afternoon."

"And…" Hope coaxed.

"She wanted to know what my intentions toward you were."

"No." Mortified, Hope buried her face in his chest. "I apologize…. Oh, Stefano, forgive her. She means no harm. It's just that…" Try as she might, Hope didn't have a prayer of explaining, because she didn't have a hope of analyzing what her mother could have been thinking. "It's just that…"

"Perhaps she believes I'm the prince she told you was coming all these years."

"Mom and her friends are romantics," Hope offered as a possible explanation. "They don't understand that life isn't filled with happy endings."

It seemed his hold on her tightened briefly. "Let's not speak of the future. Not tonight. It is selfish to indulge myself with you, I know, but it is a little thing, and I hope in time you'll find it in your heart to forgive me."

Hope didn't want to think of the future, either. It went without saying she wouldn't—couldn't be—part of his life. Like Stefano, she was content to indulge her fantasies.

They didn't seem to have a lot to say. Together they sat on a bench at the end of the pier and he wrapped his arm around her shoulder. Every now and again he'd kiss her. In the beginning his kisses were gentle, but they soon took on an intensity that left Hope breathless.

He stopped abruptly and brushed a strand of hair from her cheek, and his hand lingered there. Several moments passed before he gave in to the temptation and kissed her again. She parted her lips to him and his tongue sought hers, involving her in a slow, erotic game.

Hope's breathing became heavy and shallow and when he raised his head, his gaze sought hers in the moonlight. She noted that his eyes were dark with passion and knew her own were a reflection of his.

His mouth found hers once more and when he dragged his lips away, he pressed his forehead to hers. "I can't kiss you again," he whispered.

The funny thing with greed, Hope discovered, was that she was never satisfied. At one time all she wanted was to spend time with him, then she'd be happy, she told herself. Then he kissed her, and she never wanted it to end.

"Why can't you kiss me?" she asked, spreading a series of kisses over his face, starting at his jaw and working her way over the contour of his face, teasing his lips with the tip of her tongue.

"Hope…" He trapped her face between his hands.

"Hmm?"

He directed her mouth to his and it was as if they were reuniting after a six-month absence. When he pulled away, Hope saw that his face was tight with desire.

"We must stop," he murmured, sounding very much as if he were in pain.

"I know…but I'm greedy for you."

"That's the problem," he murmured. "I am greedy for you, too. I just didn't know…"

"Didn't know what?"

"How much I need you," he whispered. "Now, please, don't tempt me anymore. You make me weak and—" he chuckled softly "—strong."

"That makes no sense."

"I know, but it's the truth." He pressed her fingers to his lips. "I want you to tell me more of your childhood."

"But, Stefano, I'm so…ordinary. Tell me of yours."

"I have no interest in hearing myself speak. Tell me everything there is to know about you."

"What about my old boyfriends? Do you want to hear about them, as well?"

"No," he said and laughed softly. "It wouldn't take very much to make me insanely jealous."

"It would only be fair," she chided. "I've been reading about your exploits for years. You aren't called the Bachelor Prince for nothing." She meant to tease him, to make light of his reputation.

He surprised her by clasping her upper arms. His eyes locked with her.

"It's true, there've been many women in my life."

"I know." She lowered her gaze, not wanting to think about all the beautiful females who had loved him. And worse. Whom he'd loved.

He lifted her chin with his index finger. "But there's only been one woman who held my heart in the palm of her hand." He reached for her hand and kissed her palm. "That woman, Hope Jordan, is you."

Chapter 6

It was the wee hours of the morning before Stefano returned to the hotel. He couldn't remember a time in his life that he'd been happier.

All his life he'd been groomed for his position as the Prince of San Lorenzo. He'd been taught the concerns of his country must come first. Duty and sacrifice were equated with honor and character. He knew he must marry Priscilla Rutherford or some other woman who was equally wealthy. There was no other option.

Now certainly wasn't the time to fall in love. Now wasn't the time to give his heart to a woman he must eventually leave.

A week, he told himself. He would give himself that time with Hope as a gift. Seven days would be ample time to fill his heart with memories. Ones that he would need to last him a lifetime.

He'd been honest with Hope from the first. She understood and accepted that there could be no future for them. And yet she'd generously opened her heart and her life to him.

By the time Stefano let himself into his suite, he realized how exhausted he was, and yet he doubted that he'd sleep. Sleep would rob him of the precious moments he had to think about Hope, to remember the taste of her kisses and how right it felt to hold her in his arms.

"Where have you been?"

Pietro's hard voice rocked Stefano. Never had anyone dared to speak to him in such a tone.

"Pietro?" His friend stood by the picture window, his hands clasped behind his back as if he'd been furiously pacing. "Is something wrong?"

"Only that you'd disappeared!" he snapped. Walking over to the phone, Pietro punched out a series of numbers and spoke brusquely to James, Stefano's bodyguard, reporting the prince's safe return.

"I apologize, my friend. I wasn't thinking."

"What is this…this ridiculous outfit?" Pietro gestured toward the Elvis costume as if he found it distasteful to look at.

"What does it look like?" Stefano was prepared to give his secretary a little slack, but Pietro was stepping dangerously close to his limit. As the crown prince, he rarely had to account for his actions, and certainly not for his choice of wardrobe.

"It looks like you've been making a fool of yourself," Pietro said heatedly.

"Pietro," Stefano barked. "I think it would be better if we saved this conversation for morning. I've already apologized for any dismay I may have caused you and the others. It's late and you're upset."

"I'm more than upset." His secretary walked over to the desk and reached for a typewritten sheet, jerking it off the top with enough energy to send several papers fluttering to the floor. He ignored the disruption and slapped the single page down on the table next to where Stefano was standing.

"This is my letter of resignation, effective immediately." Having made that announcement, Pietro stormed over to the window and stood with his back to Stefano.

The prince couldn't have been more surprised if his secretary and friend had pulled a gun on him. The betrayal was as shocking.

Stefano sank onto the sofa cushions, hardly able to believe what he was reading. Pietro had been with him for years. He was far more than his secretary and companion. Pietro was his friend. The best he'd ever had.

"Is there a reason for your resignation, other than my tardiness this evening?" he managed to ask after a strained moment.

Pietro whirled around to face him. Their gazes locked in a fierce battle of wills. It felt as if they breathed simultaneously, each harboring his own grief.

"Yes," Pietro admitted reluctantly.

"You are free to tell me what I've done to offend

you." He wanted this confrontation to be man-to-man, not prince to subject, not employer to employee.

Pietro chose to sit in the chair across from him. His friend was a large man, and when he leaned forward their knees almost touched.

"I cannot. I will not," he amended heatedly, "allow you to treat Priscilla Rutherford in such an insulting manner. She is a woman worthy of being your bride."

"I fully intend to marry the woman," Stefano argued, but he could see that his reassurances did little to appease Pietro. "That's what you want, isn't it?" Stefano asked.

"Yes," he barked. "But give me one good reason she would want you after the horrible way you've treated her."

Stefano didn't have a clue what Pietro was speaking about. "Forgive me for being obtuse, but what terrible sin have I committed against the woman?"

It didn't take Pietro long to answer.

"First off, you visit her home and meet her family and completely ignore Priscilla."

Now that Pietro mentioned it, Stefano did recall becoming heavily involved in a conversation with James Rutherford. He'd been distracted, but as he remembered it, Priscilla hadn't seemed to mind.

"Nor can there be any excuse for this evening," Pietro continued.

"This evening at the banquet?" Stefano had thought he'd been attentive and thoughtful. It was apparent from the beginning that Priscilla had been ill. Rather than detain her while he dealt with the many women who sought an audience, he'd had Pietro escort her home.

"I never intended to insult her. I assumed she wasn't feeling well and thought to see to her comfort as quickly as possible."

True, he'd been eager to escape the banquet so he could meet Hope, but that had nothing to do with his time with Priscilla. "First thing in the morning, I'll send flowers and beg her indulgence," Stefano offered, hoping that would appease his secretary.

Pietro rubbed a hand down his face, and Stefano couldn't remember seeing his friend look more tired. "I've already seen to that."

"Thank you," Stefano murmured, inclining his head.

Pietro clenched his hands over his knees. "Answer me one thing."

"Of course."

"Do you care for Priscilla?"

If asked if he loved her, Stefano would have been honest. He liked Priscilla Rutherford, and was comfortable enough with her that in time he was confident he would grow to feel a deep tenderness for her. "Yes, I care for her."

"Then you intend to marry her?"

Stefano had no option. Pietro knew that better than anyone. "If she agrees to be my bride, then we will be married at the first opportunity."

Pietro lowered his gaze and after a long moment, said, "Good."

"My hope is that once we return to San Lorenzo, she

will follow with her family. Once she stays at the palace and samples what her life would be like there, I'll court her seriously." He hesitated, wondering if the heiress had said something to Pietro that he should know. "Do you know what her feelings are toward me?"

"No," came the stark answer.

Stefano waited a moment more, and tore Pietro's letter of resignation in half. "Now, can we forget this nonsense? It's late and we're both tired."

Pietro studied the torn piece of paper. "I will stay with you until we return to San Lorenzo," he said, his look both troubled and thoughtful. "If you want, I'll interview the applicants for my replacement, and leave as soon as one can be trained."

Stunned, Stefano nodded. "As you wish."

Stefano woke with a heavy heart. Unfortunately, the morning didn't bring any better news. He dressed, and when his breakfast arrived, he sat alone at the table and sipped his first cup of coffee.

From habit, he reached for the morning newspaper and scanned the headlines. As he reached for a baguette, his gaze fell upon the society page. The image of his own face smiled up to benignly greet him. It wasn't as though he were unaccustomed to finding his picture in the paper. Cameras routinely followed him.

But this photograph was different because Priscilla Rutherford was standing next to him. The lens had caught them at an opportune moment in which they happened to be gazing at each other. For all intents and purposes it looked as if they were deeply in love. The headlines gave way to speculation that an American had laid claim to Prince Stefano's heart.

The speculation in the article was even worse. The more he read, the more alarmed Stefano became. The entire piece was geared toward Stefano's attention to the heiress, and speculation as to where the romance would lead.

Stefano feared Hope would read this article and think terrible things of him. He must talk to her, assure her he wasn't playing her for a fool. But just as he reached for the telephone, Pietro brought him in some documents that required his signature.

Stefano didn't dare risk contacting Hope with Pietro in the room. As much as it was possible, he wanted to keep his relationship with Hope a secret. Later, when it became necessary for him to leave, he wanted to spare her any unnecessary attention and/or embarrassment.

His only opportunity to speak privately with Hope was to find some errand on which to send Pietro. "I need you to do something for me at your earliest convenience," Stefano said, reaching for his gold pen and a monogrammed sheet of paper.

"Of course," Pietro replied stiffly.

Stefano wrote out a message as quickly as his hand would move the pen. He folded the note and inserted it inside an envelope. "Personally deliver this to Miss Rutherford for me," he said, "and await her response."

Pietro hesitated long enough to attract Stefano's

attention. "Would you like me to leave right away?" Pietro asked.

"Please," Stefano said. He didn't know what was wrong with Pietro, but his tone implied that he'd rather walk off a gangplank than carry out this errand. If he wasn't so anxious to speak to Hope, he would have questioned his friend.

Pietro reluctantly accepted the envelope. Stefano waited until his secretary had left the room before reaching for the telephone. An eternity passed before the first ring. A second, third and a fourth followed before her answering machine clicked on.

He listened to Hope's voice and even though it came through a mechanical device, Stefano's spirits lifted just hearing her speak. She sounded upbeat and energetic, giving instructions to wait for the long beep.

"Hope, my princess..." Stefano hated machines. Now that he could speak, he didn't know what to say. "Please, my darling, don't be influenced by anything you read in the papers. You own my heart. Meet me this evening as we arranged. It's vital that we speak." With that he replaced the telephone receiver, convinced his message was grossly inadequate.

He covered his face with his hand and sighed heavily. If she hadn't already read the article, she would now. With one phone call he might have destroyed his relationship with the only woman he'd ever loved.

Priscilla endured breakfast with her parents while they touted the virtues of Prince Stefano as if he were a god. As far as either of them were concerned, the man was perfect in every way.

Neither bothered to ask about her evening. Apparently they assumed everything had been wonderful from beginning to end. But then Priscilla hadn't volunteered any information, either, and if the truth be known, she didn't know what she'd say if they asked.

The fever pitch accelerated when her mother read the morning paper and found Priscilla pictured with the prince taking up almost half of the society page.

By midmorning, the phone was ringing off the hook, and Elizabeth was in heaven delivering tidbits of speculation to her dearest friends.

As soon as she was able, Priscilla escaped with a book to the gazebo, one of her favorite hiding places. Her intention was to bury herself in the carefree world of a good story, but try as she might to concentrate, her attention repeatedly wandered from the printed page.

Instead of becoming absorbed in the novel, her thoughts countlessly reviewed the time she'd spent with Pietro. The man confused her more than anyone she'd ever known. But it didn't stop there. He intrigued her, as well. No other man had ever made her feel the way he did, as if she were a rare beauty, as if she were brilliant and utterly charming.

Priscilla discovered that all the things Pietro had told her about the prince were true for himself, as well. He was a gentle, kind and caring man.

"I wondered if I'd find you out here, miss," Mrs. Daily, the cook, said, sounding winded. She wore a black dress that rounded nicely over her ample hips and a white apron. "I swear I've spent the last twenty minutes searching for you."

Disheartened, Priscilla closed the novel. She'd been found. "Is my mother looking for me?"

"No. A gentleman came to call. He gave me this card."

Priscilla examined the name and sat upright so fast she nearly toppled out of the chair. Pietro. Her heart pounded with excitement. "Has he left?"

"No. Apparently he has a letter and has been instructed to give it to you personally. He explained that he needs a reply. He's waiting in your father's den."

"Does…anyone else know he's here?"

Mrs. Daily wiped the perspiration from her brow. "Not to my knowledge."

"Thank you, Mrs. Daily," she said and impulsively kissed the older woman's flushed cheek. "You're an angel." With that, Priscilla raced across the wide expanse of groomed lawn, taking a shortcut through the garden. Breathless, she came upon the den from the outside entrance.

She stood on the other side of the double wide French doors and watched Pietro, who was standing in front of the fireplace. He seemed to be examining the carved wooden ducks her father displayed on the mantel.

Pietro turned at the sound of the door opening.

"Hello," she said, terribly conscious of her shorts and T-shirt. Her mother would most definitely disapprove, but Priscilla hadn't wanted to waste time changing clothes.

"Priscilla." She surprised him and he appeared to brace himself. At once he became stiff and business-like. Opening his suit jacket, he withdrew an envelope.

"How are you this fine day?" she asked cheerfully.

"Very good, thank you," he returned crisply. "And yourself?"

"Great." Especially now, although it was hard to believe that the dignified man who stood before her was the same one who'd held and kissed her the night before.

"You might wish to read what's inside the envelope," he offered after a moment.

"Of course," she said, laughing inwardly at herself. It had been enough just to see him. Nothing Prince Stefano had written could rival that.

Priscilla felt his scrutiny as she read over the few scribbled lines. Either the prince had poor penmanship or he'd been in a terrible hurry. "I can't seem to make out a few lines," she said, using that as an excuse to move closer to him. "Can you?"

Pietro reluctantly read over the note. He frowned as if he were having difficulty reading the message, as well. "He apologizes for any embarrassment the article in this morning's paper has caused you."

"Did you see it?" she asked Pietro.

"No."

"Trust me, you didn't miss much. Frankly the prince is far more photogenic than I am. The article is nothing but speculation about our supposed romance, and nothing anyone with a whit of sense would take seriously. I know I'm not." She motioned toward the deep burgundy chairs that were positioned next to the fireplace. They both sat.

"Unfortunately," she confided, "that's not the case with my mother. You'd think I'd been awarded the Nobel Peace Prize from the way she's acting."

"So your parents are pleased with the attention the prince is paying you."

She wrinkled her nose and nodded. "I suppose I should let them enjoy it while they can. You see, I haven't given them that much to brag to their friends about. I'm not the least bit gifted."

His eyes snapped with disagreement. "That is most certainly not true."

If Priscilla hadn't already been in love with Pietro, she would have fallen head over heels right then. "I mean I'm not talented musically, or athletically or in some other way that parents like to brag to their friends about. With one exception," she amended, "I always achieved top grades. For years my mother wanted to test my intelligence quotient so she could boast to her friends that I had a genius IQ."

"Do you?" He made it sound like a distinct possibility.

"I don't know. I refused to be tested. I mean, what does it really matter if have a high IQ or don't? Knowing my test score doesn't change who or what I am, does it?"

"Not in the least."

"I didn't think so, either. Bless her heart, my mother

never understood that. And so, if she can stand in the limelight with her friends because of the attention Prince Stefano's giving me, well, I figure she's waited a long time."

Pietro's gaze found hers and she smiled at him. "What was the last part of his message? I couldn't make it out."

"He's invited you and your parents to brunch tomorrow morning at eleven."

"Oh, dear," Priscilla said with a ragged sigh. "I'd hoped the banquet might be the last of it."

Pietro frowned. "The last of it?"

"The prince's attention," Priscilla explained. "Frankly, I haven't figured out what he sees in me."

Pietro's eyes snapped the way they had earlier when she claimed she was without talent. "Can you accept Prince Stefano's invitation?" he asked brusquely.

"I'm sure we can." The truth was she'd much prefer for the prince to leave Seattle, so she could quietly return to her life. But that would mean that Pietro would be leaving, as well, so she was torn.

"Before you accept, don't you think you should speak with your parents first?"

"No," she said with frank honesty. "Because if they have a conflict, I'm sure they'll make other arrangements. It isn't every day a father has a chance to foist his daughter off on royalty." It was a joke, but Pietro didn't laugh.

"If Prince Stefano chooses you as his bride, he will be the fortunate one. How is it your parents don't recognize the rare jewel you are?" He frowned, sincerely puzzled. His words were so genuine that Priscilla developed a lump in her throat. Several moments passed before it dissolved enough for her to speak.

"Oh, Pietro, you make me feel like a princess."

He opened his mouth as if he were about to speak, when the door to the den opened and her mother abruptly appeared.

"Priscilla, I've been looking for you for a solid hour. You've been hiding from me again," she said disapprovingly until she noticed Pietro.

He stood. "Good day, Mrs. Rutherford."

"Hello, Pietro," she greeted warmly, clasping her hands together. "I wasn't told you were here."

"Prince Stefano sent me to deliver a letter to Priscilla."

"A letter?" Elizabeth Rutherford's eyes brightened. "I was just looking to tell Priscilla a gorgeous bouquet of flowers arrived from the prince. Why, it's one of the largest arrangements I believe I've ever seen." She handed Priscilla the card and then gracefully slipped the prince's letter from Pietro's fingers.

Instead of reading the card, Priscilla watched her mother's eyes quickly scan the letter. Elizabeth seemed to have no problem deciphering Stefano's handwriting. "He's invited us to brunch," she cooed.

"Yes, Mother."

"I hope you told him we'd be most honored to accept his invitation."

"Priscilla has already accepted on your behalf."

"Very good," her mother said, and the "look" came

over her as she studied Priscilla—one that Priscilla recognized all too well. The look that claimed there was nothing in three wardrobes full of clothes that was appropriate for her to wear. The look that said Priscilla was doomed to spend the entire day shopping.

"It was good to see you again, Pietro," Elizabeth said.

It demanded everything for Priscilla not to protest. She didn't want him to leave so soon. They'd barely had a chance to talk.

"Perhaps Pietro would like some refreshment, Mother," Priscilla said hurriedly.

"Of course," Elizabeth said, recovering quickly. "You must forgive my thoughtlessness. It was just that we're so very pleased to have met you and the prince. I was overcome with excitement to receive his latest invitation."

"I appreciate the offer, but I must be leaving."

"So soon?" Silently Priscilla pleaded with him to stay, but he looked away, ignoring her entreaty.

"I must return to the hotel to make our travel preparations."

Her gaze flew to his. "When…will you be leaving for San Lorenzo?" Priscilla asked, her voice hardly above a whisper. He'd casually dropped a bomb and then left her to deal with the aftermath. Not once had he mentioned returning to San Lorenzo. She knew, of course, now that the Romance Lovers' Convention was over, the prince and Pietro would be leaving, but she'd hoped it wouldn't be for a few days.

"We'll be returning to San Lorenzo as soon as I

can make all the necessary arrangements," Pietro announced.

"And that will be...?" her mother pressed.

Pietro hesitated. "Two days, possibly three."

"Oh," mother and daughter murmured together in sorry disappointment.

Hope's day had been hectic. From the moment the alarm sounded that morning until this very second, she'd been on the run. There seemed to be a million errands that had accumulated in the past few weeks. Errands she'd been putting off.

This day had been perfect. Since she had a dentist appointment in the afternoon, she decided to make a day of it. To be fair, her motives weren't pure. She needed an escape to mull over and savor the evening she'd spent with Prince Stefano.

If she followed her usual schedule, she'd face countless questions. Although Hope hadn't said anything to Lindy about the prince, she suspected her friend had heard him ask her to meet him at the ferry terminal. And then there was her mother.

Hope wanted to avoid all the questions, all the curiosity, and so she'd used this day as a convenient excuse to disappear.

Since she hadn't taken time for lunch, Hope was famished when she finally arrived home. Checking her watch, she saw that she wasn't scheduled to meet Stefano for another three hours. Briefly she wondered if he was going to opt for the Elvis costume again this evening.

The phone rang just as she opened the refrigerator door. She groped inside for a carrot and then reached for the receiver. "Hello."

"Hope, sweetheart." It was her mother. "Are you all right?"

Hope frowned at the apprehension in her mother's voice. "Of course I'm all right. Why shouldn't I be?"

"Well…I just didn't know how you'd feel after dating Prince Stefano and everything. You seemed quite taken with him."

"Mother, I thought we already went over this." Hope hadn't mentioned anything to her mother and the other self-appointed fairy godmothers about seeing Stefano again.

"I know, it's just that…well, I didn't want you to be hurt."

Hope had to bite her lip to keep from commenting on the letter Doris had written the prince, asking him his intentions. But to do so would reveal that she'd been in contact with him herself.

"I'm fine, Mom."

"You're sure?"

The line beeped, indicating that she had another call. "I have to go, Mom."

"All right, sweetie. I just wanted to be sure you weren't upset."

"I'm not." The line beeped again and she picked up the second call. "Hello."

A slight pause followed her greeting. "Hope?"

"Stefano." She said his name in a rush of happiness.

"Where have you been all day? I've been trying to reach you for hours."

"I was doing a bunch of errands I've been putting off for weeks. You wouldn't believe all the red tape involved in operating a small business. Then I had a dentist appointment. You'll be pleased to know I'm cavity-free."

"When did you arrive home?"

"Just a few minutes ago." It dawned on her then that there could only be one reason for his call. He couldn't meet her as they'd arranged, and her heart sagged with disappointment. "You can't come this evening." She said it for him, because it was easier than to have him tell her.

"Nothing could keep me from seeing you again. I swear this has been the longest day of my life." His voice was low and sensual and it was almost as if she were in his arms again. Which was exactly where Hope longed to be.

"It has for me, too," she whispered.

He seemed to hesitate. "I'm scheduled to dine with the mayor and his wife this evening."

"Yes, I know. You already explained why we can't meet until later. I understand, Stefano. Don't worry."

"I've decided to have my driver deliver me to your home directly following the dinner. You'll be there?"

"Of course, but…"

"I'm sorry to be so rude, but I must go. I'm at the mayor's home now and they tell me dinner is being served. You understand, don't you?"

"Of course."

With that, the telephone line went abruptly dead, and Hope was left to wonder at the purpose of Stefano's call. It had all been rather odd. Yes, he'd changed their plans, but she had the sinking sensation that there was far more to this than he was letting on.

Hope chewed down on the carrot as she walked back into her bedroom and sorted through her closet, reviewing her choice in outfits. She decided upon jeans and a shirt with a Southwestern pattern.

She was examining the contents of her freezer, looking for something appetizing to zap in her microwave when she remembered she hadn't checked her messages on the answering machine.

The first was from Lindy who sounded madder than hops about something. A long beep followed and Stefano's voice came on the line, claiming she shouldn't put any credence in the article in that morning's paper.

Newspaper article? She'd brought the paper in with the mail and hadn't bothered to look at it. She went through the entire front page and didn't find a single word printed about Stefano.

Not until she reached for the society page did she see it. The photograph of the prince gazing longingly at another woman seemed to slap her across the face.

For a moment, Hope actually thought she might be ill. The impact of learning the man she loved was involved with another woman quite literally made her sick to her stomach. The blood rushed out of her face so fast that she grew dizzy.

Hope slumped into the kitchen chair and waited for

the nausea to subside. Three times she attempted to read the article, and each time discovered that she couldn't get past the first five paragraphs. In those few short lines she learned that it was widely believed that the heiress, Priscilla Rutherford, had captured the Bachelor Prince's heart and that a marriage proposal couldn't be far behind.

Hope didn't know how long she sat there staring into space while she attempted to calm herself.

She was such a fool. The man was known around the world as a playboy. How could she have allowed this to happen? That was what plagued Hope the most. Within the space of two days, she'd handed this man her heart. A man who collected women's hearts the way some do foreign stamps and coins.

He was good—she had to grant him that. He'd had her believing that he actually cared for her. Perhaps because she so wanted to believe it so desperately.

She didn't cry. This was a pain too deep for tears. A betrayal. The funny part of it was that she didn't actually blame Stefano. From what she saw of Priscilla Rutherford, the other woman was quite lovely. A woman Hope would like for a friend.

Hope had nothing to offer Stefano other than her heart. Unfortunately he was already in possession of that.

The doorbell chimed and she stared at the door for several moments.

"Hope, please." It was Stefano.

"Go away," she begged. "Just go away."

Chapter 7

"I'm not leaving until we speak," Prince Stefano insisted from Hope's porch.

"I have no intention of opening this door," Hope said with equal conviction. He didn't know the meaning of the word *stubborn* until he'd crossed swords with her. "You played me for a fool!" she cried.

"All I'm asking is five minutes of your time," Stefano pleaded. "Hear me out and if you still don't want to see me, then I'll quietly leave."

It wasn't Stefano Hope didn't trust, it was herself. The prince made her vulnerable in ways no man had before. As much as she'd claimed otherwise, she'd inherited a romantic nature from her mother and her irrational heart had led her down a primrose path. What angered Hope the most was the way she'd obtusely followed. She was smarter than this. If she hadn't been so blinded by her attraction, she would have realized much sooner that a man like Prince Stefano couldn't possibly be serious about someone like her.

"Hope," he pleaded, "all I want is five minutes of your time."

"Answer me one thing," she insisted, finding herself wavering despite her earlier resolve. "Do you or do you not intend to marry Priscilla Rutherford?" The answer to that question would be all she needed to know.

The prince hesitated. "Let me explain."

"Answer the question." She trusted him to be honest. In light of what she'd learned, perhaps she was an even greater fool to believe Prince Stefano was an honorable man.

"Trust me, Priscilla has nothing to do with the way I feel about you."

"Stefano, if you want me to open this door, then you'll answer the question."

Once again he hesitated.

Fool that she was, Hope unlocked the door. Carrying on a conversation in this manner, with them both shouting to be heard through the thick oak door, was ridiculous.

The mesh screen door was solidly locked in place. She stood on one side and he on the other. The barrier was flimsy at best, but necessary.

Stefano's gaze held hers. She read the agony in his eyes, the pain of the truth.

"There are many things you don't understand," he whispered.

"I understand that you wine and dine Miss Rutherford and sneak away to meet me in a back alley. What you failed to realize, Stefano, is that I may be a nobody, but I have my pride, and frankly you've walked all over it."

By the time she finished, her voice was trembling. She stopped abruptly and swallowed in an effort to control her own pain, complicated by her considerable anger.

Stefano had made a mistake if he believed she would allow him to treat her in such a shabby manner.

Briefly Stefano closed his eyes. "I would rather die than hurt you."

Hope knew he spoke the truth, but why would he marry another woman if he cared so deeply for her? There could only be one explanation. He was ashamed of her. Her family wasn't good enough for the likes of Prince Stefano. Jordan wasn't a surname that brought instant recognition in the world of high society, whereas the Rutherford name was emblazoned across one of the finest shipping lines in the world.

"Are you going to marry Priscilla Rutherford?" she demanded, her voice strong and sure.

He hung his head and nodded. "Yes."

"That's everything I need to know," she whispered. With that she closed the door. For a moment, the pain of the truth was almost more than she could bear and she slumped against the wooden structure, letting it hold her upright.

Taking in a deep breath, she moved away from the door and looked out the window. Stefano had returned to his limousine. He sat in the backseat for several torturous moments before giving his driver the order to leave.

The long, sleek automobile moved away from the curb. Prince Stefano was out of her life. He could have lied, she realized, could have glossed over the newspaper article as gossip. Instead he'd admitted the painful truth, unwilling to spare him or her with lies.

It seemed impossible that she could still love him, but she did.

Nestled on her sofa, Hope drew her knees up and rested her forehead there. It took her a while to sort through her emotions.

At first she was steamy with resentment. She was hurt. Angry. She looked for someone to blame. Her mother was the first person who came to mind. If Doris hadn't purchased that ridiculous ticket none of this would have happened.

Lindy was the second name on her list. If her friend hadn't fed her this line about romance, Hope might have seen through the smoke screen.

But ultimately there was no one to blame but herself. She was the one who'd been foolish enough to believe in fairy tales. She was the one who'd sat in a ferry terminal at nearly eleven o'clock at night, praying Stefano would show. She was the one who'd handed him her heart on a tarnished silver platter.

Loving Stefano had seemed so right. Hope had been foolish enough to believe she had it all figured out. Him figured out. Just as if she were reading a recipe. She'd seen the look in his eyes, tasted his kisses, held him in her arms.

For a few short days she'd believed in the impossible.

It was over now. She'd made sure he understood that. All she had left were the memories, and try as she might, she couldn't make herself regret having fallen in love with the Bachelor Prince.

An hour and a half later, Hope decided against sitting inside her home on a bright, beautiful evening and brooding over her mistakes. She needed physical activity to help her out of the doldrums. With that thought in mind, she decided to water her front yard.

A bundle of nervous energy, she changed into shorts and a sleeveless top and brought the hose around to the front of the yard. Her roses needed to be clipped, and she made a mental note to put that on her to-do list for the weekend.

A roar of a motorcycle zooming down her street caused her to turn around and glare at the rider. This was a peaceful neighborhood, and the irritation of loud noises wasn't appreciated.

The rider resembled James Dean, the legendary movie actor. He wore a white T-shirt, blue jeans and black boots, and when he saw her, he roared his bike into her driveway.

"Hope."

Not until that moment did Hope realize the rider was Stefano. Her mouth sagged open in surprise.

"I can't leave matters this way between us. Unfortunately, I fear I've been followed. Come with me. Please."

"But…"

He held his hand out to her. "I will never ask anything more of you. If you feel anything for me, you'll do as I ask without question. Hurry, please, before I'm found."

Dropping the hose, Hope leapt onto the back of the motorcycle as if she'd been born on the seat of a bike, and placed the helmet he had for her over her head. She wrapped her arms around Stefano's middle and within seconds they were off.

The prince expertly wove in and out of traffic. She saw him checking his rearview mirror several times, and when they stopped for a red light, he turned and looked over his shoulder.

"Who's after you?" Hope asked, fearing he might be in some kind of trouble.

"My bodyguard," Stefano explained.

"But don't you pay him to protect you?"

"Yes, but there are times, such as these, when I need my privacy. James doesn't appreciate that, I fear."

"How often do you come up with these disguises and the sudden need to escape?"

Stefano chuckled, but his laughter lacked any real amusement. "Only since I've met you."

"Me?"

The light changed and Stefano revved the engine, drowning out her thoughts as they continued down the busy street. Hope hadn't a clue of their destination, and she wasn't sure Stefano did, either. By the time he pulled over and parked the bike at the Ballard Locks, Hope was convinced it would take a week to clean the bugs off her teeth.

Stefano removed his helmet, helped her off the motorcycle and held her hand. They walked over to the viewing point and gazed at the long line of motorboats and sailboats awaiting their turn to travel through the locks that linked Lake Washington with Puget Sound.

"Forgive me for being so demanding," he said without looking at her. "You had every right to refuse to come with me."

That was true. "I was under the impression that if I didn't come, you'd have kidnapped me."

"I was desperate enough to have considered that, although I'd like to think myself incapable of such a crime. After this evening, I'm no longer sure."

"This evening?"

"When you closed the door on me."

It hadn't occurred to Hope that this was probably the first time anyone had behaved so brusquely with His Highness. Generally, doors were opened for him, not slammed in his face.

"I can't bear the thought of leaving matters as they were between us," he explained. His gaze studied the deep green waters as if he dared not turn and look into her eyes.

"I don't know that there's anything left to say."

"Perhaps not, but I couldn't leave without telling you the truth. I owe you that much."

Frankly, Hope had had just about all of that she could take for one day. "I know you're going to marry Miss Rutherford. You told me that yourself."

"Yes, but you do not know why."

"I'm not stupid, Stefano. Priscilla Rutherford is far more socially acceptable than I am. I own a coffee shop, remember? Not a shipping line." Although she tried to keep the bitterness out of her voice, she feared she had little success.

Stefano turned and looked at her for the first time. He framed her face in his hands and gazed deeply into her eyes. His own narrowed with an emotion she was sure she misread…love. A love so strong, it left her shaken.

"No, my love, what you're thinking couldn't be further from the truth. I must marry Priscilla Rutherford because she's an heiress."

Hope blinked. "I don't understand. You're one of the wealthiest men in the world…or so I've read. It doesn't make any sense that you'd be forced to marry for money."

He hung his head as if deeply ashamed. "It's true. My country is on the brink of bankruptcy. For the last year I've drained my family fortune in an effort to keep the economy stable. Other than a meager trust to cover my personal expenses, I'm nearly penniless."

"Oh, Stefano."

"Falling in love now is God's joke on me. You see

I never really believed in love until I met you. Isn't it ironic that I should give my heart to one woman and be forced to marry another?"

Hope blinked back the ready tears that crowded the corners of her eyes.

"I promised myself a week with you. It was selfish and thoughtless of me not to have told you the truth in the beginning. I love you, Hope. I'll always love you, but within the next couple of days I'm going to walk away from you and never look back."

A tear blazed a trail down her face and she furiously wiped it aside, hating the weakness of emotion. "This is supposed to make me feel better?"

He blinked with surprise at her anger. "I…I've hurt you again."

"You couldn't leave matters the way they were? Oh, no, you had to be sure I knew you loved me. Well, that's just fine and dandy." More tears escaped, and she ran her forearm under her nose, and sniffled loudly. "This is just great."

Stefano looked utterly perplexed. "You'd rather not know how much I love you?"

"Of course I want to know that." The man simply didn't understand. "I love you, too. That much should be obvious. It's just that… Never mind," she cried. "Go and marry your heiress!" She walked several feet away from him and wiped the moisture from her cheeks while she attempted to compose herself.

She didn't hear him until he was directly behind

her. He placed his hands on her shoulders and brought his lips close to her ear. "I cannot bear to see you cry."

"Don't worry about it," she said, and shrugged one shoulder. "I'm a big girl, I'll get over you. I mean…I fell in love with you fast enough, it shouldn't be that difficult to forget you." That wasn't true, but she was looking to salvage her pride by making light of her feelings.

His grip on her tightened. "Pietro wants to schedule our return flight to San Lorenzo for tomorrow afternoon," he whispered.

She stiffened. "So soon?"

"I'll agree to his schedule if you tell me you don't want to see me again. But if…if there's a chance you'd consider meeting me for the next two or three nights, then I'll rearrange my schedule to be sure I stay in Seattle a bit longer."

"You're asking the impossible," she cried. She couldn't bear to have him hold her, knowing there would soon be another woman in his arms. Couldn't allow him to kiss her, knowing he'd soon be kissing another.

"I know," he said in a tortured whisper. "We have so little time together. Forgive me, my love, for being self-indulgent. I should have realized I've asked the impossible."

"Stefano," she whispered, and her hands covered his.

He turned her into his arms and brought his mouth down to hers in a moist, gentle kiss. The pressure of his touch changed the moment Hope responded. He kissed her again and again with a growing desperation, an urgency that left her clinging and struggling for breath when he finished.

"I'm sorry," he whispered, "I didn't mean to frighten you."

He hadn't, but she didn't have the breath to assure him otherwise.

He kissed her once more, and his lips brushed her nose, her cheek, her ear. She heard a sigh rumble through his chest. He paused, seemed to draw upon his reserve of strength, and with some effort eased himself away from her.

"I'll take you home now," he said.

She nodded.

They rode back in silence, with none of the urgency with which they'd sped away. Sometime later, he came to a stop in her driveway. Climbing off the bike first, he helped her dismount and then escorted her to the front door.

Neither spoke. Their eyes met and he smiled weakly. "Thank you, Hope." He pressed his hand against her face and rubbed his thumb over the arch of her cheek. His eyes were filled with pain. "I don't know if I have the courage to walk away from you," he told her in a broken whisper.

"Then don't," she whimpered and flung herself into his arms. "Not yet. We'll worry about tomorrow later. For now we have each other."

Stefano dared not look at his watch again for fear the Rutherfords would think he was pressed for time.

He wasn't. It was another three hours before he could see Hope again. If anything, he wanted the time to pass more quickly.

"I'm so pleased you could join me," he said, as the small group reviewed the menu selections. Personally, Stefano wasn't hungry. Hope had promised him a tour of the rain forest and a picnic. It would be a shame if brunch with the Rutherfords ruined that.

"The pleasure is all ours," Elizabeth Rutherford assured him. "Isn't that right, Priscilla?"

The woman seemed to prod her daughter at every turn. It had been a mistake to invite her parents, he realized. Stefano would have enjoyed the meal with Priscilla, but with her family present—especially her mother—the brunch was sure to be an ordeal.

"We are honored by your invitation," Priscilla said in a monotone, as if she'd been forced to rehearse the line countless times.

Stefano's gaze drifted toward Pietro who wore a deep frown. The prince didn't fully understand what was going on with his secretary. For years Pietro had accompanied him to endless state dinners and other social functions. He often used his secretary as a buffer against the curious and meddling dowagers keen on marrying him off to their daughters and granddaughters.

Stefano had sensed his secretary's reluctance the minute he asked Pietro to join him with the Rutherfords. He'd offered a weak excuse, which Stefano rejected, and afterward Pietro was tight-lipped and sullen.

Even now Pietro sat stiffly at the table as if he'd rather be anyplace else but with the prince and the Rutherfords. Frankly, Pietro's attitude was beginning to irritate him.

Stefano had once considered Pietro his friend. Now he was no longer sure. Although nothing more had been said between them regarding Pietro's resignation, it was understood that once they returned to San Lorenzo, Pietro would hire his replacement, train him and leave Stefano's employment.

Apparently the prince had committed some terrible crime, other than his treatment of Priscilla, which, frankly, Stefano didn't think was so bad.

He liked Priscilla, and knew the feeling would grow once he got her away from her mother's clutches. Already he had a tender spot in his heart for the heiress. It didn't compare to the fiery intensity of feeling he shared with Hope, but over time he believed Priscilla and he would be happy. As happy as any man could be who was in his situation.

"My husband and I were discussing your invitation to visit San Lorenzo," Elizabeth said, breaking into his thoughts.

Stefano focused his attention on Priscilla's mother. "Naturally I'd want you to stay at the palace."

Elizabeth exchanged appreciative looks with her husband as if she'd somehow manipulated the invitation from him.

"We certainly wouldn't want to intrude on your royal business," the elder Rutherford inserted.

"Darling, the prince wouldn't have invited us if we were going to be a nuisance, isn't that right, Prince Stefano?"

"Most certainly."

"From what I understand, San Lorenzo has some of the best hotels in all of Europe," Priscilla's father said, as if he'd be just as happy in a hotel as a guest in the palace.

"That's true." Stefano didn't mention that a good portion of those world-class hotels sat vacant and were struggling to stay afloat in the current economic slump.

"If you wish," Stefano said, glancing at his secretary, "I could have Pietro arrange rooms for you at the Empress at my expense. It is our finest hotel, and I'm sure you'd be most comfortable."

"Nonsense," Elizabeth said quickly. "We'd prefer the palace. It isn't everyone who can say they've slept there, now can they?" She laughed lightly at her own joke, but Stefano noticed no one joined in her amusement.

After an uncomfortable moment of silence, Elizabeth once more picked up the conversation, directing her comment to her daughter. "You should tell the prince about your charity work, Priscilla."

"Mother, please. If Prince Stefano wants to hear about my work at the Children's Hospital, he can ask me himself."

It pleased Stefano that the Rutherfords' daughter revealed a little pluck. He was beginning to despair.

Priscilla glared at her mother and it did Stefano's heart good to see her mother squirm just a bit. He might have lessened the older woman's discomfort by inquiring about Priscilla's charity efforts, but he decided against it.

"How long will you be in Seattle?" the elder Rutherford inquired of Pietro.

"I've arranged to depart early tomorrow morning," his secretary answered.

"Change that," Stefano said.

"Change the arrangements?" Pietro asked and glared at him.

"I've decided to remain in this beautiful city for three more days. There's some sightseeing I want to do. With my current schedule I rarely have the opportunity to become properly acquainted with an area. Seattle strikes my fancy."

If looks could kill, Stefano would be mortally wounded. Pietro all but rose from his chair. Although he did an adequate job of restraining himself, Stefano wasn't fooled.

Whatever it was that was troubling his friend had gone on far too long. At first opportunity Stefano planned on confronting his secretary. The man hadn't been the same from the moment they landed in Seattle.

As it happened, the opportunity arose soon after the meal with the Rutherfords. Stefano and Pietro rode up in the elevator to the series of suites set aside for him on the nineteenth floor.

"I'd like a word with you," Pietro said the moment they were alone.

"If you insist."

"I do." It seemed Pietro was about to explode. His jaw was set and tight, and his hands were clenched at his sides.

The elevator doors rushed open and Stefano led the way into his private quarters. "What's wrong? Something's been troubling you from the moment we arrived, and I want to know what it is."

Pietro started to pace, a habit that relieved his tension. "I'd already made the arrangements to leave Seattle tomorrow morning."

Stefano shrugged. "Change them. You've done so often enough in the past. Why does it bother you so much now?"

His friend's mouth tightened. "If you insist upon staying this additional time, then I'd like to request your permission to return to San Lorenzo on my own."

"Absolutely not." Stefano didn't need time to consider his response. Not a day passed in which Stefano didn't require his secretary's assistance. To have Pietro return ahead of him would place an unnecessary burden on Stefano.

Pietro mumbled a profanity under his breath.

"Pietro," the prince said, thoughtfully studying his friend. "Can you tell me what plagues you?"

His secretary stiffened. "No."

"I can't order you, but as your friend, I would hope you could share with me what's wrong. If I've done something to offend you, let's clear the air."

"It's nothing you've done," Pietro assured him. He

slumped into a chair and buried his face in his hands. "I apologize for my behavior."

Stefano could press his friend for details, but he preferred that Pietro would offer them willingly. He didn't.

"I have an appointment this afternoon," Stefano said.

Pietro nodded, without inquiring as to the prince's plans. Generally his secretary was as conscientious as his bodyguard of his whereabouts and schedule.

"Perhaps we can talk more later," Stefano suggested.

"Perhaps," Pietro agreed.

But Stefano doubted they would. It saddened him to think he had lost the best friend he'd ever had, especially when he hadn't a clue why.

Pietro sat in his compact office, staring out of the window. The view from the nineteenth floor was spectacular. Puget Sound shone like a polished jewel in the sunlight. Ferries and an abundance of oceangoing vessels patrolled the waterways. But the beauty of the scene escaped him.

A knock sounded against his door. "Come in," he called.

A footman opened the door and approached the desk. "The front desk sent this up. It's addressed to you."

"Thank you." Pietro waited until the man had left the room before tearing open the envelope. He knew before he read a single word that the message was from Priscilla.

*I'm sorry to trouble you, but it's vitally important
that I speak to you at your earliest convenience.
I'll wait in the lobby for your reply.*

He read the note and wiped a hand down his face.

After having spent an uncomfortable hour and a
half in her presence, Pietro wasn't sure he could endure
much more. His restraint was stretched to the breaking point. It had demanded every ounce of self-control
he possessed not to make a scene with Priscilla and
her mother. Elizabeth Rutherford was a fool. Somehow
he didn't think the prince would appreciate it if he'd
pointed it out to him.

Knowing there was no help for it, Pietro rang for
the footman and asked that Priscilla be escorted to his
office.

The pair returned within five minutes. It was clear
that Priscilla had returned home and changed clothes.
Instead of the dove-gray suit that didn't do her beauty
justice, she wore a simple sleeveless summer dress and
a wide-brimmed hat.

Pietro was literally stung by her beauty. It took him
a moment to recover.

"Hello, Priscilla," he offered, and gestured for her
to sit down.

"Pietro." She sat and clasped her hands in her lap.
"Thank you for seeing me. I imagine after the spectacle
this morning, you were wishing you never had to lay
eyes on me again."

Actually, quite the opposite was true. The temptation to carry her away had nearly been his undoing. He couldn't tolerate the demeaning way in which her family treated her, as if her personal value rested solely in Prince Stefano's attention.

That Prince Stefano was prepared to marry Priscilla for her fortune troubled him. But seeing that he'd been the one to handpick Priscilla Rutherford from the list of potential brides, he couldn't very well object. He, too, had discredited the woman who innocently sat across from him. Now he was left to pay the piper.

"I don't mean to be a nuisance," she said, her gaze avoiding his.

"You could never be that," he assured her, hoping to keep their conversation on a professional level, and immediately failing. It was when it swayed toward the personal that he lost control. Twice now he'd held and kissed the woman who was destined to be the princess of San Lorenzo. If Stefano had so much as a hint of his feelings for Priscilla, he'd have him banished, and with reason.

"I was wondering if you could arrange for me to meet the prince alone," Priscilla asked.

"Alone?"

"Yes. Wherever we're together, there are always a number of people around…and that makes it extremely difficult for us to speak privately."

"I see." His mind was working double-time, wondering what it was Priscilla Rutherford had to say to the prince that had to be said when they were alone.

"Since it appears we're going to be in the area a few

days longer than I'd anticipated, I'll see what I can do," Pietro said. He opened a small ledger where he wrote in the prince's appointments.

He paused when he saw that there was nothing written down for the prince that afternoon. Yet he distinctly remembered Stefano mentioning an appointment.

"If you'll excuse me for a moment."

"Of course."

Pietro stepped out of the office and called for a footman. "Is James with the prince?"

"No, sir. We assumed Prince Stefano was with you."

"He isn't." Pietro didn't know what kind of childish games the prince was playing, but this was getting out of hand. "Send James up to my office right away."

"Yes, sir." The footman disappeared and he stepped back inside his office and smiled at Priscilla.

"I'll contact you later with a time," he said.

"Thank you."

She didn't leave as he expected she would. "There's something else," she said, and her shoulders rose as if it had required a good deal of courage for her to broach the subject.

"Yes?" Pietro said, looking at his watch. He didn't want to be rude, but he had a minor crisis on his hands.

"It's about—"

She was interrupted by a loud knock against the door.

"If you'll excuse me."

Defeated, she lowered her head and nodded.

"I apologize, Priscilla, but this is necessary."

"I know," she said, smiling bravely up at him.

Pietro met the bodyguard on the other side of the door and glared accusingly at the muscle-bound young man. "Where's the prince?"

"I'm...not sure."

"As I recall, this is the second time the prince has left without your protection."

"Sir, I don't mean to complain, but how was I supposed to know the man who'd dressed up like Elvis was Prince Stefano? And then last night..."

"You mean he left unescorted last night, as well?"

"Yes. I thought you knew."

Pietro ran his hand through his hair. "No. Where did he go this time?"

"I don't know. I lost him someplace in Ballard. His motorcycle squeezed between a bus and a car, and I couldn't catch him after that."

"He was on a motorcycle?"

"Yes. From what I understand, he paid one of the hotel staff for the use of it."

Pietro splayed his fingers at his sides in an exercise in frustration. "And you don't have a clue where he is right now?"

"Not exactly."

"How about a wild guess?" Pietro was desperate. He was willing to speculate.

James shrugged his massive shoulders. "I can't rightly say."

It came to Pietro that he should fire the man on the spot, but he'd wait until later after he'd confronted Stefano. He didn't know what had gotten into the prince.

Dressing up like Elvis, riding around on a motorcycle and now this.

"I want you to report to me the minute the prince returns."

"Yes, sir," James said stiffly.

Dragging a calming breath through his lungs, Pietro opened the door and entered his office. To his surprise Priscilla was standing.

"My apologies, Priscilla. There was something you wanted to tell me."

She nodded, smiled and then casually, as if she'd been doing so for years, she looped her arms around his neck and kissed him.

Chapter 8

Hope studied Prince Stefano's features as they stood inside the Visitor Center at Hurricane Ridge. The unobstructed view of the Olympic Mountain range with its peaks, deep valleys and ridges stretched before them, paralleling the Strait of Juan de Fuca.

Hope had never been to Europe or witnessed the splendor of the Alps, and she wondered what the prince would think of her world, so different and yet so much like his own.

"It takes my breath away," he said in awe.

"Some of those mountains remain unexplored," she told him.

"No." He raised his eyebrows dubiously. "How can that be?"

"Look at the ridges. In order to reach one mountain, you must climb a number of others. Several planes have crashed in the region, but there's no hope of ever recovering the bodies."

"How tragic. They are beautiful, these mountains of yours."

Hope smiled. "I don't exactly own them, but thank you anyway."

"You love your state?"

"Very much. Washington is quite diversified, you know. We're standing in a rain forest and in less than three hundred miles there's desert. In some areas in the eastern half of the state, the growing season is only two weeks too short for cotton."

Once more Stefano's eyebrows shifted upward. "This state of yours is amazing." His arm circled her waist. "You're amazing."

Hope smiled up at him. He hadn't worn a disguise this afternoon, at least none that required a wig. He came as himself, wearing jeans, a Western-style shirt and snakeskin cowboy boots. He looked more like a country-western star than a European prince.

"Are you hungry?" she asked.

"Famished."

She led him outside the Visitor Center. Her car was parked across the road. "There's a picnic area this way," she said, unlocking the trunk of her red Saturn.

Stefano lifted out the wicker basket and she reached for the Scottish plaid blanket. A rainbow of colorful wildflowers brightened the slopes. They trudged uphill for several moments until they found an appropriate site for their lunch. They chose a spot that offered a maximum of privacy beneath a forest of tall conifer trees.

Spreading the blanket out beneath the shelter of a Douglas fir, Hope and Stefano sat down. The area was sunny and warm and Hope welcomed the shade.

"What have you packed?" Stefano asked, kneeling down next to her on the blanket. He opened the basket and smiled when he viewed the contents.

"What's this?"

"Blueberry pie, fresh from the oven," she explained proudly. Now wasn't the time to let him know Lindy was the one responsible for this delectable delight.

"Ah, yes, American fruit pie," Stefano said. "I tasted it once in New York."

"You mean to say you don't have pies in San Lorenzo?"

"Not the way you do in America. You must remember fruit pies are a product of your country."

"But what about France? They're known all over the world for their pastries."

"Tarts, yes, but not pie. Generally our pies are filled with meat," he explained matter-of-factly.

Hope digested this latest bit of information. "There are more differences between our two countries than I realized."

"Many, many differences." A note of sadness entered his voice and Hope knew he was thinking about his duty to his country to marry a woman he didn't love. A woman who would save his tiny country from financial ruin.

"And what are these?" Stefano brought out the thick submarine sandwiches she'd built.

Smiling, she explained the history of the oblong sandwiches. They ate then, companionably. The sun wove its way through the limbs of the Douglas fir, leaving a lacework pattern that slowly traveled over them as it crossed the brilliant, blue sky.

Afterward they went on a short hike and Hope pointed out a number of different ferns. Stefano listened politely while she spread out the leaf of a sword fern, then a bracken fern and then that of the evergreen. She found herself chatting as if it were important to relay as much information about indigenous plants as possible. If she could fill the silence with words, then she wouldn't need to think about the future and how empty it would seem without him.

"Hope?"

She closed her eyes, and he pulled her softly into his arms. There was no need for words, no need to speak what was on both of their minds.

"I knew this wouldn't work," she whispered against his shoulder. She clung to him for fear that once he released her, her arms would feel forever empty.

"I thought if I kept you to myself for two more days I would have the strength to leave you. Now I wonder." His arms tightened about her. "I have no choice, my love. The fate of my country rests on my bride."

"I know. I know." Hope did, but that didn't make it

any easier, loving him like this. In thinking over Stefano's plight, she'd attempted to come up with a solution that would allow them to stay together. But she could see no way out for them.

"Come," Stefano said with some effort. "Let's not think about the future. We're together now and that's all that matters."

Hope struggled to hold back the tears.

They made their way back to the picnic area. An eagle soared overhead and Hope pointed out the magnificent bird with its huge wingspan. They stood watching the eagle making a sweeping turn over the horizon. Stefano was enthralled by the grandeur of the bird that had come to represent the United States.

Sitting back down on the blanket, Hope lowered her head, fighting back the emotion. To her surprise Stefano wandered away. He stood no more than a few feet from her, but it felt as though the Grand Canyon divided them. As she watched, it seemed his shoulders slouched forward as if the weight of his burden had increased a hundredfold.

Hope did the best she could to compose herself, and once she was relatively sure she could speak without tears leaking into her voice, she stood and moved to his side.

For a long time neither of them spoke.

"I need your forgiveness, Hope," he whispered.

"My forgiveness?"

"For being so selfish. To want you so badly, to hold

on to you these few days, when my presence brings you pain."

"It brings me joy, too."

"I've been unfair to you. I see that now. It is better for us both if I left Seattle."

"No." Her cry of protest came automatically. "Not yet."

"It's impossible for us. Being with you makes it even more impossible. I've done you a grave injustice and Priscilla, too. While it's true I don't love her…"

"It would hurt her if she ever found out about me," Hope finished for him.

"Yes." The lone word was barely above a whisper.

"Then she must never know." Her words were stronger and braver than her heart. She wasn't intentionally sparing the heiress who would marry Stefano. She did it for the prince. Her prince.

"You understand why this must be the last time we meet?"

"Yes," she returned in a broken whisper.

"But we have today," he returned, gripping hold of her hand. He gestured toward the sky. "The next time you see an eagle, remember me…and that I will always love you. Hold that knowledge in your heart forever." He turned to her and cupped her face between his hands. For a long moment, he gazed into her eyes, his expression deep and troubled. "In time I fear you'll grow to hate me…that you will think me a coward," he murmured.

"I won't…I couldn't."

Briefly he closed his eyes, and shook his head. "When that happens I want you to know that leaving you has been the most difficult thing I've ever done. Please remember that, Hope, above all else. You own my heart, and always will." He paused and then gently kissed her. "As the years pass, if there's ever a time you should need me, ever a time you're in trouble—"

"No," she said, cutting him off. "It has to be over here and now, Stefano. Promise me you won't come back into my life. You must," she insisted, before he could protest, "otherwise I'll find myself waiting for you, for the opportunity for you to return. Promise me that after today I'll never see or hear from you again."

It looked as if he couldn't make himself do it.

"Above all else, I know you to be an honorable man, Stefano. If you give me your word never to see or contact me again, then I'm free to do as you ask and treasure the days we shared. Free to take our time together and place it in the tenderest part of my heart, and cherish it. I'll be free to go on with my life."

She watched as his Adam's apple worked in his throat. "I give you my word," he whispered. "You will never see or hear from me again after this afternoon."

Hope looked away for fear he would see the tears glistening in her eyes. "Thank you," she whispered.

Priscilla knew she'd shocked Pietro by tossing her arms around him and kissing him. But she'd intended to catch him off guard. That had been part of her plan.

At first, he attempted to gently push her away, but she resisted and clung to him.

Then her hat fell on the floor and his hands were in her hair and he was slanting his mouth over hers. This must be what it would be like in heaven, Priscilla mused with a deep sigh of pleasure.

Pietro kissed her again and she gloried in his lack of control. It had happened just the way she'd planned. Once she was in his arms, he wouldn't be able to deny his feelings, wouldn't be able to brush her off with lies. He wouldn't be able to pretend.

"Oh, Pietro," she whispered, "don't stop, don't ever stop."

He stopped.

Priscilla sighed with disappointment and frustration.

They were both breathing hard, and it seemed to require several moments for Pietro to compose himself. "That shouldn't have happened," he said, his words taut with tension.

"I kissed you, remember? You did nothing improper."

"I kissed you back." He made it sound as if he should be dragged before a firing squad.

"Don't be ridiculous, I encouraged you. I wanted you to kiss me. You might think I'm being fanciful, but I knew in the beginning that you were going to be someone special in my life."

His face tensed as if he didn't want to hear what she had to say. "Priscilla..."

"You called me your love once. Remember?"

His eyes narrowed as if to say he'd give anything

never to have uttered those words. "You don't understand about such things," he said stiffly.

"I understand everything I need to," she returned with a righteous tilt of her chin. "All my life everyone else—my parents, my teachers, everyone—have seemed to think they know what's best for me. And I listened. Well, no more!" She braced her hands against her hips.

"Perhaps you should discuss this with them."

"I'm going to discuss it with you."

"Priscilla…"

"Hear me out, please," she said, and as an inducement, she stood on the tips of her toes and gently brushed her lips over his. "I know now that you were lying when you said you weren't attracted to me. I'm not sure why you'd hide the truth, but that doesn't matter any longer, because I know everything now."

"About what?" Pietro challenged.

"Your feelings for me."

A sad, intense look came over him. "I find you to be an attractive, generous young woman."

"Do you often kiss attractive, generous young women the way you do me?" she challenged. She knew he didn't.

"No," he admitted reluctantly, "but then it isn't often that one throws herself into my arms."

Although he spoke without criticism, Priscilla could feel her cheeks filling with color. "What about the time before that?" she asked. "The night of the banquet. As I recall you were the one who kissed me."

"Yes, that's true but…"

Again she sensed his reluctance, his hesitation. "But what?" she prodded.

"I'm afraid I've given you the wrong impression," he murmured. "That was the night you were feeling ill and I was attempting to comfort you."

Priscilla wasn't about to accept that excuse, either. She laughed softly and shook her head. "You're going to have to come up with a better excuse than that. I may not be as worldly and sophisticated as some women, but I know the kisses we shared were far more potent than a couple of aspirin."

As if he needed to put some distance between them, Pietro returned to his desk. Priscilla claimed the chair on the other side. He reached for a pen and rolled it between his palms.

"Hurting your feelings would greatly distress me, but I don't feel I have much—"

"Then don't." Priscilla felt on a natural high from his kisses. Little he could say or do would discourage her now that she'd discovered the truth.

"Priscilla, you're making this difficult."

"That's the reason I'm here." She beamed him a wide smile. He hesitated and looked almost grateful when the phone rang.

"If you'll excuse me a moment."

"Of course. Do you want me to leave?" she asked, thinking he might prefer privacy.

"That won't be necessary," he said, reaching for the telephone.

From her position on the other side of the table, Priscilla knew the call must be important from the way Pietro straightened his shoulders. He reached for the appointment book and flipped through the pages.

From the gist of the conversation, Priscilla could tell that he was scheduling a meeting for Prince Stefano. She couldn't be sure who was on the other end of the line, but it seemed to be some United States government official.

Pietro's look was thoughtful when he replaced the receiver. His gaze lingered there for a moment before lifting and meeting hers.

"Now, where were we?"

"We were discussing us," she said brightly.

His frowned deepened. "I didn't know there was an *us*."

"All right, I'll rephrase that. We were discussing our feelings for each other."

"I thought I'd already explained that I find you to be an attractive, likable young woman, but that I don't have any strong feelings for you one way or the other."

"I don't believe that."

He gestured weakly with his hands. "I realize that I might have given you *some* cause to think I was romantically interested in you. If that's the case, I apologize. You're a beautiful woman and I wanted to kiss you. A kiss is a little thing, don't you think?"

Priscilla blinked, her confidence shaken. "Yes, but there was a whole lot of emotion in those kisses…for me, at any rate."

"I'm honored beyond words that you find me attractive."

Find him attractive! The man didn't seem to have a clue that she was crazy in love with him. Perhaps he did, she decided, and he wanted to extract himself from the relationship as gracefully as he could.

"But," she said it for him, rather than wait.

"But you're young and impressionable, and I fear you've placed far more credence on the few times we kissed than is warranted. I don't mean to hurt you, but it would be cruel to continue in this vein."

From force of habit, she gnawed on her lower lip. "I apologize for causing you this embarrassment," she said, her pride giving her the strength she needed.

"It's not that," he said gently. "I'm honored that anyone as lovely as you would have these feelings for me."

"Yeah, right," she murmured and stood, eager now to make her escape. She turned and paused at the door. "I have an appointment with the prince tomorrow."

"That's correct."

"I'd appreciate it if I could be alone with him." In other words, she didn't want to see Pietro again.

"I'll see to it."

Her hand tightened around the doorknob and gathering her resolve, she pivoted around to face him. Their gazes met and held as if in a great unspoken battle of wills.

"Before I leave, I want you to know something." Her voice trembled a bit and she paused until she could be certain it would stay even and unemotional. "You're lying and I know it. I'm not exactly sure why you're sending me away.... Actually it doesn't matter. I'll walk out this door and we'll probably never see each other again. You've made it clear that's the way you want it, and I have no choice but to accept your wishes.

"You almost convinced me you don't love me," she continued and her voice wavered slightly, "but you didn't convince my heart."

She felt the tears burning for release and knew she had to leave soon. "Goodbye, Pietro," she whispered, and with nothing more to say, calmly left. The door softly clicked closed behind her.

Stefano returned to the hotel emotionally depleted. He met Pietro in the hallway outside his private quarters and their eyes clashed.

Instead of retreating to his own quarters, Stefano moved into the larger room where he'd shared tea with Priscilla Rutherford. Pietro followed.

For a long time neither spoke.

Stefano wasn't prepared for the litany of irate questions regarding his whereabouts. Not this time. He felt as if he'd been wrenched apart and was in no mood for an interrogation. Gratefully Pietro appeared to understand this.

"I see you're back." Pietro spoke first. "Will you be leaving again anytime soon?"

"No." Pain tightened the area around his heart. "I'd like for you to arrange our departure as soon as possible. Tomorrow, if we can be accommodated." If anything, this should please Pietro, who'd been eager to return to San Lorenzo for the past several days.

"You have two appointments in the morning," his secretary informed him. "The first is with Priscilla Rutherford."

"Priscilla?"

"Yes, she stopped by this afternoon to schedule the meeting."

"But I saw her earlier in the day. She didn't mention anything then."

"I was curious myself, but she gave no indication of what she wanted to discuss, although she made it clear she preferred that the two of you speak in private."

This piqued Stefano's interest. "In private?"

Pietro nodded. "The second appointment is with a representative from the American State Department. The call came in this afternoon and he requested an audience. He said it was essential that he speak to you at your earliest convenience."

"Regarding?"

"Again there was no indication."

"I see." Stefano was curious, but with other matters on his mind—mainly Hope—he didn't give the appointment much deliberation. Soon he'd be back in San Lorenzo. There he would find his peace. There he would have less difficulty accepting his duty. There he'd be surrounded by all that would remind him of his responsibilities to his country and his people.

"Would you like your dinner sent up?" Pietro asked, breaking into his thoughts.

"Dinner," Stefano repeated, then shook his head. "No, thanks, I don't seem to have much of an appetite." He walked toward the window, wanting the conversation to be over so he could escape.

"Will that be all for this evening, then?" Pietro inquired.

"Yes," Stefano said evenly.

Stefano could hear his secretary hesitate. "Are you ill?"

Yes, his heart cried. "I'm fine." More than anything, he wanted to be left alone.

"Good evening, then."

"Good evening, my friend," Stefano whispered, and rubbed a weary hand down his face. His secretary left the room and, after a few moments, Stefano sank into a chair and waited for the darkness of night to claim the room and his heart.

In the morning, the suite bustled with activity as the entourage that had arrived with him prepared for the flight to San Lorenzo that evening. Never had Stefano been more eager to be on his way. As soon as he departed Seattle, his heart was free to mend. While he remained in the city, his every thought centered upon Hope.

Pietro came to him around ten and it looked as if his friend hadn't slept all night. He wondered what could be troubling his companion. In light of their recent differences, he didn't feel he could pry.

Pietro's eyes were bloodshot. If he didn't know better, he'd think his secretary had been drinking. It happened rarely and generally when Pietro had something to celebrate. If he were happy it certainly didn't show.

"The front desk phoned," Pietro annnounced. "Apparently Doris Jordan and a few of her friends have asked to see you. Actually, it's more of a demand."

Stefano hesitated, unsure if he was up to a confrontation with that group. Generally he was amused by their antics, but it would take more than four romantics to entertain him this day.

"Should I have them sent away?"

Stefano hadn't the heart for that. "No." He would prefer to avoid a confrontation, but he found he couldn't refuse the fearsome foursome. "Send them up," he instructed reluctantly.

"I could meet with them, if you wish." Pietro checked his watch. "Priscilla Rutherford will be arriving momentarily."

The generosity of Pietro's offer to deal with Hope's mother surprised Stefano. "I'll keep the time in mind," he assured his secretary.

Within a matter of minutes four women marched into his suite as if they were looking to draw blood. Hope's mother, who'd swooned when she'd learned she held the winning ticket, looked anything but fragile. Her eyes sparked with outrage.

"We want to know what you've done to Hope."

"Please sit down, ladies," Stefano instructed.

"We'll stand, thank you very much," Doris announced righteously.

The footman arrived just then, carrying a silver tea service. Another followed with a display of delicate pastries. Both were set on the table. The two footmen stood back and folded their hands behind their backs.

"Perhaps we have time for tea," the one Stefano remembered as Hazel said, tugging at Doris's shirtsleeve.

"Aren't those petits fours?" she asked as her voice dipped. "We might have been a bit hasty, don't you think?"

"Since the prince has clearly gone to all this trouble, I think we should stay for tea," one of the others whispered.

Stefano hadn't the heart to tell them the tea had been arranged for Priscilla Rutherford.

"First answer me one thing, young man," Doris said heatedly.

In all his life, Stefano couldn't once remember being called "young man." "Of course," he said, as formally as he could, without smiling.

"I want to know why my daughter spent the entire night in tears. She wouldn't say a word, but I know it has to do with you. What have you done to her? That poor girl's suffering with a broken heart, and nothing you say can convince me otherwise. She won't even speak to me—her own mother."

"That's not the only thing," Hazel said, wagging her finger as if she were keeping time with the music. "We aren't old fools, you know. Something's been going on between the two of you ever since the night of your date."

"I want to know about the scarf she claims she got from Elvis!" Doris demanded.

"Elvis?"

The four women broke into excited chatter all at once.

"Hope Jordan?" It was Pietro's voice that cut through the prattle. His eyes linked with Stefano's and he watched as his secretary seemed to put everything together in his mind.

"Ladies, ladies," Pietro said, "I'm sorry to cut your visit so short, but the prince has an appointment in five minutes."

"But the tea…" Hazel cast an appreciative eye toward the plateful of delectable pastries.

"I don't think those were for us," Doris said, under her breath.

There was a chorus of disappointed sighs.

"Whatever questions you have for the prince can be directed to me," Pietro said. "If you'll come to my office, perhaps we can sort all this out."

Stefano shouldn't have been so grateful to be rescued from painful explanations, but it was a sign of how battered and spent he felt.

A short ten minutes later, Priscilla Rutherford was escorted into the suite. Clearly there was some sort of malady that had affected everyone, because he couldn't recall ever seeing anyone look more unhappy. She, too, had apparently spent the night pacing the floor. The circles around her eyes were dark, and even expertly applied cosmetics couldn't hide the sadness he sensed in her.

"Please sit down," he said, gesturing toward the davenport.

She shook her head. "No, thank you. This will only take a moment."

Stefano remained standing because she did. "Have I done something to offend you?" he asked, wondering at her strange mood.

She shook her head. He noticed the nervous way she rubbed her palms together. "I've spent a good portion of the time since we had brunch yesterday speaking to my parents. I'm afraid they're rather upset with me at the moment, but they'll recover." She seemed to reach some kind of conclusion. "For that matter," she added sadly, "so will I."

"I'm afraid I don't understand."

"I don't expect you will." All at once it seemed she needed to sit down because she slowly lowered herself into a chair.

"Priscilla, are you feeling all right?"

She smiled weakly. "If you want the truth, I've never felt worse."

"Is there anything I can do?"

She looked down and shook her head. "I wish there was, but unfortunately there isn't."

He waited for several moments for her to speak, then prompted her. "You asked to see me?"

She nodded and slowly raised her eyes to his. "I think you're probably the most attractive man I've ever met."

"Thank you." He didn't like the sound of this. Generally, such compliments were followed by words he found to his disliking.

"No man has ever paid me the attention you have. On a bright note, you've made my mother a happy woman. My father thinks you're the best thing since sourdough bread and frankly, I don't know if either one of my parents intends on speaking to me ever again."

"What could you have done that's so terrible?" Stefano pressed gently. Priscilla was as nervous as a filly, and he feared she'd burst into tears at any moment.

She folded her hands together as if she were about to pray. "I could see the handwriting on the wall," she said, studying her fingers as though the script were written out for her there. "Mom and Dad were hearing wedding bells and I'm afraid the sound of them drowned out all reason."

"How's that?"

"You see, I like you and everything and...well, if we got to know each other a little better, we'd probably become good friends, but I don't love you."

"Love is something that's nurtured," Stefano explained thoughtfully. "After the wedding, I feel we'd develop a deep friendship, in time."

Priscilla's eyes widened perceptively. "It's true, then?" she whispered, as though he'd somehow shocked her.

"What's true?"

"That you were serious about...marrying me."

He nodded. "My thoughts had been running along those lines."

"My heavens." She leapt to her feet and then just as quickly sat down again. "You see, I told my parents you had no such intentions."

"All in good time, Priscilla. I didn't intend to rush you."

"But you see, I don't want to marry you."

Funny as it seemed, her reluctance to take him as a husband had never occurred to him. There could only be one reason. "There's someone else?"

Her head bent lower, before she slowly raised her eyes to meet his. He saw in her a pain he hadn't earlier, a pain that was a reflection of his own. "There was," she admitted in a choked whisper. "But he doesn't share my feelings."

"The man is a fool."

She was saved from explaining further by Pietro who abruptly stepped into the room. His gaze honed toward Priscilla as if drawn by a powerful magnet. For a breathless moment they stared at each other, and then as though by remote control, they both looked away.

"Excuse me," Pietro murmured apologetically.

"You wanted to see me?" Stefano asked.

"It can wait." He left as hastily as he'd arrived.

Stefano watched his friend and then looked to Priscilla. She'd composed herself, but in that instant he knew the man the heiress loved, the one she wanted over him, was none other than his own secretary.

Chapter 9

Priscilla was in love with Pietro. Stefano couldn't believe that he could have been so obtuse. The evidence was all there for him to see. Poor Pietro. No wonder his secretary had been surly and short-tempered of late. Pietro had been caught between loyalty and friendship, trapped in a no-win proposition. If Stefano hadn't been so blinded by his love for Hope, he might have been able to help them both.

Priscilla studied him, and Stefano realized he was staring at the door, after his secretary. "I appreciate your honesty," he said thoughtfully, his mind working hard and fast. "Would you excuse me a moment?"

"Of course."

"Make yourself comfortable. I'll be back momentarily."

Stefano made a hasty exit and went in search of Pietro. He found his companion in his office. "You wanted to see me?" Stefano asked.

"Has Miss Rutherford left?" It seemed Pietro's gaze bore straight through him, as if he were holding himself in tight resolve until he could be certain Priscilla had gone.

"She's waiting for me," Stefano announced and plopped himself down on the chair. "We have a problem," he announced, as though the weight of this latest development were more than he could bear.

"A problem with Priscilla?"

"Yes," Stefano confirmed. "She's afraid her family is going to manipulate her into marrying me. This is the reason for her visit. She's come to explain that, although she thinks highly of me, she'd rather not be my wife. Can you believe that! The woman has no idea she's ruined our plans."

Pietro's frown deepened.

"To complicate matters, she claims she's in love with someone else—or so she says. I pried, but she wouldn't talk about him. But from what little she did tell me, she cares deeply for this other man. The cad!"

Pietro ignored the last remark. "I'm sure that in time Miss Rutherford's feelings will change. She'll grow to love you."

"We don't have the time to wait around to be sure that happens." Keeping a straight face was becoming something of a chore, but Stefano managed. "The situation is grave—you know that as well as I do."

"True." Pietro shifted uneasily in his chair.

"It's clear to me that her parents are keen on the idea of their daughter becoming my princess."

"They wouldn't object to a union between the two of you," his secretary agreed stoically.

"My thoughts precisely." Prince Stefano beamed his friend a wide grin. "That's why I believe there's only one solution to all this." He gestured with his hands, expressing his exasperation with the whole business. "We're going to need to kidnap her, and force her into marrying me."

"What!" Pietro vaulted to his feet. "You can't be serious."

"We don't have any choice. Priscilla assured me she's in love with someone else, but when I pressed her, she admitted that this other man didn't return her feelings. That being the case, we really can't allow her to throw her life away."

"Aren't you being a bit dramatic?"

"I thought that at first, but the longer we talked, the more I realized how serious she is. Priscilla's prepared to wait for this…scoundrel to come to his senses, and if he doesn't, then, well, she never intends to marry."

"She told you that?" Pietro's frown was dark and brooding.

"Why else would I be telling you this?"

His secretary wiped his hand over his eyes in a gesture of fatigue. "You can't be serious about kidnapping Priscilla."

"Desperate times call for desperate measures," the prince returned flippantly.

Pietro's fists knotted at his sides. "I won't allow it."

Stefano arched his brows in fabricated shock. "Not allow it?" he repeated slowly.

"There are laws against such matters."

"Fiddlesticks. After a month or two, Priscilla will have forgotten about the man she thinks she loves. She'll be grateful that I had the foresight to arrange our wedding. Given the circumstances, I believe her family will fully cooperate with the idea." He paused and waited for Pietro's reaction.

"I want no part of this."

"Oh, I wasn't asking you to collaborate. I was just bouncing the idea off you."

His gaze focused away from Stefano. "This is by far the most outrageous thing you've ever suggested. Are you foolish enough to believe she'll forgive you for something so underhanded?"

"It won't matter if she forgives me or not. We both know this isn't a love match. I need her money, not her." He made his voice as frigid and calculating as possible.

Pietro's eyes narrowed to points of steel. "You're a coldhearted son of a—" He stopped himself in time to keep from swearing.

Stefano pretended to be shocked. "Why should you care? From what you claimed, your resignation will be in effect as soon as we return to San Lorenzo. You won't be around to witness any of this."

"I care," Pietro snapped.

"Apparently not enough," Stefano returned casually. He leaned back in the chair and crossed his legs.

"I was the one who chose Priscilla. You don't seriously believe I'd sit back and allow you to follow through with this preposterous idea of yours, do you?"

"Frankly, Pietro, I don't understand your objection."

"It doesn't matter if you understand it or not. I refuse to allow you to abuse Priscilla. She's warm and loving. Heaven knows she deserves better than to be treated like an object with no feelings, no heart."

The angry words fell into the silence. This was what Stefano had been waiting to hear, what he'd been waiting for his friend to admit. "Isn't that what you were planning to do?" he asked starkly. "Abandon her to a loveless marriage?"

Pietro glared at him as if he didn't understand.

"It's you she loves, you fool, not me," Stefano said smoothly. "And, no, she didn't tell me. She didn't need to. I saw the way the two of you looked at each other just now. The woman's crazy about you, Pietro, and any fool could see you feel the same way about her."

"But—"

"I believe we've already been through this argument," Stefano cut in. "She has no intention of ever marrying me. I believe she said she'd like to consider me a friend."

Pietro said nothing for several seconds, then slowly lowered himself back into the chair. "I apologize, Stefano. When I realized Priscilla was attracted to me, I did what I could to discourage her."

"Don't apologize. It's more clear to me than ever that the two of you are far better suited than Priscilla and I would ever be. You'll make her a better husband. A woman deserves a man who deeply loves her. Don't you agree?"

It took Pietro a long time to answer. "What about you?"

Stefano laughed softly. "The only thing that's injured is my ego, and that was only dented. I'll manage, and so will San Lorenzo, at least for now."

Something would need to be done to secure his country's finances, but he didn't want to think about that. Somehow he'd find a way to manage. His country had survived seven hundred years of war and plague. A little thing like financial ruin didn't seem so daunting. He'd survive without Hope, just as his country would survive without Priscilla Rutherford's money.

Priscilla shifted her weight in the chair and glanced at her watch. Stefano had already been gone several minutes, and she wasn't keen on waiting much longer. Everything she'd come to say had already been said. She hoped she hadn't hurt the prince's feelings, and frankly she wasn't willing to argue. She wouldn't marry him, or anyone, to gain her parents' approval.

The door opened from behind her just when she'd decided the best course of action was for her to silently slip away, and hope no one noticed.

"Priscilla."

It was Pietro, and the sound of his voice, saying her

name in that special way of his, was enough to cause her heart to painfully constrict.

She stood and braced herself, knowing she'd need to be strong. "Hello, Pietro. Where's the prince?"

"Please sit down."

"Is the prince coming?" She looked behind him, thinking it would be much easier to maintain her composure with Stefano in the room. Otherwise, she feared she'd do something to make an even greater fool of herself than she had already.

"No," Pietro said starkly. "The prince won't be returning."

"I…see." She didn't, but it was difficult to concentrate. Slowly she sat back down, and fiercely clenched her hands together.

He claimed the chair the prince had vacated, and leaned forward slightly. "You were correct when you said I lied," he said after a tension-filled moment.

Priscilla frowned, thinking he was about to apologize for some unconfessed sin. She looked away, not having the heart for this. "It doesn't matter, Pietro."

"That's where you're wrong. It does matter. You're right, I love you, and little in this world would make me happier than for you to be my wife."

Nothing he might have said could have shocked or outraged her more. "You love me!"

"That's what I just said." He was smiling and his eyes sparkled with happiness.

"You love me and…and yet you were willing to let me walk out of your life?"

"Yes," he admitted reluctantly. "Although I swear by all that is holy, it was the most difficult thing I've ever done."

"But why? Because you believed Stefano was in love with me? That's ridiculous and we both know it."

"Priscilla," he said gently, coming off the chair. He got down on one knee before her, and captured both her hands in his. "We can argue about my foolishness for many years to come if you wish. For now, all I need is your answer to my proposal. Will you be my wife?"

It greatly perturbed Priscilla that at the most important moment of her life tears would fill her eyes and blur out Pietro's face. She wiped the moisture from her face and sniffled. "There's something you should know first."

"Yes?"

"I...I have ugly feet."

Pietro burst out laughing, which was not what she'd intended for him to do. She was serious. She didn't object, however, when his arms circled her waist and he kissed her with a hunger and longing that matched her own.

"Pietro," she whispered between kisses, "you're a fool."

"Never again, my love, never again."

Chapter 10

Stefano found a certain solace in his homeland. One that helped ease the ache in his heart. He didn't expect the longing for Hope to fade completely, and so he savored the memories of her and the all-too-short time they'd shared. Like a young boy who buries a secret treasure, Stefano clung to the memory of Hope Jordan, the woman who'd stolen his heart.

The entire country of San Lorenzo was abloom in mid-August. Although Stefano tried not to think about Hope, he found her creeping uninvited into his dreams. She came to him a vision of warmth and beauty in his sleep, when his defenses were lowered and he hadn't the strength of will to resist.

Almost always they were at Hurricane Ridge, as

they'd been the last time they were together. She'd collect a bouquet of wildflowers to bring to him, her face bright with love, her eyes filled with promises he'd never collect.

Although Stefano had vowed never to contact her again, he'd hired a detective agency to report back to him with their findings. It was vital that he learn she was getting on with her life and that she was happy.

From what he'd learned, that was true. Hope's coffee delivery business was thriving, and the last and final report he'd received said that she was dating. Stefano had suffered the agonies of the damned, wondering about the young man she was seeing.

The prince hadn't returned to Seattle for Pietro's wedding to Priscilla Rutherford. The temptation to see Hope would have been far too strong, and he'd given her his word that he would forever stay out of her life. He'd honored his promise, but at a costly price.

Priscilla and Pietro's wedding was said to have been the social event of the year. Dignitaries from around the world had attended the festivities. From what the prince understood, the happy couple were honeymooning in Australia. Stefano wished the two every happiness.

"Your Highness." His newly hired assistant, Peter Hiat, timidly interrupted him. "Mr. Myers is here to see you."

"Ah, yes," Stefano said. "Please show him in."

Stefano stood at his desk while the other man was escorted into his private office. He'd met briefly with Steven Myers shortly before he left Seattle. Myers's purpose had to do with a proposal from the United States government regarding leasing land in San Lorenzo. Because of the emotional upheaval of those last hours in Seattle, Stefano had suggested the State Department contact him again, after he'd returned home.

When Stefano didn't hear immediately back again, he had assumed the project was no longer of any interest to the United States.

"Prince Stefano," Steven Myers said as he walked into the office. "I appreciate your time."

"Please sit down." He gestured toward the chair.

Myers sat and lifted a briefcase onto his lap. "Thank you for seeing me."

"The pleasure is mine. What can I do for you?"

"I've come to make San Lorenzo an offer you can't refuse," Myers said with a broad smile.

Four hours later, Stefano felt as though he were walking on air. The United States, whom Myers reminded him, had always been San Lorenzo's friend, had come seeking a favor. They were looking to establish an air base in San Lorenzo. The government of the United States was offering his country more money than Stefano had ever dreamed possible. Naturally, the decision wasn't his to make alone, but the positive side of the proposal far outweighed the negative. All it would take was a simple parliamentary vote to gain approval.

His country was saved.

Once the relief hit him, Stefano's first thought was to contact Hope and ask her to be his bride. His princess. He loved and needed her.

Then he remembered his promise to stay out of her life forever. Already she'd found another. Already she had forgotten him.

"So," Lindy said, slumping into a chair, "you going out with Cliff again this evening?"

"I wish you wouldn't make it sound like he's the love of my life. He's my cousin," Hope explained for the tenth time that day.

"I know you're related," Lindy said, biting into one of her own low-fat muffins, "but getting out again has done you a world of good. I've been worried about you lately."

This was territory Hope didn't want to traverse. Not with her friend. Especially since her own mother had been treating her as though she had a case of the measles instead of a broken heart.

Hazel and her mother's other friends were equally certain their efforts would aid Hope's recovery. They brought her jars of freshly pickled corn relish, in addition to working on a hope chest, filling it with items she'd need when she found "that special man" who would make her forget all about Prince Stefano.

As much as she loved them all, Hope felt smothered. When Cliff, a distant cousin on her father's side, arrived in town, she leapt at the opportunity to break away from the condolences being heaped upon her, and spend some time with him.

"Has Cliff found an apartment yet?" Lindy asked, carefully peeling the paper bottom off the muffin.

"I helped him move this weekend."

"Ah." Lindy's eyes avoided hers.

"What makes you ask?" Hope inquired.

Briefly, Lindy looked up and then shrugged. "No reason."

"He enjoyed the apple pie you sent over."

"He did?" Lindy's gaze widened. "Why didn't you say something sooner?"

Hope laughed and propped her feet on the seat of the chair opposite her. "I wanted to see how long it would take you to ask."

"Hope! That's cruel."

"He asked about you, too."

"He did?"

"Yep, but I told him to look for greener pastures."

"Hope, you didn't. Tell me you didn't!"

Hope laughed. "I didn't. In fact, I gave him your phone number and he told me he'd be calling you this evening."

"He only met me the one time...." Lindy's hands nervously set aside the muffin.

"You made quite an impression on him. Then again, it might have been the apple pie," she said, giggling. It felt good to laugh again. She hadn't had much reason to laugh of late, but she was learning.

The bell above the door to the coffee shop sounded and Hope plopped her feet onto the floor. "I'll get that," she mumbled. This was the first break Lindy had taken all morning, and Hope didn't want her friend to wait on walk-in customers. Not when the kitchen demanded so much of her time.

"Hello," Hope greeted the smiling young woman. She looked vaguely familiar, but Hope couldn't place her. "Can I get you something?"

"You don't know me," the other woman said, extending her hand. "I'm Priscilla Rutherford—or rather, that was my name. I recently married Pietro. You know him as Prince Stefano's secretary."

Hope's body froze. *Not now,* she silently begged. *Please not now. Not when I'm just getting my life back together. Not when I've convinced myself I can be happy without him.*

"How can I help you?" she asked once more, stiffly this time, protecting her heart as best she could.

Priscilla smiled gently. "You can't. Pietro and I are here to help you."

Three weeks following their marriage, Pietro and Priscilla arrived home at the palace.

"Pietro," Stefano shouted when he first saw his friend. He rose from behind his desk and the two men exchanged hearty hugs. Stefano briefly kissed Priscilla's cheek. It amazed him how radiantly beautiful the heiress looked. Apparently, married life agreed with them both. Pietro had never looked better.

"I thought you two were on your honeymoon," he said, ringing for the footman and ordering a tray of coffee to be sent up.

"We cut it short," Pietro explained. Husband and wife

sat next to each other, holding hands. "We read about the agreement between San Lorenzo and the United States," Pietro explained. "It made the Australia newspapers. It's true, isn't it, about the air base?"

"Yes." Stefano beamed Pietro a smile. "We're more than pleased. The parliament voted on the proposal in record time, and construction is scheduled to begin on the project after the first of the month."

"Congratulations."

"I'm grateful for the turn of events." Which was an understatement only Pietro could fully appreciate.

"What about the wedding?"

Stefano stared at his friend. "Wedding? Whose wedding?"

"Pietro," Priscilla said softly, casting a disapproving glance toward her husband, "you're going to ruin the surprise."

"Surprise?" Stefano was beginning to feel like a parrot, repeating everything said.

"We brought you back something from our honeymoon," Pietro explained. "Would you like to see it?"

"In a minute," Stefano said. He was more eager to talk to the two. He'd deeply missed his friend. His newly hired secretary was efficient and organized, but he lacked Pietro's skill in several areas, the least of which was the sword. It'd been weeks since Stefano had been challenged. Never had he felt more alone than in the past month without Pietro at his side.

"Tell me about the wedding," Stefano instructed.

The footman delivered a silver tray with a pot of coffee and three cups. Priscilla poured, while chatting.

"First off, Mother and I had quite a discussion. She wanted a wedding that would rival something coming out of Buckingham Palace."

"It didn't help matters," Pietro said, smiling at his wife, "that you had me knighted before the wedding. Elizabeth felt that if Priscilla was going to marry a knight, she should have a wedding fit for a queen."

"Despite everything, the wedding was lovely," Priscilla assured him.

"We missed you, however," Pietro said.

"My mother was convinced you didn't attend the wedding because I'd broken your heart by choosing Pietro over you."

"That's very nearly true," Stefano returned, and shared a secret smile with his former secretary. "Now, what is it you're so eager to show me?"

"Shall we make him close his eyes?" Priscilla asked her husband.

"I don't think that's a good idea." Pietro stood and walked over to the large double door and disappeared momentarily. When he returned, Stefano was convinced he'd lost his mind—he couldn't believe what he saw.

Hope Jordan stepped into the room and smiled serenely at him.

"Hope." He rasped her name as if he were saying a prayer, pleading to the powers on high.

"Hello, Stefano."

He couldn't believe how lovely she was. Had he forgotten so much about her, so soon? It was as though she were a vision, a figment of his imagination.

"You might want to ask her to sit down," Pietro prodded.

"Of course. Forgive me."

"Pietro, don't you think we should leave these two alone for a few minutes?" The sound of Priscilla's voice drifted to Stefano but it seemed as if it were coming from a great distance.

"I suppose.... We'll be waiting in the rose garden," Pietro said as he followed his new bride out the door. Stefano barely heard his friend.

Each one of his senses was centered on Hope. "I wasn't sure I should come," she said, and for the first time he realized she was ill at ease.

"Not come?" He sat across from her.

"I wasn't sure your feelings for me hadn't changed."

"They haven't. You hold my heart in the palm of your hand. You always will."

She lowered her head and he noted the nervous way in which she nibbled at her lower lip. "You didn't contact me. Not even after you learned about the air base. I'd never have come to San Lorenzo if it hadn't been for Pietro and Priscilla."

"I'd given you my word of honor that I'd never see you again."

"But that was when you were planning to marry Priscilla Rutherford. That was when there was no future for the two of us. I thought…when I learned about the air base, what else could I think but that…well, that

I'd been a passing fancy who'd amused you while you were in Seattle."

"Hope, no. Never that." He'd hurt her so much already, knowing he'd caused her additional pain brought a surge of bitter regret.

"Then why didn't you come for me?"

It wasn't easy to admit what he'd done. "I learned you were dating, and felt it was best to let you get on with your life. I'd hurt you already."

"You learned I was dating! Who told you that?" She sounded agitated, as well she should.

"I'm not proud of this…but you need to understand my state of mind. I hired a detective agency to check up on you." He drew in a deep breath and held it for fear she'd never forgive him for invading her privacy. "I had to know that you were well…I couldn't have gone on without that peace of mind."

"Oh, Stefano…"

He couldn't resist holding her a moment longer. He gathered her in his arms and absorbed the feel of her, her softness, her gentleness. Her love. For weeks Stefano had felt as if he were adrift on a wide ocean with no land in sight. He'd suffered deeply, believing Hope had found another man. He'd been torn in different directions, seeking her happiness above his own.

They kissed and it was as it had always been between them. Soon his hands were in her hair and he was drinking in the taste of her, the feel of her.

"Promise me you'll never leave me again," Hope asked.

"On one condition." He kissed her, not giving her time to respond for a long, long time.

"Anything you ask," she said with a sigh between deep, slow kisses.

"Marry me. Stand by my side the rest of my life. Be my princess."

"I'll need to think about it," she whispered. Stefano lifted his head, surprised by her response. She smiled up at him, wove her fingers into his thick hair and laughed softly, before bringing his mouth back to hers. "I thought about it."

"And?" With a great deal of restraint, he held his lips a mere inch away from hers.

"And, the answer's yes. A thousand times yes." Stefano let out a triumphant cry, wrapped his arms around Hope's waist and whirled her around. It was a fitting gesture, since she'd sent his world spinning from the first moment he'd seen her. He had a sneaking suspicion this was one joyride that was never going to end. The Bachelor Prince had met his match. His mate for a lifetime.

* * * * *

YESTERDAY'S HERO

Chapter 1

"**Y**ou must understand that the government of the Diamantina Islands is understandably circumspect. The people are the direct descendants of Puritan missionaries." Dr. David Brewster took a clean handkerchief from his pocket and wiped his perspiring face.

He's flustered, Leah Talmadge mused. Dr. Brewster, California's most renowned marine biologist, man of steel at seventy-five, the solid department head, was obviously nervous. Something had gone wrong. Disconcerted, Leah stiffened in the high-backed leather chair. A cold sweat broke out across her upper lip, and she nervously ran her finger over it. Dear heavens, this expedition was the chance of a lifetime.

"Just what are you saying, Dr. Brewster?" Cain Hawkins interrupted abruptly.

Leah's gaze skidded to the world-famous photographer who would be accompanying her on this whale watch. Cain's work had appeared several times in *National Geographic* and other nationally known magazines. The talented photographer had made his name taking spectacular shots of wildlife, landscapes and people; his skill wasn't limited to any one subject. His work hung in some of the best art galleries in the world. The entire department was elated that he'd been assigned to accompany Leah on this expedition to the islands.

His pictures might be fantastic, Leah reflected, but the man was a disappointment. He didn't look anything like what she'd expected. In some ways he resembled a hippie left over from the nineteen-sixties. His chestnut hair was unfashionably long, and he wore it brushed away from his face. It curled out just below his collar, and an unruly patch defiantly brushed his brow. His face was weathered from exposure to the elements, and he looked closer to forty than the thirty-five she knew him to be. Of course, she'd heard the rumors. Her colleagues had delighted in feeding her tidbits of information about the unorthodox Cain Hawkins. A rebel. A nonconformist. Tough as leather. Hard as nails. Leah had heard it all and secretly hadn't believed a word. His pictures told a different story.

David Brewster paused and cleared his throat. Again he wiped his face with the wrinkled linen cloth. "I was in communication with the governor of the Diamantinas this afternoon."

Apprehensively, Leah scooted to the edge of her seat. "And?" she urged.

"In light of the fact that you two unmarried adults would be spending considerable time in the uninhabited archipelago together, the request has been denied."

Leah felt her heart drop. "Denied," she repeated in shocked disbelief. The opportunity of a lifetime washed away by the moral righteousness of a government official.

"Good grief, man. We live in the twenty-first century." Cain Hawkins's dark eyes sparked with disbelief and irritation.

"Indeed," David Brewster agreed, "but no one bothered to inform the islanders of this. The people in these islands are deeply religious."

"But, Doctor," Leah said, struggling to disguise her exasperation, "surely you explained that Mr. Hawkins and I are professional people. Our purpose isn't to…" She left the rest unsaid as hot color invaded her pale face. The worst part of being a blonde was the way her complexion signaled her thoughts.

"I fear we must either find a female photographer or make the—"

"Oh no you don't." Cain shot to his feet and glared intimidatingly at Leah, expelling an angry breath. The dark eyes narrowed to points of steel that looked capable of slashing through any barrier, any defense. "You can just as easily find a male marine biologist. I'm not giving up this opportunity because of her." An accusing finger was pointed at Leah.

"How...how dare you," Leah stuttered. "I've waited years for this and I won't be denied my chance because—"

"Children, children." Dr. Brewster waved his hand authoritatively.

So angry she could barely speak, Leah defiantly crossed her arms. Whom did Cain Hawkins think he was dealing with, anyway? She hadn't worked this hard and come this far to let a boorish chauvinist walk over her because she was a woman.

"If you two would consider marriage..."

"What?" Leah spat. "Surely you don't mean to each other." Slowly, deliberately, she gave Cain Hawkins a practiced look of distaste.

The corner of his upper lip curled into what she assumed was humorous disdain. He was telling her without words what he thought of that idea.

Leah forced herself to think through this sudden obstacle. Finally she suggested, "Surely, if I were a married woman and Mr. Hawkins a married man—not to each other—then this expedition would be sanctioned by the governor."

David Brewster loosened his tie and ran a finger along the inside of his collar in an agitated movement. "That's a possibility, of course—and, frankly, one I haven't considered."

"I'm sure that once I talk to Siggy he would be willing to move up our wedding plans."

"Siggy?" Cain repeated, and his voice dripped with sarcasm. "You look like the type of woman who would marry a man named Siggy."

Despite her attempt at disciplined self-control, Leah bit off an angry retort. "Siegfried Harcharik is an honors graduate of MIT and is currently employed as a biochemist for the largest drug company in the United States." Siggy's credentials, she thought, would quickly put Cain Hawkins in his place. "I consider myself fortunate to be his fiancée."

Cain's low snicker filled the room. "Honey, if I were you, I'd consider myself lucky to be any man's future wife."

The words came at Leah like the cutting edge of a sword, and with as much power to inflict pain. She hated herself for wincing. No one needed to remind her that though she was blonde she wasn't beautiful. Too tall. Too thin. Too…no need fencing around the word…ugly. From the time she was in junior high she'd known her uneven features weren't likely to attract a man. All brains, no beauty, was what the boys in high school used to say.

Standing, Leah clenched her hands together in a show of determination. "I can see that Mr. Hawkins and I are only capable of hurling insults at each other. I suggest we schedule a meeting for a later date. Tomorrow, perhaps, when we've both had the opportunity to cool our tempers."

"I couldn't agree more." David Brewster's pained,

wrinkled face relaxed. "Shall we say Thursday at the same time?"

"Fine." The clipped response was followed by the scraping of a chair as Cain left the room.

Leah avoided looking in his direction and lingered in the office an extra moment.

"My dear," Dr. Brewster said, and cupped Leah's elbow. "I know this announcement has come as a surprise to us all. But I personally chose you for this whale expedition, and I won't easily be dissuaded. So rest assured, things will work out."

Leah's returning smile was feeble at best. "Thank you, Doctor." She didn't know that she should be all that reassured. Dr. Brewster had also handpicked Cain Hawkins.

"I'll talk to Siggy tonight."

"You do that," he returned, patting her back. "I'm confident we'll find a way around this."

Leah was skeptical, but she gave him a polite nod on her way out the door.

The long drive down the San Diego Freeway was accomplished by rote. Traffic, smog, faceless people were all part of life in southern California. Leah learned early that she must either accept it, or be defeated by the congestion that met her morning and night. But this afternoon, California had never seemed farther from the rolling hills of wheat in her home state of South Dakota. It had been a long time since she'd visited her family. When she returned from the Indian Ocean she'd make a point of doing that.

The first thing Leah did when she entered her condominium was pull Cain Hawkins's book of photographs from the shelf beside the fireplace. With a sense of incredulity, she ran her fingertips over the bottom of each page. The photos were beautiful. Each one looked as if the man who took it was revealing his soul.

But Cain Hawkins wasn't anything like these pictures. The ruthless quality in him had astonished her. In her mind, she had formed an image of what he would be like. Not so much his looks, but his personality. Any man who could reveal so much with his camera must be capable of deep insight. Today she had learned that he was ordinary. Hurtful. Arrogant. And, indeed, insightful. Within fifteen minutes of their meeting, he had found her weakest point and attacked.

Angry with herself for letting his cutting words disturb her so much, Leah reached for her cell to connect with Siggy.

The phone rang only once. "Harcharik here."

"Siggy, it's Leah." A short silence followed her announcement.

"Hello, darling."

Leah knew Siggy didn't like it when she phoned him at the office, but she couldn't help it. This was important. "Can you stop by for a few minutes after work?"

Again he hesitated. Siggy had never been one to move quickly on anything. The trait was part of the scientist in him. "Yes, I suppose I could."

In her mind Leah could see him pushing up the bifocals from the bridge of his nose, and she smiled softly, appreciating him.

"Good, I'll see you then. Goodbye, darling." The word stuck in her throat. So far in their relationship, they'd never done anything more intimate than call each other darling, and that had troubled her from the beginning. But the time was fast approaching when she'd be far more intimate with him. She liked Siggy. No, she corrected herself mentally, she loved Siggy. She wanted to be his wife. They shared so many of the same interests. They were perfect for each other. Everyone said so. And Leah was the first woman Siggy had introduced to his family that his mother approved of. That said a lot.

After tucking Cain's book back onto the shelf, Leah delivered her briefcase to her small office in the back of the condominium. For the hundredth time in as many days, she read over the Australian government's report of the sighting of an ancient whale. The report had been received with a high amount of skepticism since ancient whales were assumed to be extinct.

But when the corpse of an ancient whale had been found washed up on one of the Diamantina Islands, the world had taken serious note. Scientists from all over the globe had converged on the tiny cluster of islands a thousand miles southwest by south of Australia and found nothing. Now, a year later, Leah was going during migration time, when she could study the pods and keep meticulous records. This was more than a golden opportunity; it was one that wasn't likely to be repeated.

By the time Siggy arrived Leah had released her

tightly coiled hair so that it cascaded down the middle of her back. Siggy had always loved her hair down. She prayed now that it would be all the inducement she needed for him to agree to her plans.

"Hello, darling." He brushed his lips across her cheek.

"Come in." Nervously, Leah gestured toward the fashionably furnished living room. "Would you like something to drink? Coffee's on."

"That'll be fine."

With Siggy, Leah was forced to wear flat-heeled shoes. He exactly equaled her five-foot-eight stature and disapproved when she wore anything that made her taller. And although he claimed to like her hair worn down, Leah sometimes wondered if it wasn't that, with the blond length piled on her head, it gave an illusion of height. Not that any of this mattered; she was happy to do anything to please Siggy.

"I had a meeting with Dr. Brewster and Cain Hawkins today," she said, forcing a casual note into her voice as she delivered his coffee.

"Yes, I remember your saying something about that. How did it go?"

Sitting across from him on the white leather couch, Leah expelled a shaky breath. "Not so well."

"Why not? Isn't this Hawkins fellow what you expected?"

"Not at all." She pushed the hair away from her face. "Siggy, has it ever bothered you...I mean, have you ever been concerned about the fact that I'll be spending several weeks alone with an unmarried man?"

Straightening the corner of his bow tie, Siggy stiffened slightly. "Of course not. You're going to be my wife, Leah. I trust you implicitly."

Leah's heart softened, and she gave him a loving look. "Oh, Siggy, you're so good for me."

His returning smile was brief. "You are for me, too, darling." Fidgeting, he glanced at his wristwatch, then cleared his throat. "Mother's holding dinner."

"Oh...well, the reason I asked you over tonight was..." she began, and her hands were so tightly clenched she felt the blood supply must be cut off. Suddenly Leah felt unsure that she was doing the right thing. Marriage, after all, was forever. "I've been thinking that I'd like us to be married before I leave for the Diamantina Islands." Leah watched him closely, but no emotion showed in his blue eyes.

"Leah, I'm afraid that's quite impossible. Mother doesn't know yet that I've asked you to be my wife."

"Then don't you think it's time Mother did?" she said crossly. "You told me yourself that your mother approved of me. I can't see the necessity of putting my life on hold because you're afraid of your mother."

His coffee cup made a clanking sound as he set it roughly on the coffee table. As far as Leah could remember, this was the most emotion she had ever seen from Siggy. "I find that comment unforgivable."

The flaxen length of Leah's hair fell forward as

she bowed her head. "Maybe you should leave then. I wouldn't want you to be late for dinner with Mother."

Standing, Siggy straightened his pant legs. "I don't know what's come over you, Leah. You're hardly the girl I fell in love with anymore."

"Woman," she corrected brittlely. "I'm not a little girl who can live on promises. I'm a woman."

Her back was ramrod straight as Siggy walked across the carpet and paused at the door. "I'll phone you tomorrow. You'll have come to your senses by then."

Refusing to answer. Leah pinched her mouth tightly closed until her teeth hurt. Her lashes fluttered closed when the front door clicked, telling her that Siggy had left. Frustration came in waves, lapping at her from all sides, until she wanted to lash out at anyone or anything. Naturally, she didn't.

An hour later, disheartened and miserable, Leah tossed a TV dinner into the oven and set the timer. The local evening news was blaring from the TV when the doorbell chimed. Leah's heartbeat quickened. Siggy had reconsidered.

She fairly flew to the door, but her welcoming smile died an instant death when she saw it was Cain Hawkins and not Siggy.

"Can I come in?" he asked brusquely, and paraded past her, not waiting for a response.

"Feel free," she returned mockingly. "Make yourself at home while you're at it." She stepped aside and closed the door with her back, suddenly needing its support. "What can I do for you?"

"You and I have to reach an understanding."

"I'm going, Mr. Hawkins. There is nothing on God's green earth that's going to keep me from the Diamantinas."

Cain jerked a hand from his pants pocket and ran it through the dark hair along the side of his head. "Me, either, lady."

Lady! Well, at least that was an improvement over Siggy, who apparently viewed her as a disobedient child.

"Did you talk to this Sidney fellow?" he demanded, pacing in front of the sofa.

"Siggy," Leah corrected calmly, still standing at the front door.

"Whoever." Impatiently, his hand sliced the air.

"Yes, as a matter of fact I did discuss the situation with Siggy." Primly, Leah folded her hands. She wasn't about to announce to this arrogant male that Siggy hadn't asked his mother's permission yet.

His hand returned to the corduroy pocket. "I don't suppose you've got a beer?"

"You're right. I don't."

He gave a look that said he'd guessed as much. "Well, what did ol' Sidney say?"

Leah lowered her gaze. "He's…he's thinking about it. And it's Siggy," she returned with marked patience.

"Whoever," they said together in perfect unison.

For the first time, Leah saw Cain smile. Despite everything she felt about this man, she had to admit she liked his smile. His rugged face was affected by the movement of his mouth. His eyes grew a richer shade of brown until they looked almost black, and she saw a glimpse of the man she'd always thought him to be.

"Did I hear something ding?" Cain turned his ear toward the kitchen.

Leah nodded. "Yes. Please excuse me a minute."

He followed her into the compact kitchen and idly leaned against the counter as she opened the microwave and took out the packaged meal.

"You don't honestly eat that garbage, do you?" he asked, his voice rising with astonishment. "Good grief, no wonder you're so thin. Come on, I'll take you to dinner and feed you properly. You need some meat on those bones."

Leah bristled. "How could I possibly turn down such a flowery invitation?" she asked with more than a trace of sarcasm.

"Right." A reckless grin slashed his mouth. "How could you?"

The next thing Leah knew, she was being ushered out the front door and into the lot where a red Porsche speedster was parked.

Stopping, Leah ran her hand along the polished surface of the car and shook her head knowingly. "Honestly, Hawkins, you're so predictable."

He mumbled something under his breath and left her to open her own door and climb inside.

Leah had barely snapped the seat belt into place when Cain revved the engine and shoved the gear into place. They left the parking lot with a spray of gravel kicking up in their wake. The tires screeched as they came to the first red light.

"Do you have to… Is it necessary to drive quite so fast?" Leah asked, holding on to the seat with both hands.

"Just wait. This baby does one eighty-five."

"Not with me, it doesn't." Leah reached for the door handle to climb out, but the light changed and Cain shot across the intersection like a bullet out of a gun. Leah's head was jerked back with such force that it bounced against the headrest.

"Isn't this great?"

"No." Leah screamed, instinctively reaching for the dashboard. Her heart was pounding so fiercely she didn't know which was louder, her pulse or the roar of the engine.

Suddenly, Cain slowed down to a crawl and laughed. That mocking, taunting laugh Leah hated. She was so angry, she couldn't breathe.

"Now." He pulled over to the curb and parked. "Isn't that what you expected? You took one look at my car and immediately assumed that I was a crazy man at the wheel."

Unable to answer, Leah placed her hand over her heart and shook her head.

Cain's fingers tightened around the steering wheel. "We'll get along a lot easier if you learn something right now, lady. I'm never predictable. I do what I want, where I want and when I want. Got it?"

The grip on her anger was so fragile that Leah's voice

shook dangerously. "Don't ever do that to me again. And...and you get one thing straight. I have a name, and it isn't lady or honey or princess. It's Leah." Her shoulders were heaving, her breasts rising with every panting breath.

Their eyes locked, hers filled with determination and pride, his with an unreadable quality she couldn't quite define. She hoped it was grudging respect. When his hands loosened their grip on the steering wheel, she relaxed.

"Hello, Leah, my name is Cain Hawkins." He extended his hand to her, and with a trembling smile she placed her much smaller one in his.

"Hello, Cain."

A smile briefly touched his eyes before he checked the side mirror and pulled back onto the street. "I hope you're hungry," he said with a laugh.

"I don't know." Leah's returning laugh was shaky. "I think you might have to go back the way we came. My stomach is about a mile behind us."

He didn't laugh; his concentration was fixed on the road. Trying not to be obvious, Leah studied him from beneath long lashes. He was a complicated man, and she doubted that anyone could truly understand him. A genius. Few would deny that. For the first time she noticed a small dimple in his cheek. It wasn't apparent except when his face was relaxed, Leah concluded. His hair was unkempt and his beard showed a five o'clock shadow. She wondered if he often forgot to shave, then smiled because she knew intuitively that he did.

They arrived at an Italian restaurant that emitted the aroma of pungent spices and tomatoes. It seemed like weeks since Leah had eaten a decent meal.

Cain was recognized immediately, and there were shouts from the kitchen as a short, stout man came through the swinging doors, wiping his hands on a white apron. A flurry of Italian flew over Leah's head.

The man from the kitchen, whom Cain called Vinnie, directed his attention to Leah and nodded approvingly. He shook his head dramatically, his white teeth gleaming.

Never had Leah felt more as if she was standing on an auction block. Nervously she tucked a strand of hair around her ear and shifted her weight from one foot to the other.

A woman with a lovely olive complexion appeared, her dark hair filled with strands of silver. She, too, joined in the conversation, then slapped her hands with apparent delight.

Leah recognized only a few words of Italian, but *bambino* was one of them. Leah surmised that the restaurant couple were expecting their first grandchild and offered them a smile of congratulations.

Smiling happily, the woman took Leah by the shoulders and nodded her head several times. Again a flurry of Italian was followed by laughter.

When Cain put his arm around her shoulder, bringing her close to his side, Leah was all the more confused.

The couple led Cain and Leah into a secluded corner of the restaurant and smiled broadly as they held out the chairs. Almost immediately, a flurry of activity commenced. A large loaf of freshly baked bread and a thick slab of cheese were delivered to the table.

"You speak Italian," Leah said to break the silence between them. It wasn't one of her more brilliant deductions.

"I picked it up as a kid in Europe," Cain explained, pulling apart a hunk of bread and cutting off a slice of cheese.

Leah followed his example, taking a smaller piece of both the bread and the cheese. "You were born in Europe?" She wouldn't have guessed it.

"No, I was an Army brat. My dad was stationed all over the world. My mother and I were with him much of the time."

"How interesting." Leah realized her comment sounded trite, and she regretted having said anything.

"Actually, I was born in California, but soon afterward we were stationed in Formosa." He paused and took a sip of wine. "That's Taiwan now."

She knew that much from Trivial Pursuit.

"What about you?"

Her fingers worked the stem of the wineglass. "I'm originally from South Dakota. My father's a farmer. Wheat, barley, soybeans." She didn't mention how much she loved Cain's photos of America's farmlands and how she'd given that book to her father for Christmas last year.

If Cain was surprised by her homey, Midwest background, he didn't show it. But Leah was quickly learning that Cain didn't divulge anything unless it suited him. Something told her that he usually didn't talk about himself. Even in his books there was little information given about him. Most of what she knew she'd heard through gossip.

The bread and cheese disappeared, to be replaced with a relish plate filled with crisp, fresh vegetables and dark olives. Their wineglasses were replenished.

"You must come here often." Leah felt as if she had to carry the conversation. The looks Cain was giving her were unsettling. His thick brows were drawn together as if he were seeking something beyond her obvious lack of beauty. Either that, or something was troubling him. Lowering her eyes, she cursed their color for the thousandth time. They weren't quite green, nor dark enough to be brown, but some murky shade between.

She reached for a celery stick, then laid it against the side of her plate. Opening her mouth would only have drawn attention to how full her lips were.

"Your eyes are the most unusual color," Cain commented thoughtfully.

Leah's hand gripped the linen napkin in her lap. "Yes, I know." It looked for a minute as if Cain would say something else, but the waiter interrupted to deliver a small salad covered with a creamy herb dressing.

"You obviously know these people," Leah tried again.

"We go way back."

That absent, thoughtful look returned, and if Leah didn't know better she'd have said he was nervous about something. "I thought you must. They were saying something about a baby. Are they expecting a grand-child?"

Cain regarded her blankly. "No."

Leah's fork played with a lettuce leaf. "Oh, I thought I heard her say *bambino,* but then I'm not exactly fluent in Italian."

"You did," he said, but he didn't elaborate.

The salad was taken away and quickly followed by a plateful of spaghetti with a thick, rich meat sauce.

"I don't know if I can eat all this," Leah said with a wistful sigh.

A half smile deepened the grooves on one side of his face. "Be sure and save room for the main course."

"The main course," Leah repeated, her round eyes giving him a shocked look.

"I guess I should have warned you." His smile was replaced with a frown of concentration as he wove the long strands of spaghetti around his fork, using his spoon as a guide.

Leah watched him for a minute and shook her head, unwilling even to attempt his method. Setting her fork aside, she studied Cain. There was something bothering him. She could sense it in the way his brow knitted as he manipulated the spaghetti.

Cain looked up and their eyes clashed. "What's wrong?" she asked softly.

Cain heaved a sigh and set his fork aside. "I'm no good at this."

Leah blinked uncertainly. *Good at what?* she wondered.

"I thought if I created a romantic mood it would help. But, I don't go in for this romance garbage."

Leah was stunned into speechlessness. She'd never thought of herself as stupid, but at the moment she felt incredibly so. Cain looked as if he wanted to punch a hole in the wall, and she hadn't an inkling why.

"You know what's going to happen Thursday, don't you?"

She shook her head, more confused than ever.

"Brewster's going to come up with a compromise team."

Forcefully, Leah shook her head. "He wouldn't do that." He couldn't. David Brewster knew how much this trip meant to her.

"Of course he would. It's the only answer. If he doesn't he takes the risk of offending us both. And whether he feels like admitting it or not, we're both valuable to the university."

It didn't take much thought for Leah to recognize that what Cain was saying was true.

"And—" he tossed his napkin onto the table "—you may have this Sidney fellow to solve your problems, but there isn't anyone I can marry at the drop of a hat."

Leah couldn't believe that. "What…what are you suggesting?"

"There's only one thing to do." Cain looked thoroughly miserable. He reached for his wine and took a gulp. "Leah…?" He hesitated.

"Yes."

"Damn it anyway. Will you marry me?"

Chapter 2

"Marry...you," Leah repeated, dumbfounded.

"It isn't like this is any love match," Cain inserted, clearly angry. "We're adults. How old are you, anyway?"

"Twenty-eight." That, at least, was easily enough answered.

Cain looked surprised. "You look younger. I checked with a judge friend of mine this afternoon and found out all we need are blood tests. We can have those done tonight, get the license and be married before your first class in the morning."

"I...I suppose we could." A cauldron of doubts bubbled in her mind, but Leah could marshal no argument. Cain was right. They were adults, they were professional people and they both desperately wanted to be a part of this expedition. The choice was clear.

"Does that mean yes?" Cain demanded.

Leah chose to ignore the warning lights blinking in her brain. "Yes," she murmured.

"Thank you," Cain said with an exaggerated sigh. He called out something in Italian, and the entire kitchen staff appeared. Someone brought out an accordion, and the man Cain had called Vinnie pumped Cain's hand and kissed him on both cheeks.

Music filled the restaurant. Violins, accordions, guitars. Champagne flowed freely, and Leah quickly lost count of the number of people who congratulated her with kisses on both cheeks. It seemed she waltzed with more men in that one night than she had in her entire life.

The next thing she remembered was Cain delivering her to her apartment and asking her if she was going to be sick. The whole world was singing and dancing, spinning and weaving, and it was all she could do to wave him aside. Leah didn't know if she was going to be sick or not. But if she was, she didn't want Cain around.

The next morning Leah awoke in the clothes she'd worn to dinner the night before. She was suffering from the worst headache of her life. The base of her skull was throbbing as if an avenging demon were hammering on it.

Leah staggered into the bathroom and brushed her teeth but the sound of running water only intensified the ache in her head, and she turned off the faucet. Pressing a hand against her forehead, she took in deep breaths and winced when the doorbell chimed. With her hand still to her head, she moved to the living room and, as quietly as possibly, undid the dead bolt lock and opened the front door.

"Morning," Cain greeted her stiffly. "How do you feel?"

"About the same as I look," she whispered.

Idly he stuck his hands in his pockets and cocked his head to one side. "That bad, huh?"

Leah gave him a frosty glare. "I just woke up. I'd like to shower and change first."

"Sure. Do you mind if I make myself a cup of coffee?"

In her worst nightmares she had never dreamed that her wedding day would be anything like this. Cain wasn't even wearing a suit. He was dressed casually in dark cords and a sport shirt. She watched as he removed his leather coat and draped it over the kitchen chair, then paused to look at her expectantly. "The coffee?"

"Go ahead."

She left him to his own devices while she surveyed the contents of her closet. She didn't have a thing to wear. And the urge to use that as an excuse to back out of the wedding was almost overwhelming. Finally she chose an olive-green dress. The color matched her mood.

The shower took some of the ache from her bones, but the whine of the hair dryer nearly drove her insane.

Before twisting the blond strands into her usual chignon, Leah stepped into the kitchen. Cain was at the table reading the morning newspaper.

"Would you prefer my hair up or down?" she asked as she poured herself a cup of coffee.

Cain glanced up and blinked. "Would I what?"

"My hair," she returned with marked patience. "Should I wear it up or down? Siggy prefers it down."

Cain's blank stare continued. "Good grief, why should I care? You could be bald and it wouldn't make any difference."

Leah successfully resisted the urge to shout at him that this whole thing was ludicrous and she wouldn't have anything to do with it. "I'll leave my hair down then."

"Fine." Already his attention had reverted to the newspaper.

Leah had hardly taken more than a few sips of her coffee when Cain straightened and checked his watch. "The courthouse is open. Let's get this over with."

"Before we do anything with legal ramifications, I think we should make certain aspects of this relationship clear," Leah asserted.

"Of course." Cain gave her a strange look. "I've already thought of that." He lifted his coat from the chair and took out a folded piece of paper. "Read this over and see if I've left out anything."

Scanning the list, Leah was impressed with his thoroughness. Everything she'd thought to mention was there. She didn't want him to have any legal claim to her assets, and she wanted to keep her surname. "I'd like the divorce proceedings to start the first week after our return instead of a month later."

Cain hesitated. "Fine. Write that in if you want, but I can't have my time tied up in court. I'll be working day and night developing the film."

"I'm sure it will be a relatively painless process." Leah spoke with more confidence than she was feeling. "If it would make things simpler, we could make a quick trip into Nevada."

Again Cain glanced at his watch. "Let's decide that later."

"Fine," was Leah's clipped response. He didn't care how she styled her hair, and she didn't care how they went about the divorce as long as there was one.

"You'll notice that I've left a space for each of us to sign. You can keep a copy and I'll take the other."

"Good." Leah penned her name in flowing, even strokes and handed the ballpoint to Cain, who scribbled his signature below hers.

"You ready now?" he asked.

Leah answered him by reaching for the short olive jacket that matched her dress.

Obtaining the license was a simple matter of handing the clerk the results from the blood tests, penning their signatures and paying the fee. Leah watched the money change hands and felt they were selling themselves cheap.

Recognizing how strange it would sound, Leah resisted questioning the clerk about where they could file for the divorce. That would be easy enough to find out when they returned from the Diamantinas.

Judge Preston's quarters were in the same building, only a matter of a short ride in the elevator.

Leah paused outside the door, staring at the evenly printed letters on the glass door. Nervously, her fingers toyed with the strap of her purse as she bit into her quivering bottom lip.

Cain opened the door and pressed a hand in the small of her back, urging her forward. "Come on," he said impatiently, "we're running on a tight schedule."

Squaring her shoulders, Leah stepped into the office. Her throat was desert dry with apprehension.

"Judge Preston is expecting us," Cain announced to the receptionist.

The attractive young woman flashed them an easy smile. "You must be the young couple the judge mentioned this morning. He asked me to be your witness. That is, if you don't mind?" She directed her questions to Leah.

Both the receptionist and Cain seemed to be waiting for Leah to respond. "That's very kind…thank you."

They were ushered into the judge's quarters, and the gray-haired, fatherly-looking man stood immediately. "Welcome, my boy. It's good to see you." Enthusiastically, he shook Cain's hand and turned to Leah. "You've chosen well, Cain. Your father would be proud." He centered his attention on Leah and smiled at her with blue eyes that had faded with age but retained their sparkle. Taking her cold, clammy hand in his, he said, "There's no need to be nervous. Cain Hawkins took his time in choosing a bride. He'll make you a good husband."

Obviously Cain hadn't explained the situation to anyone, and Leah was supposed to fall in with this happy-bride act.

Leah saw Cain glance at his watch, and she seethed silently. If he announced once more that they were on a tight schedule, she swore she was going to turn around and walk out that door.

The judge leaned forward and flipped a switch on the intercom. "We're ready now, Joyce. Would you ask Mr. Graham to step into my office?"

At Cain's look of surprise, the judge explained, "Your other witness."

Cain looked uncomfortable as he took the license from his coat pocket and gave it to his friend.

As soon as everyone was in their place, the judge reached for his little black book and flipped through the pages.

"We are gathered here today...."

The words droned in Leah's ear as she struggled to pay attention. This wasn't right. Marriage was forever, a commitment meant to last a lifetime. Her parents had recently celebrated their thirtieth wedding anniversary. *Divorce* was such an ugly word. No one in her family had ever been divorced. Panic grew within Leah until she wanted to turn and bolt from the room and Cain Hawkins's craziness. Nothing was worth compromising everything that she believed was right.

"Do you take this man to be your lawfully wedded husband, in sickness and in health…?"

"I don't know," Leah cried, desperately close to tears.

Four stunned faces turned to her. Cain looked as if he wanted to wring her neck, and she couldn't blame him. Leah swallowed and fought back the rising hysteria. "It just doesn't seem right to talk about divorce on the way to the wedding. I…I was raised to believe in the sanctity of marriage."

"Leah," Cain's low voice threatened, "we agreed."

"I know." Her newly discovered resolve was faltering.

"Think of the whales," he whispered enticingly.

Oh how she loved those marvelous creatures. Her hazel eyes pleaded with Cain to understand.

"Miss Talmadge," the judge spoke gently. "If you have any questions about this ceremony…"

Cain's eyes sharpened with determination. "There's no problem. Carry on."

"Miss Talmadge?"

Leah could feel Cain stiffen at her side. His hand at the back of her waist pressed into her painfully. She couldn't believe he was hurting her consciously.

"Leah," Cain urged.

"I do," she screamed. "All right, all right, I'll go through with it."

A minute later a recognizably flustered judge asked for the ring. Cain and Leah looked at each other with growing frustration. They'd completely forgotten the wedding bands.

In an apparent move to stall for time while he thought of something, Cain pretended to search through his pockets.

"I think we may have left those at Leah's apartment," Cain murmured, and gave Leah a panicked look.

"You can borrow mine," the receptionist offered generously, slipping the small diamond ring from her finger.

"No...I wouldn't want to do that." Marrying under these circumstances was difficult enough; Leah refused to borrow a ring. "Molly Brown wore a cigar band," she offered, hoping to lighten the mood.

"Who?" The same four faces glared at her.

She swallowed uncomfortably. "*The Unsinkable Molly Brown*...it was a movie with Debbie Reynolds, one of my mother's favorites."

"Will this do?" The young attorney who was standing next to Cain withdrew a pull tab from a soda can out of his pocket. "As I understand the law, a ring isn't actually required. This will do until you replace it later."

"Good idea." Cain brightened. "Thanks."

Fifteen minutes later, Cain and Leah were on the freeway, heading toward Leah's apartment.

"Well, that wasn't so bad, was it?" Cain broke into the oppressive silence that filled the car.

"Not bad?" Leah returned, shocked. "It had to be the most horrible experience of my life."

"You're letting your emotions get in the way. The little girl in you is waiting for orange blossoms and the flowing white gown and veil. You can have that the next time."

Leah wanted to hate him for being so analytical. None of this had troubled Cain.

"I...I don't care what you say, I don't feel right about this."

"Honestly, Leah, it isn't like we did anything wrong."

"Then why am I filled with regrets? Why is there a lump in my throat and I feel I could cry?"

"Oh, good grief, here it comes."

Leah ignored him as best she could. If she couldn't disregard Cain's sarcasm, she'd end up looking for some painful way to lash out at him. "We were wrong to have married like this. And whether you admit it or not, we've lost something we'll never be able to recapture."

Cain stopped at the light at the bottom of the exit ramp and thumped his fingers against the steering wheel. "You've been a good sport until now. Don't go all melodramatic on me."

Staring straight ahead, Leah murmured caustically, "Right."

Cain came to a halt beside her car in the parking lot. She slipped the ridiculous soda can ring from her finger and left it on the console.

"I'll stop by tonight," Cain said as he leaned across the car seat when she climbed out. "We've got lots to discuss."

Leah couldn't think of a thing she had to say to him.

"About the trip," he said, apparently having read her thoughts. "I'll see you about seven. Okay?"

She never wanted to see Cain Hawkins again. "All right," she found herself agreeing.

Leah's classes that day were a disaster. It would have been better to have phoned in sick, for all the good she did. Her mind refused to function properly, and she made several embarrassing mistakes. All she seemed able to think about was that this morning she had married a man she didn't know, who was probably the coldest, least demonstrative, most analytical being on earth. Cain Hawkins's pictures may have been wonderful, but they were nothing like the man.

As promised, Cain was at her apartment at seven, bringing a six-pack of beer with him. He delivered it promptly to the refrigerator.

"Feel any better?" he asked on his way out of the kitchen.

"No," she answered stiffly. She was about to tell him what he could do with his beer, when he spoke.

"This should improve your mood." He took a plain gold wedding band from his pocket. When she ignored it, he reached for her hand and pressed it into her palm. "It was my mother's."

The ring warmed her hand, and Leah realized he must have been holding it for quite some time before giving it to her. Leah stared at it, unable to believe Cain would do something like this. "I…I appreciate the thought, but I don't want your mother's ring."

"What am I going to do with it, anyway?"

Leah gave him a look of disbelief. "Someday there'll

be a woman you love that you'll want to give this ring to." Someone beautiful, no doubt, she added silently.

Cain removed his jacket and tossed it over the leather love seat. "If I can go thirty-five years avoiding the marriage trap, then…"

Leah started to giggle. She couldn't help it. Laughter consumed her, and she covered her mouth. Giant tears welled in her eyes and rolled down her pale cheeks.

"What's so all-fired funny?"

"You…us," she managed between peals of laughter. "Avoiding the marriage trap, indeed. You *are* married. *We're* married."

His mouth was pinched as he went back into the kitchen and returned with a can of beer. "Wear the ring. You'll need to have one or there'll be questions."

"But not your mother's ring." Leah watched him with mounting incredulity. Maybe he didn't care. Apparently there was little in life that did concern him.

"Yes," he insisted tightly. "My mother's ring. What do I want with it?"

His face tightened with anger. Or perhaps it was pain; Leah couldn't tell.

"It's obvious this sort of thing means something to you," he continued. "So keep it."

"Don't you care about anything?" Leah asked, perplexed by this complicated man. True, the ring wasn't worth much, but it must have had some sentimental value if he'd kept it all these years.

"I care about a lot of things," he countered swiftly. "Good beer." He saluted her mockingly by raising the aluminum can. "And gourmet food, which reminds me, have you eaten yet?"

"Stop it," she shouted unreasonably. For the first time since they'd met, Leah felt she was close to understanding this man. So this was how he'd remained single all these years. He allowed people to get only so close before shutting them out. Cain Hawkins was running from life, from commitment, from everything that his photographs revealed. Only when he was behind a camera was he comfortable.

"I take it you ate," he prompted.

She hadn't been able to down anything all day. "No."

"Good. Why don't you throw two of those frozen dinners in the microwave? I could eat a cow."

Ignoring him, Leah fingered the plain gold band. Cain hadn't fooled her. The ring meant a great deal to him, and he was giving it to her to prove to himself in some perverse way that it meant nothing.

"I can't accept this," she said, holding out the ring.

Cain looked stunned. "Why not? It isn't like it was all that important to my mother." He laughed mirthlessly. "She left it on the kitchen counter when she ran off."

Just by the way his voice dipped to a low, husky tone, Leah realized how painful that episode must have been for Cain. "But you kept it?" she prompted softly.

"No." He took a long drink from his beer. "My father did. I found it recently when I was going through Dad's things." A glazed look flitted across his face as he explained softly, "He died six months ago."

"I'm sorry."

"Why? Was it your fault?" The sarcasm laced through his words said she was getting too close and it was time to push her away. He took another swig of his beer and took a small pad from his coat pocket.

Leah moved into the kitchen, took out two frozen dinners and set them in the microwave. The ring sat on the white countertop and magnetically drew her attention. No matter where she was in the kitchen, her gaze was attracted to it. Finally, she picked it up and slipped it on her finger. The fit was perfect.

In a way she couldn't explain, Leah *felt* married. And although they'd only met a day ago, there was a bond between them. A spiritual bond. Cain didn't go around telling people about his mother, she was convinced of that. Nor would he mention to a mere acquaintance that his father had recently passed away.

When they'd agreed to get married, neither of them had expected it to have any effect on their lives. Not really. This marriage was for one purpose—so they could both be included in the ancient whale expedition to the Diamantina Islands. Yet it was only hours after the wedding and Leah felt indelibly marked. An invisible link existed between them, and Leah doubted that either one of them would ever be the same again.

Carrying a cup of coffee with her, Leah moved into the living room. She sat opposite him and crossed her long legs. "I thought we might talk about the goals of the expedition."

"First tell me something about the ancient whale."

"All right," Leah agreed. "There are about a hundred

known species of whales divided into two suborders. The scientific names are *Mysticeti* and *Odontoceti*. Or to say it another way, whalebone whales and toothed whales."

Cain nodded, his eyes lowered. Leah realized that she was probably giving him more information than he wanted. But it was important that he understood the significance of the discovery of this whale last year.

"Ancient whales," she continued, "are in a third separate category. The reason they're called ancient whales is because it's been presumed for years that they were extinct."

"What are our chances of photographing one?"

Leah wouldn't be anything but truthful. "Slim, at best."

"But there will be ample opportunity to view the other species."

"Definitely. Probably closer than you've ever thought you would get to a whale. There's been a boat supplied and—"

"You're wearing the ring."

His statement caught her off guard, and her gaze fell to her left hand. "Yes." She didn't elaborate, not sure why she'd relented and slipped it on her finger. "As I was saying about the boat—" she swallowed, suddenly ill at ease "—I'm hoping that we can get—"

"Why?"

"For the photos, of course."

"I'm asking about the ring. What made you decide to wear it?"

Leah didn't know how to explain something she wasn't sure of herself. "I only hope there's enough time to gather all the material I'll need."

The room became quiet. "That wasn't what I asked."

Deliberately, she uncrossed her legs and stood. "I think I'll check the microwave, I think I heard it ding."

"I'll only follow you."

"I don't know why," she shouted, unreasonably angry that he would demand an answer when she obviously didn't have one. "It was there, and you're right, I'm going to need one. And this will save us the trouble of going out and buying one. Now, are you satisfied?"

The doorbell chimed before Cain had the opportunity to answer.

Leah glared accusingly at the door, marched across the room and turned the handle. "Yes," she said heatedly.

"Darling." Siggy stood on the other side. Shock moved across his eyes. "Is something wrong?" he said gently, reaching for her limp shoulders and bringing her into his embrace. "Of course you're upset. It's about yesterday, isn't it?"

"Siggy."

"No, no. It's my turn. You're right, so right, my love. I was cheating us both by not telling Mother about us. I talked to her this evening and—"

"Siggy, please, let me explain," Leah pleaded as she stepped back out of his arms.

"Mother approves, darling. Do you understand what that means?"

The urge to laugh was almost overwhelming. "Mother approves," Leah echoed.

Cain stood and moved behind Leah, placing a possessive hand on her neck. "Is there a problem?"

Siggy stiffened, then straightened the corner of his bow tie. "Who is this man?" He directed his question to Leah.

"Is there something I can do for you?" Cain answered stiffly. "I'm Leah's husband."

Chapter 3

"Leah?" Siggy couldn't have looked more stunned. His eyes rounded and his cheeks puffed out like someone who had come under sudden attack. Slowly he regained his composure enough to continue speaking. "Is this true?"

Frustrated and impatient, Leah glared angrily at Cain. He had no right to adopt this high-handed attitude. From the smug smile that played across his mouth, he was obviously enjoying her fiancé's discomfort. "Siggy, let me explain," Leah pleaded, a thread of despair weaving its way through her voice.

The hand at the base of her neck tightened as Cain drew her possessively closer. "Just answer the question, darling."

"Leah?" Again Siggy's shocked, hurt gaze sought hers. "Is it true?"

"Yes, but there are…extenuating circumstances."

The smile Siggy gave her was decidedly dispirited. "There'd have to be. Only yesterday you wanted to be *my* wife."

Her heart leaped with pity at the hurt-little-boy look in his pale-blue eyes.

Siggy took a step in retreat, his shoulders hunching. "Everything would have been all right now that Mother knows. Couldn't you have waited?"

"No, we couldn't." Again Cain had answered for her.

Siggy's gaze skidded from Leah to Cain and then back to her again. Confusion and pain marked his expression. "Then there's nothing left to say. Goodbye, Leah."

"Siggy." The aching sigh of his name must have caused him to hesitate.

"Yes?"

"I'll give you a call in the morning." She ignored the way Cain's fingers were digging into the nape of her neck. "All this can be explained quite simply."

"You won't have time, darling," Cain insisted, his eyes narrowing. "We're both going to be extremely busy from now on."

If possible, Siggy went all the more waxen. A figure of rejection, he turned and walked away, closing the door.

Anger washed over Leah in turbulent waves. The first swells rose quickly to storm intensity, so that she had difficulty forming her thoughts.

"How…how dare you!" With a sweep of her hand she slammed the front door closed and turned on Cain like an avenging archangel. Quivers of rage sharpened her voice. The sound of her anger vibrated through the room like a violent ocean storm attacking the shore. This was no squall, but a full-blown tempest.

Even Cain looked shocked at the extent of her wrath. "You can't honestly love that pompous, bureaucratic windbag."

"Why should you care one way or the other? Siggy is part of my life. He had nothing to do with you." To her horror, stinging tears pooled in her eyes, so that Cain swam in and out of focus.

"But he doesn't love you," Cain argued. "Can't you see what he—"

"And you do love me, is that what you're saying? Are you such an expert in love that you know instantly who does and doesn't?" Pride was the only thing that carried her voice now as it quivered and trembled with every word.

His gaze narrowed as he plowed a hand through his hair. "You're misinterpreting everything."

"I am?" She gave a weak, hysterical laugh. "Weren't you the one who said I'd be lucky to be any man's wife? Look at me. Do you think I don't know I'm no raving beauty?"

Clearly flustered now, Cain stalked to the other side of the room. "You're not that bad."

"Oh, come now. Be honest. If it hadn't been for this assignment, you wouldn't have given me more than a passing glance."

He gestured indecisively with his hand. "How am I supposed to know that? If it weren't for this assignment we wouldn't have met."

"I'm too tall, too thin and blatantly unattractive. Do you have any idea what that means to someone like me? Siggy cares. For the first time in my life there was a man who looked beyond my face and loved me enough to want to share his life with me. And…" She paused as her voice cracked. "And now, you've done your best to ruin that."

"Leah." He clenched his hands into tight fists. "I apologize. I have no excuse. My behavior was stupid and irrational."

She sniffled and reached for a tissue to blow her nose. "An apology isn't going to reverse what just happened. You may very well have ruined my life."

"All right, all right. Call…Sidney, and we'll get together and explain everything."

"When?" she demanded.

"Whenever you like."

She reached for her phone and left Siggy a message in voice mail. "He'll return the call," she murmured confidently. Siggy would be willing to clear away any misunderstandings. It didn't matter what Cain Hawkins thought, Leah reminded herself. Siggy loved her and that was the most important thing. When she returned from the Diamantinas her routine could return to normal. Cain would want her out of his life as quickly as possible.

While she was phoning, Cain had gone into the kitchen, and he returned now with a strong cup of coffee. "Here." He set it on the glass coffee table. "Drink this."

The gesture surprised Leah. Cain had already apologized and had promised to make things right between her and Siggy. Now he was thoughtfully taking care of her. "Thank you."

"Do you feel like going over the list of supplies?" He sat across from her and leaned forward as he pulled the tab from his beer can.

Leah waited until he'd taken his first long drink before she answered. "I hope you're not planning to bring that stuff along."

"What?" His gaze followed hers, and a low, husky chuckle escaped. "This, lady, is as essential as film for my camera. Don't worry, I seldom drink more than one or two at a time. Think of it as my brand of cola."

Leah wasn't convinced. If they were going to be spending a lot of time together, alcohol could be a dangerous thing. But the dark gleam in his eye discouraged argument. This was one area where Cain wouldn't compromise. His look confirmed as much.

"Here, take a look at this." He withdrew a pad from his jacket and handed it to Leah.

She glanced over the itemized list of food supplies Cain had typed. The list was extensive and seemed far beyond what they could possibly eat during the course of their trip.

"You've got that look in your eye again," Cain grumbled.

"What look?"

"The one that says you disapprove."

A smile danced across her face, her first since Siggy had come…and gone. "It's just that it seems like so much."

"Perhaps it is, but I'd like to fatten you up a little while we're there."

A small laugh escaped. "My dear Mr. Hawkins, better men than you have tried."

At ease now, Cain chuckled, but the amusement slowly drained from him as his gaze captured hers and the room went still. An expression she couldn't read filtered over his features, an odd mixture of surprise and incredulity. Silence fell between them.

"Is something wrong?" Concerned, Leah wondered what had happened to alter his mood so quickly.

"You're not ugly—or even plain. In fact, you're lovely."

His announcement came out of nowhere. Self-conscious, Leah dropped her gaze to her hands. With the movement, her long hair fell forward, wreathing the delicate features of her oval face. "Don't, please," she whispered entreatingly.

"No, I'm serious. You were laughing just now, and your eyes sparkled, and it struck me—Leah Talmadge is really pretty."

Involuntarily, she flushed. "Cain, I know what I am." In many ways, she knew, she was like the Leah from Scripture, the plain, weak-eyed first wife of Jacob. The unloved one.

"And you think I'm making it up?"

No, she knew exactly what he was doing. In his own

way, Cain was trying to make up to her for what had happened with Siggy.

"Believe what you want, then. But I didn't imagine what I just saw."

Where only minutes before they had been fiercely arguing, now there was kindness in his words. For a time, it had seemed impossible that they would ever manage to work together. Now Leah had no doubts that they could and would.

"Everything's going to work out fine," Cain said with a confidence that was irrefutable. "Tomorrow we'll meet with Dr. Brewster and your…Sidney. I'm hoping that we'll be ready to leave by the end of the week."

Leah was stunned. "So soon?"

"The faster we're out of here, the better. If we stick around California another week, something else might crop up that could cause a change in plans. Can you be ready?"

"If I can meet a man one day and marry him the next, I can do anything. Lead the way, partner."

"Now you're talking. We're a team. We can't forget that."

The microwave dinged again, reminding Leah their dinner was ready. Cain followed her into the kitchen, and while she took them out of the microwave he set the table. Wordlessly, they worked together. What Cain had said was true—they were a team. In the coming weeks they'd be spending a lot of time together. Yesterday the thought had terrified her, but tonight she felt at ease with Cain Hawkins. Their peace would hold because they both wanted this expedition to succeed.

With all that needed to be discussed and planned, Cain didn't leave her apartment until the early-morning hours. She turned the dead bolt lock after he'd gone and leaned wearily against the door. Releasing a soft yawn, she brushed the hair off her face with her hands. Surprisingly, Cain was a meticulous organizer; his expertise was undeniable. The opportunity of a lifetime was opening up for them and her heart swelled with excitement.

Not until Leah had undressed and climbed into bed did the realization come. A chill raced up her spine, and her fingers went cold as they gripped the sheets. Her chest ached with the unexpected pain of it, and she pressed her palm over her heart.

Tonight was her wedding night!

A heavy frown formed deep creases in her brow as Leah's gaze slid to the simple gold band on her ring finger. This so-called marriage was wrong. Her heart had known that from the beginning. The uncertainty she'd experienced as she stood in front of Judge Preston was only a foreshadowing of what was sure to follow.

Slowly Leah lay back and stared at the ceiling. A flip of the lamp switch and the room was cast into instant blackness. The night seemed to press down on Leah. As a teenager, she had often dreamed of her wedding, seeing it as the one day in her life when she was sure to be beautiful. Wearing a long white gown and flowing veil, she would stand before friends and family and give testament to her love. A love that was meant to span a lifetime. Her wedding night would be one of discovery and joy. Not in her cruelest nightmares had she suspected that she would be spending it alone.

Moon shadows flickered across the walls as Leah rolled over, pulled the blankets over her shoulders and took in a shuddering sigh. Even ugly women should be allowed their fantasies. But not Leah. So much for dreams. So much for romance. So much for love.

The relief on Dr. Brewster's wrinkled face was evident in every craggy line. "My children, I couldn't be more pleased." He slapped Cain across the back and shyly kissed Leah's cheek. "I realize that marriage must have sounded a bit drastic, but I can't imagine sending a better team to the islands. Everything will work out splendidly. Just you wait."

"I think it will," Cain agreed.

Perhaps the project would work out well, but as to carelessly linking their lives, Leah wasn't nearly as confident. Their marriage was supposed to be a two-month business arrangement, but the gold band around her finger felt as if it weighed a hundred pounds. Leah knew that when she slipped it from her hand to return to Cain after the expedition, her finger would be indelibly marked by its presence for all her life.

They left Dr. Brewster's office with their travel documents, airline tickets and a list of contacts in Australia and New Zealand.

"Where to from here?" Cain questioned once they'd reached the university parking lot.

With a false smile of courage, Leah lowered her chin fractionally. "I'm having lunch with Siggy."

"You, not us." Cain's voice was clipped and direct. "In that case, I'll drop you off at your apartment." He held the car door open for her, and she gracefully swung her long legs inside.

"It's not that I don't want you to come." She felt obliged to explain, and her soft voice thinned to a quivering note. "But I think it will be a lot better if I see Siggy alone."

"Sure." His gaze seemed to lock on the pulsing vein in her neck, and it was all Leah could do not to turn up her collar. While she stared ahead, unnerved by his sudden interest in her heart rate, Cain started the car and pulled into the heavy traffic in the street.

"Without getting too personal, maybe you can tell me what you find so intriguing about Sidney."

Leah had difficulty disguising her grimace. If Cain called Siggy Sidney one more time, she'd scream. From the first, she'd known his game. He did it on purpose, just to get a rise out of her, and she refused to give him one.

"Well?" Cain prompted. "You were going to marry the guy. Certainly you saw something in him."

"Of course I did...do," she corrected hastily. "Siggy's intelligent, sensitive, hard-working."

"From what he said about *Mother,* I'd say he's tied to the apron strings, wouldn't you?"

Leah had despaired over that herself, but there wasn't anything that she and Siggy couldn't settle once they were married. "Siggy has a strong sense of family."

Cain's attention shifted from the slow-paced traffic to her. "Are you always this loyal?" The lines etched about his eyes crinkled as he studied her. But it wasn't a smile he was giving her.

"When you care deeply about someone, then it's only natural to want to defend him."

"Care deeply or love?" Cain demanded.

His question struck a raw nerve. Leah had trouble herself distinguishing between the two when it came to Siggy. She cared about him. She was planning on being his wife. Of course she loved him.

"You can't answer me, can you?"

"I love him." Leah tore the admission through the constricted muscles of her throat. "No woman agrees to be a man's wife if she doesn't love him."

Cain's thick brow arched mockingly. "Oh?" Pointedly, his gaze fell to her ring finger as a mocking reminder that only yesterday she had married him without love or commitment.

For a mutinous moment, Leah wanted to shout at him for being unfair. Instead, she pressed her lips tightly closed and stared out the side window.

They didn't speak again until Cain dropped her off in her parking lot. Leah started to let herself out.

"What time will you be back?" Cain wanted to know.

Leah shrugged noncommittally. "I haven't any idea." At the scowl he was giving her, she added, "Did you need me for something?"

"No." His gaze refused to meet hers. "Enjoy yourself."

The instant Leah closed the car door, Cain sped away, his tires screeching as he pulled out of the parking lot.

Bewildered, Leah watched him go. Cain was acting like a jealous husband. Not that he cared for her himself; he just didn't like the idea of her seeing Siggy. Why, she didn't know. But Cain Hawkins wasn't an easy man to decipher.

Siggy was already seated at their favorite restaurant when Leah arrived. As a vegetarian, Siggy would dine at only a handful of restaurants, even though Leah had often argued that he could order a meatless meal almost anywhere.

"Leah." As she approached the table, he stood and held out a chair for her.

"Hello, Siggy," she murmured self-consciously. "I'm so pleased that you agreed to see me."

"Well, yes, that was rather considerate of me under the circumstances."

Unfolding the napkin gave her something to do with her hands as Leah struggled with her explanation. "Marrying Cain isn't what it seems," she began haltingly. "Cain and I were forced to marry or give up the expedition."

A smile relaxed Siggy's tense features. "I thought as much. I knew you'd never do something like this without good reason. It's not a real marriage, is it? I can't imagine you making love with that unpleasant fellow."

Leah could feel the color flowering in her face. Two bright rosebuds appeared on each cheek and flashed like neon lights for all to witness her embarrassment. "Of course we haven't."

Siggy's chuckle was decidedly relieved. "This is strictly a business arrangement then."

"Yes, strictly business." This entire discussion was humiliating.

"And..." Siggy hesitated, obviously disconcerted. "How shall I put this?"

"I don't plan to ever sleep with him, if that's what you want to know."

Clearing his throat, Siggy flashed her a warm smile. "I had to be sure you weren't going to mix business with pleasure." Finding himself highly amusing, Siggy snorted loudly.

"Siggy," she flashed. "I'm a scientist with a mission. Just because Cain and I will be alone on the island together doesn't mean I'll find him attractive."

"You may be a scientist, my dear, but you're also a woman. A man like Cain Hawkins herds women in unconsciously."

Cain wasn't a ladies' man, Leah knew that much. If anything, he avoided relationships. His camera and his pictures were his life; he didn't need anything else and made a point of saying so.

"Now you're being unfair. Cain's not like that," she said, fighting back the urge to defend him even further.

Siggy's response was a loud cough as he lifted the menu and studied it carefully. Leah wondered why he bothered to read it. He never ordered anything but the zucchini quiche anyway.

The waitress arrived and took their order. True to form, Siggy ordered the quiche; Leah asked for the spinach salad.

Their meals arrived a few minutes later. As Leah dipped her fork into the bowl of greens, an unexpected smile quivered at the corners of her mouth. She knew exactly what Cain would say about this meal. He'd insist that she have pasta on the side and cheesecake for dessert.

Obviously troubled again, Siggy toyed with his meal. "You do plan to divorce the man."

"Of course," Leah returned instantly. "We've agreed to take care of that the first week after we return."

Siggy seemed to breathe easier. "Mother must never know. You understand that, don't you, Leah?"

"I won't say a word," she promised. "It isn't as if it's a real marriage," she went on, "but one of convenience strictly for professional reasons." She couldn't understand why she felt compelled to repeat that. The thought flashed through her mind that she was saying it more for her benefit than Siggy's.

"I understand why you've done this," Siggy continued. "But I can't say I'm pleased. However, trust is vital in any relationship, and I want you to know I trust you implicitly." Having said his piece, Siggy nodded curtly.

"Thank you," Leah murmured, and bowed her head. A ray of light hit the gold band on her finger, causing her to catch her breath softly. This marriage was one of pretense. Deep down in her heart, she doubted Cain Hawkins had it in him to love someone of flesh and blood. His wife was a camera, his children his pictures. Then why, oh why, did she feel so married?

The Los Angeles airport was crammed with people, all of them in a hurry. A blaring voice over the loudspeaker announced a flight's departure gate, and Leah paused to be sure it wasn't hers. Nerves caused her stomach to knot painfully. Excitement seared through her blood. It had been a test of endurance, but together she and Cain had managed to meet the deadline they'd set for themselves. Barely. Leah was convinced that the first week she was on the island, all she'd be able to do was sleep.

Showing his concern for her well-being, Dr. Brewster had kindly arranged hotel accommodations in Sydney, Australia. From Sydney they would fly directly to Perth and meet with the contact, Hugh Kimo.

"Excited?" Cain's eyes smiled into hers.

"I don't think I can stand it." Her gaze scanned the milling crowd. They'd be heading for security any minute, and Siggy had said he'd be there to see her off. That was one thing she could count on: if Siggy said he was going to be someplace, he'd be there. Of all the people Leah had known in her life, Siggy was the most dependable—and predictable.

"Looking for someone?" Cain's mouth was pulled up in a mirthless smile.

He knew exactly whom she was expecting. "I don't understand it—Siggy's never late."

"I hope I didn't inadvertently give him the wrong flight time."

"Cain!" She expelled his name with the cutting edge of anger. Neither man had made any pretense of liking the other, but to have Cain stoop to lying was unfair.

"Leah, Leah, there you are." Breathlessly, Siggy arrived, flustered and obviously relieved to have found her in time. "I've had the most horrible afternoon. This place is a madhouse."

Cain's gaze was hard and disapproving as he made no attempt to disguise his dislike of Siggy.

Apparently not wishing to cause a scene, Siggy ignored Cain and reached inside his jacket pocket for a jeweler's box. He handed it to Leah.

"Siggy," she breathed in surprise.

"Go ahead," he urged, "open it."

Lifting the black lid, Leah discovered a small gold heart and a delicate chain, nestled in a bed of velvet. "Siggy, it's beautiful." Tears stung the back of her eyes. The gesture was so unexpected and so thoughtful that she gently brushed her lips over his cheek, finding no better way to express her appreciation.

Her genuine pleasure caused Siggy to flush with satisfaction. "I want you to wear it while you're away so you won't forget me." He fixed his gaze pointedly on Cain.

"I'd never forget you." She hardly knew what to say. Siggy wasn't much for gifts. "I don't know how to thank you."

The grim set of Cain's mouth told her that he didn't care for this sentimental exchange. His attitude was difficult to understand. She supposed that in some mysterious way his male pride had been challenged by Siggy, although she couldn't understand why.

Lifting the delicate necklace from its plush bed, Siggy held it up, prepared to help Leah put it on. She turned and lifted her hair as he placed the heart in the hollow of her throat and closed the clasp. Never one to display his affection publicly, Siggy was somewhat clumsy as he turned Leah around and kissed her soundly. The unexpected force of his mouth grinding over hers shocked Leah; his violent embrace knocked the wind from her lungs. Instinctively her hands sought his shoulders to maintain her balance.

Releasing her, Siggy gave Cain a self-satisfied glare. "Don't you so much as touch her," he warned smugly. "Leah's mine."

With a savagely impatient movement, Cain turned and stalked away.

Looking pleased with himself, Siggy stood in front of Leah and placed his hands on her shoulders. "Remember that I'll be waiting for you. Be true, my love, be true."

"You know I will." Lowering her gaze, Leah fought the urge to wipe his kiss from her mouth and was relieved to see it was time to get to her gate. Their flight would be boarding soon. She had wanted Siggy to come to the airport, but his selfish, brutal kiss had ruined her enjoyment of his unexpected gift. Siggy had come to stake his claim on her so that Cain would know in unconditional terms that she was his. Maybe, after all these months, she should be glad that Siggy was finally showing some signs of possessiveness. But she wasn't.

A quick survey of the area confirmed that Cain had already gone to the gate and had entered the line for security without her. Securing the strap of her carry-on bag over her shoulder, Leah offered Siggy a feeble smile.

"I'll call you in two months," she said, eager to be on her way.

Hands in his pants pockets, Siggy gave her his practiced hurt-little-boy look. "Hurry back."

Not goodbye, not good luck, just a reminder that he wanted her to hurry through the most important assignment of her career.

"Goodbye, Siggy." Turning, she handed the TSA agent her passport and proceeded to the gate. Their flight had already started boarding the 747.

Cain was in his assigned seat when Leah joined him. His attention was focused on a magazine taken from the pocket in front of him. After she'd stored her carry-on bag in the compartment above their seats, she joined him.

Their eyes met, and his gaze raked her face, pausing on her swollen lips. The look he gave her made her feel unclean.

The silence stretched between them oppressively. Within minutes the huge aircraft was taxiing down the runway. The roar of the engine was deafening as a surge of magnificent power thrust them into the welcoming blue sky.

Still Cain didn't speak, and in agitated reaction, Leah fingered the gold heart at her throat. The movement attracted Cain's attention.

"You must be pleased with yourself," he declared cruelly. "There aren't many unattractive women who can be married to one man and engaged to another."

Leah struggled not to react to his taunt. "Not many," she agreed, her voice sarcastically low and controlled to disguise her anger. It cost Leah everything to meet his gaze with a look of haughty indifference. That accomplished, she swiveled her head and closed her eyes. Cain had attacked her where he knew he would inflict the most discomfort, and he had succeeded beyond anything he would ever realize.

"Leah," he murmured her name with what sounded like regret. "I didn't mean that."

"Why hedge now? It's true. A girl like me is lucky to have any man want to marry her."

Cain's features hardened. "I didn't mean it." His hand reached for hers and squeezed so hard it almost hurt.

Her eyes blazed for an angry second. "Whether you meant it or not is immaterial. What you said is true." Jerking her hand free from his grasp, she continued to stare out the window, blind to anything but the ache that throbbed in her heart.

The next thing Leah knew, she was being gently shaken awake. "Leah," Cain whispered beside her ear. "Lunch is arriving."

To her acute embarrassment, Leah realized that in her sleep she had used Cain's shoulder as a pillow.

"I would have let you sleep, but I don't want you missing any meals." Her fiery gaze produced a soft chuckle from him. "Now, now, my dear, we're going to spend two months together. There's no call to be testy at the start of our adventure."

Their flight between Los Angeles International Airport and Sydney, Australia, was fourteen hours and spanned two calendar days because they crossed the international date line.

Although Leah slept—or made a pretense of sleeping—almost the entire time, she was exhausted when they touched down in Sydney.

Like a puppet with no will of its own, she followed Cain out of the plane, through customs and into the taxi that delivered them to the hotel.

Not until they were in the lobby, with people bustling around them in a flurry of activity, did Leah acknowledge how drowsy she was. Sitting on the edge of her suitcase, Leah waited while Cain signed the register and murmured something that caused the man at the counter to smile.

"Welcome to Sydney, Mr. and Mrs. Hawkins," the bellhop said in greeting as he held up the key to one room.

Chapter 4

"Just what do you think you're doing?" Leah whispered fiercely while they waited for the elevator. "I insist on having my own room."

"Leah, darling," Cain murmured, smiling beguilingly behind clenched teeth. "Let's not air our dirty laundry in the hotel lobby."

"I refuse to sleep in the same room with you. Isn't that clear enough, or do I need to shout it?" She ground out the words angrily, unconcerned if anyone was listening or not. She was tired and crabby, and she didn't want to stand outside an elevator arguing with the infuriating Cain Hawkins.

Whistling, his hands clasped behind his back, the bellhop gave no indication he heard any of her angry tirade, although Leah noticed that he avoided looking directly at her.

The heavy metal doors of the elevator swished open, and pressing a firm hand at the small of her back, Cain escorted Leah inside. "We'll talk about it later," he returned just as insistently. "Not here and not now. Understand?"

With cool haughtiness, Leah stood with her back ramrod straight, counting the orange lights that indicated the floors they were passing. Chancing a glance at Cain as they left the elevator, Leah found that his gaze was opaque, his face schooled to show none of his thoughts. Not so much as a twitch of a nerve or a flicker of an eyelash disclosed his feelings. And yet, she could feel the frustration and anger that exuded from him with every breath.

The bellhop opened the door to the suite and delivered their baggage with an economy of movement, seemingly eager to be on his way as quickly as possible.

Leah offered him an apologetic smile as he hurried past her. With her arms crossed, Leah was determined to stand in the outside hall until Cain acquiesced to her demand to sleep in a room of her own.

"Are you coming in or not?" Cain's eyes sliced into her from the other side of the doorway.

"Not."

"For for the love of heaven, be reasonable, will you?" Cain's weary frown revealed the extent of his fatigue and the fragile thread that held back his anger. "If you think I'm going to attack you, then rest assured, I'm too tired to do anything, and that includes arguing with you."

"It's not unreasonable to want some privacy."

"I requested two beds. That, at least, should please you." A hint of amusement touched his dusky, dark eyes. "I told the hotel clerk that my wife snores."

"There's no way I'm going to spend the night in that room with you," she replied in a taut voice. "And, for your information, I don't snore."

Rubbing a hand over his tired eyes, Cain released an irritated breath and slowly shook his head. "All right, come in and I'll phone the front desk and arrange for another room. You can have this one. I'll move."

"Thank you." But there was no sense of triumph as Leah crossed the threshold into the hotel room.

The suite was surprisingly large, with huge picture windows that granted a spectacular view of Sydney and the harbor below. Leah's eye caught a fleeting glimpse of the renowned Sydney Opera House, and her first impression was that the huge white structure resembled oversized sails billowing with wind.

The two beds dominated the room and shared a common nightstand where the telephone rested. Cain sat on the edge of the mattress and reached for the phone.

"Leah, won't you kindly reconsider? What if the government official for the Diamantinas hears that we insisted on separate rooms? He may wonder if we're really married."

"I brought a copy of the wedding certificate." She had already anticipated a problem there. "We were married in a civil ceremony and I have the paper that proves it."

"Barely civil, as I recall."

Cain's sarcasm was lost on her. He could throw all the barbs he wished and nothing would affect her. She was simply too tired to care.

The silence became oppressive as Leah lifted her overnight bag onto the top of the mattress and removed the things she needed. Her fingers shook slightly, and she could feel Cain's gaze following her movements, his mouth ominously taut.

Without another word, he called the front desk. She waited until he'd finished before she spoke. "If you'll excuse me, I'd like to freshen up before going to bed." With her nightgown and bathrobe draped over her arm, she paused. "You will be gone before I'm finished?"

His look was filled with angry resentment. "Would it be too much to ask to let me stay here until there's another room available?"

"Of course not. I didn't mean…" Everything was going wrong. She hadn't meant to sound like such a prude, but if he were to see her in the revealing nightgown, he'd know how thin she was, and how flat-chested. She might be exhausted, but this was a matter of pride.

"Take your bath," he demanded tightly. "I'll do my best to be out of here."

"Thank you." An odd breathlessness came over her. The door to the bathroom clicked closed, and she prayed the soothing water would dispel the black mood that wrapped itself around her like a cloak of gloom. His heartless words on the plane returned to taunt her. Cain believed she was ugly. She knew that herself, so it shouldn't bother her. But for a minute, just one moment, he had made her believe that she could be beautiful. His cruelty had ruined that and set the record straight.

The water lapping against the edge of the tub had cooled before Leah could summon the energy to climb out of the comforting water. She took longer than usual drying off in the hopes that Cain would have gone and he wouldn't see her. But if he did, that couldn't be helped, and she was determined to hold her head high and ignore any sarcastic comment. Loosely tying the sash around her narrow waist, she squared her shoulders, mentally preparing herself for the coming assault. She'd known from the beginning how intuitive Cain Hawkins was, but she had only suspected his ruthlessness. Within minutes he had recognized her vulnerability, and he had no compunction against using it to his advantage.

The sun had set, casting the room in hues of pink. As she opened the bathroom door, Leah's gaze was drawn magnetically to the scene outside her window. It reminded her of some of the magnificent sunsets she'd seen in Cain's books—the brilliant golden orb low on the horizon; the silhouettes of a hundred skyscrapers reflected in shades of red. From the scene outside her window, Leah's gaze sought the man who dominated her thoughts. A soft smile touched her eyes as she found him sprawled across the top of the mattress sound asleep. Slumber relaxed the lines of his face and made him seem younger. Unexpectedly, a surge of something akin to tenderness brushed her heart. She admired and respected Cain the photographer, but Cain the man was a dangerous puzzle.

An extra blanket was folded on the shelf in the closet across from the bathroom. Standing on tiptoe, Leah brought it down, then gently laid it over his shoulders.

Standing above him gave her the opportunity to study his face. Relaxed, it had a childlike vulnerability. The deeply etched lines about his eyes showed faded areas where the sun hadn't tanned his skin. His hair needed trimming; it curled upward slightly at the base of his neck. Leah had thought he would cut it before they left California, but clearly she couldn't second-guess Cain. He was his own man and would wear his hair down the middle of his back if he wanted. A lazy smile curved the corners of her mouth. The urge to reach out and touch him was almost irresistible. What she was experiencing, she decided, was a latent maternal instinct.

Leah had just peeled back the sheets to her bed when the phone rang urgently. She grabbed it and whispered into the receiver, not wanting to wake Cain. "Hello?"

"Mrs. Hawkins?"

"Yes…" It was on the tip of her tongue to correct him and explain that her name was Talmadge.

"Your husband requested another room. We have that suite available for him." The clerk sounded friendly and helpful.

"I apologize for any inconvenience, but we won't be needing the extra room."

"That's no problem," the man assured her. "Gudday."

"Gudday," Leah answered with a tired smile, and replaced the receiver.

A glance at Cain assured her that the phone hadn't awakened him. With the alarm set on her cell, Leah slipped her long legs between clean, fresh sheets. Her forearm was tucked under her pillow as she stared across the narrow space that separated her from Cain. Her eyes drifted closed, but she forced them open again, desiring one last look at Cain before she slept. Her last thought before she slid into peaceful surrender was that she was glad he was there.

A sharp clicking noise found its way into her warm dream and Leah winced, irritated to have her fantasy interrupted. She was on the rubber raft off Kahu, the island where they'd be staying, when forty tons of whale broke the surface amid a storm of spray. Excitement caused her heart rate to soar. These marvelous giants of the sea were her greatest love.

The clicking sound returned and was soon followed by another. Grumbling at the intrusion, Leah rolled over, bringing the sheets with her.

"Good morning, lady."

Cain. Her eyes flew open. He was in the room with her, and that awful sound was his camera.

"It's a beautiful morning," he continued, undaunted by her irritated grumble.

She struggled to a sitting position, keeping the blanket under her neck. "What time is it?" she asked, rubbing the weariness from eyes that refused to focus.

"Six." Cain was balanced on the arm of the chair and leaned against the window, snapping pictures of the city below. "Breakfast is on the way," he announced without turning around. "And you're right, you don't snore." He paused and turned to her, his gaze gently examining her face, lingering for a heart-stopping second on her lips. "But you do gurgle."

"I don't, either," she snapped.

"Oh." He jumped down from the chair and smiled broadly. "And when was the last time you slept with someone who'd know?"

The quick flow of color into her face caused Leah to cover her hot cheeks with her hands.

Cain's laugh was low and sensuous. "Just as I suspected."

"I should have had you carted out of here." She wasn't up to trading insults with him. Not this early in the morning, when she hadn't had her first cup of coffee.

"You probably should have," he agreed. "But I'm glad you didn't."

"How could I? You were sound asleep by the time I got out of the bath."

"Was I?" Cain teased softly, sitting on the edge of his unmade bed and fiddling with his camera lens.

Leah went cold, then hot. "You mean…" Flashing hazel eyes darted him a fiery glare. So he'd been playing a game with her last night as she stood above him and felt that surge of tenderness. Siggy was right, Cain Hawkins wasn't to be trusted. Not even for a minute.

A suggestion of controlled amusement was in the slight curl of Cain's upper lip, and her palm itched to slap that awful grin from his face.

"That was a rotten thing to do," she stormed, reaching for her robe at the end of the bed. "You really are unscrupulous. Siggy warned me about you. He said—"

Cain's sword-sharp gaze silenced her immediately and pinned her against the bed. "Listen and listen good, Leah. I won't have lover boy's name tossed at me for the next two months. Yearn for him all you want, but don't mention his name again. Understand?"

The violence with which he spoke shocked her, and she blinked back in surprise. She didn't know why Cain disliked Siggy so much, but it put her in an uncomfortable position. If he didn't want her to mention Siggy, then she wouldn't. But it didn't make sense. Cain stood and crossed the room, his hands stuffed into his pockets. He stood with his back to her, granting her the privacy to climb out of bed. "Breakfast will be here any minute. Maybe you should dress now."

Heeding his advice, Leah fairly flew into the bathroom, dragging her overnight case with her.

The flight between Sydney and Perth took the better part of the day. As a seasoned traveler, Cain didn't seem to be troubled with jet lag, but Leah felt as if she'd been turned inside out. Not only were they eighteen hours ahead of California time, but the seasons were reversed, and what had been lingering autumn days in San Diego had turned into early spring "down under." Dr. Brewster had warned her that it would take several days for her body to adjust, and Leah acknowledged wryly that he was more than right. It didn't seem to matter that she'd had a good night's sleep in Sydney and had slept extensively on the flight from California. She felt a weariness that reached all the way to her bones.

They were met at the airport in Perth by a government official from the Diamantinas. Dressed in a dark business suit, he was tall, with intensely dark eyes.

"Welcome to Perth," he said, shaking Cain's outstretched hand, then doing the same to Leah's. "My name is Hugh Kimo."

Dr. Brewster had mentioned that Hugh would be contacting them in Perth, and would later escort them to Ruaehu, the Diamantinas' capital city.

"My government is most anxious to have your stay in the Diamantinas be profitable to science and to man's understanding of our friends the whales." The formal speech was followed by a warm smile of welcome.

"Thank you," Cain said for them both. "And we're most eager to arrive and begin our study."

Their luggage was beginning to appear on the carousel, and Cain reached for a heavy suitcase.

"First," Hugh continued, "I want to assure you that the supplies you requested have been delivered."

"The parabolic microphone?" Leah questioned eagerly. The device would be invaluable for recording whale location, especially at night when she would be unable to view their progress from the lookout post hewed out of the rock cliff. In addition to studying migration routes, Leah hoped to investigate the sounds of the whales and their correlation to behavior. But that goal was secondary.

"Yes, the antenna has been installed according to your instructions." Hugh's smile was filled with pride. Leah's happy eyes met Cain's. They were so close now, that she regretted they wouldn't be leaving immediately for the islands. An extra day in Perth would only delay their study. Cain's look revealed that he, too, was eager.

"How soon can arrangements be made to leave for Ruaehu?" Cain asked. "As you can understand, both Mrs. Hawkins and I are eager to begin our research."

Research! Leah nearly laughed out loud. Cain's camera finger had been itching since before they left the airport. Already he'd taken scores of pictures of Sydney. And they'd only been there overnight.

Hugh Kimo laughed outright. "Dr. Brewster said that he doubted you two would remain in Perth for long. I'll make arrangements for you to fly to Ruaehu in the morning."

Leah was so excited that she had to restrain herself from throwing her arms around Cain's neck. Her goal was only hours away, and a deep sense of unreality remained. This adventure had been a dream for so many months that even now, when she was preparing to arrive, she couldn't believe it was all going to happen.

Early tomorrow morning they would fly to the island's capital and leave the same afternoon for the cliff hut.

Cain's arm came around her shoulders and tightened in a brief hug.

"I'll be dropping you off at the hotel. Perhaps we could meet for dinner later?" Hugh Kimo continued. "There remain only a few details we need to discuss."

"We'll look forward to that," Cain assured the tall man.

The hotel was close to the airport, so that the drive was accomplished in only a few minutes. Hugh Kimo didn't come inside, but asked that they meet him in the lobby later that evening.

As the bellhop loaded their luggage onto the cart, Cain smiled down at Leah. Their delicate truce was holding, and she was convinced that maintaining peace between them was as important to Cain as it was to her.

A hand at her elbow, Cain directed her through the large double glass doors and into the hotel lobby. "I'll see about getting connecting rooms this time," he said somewhat dryly.

"I'd appreciate that," she murmured, feeling ridiculous.

Leah's room was connected to Cain's by a common door. With less than two hours before their dinner date with Hugh, Leah spent the time taking a long, luxurious bath and doing her hair. Rarely did Leah spend so much time on her appearance. But she reasoned that it would be a long time before she could pamper herself this way again.

Leah's spirits soared at the look Cain gave her when he joined her in her half of the suite. Automatically, he reached for his camera and was snapping pictures before she had a chance to protest. Long ago, Leah had learned to hate the camera. Her mother had claimed that Leah wasn't photogenic and that that was the reason her photos turned out as they did but Leah knew differently. A camera might distort a likeness to some extent, but mirrors didn't lie.

"Don't, please," she begged, casting her gaze down to the carpet.

"What's wrong?" Cain's look was bewildered as he lowered the sophisticated camera.

Turning, Leah made the pretense of checking inside her purse. "I just don't like having my picture taken, that's all."

"Why not?" he asked curtly.

"Because." She hated him for dragging this out.

"That's no reason." He was as determined to find out as she was not to tell him.

"Leah?" A hand at her shoulder turned her around. "Answer me." His enticing, velvet-smooth tone added to her confusion. She kept her eyes centered on the pattern of the carpet, unwilling to meet his gaze.

"Shouldn't we be in the lobby?" Her heart was doing a maddening drum roll that affected her voice so that it trembled softly from her lips.

"Hugh won't be there for another fifteen minutes."

"Please," she begged, hating the crazy weakness that was attacking her knees. His hand that cupped her shoulder seemed to burn through the navy-blue wool dress and sear her sensitive skin. It was unfair that his touch should affect her this way. Her fingers were clenched in front of her, her knuckles white.

"All right, I won't force the issue." He dropped his hand and returned briefly to his room to store the camera.

When he returned, Leah noted that his mouth was curved cynically, adding harshness to his uneven features.

"Are you angry?"

He looked up, surprised. "No, should I be?"

Gently, she shook her head and reached for her room key, which lay on top of the dresser. Forcing her chin up, she offered him a weak smile. "Shall we go?"

Hugh Kimo was waiting for them in the lobby as arranged. His car was just outside the hotel. The restaurant on the beach where he took them specialized in lobster, one of Leah's favorite foods.

Although she joined in the conversation, her gaze drifted constantly to the ocean and the pure white beach. Cain's eyes followed hers, and when their gazes met once, briefly, he smiled, letting her know he thought the scene just as beautiful as she did.

The meal was fantastic, and just when Leah was convinced she couldn't eat another thing, Cain ordered dessert for her.

"Cain," she whispered nervously as she smoothed her hand over the white linen napkin on her lap. "Really, I couldn't eat anything more."

"I'm fattening her up," Cain explained with a chuckle to Hugh Kimo.

His laugh infuriated her all the more, and her heart beat with frustration. When the chocolate torte was delivered, Leah tilted her chin a fraction of an inch in a gesture of pride. Her murky brown eyes flashed with avenging sparks that told Cain exactly what he could do with his high-handed methods.

Shaking his head in mock disgust, Cain reached over and took the dessert and ate it himself.

Leah was surprised when Cain suggested that he and Leah would return to the hotel by taxi. Outside the restaurant, they shook hands with their host and agreed upon a time to meet in the morning, then watched as Hugh drove away.

"You don't mind, do you?" Cain asked, casually draping his arm across her shoulders. "A walk along the beach will do us both good."

"I'd like that." She forgot about being angry over the dessert. Having lived in Southern California all these years, Leah was ashamed to admit that the only time she had been to the beach was for her work.

She didn't protest when Cain's arm moved to her waist. As he'd mentioned several times, they were a team. And if she was honest, she'd admit that she enjoyed being linked with Cain.

A crescent moon lit their way down the flawless beach. Sand sank deep into her pumps, and Leah paused to slip her shoes from her feet, loving the feel of the cool, damp sand.

"Tomorrow night we'll be on the island," Cain said, his voice coated with eagerness.

"I've waited so long for this." She recalled how excited she'd been when Dr. Brewster first considered her for this assignment. And later, how thrilled she'd felt when she learned that the world-famous photographer Cain Hawkins would be coming with her. Little had she dreamed that she would be accompanying him as his wife.

They walked so far that the lights of the restaurant behind them looked like fireflies on a summer's eve.

"Cold?" Cain's deep voice was disturbingly close to her ear.

"No," Leah breathed with difficulty. Cain was pressed much closer to her side than necessary. His hand at her waist had slid up so that it rested just beneath her breast. Unbidden, unwanted, the thought came to her, and she wondered insanely what it would be like if Cain were to caress her breasts. Would their smallness disappoint him? A shudder of longing shook her.

"You are cold." Cain sounded almost angry as he released her and yanked his jacket from his arms to place it over her shoulders.

Humiliating color flowed into her face, and she lowered her gaze, afraid he would read the desire in her eyes.

"Are you warmer now?" he asked. His hands remained at her neck.

"Yes…yes." Her voice was low and throbbing.

"Leah." His finger under her chin raised her eyes to his. "What's wrong?"

Desperately she shook her head. A bubble of apprehension was lodged in her throat; she doubted she could have spoken if her life depended on it.

"Leah." Her name was a whispered caress. In the dim light of the moon, he lowered his mouth to hers in a feather-light kiss that lasted but an instant.

Closing her eyes to the delicious sensations that wrapped themselves around her, she swayed toward him slightly.

Hands at her shoulders, Cain paused and waited as if he expected her to reject him. But she couldn't. Not when for days she'd really been wanting him to kiss her. Not when she yearned for the feel of his body close to hers. Not when the man holding her was her husband.

His hands eased up from her shoulders to the smooth line of her jaw, directing her face upward to meet the hungry descent of his mouth. With a small sigh of surrender, she parted her lips, eager to experience the depth and passion of his kiss.

Cain's mouth was on hers, hard and compelling, kissing her with a fierceness that stole her breath and rocked her to the core of her being. Again and again his mouth sought hers until her arms slid convulsively around his neck and she clung to him. Her fingers ruffled through the thick growth of his dark hair, loving the feel of it.

"Leah?" He was asking so much with just the sound of her name. He wanted her. Now. Here. On the sand. And she hadn't the will to refuse him.

"I need you," he whispered urgently against her lips. He seemed to want her to tell him how much she needed him. But she couldn't. The only sounds that passed from her lips were small, weak cries of longing. She had never felt anything this strong and overpowering.

"Tell me you want me." His voice was a hoarse whisper as he ordered her to answer him. His hands were driving her to the limit of her endurance as they roamed her back and buttocks, arching her against his hard body. Still she couldn't; words were impossible as she struggled to speak. Cain buried his face in the gentle curve of her neck, kissing her hungrily.

Suddenly, abruptly, he stopped, and with a tortured sigh, he pushed himself away.

Bereft, Leah was left to face the cold, her shoulders heaving with shock. Cain was taking in deep breaths of air, fighting for control.

"Cain?" She blinked, still not comprehending what had happened.

Without a word, Cain reached out a hand and lifted the small gold heart that was nestled in the hollow of her throat. The heart Siggy had given to her.

"I promised that I'd send you back pure as the driven snow to that bastard. And I intend to keep my word." He let the heart drop back against her skin.

Instinctively her hand reached for the heart, her fingers nervously toying with it.

"As long as you continue to wear that necklace, I won't touch you. Understand?"

Wordlessly Leah nodded, telling him that she did.

"Then let's get back to the hotel. We have a big day tomorrow. We'll need a good night's sleep."

But neither of them got one, Leah was convinced. Back at her suite she lay awake, thinking of Cain.

The fierce wind bobbed the motorboat like a toy upon the rough waves.

"There's a storm coming," Hugh Kimo shouted, trying to be heard above the roar of the wind and sea. "I'm afraid I won't be able to stay on the island long."

"Don't worry. Once our things have been unloaded, there isn't any reason for you to stay."

Hugh looked relieved and nodded appreciatively.

The spray from a large wave splashed against Leah's face, and she wiped the moisture aside. No longer was she able to keep watch ahead as the wind and sea tossed their craft at will.

Everything had been going smoothly as they crossed the five miles of water that separated the main island from the smaller one of Kahu. The squall had come on quickly and without warning.

Suddenly a cloud burst overhead and thick drops of rain began pounding at them from every side. Someone handed Leah a slicker to protect her from the downpour. She slipped her arms into sleeves that were miles too long.

The motorboat hit the sandy beach with a heavy thud, and Leah was jerked forward unexpectedly. Cain's arm prevented her from slamming into the side of the boat.

She tried to thank him, but the wind carried her voice in the opposite direction.

Once they were beached, there was a flurry of activity as the boat was unloaded and the luggage carried up the rickety stairs that led to the cliff house. Leah stayed at the boat to make sure nothing was left behind.

"The radio…" Hugh began haltingly.

"Yes…yes." Cain nodded sharply. "I've worked one before. Don't worry, I'll take care of everything. Go while you've got the chance." He waited until Hugh and his men were back inside the boat before pushing against the side of it, guiding it back into the water.

Leah returned Hugh's hand signal. They had arrived and were safe.

Cain didn't try to speak as he helped her up the wooden steps built into the steep cliff. Leah was panting when they reached the top, and she paused for a moment to catch her breath.

The heavy wooden door to the hut was open, their luggage set just inside. Leah and Cain stumbled into the large room. The area to her left would serve as their kitchen. An old black stove and a small table were set against one wall. To the right was a much larger table stacked high with the equipment they had requested. Two doors led off from the main room.

Stripping the wet coat from her arms, Leah moved into the place she would call home for two long months.

Cain closed the door, blocking out the fierce sound of the wind. "That was quite a welcome," he murmured, removing his drenched jacket.

"I'm hoping this storm moves out as fast as it came."

"It should." But Cain didn't sound overly confident.

Now that they had arrived, their work was only beginning. Lifting a suitcase, Leah moved to carry it toward the bedroom.

Cain stopped her, his large frame blocking the door. "Before you go in there, I think I should tell you there's a small problem."

Her searching gaze sought his. "What?"

As Cain swung open the door, Leah felt a sinking feeling attack her stomach. The room—indeed, the entire hut—contained only one bed. A double one.

Chapter 5

"I assumed...I thought..." Leah stuttered, feeling the blood drain from her face, leaving her waxen and unnaturally pale. In the past week they'd nearly worked themselves to exhaustion to meet their self-imposed schedule. The sleeping arrangements hadn't crossed Leah's mind. Not once. How incredibly stupid she'd been.

"I take it you don't want to share the bed?" Cain mocked lightly.

"Absolutely not. I don't even want you in the same room." Crossing her arms to ward off a sudden chill, Leah paced the compact area that comprised their living quarters.

Doing a quick survey of their stark quarters, her eyes

gleamed with satisfaction. "That table would work." She pointed to the one stacked with boxes at the other end of the room.

"As a bed?" Cain looked shocked. "Leah, that table is meant to be used as a desk. We're going to need it. Be reasonable, will you?"

"So what's to say we can't clear it off every night? You don't have to do it, I will," she volunteered, her voice sharp and vigorous. "It'll be my responsibility."

"Are you offering to sleep there as well?" Cain cut in sarcastically. "Because I have no intention of doing so. I have work to do, and there's no way I'm sleeping on a narrow table to satisfy your perverted sense of modesty."

"All right, I don't blame you. I'll sleep there." Her fingers closed tightly over the back of the chair until she feared her nails would snap. "I don't mind. Really."

The scowl darkening Cain's features revealed what he thought of the idea. But the shrug he gave her was indifferent. "If that's what you want, feel free."

The storm grew in intensity; a demon wind howled outside until Leah was sure the small dwelling would be torn from its foundation. The storm in her heart raged with the same intensity. This situation was quickly going from bad to worse and she didn't need it. Of course Cain wanted to share the bed—and probably whatever else he could take. He didn't have anything to lose. But Leah wasn't fool enough to believe that once they returned to California it would make a difference. Without a care, without a thought, Cain would be on his way to the next adventure, to another assignment. After all, that was their agreement.

Her mind buzzing, Leah inspected the supplies she'd requested. Cain lit a fire in the cast-iron stove that would serve as a means of cooking and as their only source of heat.

"Where's the bathroom?" she asked shyly after a while. "I like to freshen up before dinner."

"Bathroom?" He cocked his brow in sarcastic amusement. "If you mean the outhouse, it's outside and fifty yards to your left."

Leah spun around. "You've got to be joking."

"Leah, this isn't exactly the Hilton. Didn't you stop to think about the living arrangements?"

Perhaps it was stupid not to have considered the more mundane aspects of this expedition, but this cliff house hadn't entered her thoughts once. She wasn't here to vacation. "No," she admitted somewhat defensively. "There was so much else to consider that the living arrangements didn't enter..." Flustered now, she wiped her hand across her face. "I came to study the whales."

"And I came to take their pictures." His words were a subtle reminder that he wasn't on Kahu to steal her virginity. When she didn't respond, he turned his back to her. "I'll cook tonight and you can do the honors tomorrow."

"Fine."

Determined to make her plan work, Leah stepped to the table. She'd sleep there and make the best of it. Several boxes were stacked on top of each other, and

Leah realized it would be a monumental task to unpack and assemble them tonight. Already she was tired, the effects of jet lag having hit her with as much impact as the storm.

While Cain worked silently in the kitchen area, Leah feverishly took down the boxes, examined their contents and set them aside. Most of the equipment, the telescopes and recorders, would be used exclusively by Leah. Since many of the tools she'd requested had to be run with batteries, she would need to conserve power.

The dim light cast from the two lanterns was barely enough to work by, and before she was halfway finished, it became necessary to move one closer.

"Dinner's ready," Cain announced.

"I'm too busy right now."

A disgusted sound of exasperation came from him. "I don't care if you're busy or not, you're eating now."

If he made so much as one wisecrack about how she couldn't afford to skip meals, Leah was determined to dump his dinner over the top of Cain's arrogant head.

"In a minute."

"Now, Leah!" Cain repeated his demand. A muscle twitched warningly along the side of his jaw.

"Oh, all right," she conceded ungraciously, knowing it would be useless to argue. There would be far more serious matters to expend her energies on later. Like the matter of the bed.

They ate in silence, and afterward Leah washed the dishes, using water heated by the stove. Not until she'd finished did she realize that the storm outside had abated. Unfortunately, the one in her heart continued to rage.

"It's late," Cain announced without preamble.

He didn't need to remind her; she felt bone weary. "You go to bed.... I'll make do out here."

The deep-grooved lines beside his mouth went white. "Have it your way. There's a soft mattress in there or a hard, cold tabletop out here."

"I know," she replied miserably. The crazy part was that if she were shapely and beautiful, she wouldn't have minded nearly so much. Logic had nothing to do with it. Cain felt no constraint when commenting on her looks and figure. Long ago she had come to terms with her plainness, but at the same time Cain's remarks had the power to sting. Every thoughtless word he uttered cut her to the bone. With Cain out of the room, Leah examined the gold band on her ring finger. This single piece of gold Cain had placed on her finger had somehow allotted him the power to inflict pain. Leah could toss aside thoughtless, cruel words from other men. But not from Cain.

Carrying an armload of blankets, Cain returned to set them on top of the table. He hesitated. "Leah," he breathed slowly, carefully choosing words. "I swore I wouldn't touch you as long as you continued to wear... what's his name's...heart."

Unconsciously she reached for the necklace, rubbing the gold trinket between two fingers.

Her actions produced a heavy scowl from Cain.

"We're here alone. Trust is essential. I promised not to touch you, and I'll keep my word."

Holding a thick wool blanket against her stomach, Leah cast her gaze to the plain wood floor. "I...prefer to stay out here." In some ways Leah was more afraid of her response to Cain than any fear that he would take her against her will.

Cain threw up his hands. "Have it your way, then." He returned to the bedroom and left the door ajar.

Mumbling under her breath, admitting she was a fool, Leah spread out a couple of blankets for padding on the table's hard surface. With the pillow in place, she climbed on top and spread the warm wool blanket over her. The first thing she readily acknowledged was how incredibly unyielding a table was. And dressed in jeans and a sweater wasn't exactly conducive to a good night's sleep, either. Lying on her side with her forearm tucked under the feather pillow, she leaned over and turned off the lantern. The hut became pitch-black, so dark that a shiver of nervous apprehension raced up her spine.

"Good night," Cain called out, and she cursed him silently for sounding so comfortable.

"Good night," Leah returned, forcing a cheerful, happy note into her voice. After everything else she'd gone through to come to this island, a tabletop for a bed was something she could do without.

Ten minutes later, her own bones causing her the most discomfort, Leah rolled over. The wool blanket fell to the floor. "Damn," she muttered impatiently, and reached for it. To her horror her whole body slid off the table, and with a frightened cry she landed with a loud thump on the cold, hard floor.

"What happened?" Cain shouted.

Although she couldn't see him in the dark, she knew from the direction of his voice that he was standing in the doorway of the bedroom.

"Nothing, I...I fell off the table, that's all."

"Are you okay?"

He didn't need to sound so smug, she fumed. "Fine," she answered, doing her best to sound just as amused.

Situated atop her makeshift bed once again, Leah forced her eyes closed and did her utmost to fall asleep. An hour later, cuddled in a tight ball to keep warm, she rolled over and, to her horror, tumbled off the side of the table again. Landing with a jarring thud, she was too stunned to move. Her breath came in uneven gasps.

"That does it." The unrestrained fury in Cain's voice tightened the muscles of her stomach. " I've had it."

"I'm fine...I just fell...again, that's all." Her voice thinned to a quivering note as she heard Cain storm into the room.

"Where's the lantern?" he shouted at her. Before she could answer, he crashed into a cardboard box, knocking it over. His cry of pain filled the room as the contents of the crate spilled onto the floor.

Struggling to a standing position, Leah blindly reached out for him. Her groping arm came in contact with the solid wall of his chest. "You okay?"

"No, and I'm damn mad. You're coming into that bed before your stubbornness kills us both."

"I won't."

Cain snorted.

"I won't," she repeated.

Cain said nothing, but an arm looped around her waist and lifted her off the floor. Against his superior strength her weak struggles were a futile effort.

The next thing Leah knew she was falling through space to land on a soft cushion of comfort and warmth. A hand on each shoulder held her in place. "Now listen, and listen good." Cain spoke with infuriating calm. "You're sleeping here tonight and so am I. To soothe the outraged virgin in you, I'll remain outside the covers. Understand?"

"Yes." Her soft voice was pitifully weak.

He released her and pulled back the thick layer of blankets. "Get in."

Wordlessly she did as he demanded, feeling incredibly small and stupid.

Once she was in place, he lowered his weight beside her and rolled over so that she was presented with a clear view of his back. Within minutes his even breathing assured Leah he was asleep. Soon after that she fell into an uneasy slumber.

And so their adventure began. The first week was spent unloading and setting up the monitoring equipment. In this area, Cain was an invaluable aid. At night, exhausted, they fell into bed, Leah under the covers, Cain curled up with a wool blanket on top of them. And every morning, to her utter embarrassment, Leah woke with her arms wrapped around Cain's lean ribs, her head pillowed by his broad chest. Drawn by his warmth and comforted by his arms, she came to him naturally in her sleep.

Waking first, Leah would slip from his loose hold, praying that he would never be the wiser. If he was aware of the way she unconsciously reached for him, he never spoke of it. For that, Leah would be eternally grateful. She found the situation embarrassing in the extreme.

The sixth day after their landing, Leah spotted her first whales. She'd discovered that, although the telescopes allowed her to view miles of water, it was easier to stand and look over the rolling waves of the Indian Ocean using her field glasses.

The vast, dark shapes resembled huge black submarines. As the massive forty-ton creatures came closer to shore and into her view, Leah realized that these were the first in the large family of right whales, southern right whales, a once-abundant species that was now among the rarest.

"Cain," she screamed, pointing toward the lolling creatures. "They're here."

Standing on the beach far below, Cain shielded his eyes from the sun to study the swelling seas. Turning, he signaled that he'd be right up. In record time he was at her side.

"Holy Moses, look at those babies." Crouched down behind his camera, Cain began working at a furious speed. The clicking noise was repeated so fast that the sound blended to a low hum. "Humpbacks, right?"

"No." Laughing, Leah shook her head. "Southern rights."

"Right? That's not any kind of name for a whale."

"The sailors of old named them that because they were the right ones to hunt," Leah explained. "They float after death and can easily be towed to shore or butchered at sea." She winced as she explained, hating the thought of any of these lovely, graceful creatures dying such a brutal death at the hands of man.

The entire afternoon was spent watching the herds frolic close to shore. Cain was in photographer's heaven, carrying cameras and equipment between the beach and Leah's perch on the cliff top.

Now that the first herds were arriving, Leah wanted to secure the sonar equipment in place. In the morning they would take out the motorized rubber raft and anchor three transmitters. The underwater microphones suspended from them would catch the whales' sounds.

In the evening, when Cain radioed his report to Hugh Kimo in Ruaehu, he asked Hugh to send up a spotter plane in the morning to report the whales' course.

"What's all this sonar equipment going to tell you?" Cain asked as she finished with the evening dishes.

Leaning a hip against the sink, Leah wiped the last plate clean with a dishcloth, her hands continuing to rub in a circular motion long after the plate was dry. "Several things. First, I don't need to keep my eyes peeled on the ocean or count on the Cessna to know when they're coming. And second, I'm hoping to monitor and record the whale sounds. Later, when I'm back at the university, I'll study the sound waves to see if I can further decipher their meaning."

"Like breaking a code?"

"Exactly." She smiled, pleased at his interest. "Oh, Cain, this is so exciting I can hardly stand it." Her heart swelled with joy.

Gingerly, she put the plate aside and set the kettle back on the stove to heat. "Coffee?"

"Please." Cain delivered his cup to her, coming to stand at her side. His eyes studied her, narrowing slightly. The last time he'd looked at her that way had been in California, when he'd told her she was lovely. Her cheeks warmed with rising color, and she glanced away.

"It's been quite a day," she murmured as a means of breaking the uneasy silence. When she did look up, it was a mistake; she recognized it immediately. The warmth and nearness of his body were distractions she couldn't ignore.

Those wonderful, intense eyes were fixed on her moist lips. Leah couldn't stop staring at him. Nervously, her fingers tightened around the empty mug. His gaze was bright and glittering, his desire evident with every breath he drew. A mere inch separated them, and Leah could see every line in his sun-bronzed face, every pore, every lash. His mouth, hard and straight, was silently beckoning her to come taste the pleasure of his kiss.

A surge of longing raged through her, and Leah

shuddered slightly. Cain saw it and his nostrils flared. Their eyes were locked in a silent battle of wills. He wanted her to come to him, to make the first move. She couldn't. How much better it would be if Cain had never kissed her, had never shown her the marvels of his touch. For today, this minute, he filled her senses. But reality was only weeks away, and she couldn't allow the beauty of this island, of this time, to sway her.

Every beat of her heart was demanding that she step into his arms, but somehow, somewhere deep inside a strength she didn't know she possessed came to her rescue and she resisted.

"You said you wanted coffee?"

"Yes, I did."

Her hand shook as she poured him a cup. Cain took it and returned to the desk, sitting with his back to her.

Several hours later, Leah pretended she was asleep when Cain came to bed. Her back was to him as he eased his weight onto the soft mattress and stretched out beside her. Leah didn't know how any two people could be so close and yet have the whole universe stretch between them.

The wind whipped Leah's long blond hair about her face as the rubber raft skipped across the top of the waves. A feeling of exhilaration caused her heart to soar. Behind her, in the rear of the raft, Cain sat beside the motor.

Leah planned to place the sonar equipment in a huge triangle, each underwater microphone separated by half a mile. Earlier, Hugh had radioed the location of approaching whale pods, and it was now their job to get the equipment in place before the whales arrived.

They had just finished placing the third and final orange buoy in the swelling water when Cain pointed to a huge shape in the distance. Leah turned just in time to see the great right whale hurl itself out of the water. The huge mammal was as black as a raven's wing and as sleek as silk. It hit the ocean surface with a boom that sounded like a cannon blast. Water sprayed in every direction, and although they were a safe distance, a few drops managed to wet them.

Cain, with his ever-ready camera, took a series of shots and beamed her a brilliant smile, giving her the thumbs-up signal. The triumph, however, soon drained from Cain's eyes to be replaced with a wary light. "He's coming our way. Should I try to outrun him?"

"We can't." Leah's heart moved to her throat as the creature, fifty feet long and weighing at least a ton for every foot, approached and circled their rubber raft. "Cut the engine," Leah cried.

Cain did as she asked, but his look was skeptical.

"She may have a calf in the area and just wants to check us out to be sure we mean her no harm." Although Leah wouldn't admit it, she was frightened. Their rubber raft could be easily overturned, and with all the equipment Cain insisted on keeping around his neck, he'd sink straight to the bottom. Mentally, Leah chided herself for her crazy thoughts. They were about to become whale fodder, and she was worried that Cain wouldn't be able to stay afloat.

"Would it help if I promise to touch up her photo—you know, hide a few of those extra pounds?"

Before Leah could respond, the whale turned its tail flukes and swished the raft strongly from side to side, with Leah and Cain clinging for their lives. Leah held on to the edges in a death grip, closing her eyes to the terror that strangled her throat muscles. Their small raft was tossed about like a trembling leaf caught in an autumn windstorm.

A cry of pure terror froze in her lungs as the mammoth creature, tired of its game, backed up and, with its giant flukes, lifted the rubber raft, Cain and Leah inside, about six inches off the water's surface.

Tense, every cell, every muscle alert, Leah began to shake violently. Panic wouldn't allow her to breathe, and when she did, the air rasped painfully in her throat. Finally a noise penetrated her dulled senses: a clicking sound, followed by another and another, with whispered phrases of "Wow, fantastic, unbelievable."

Their lives were balancing precariously on the whim of a fifty-ton whale and Cain was taking pictures.

The rubber raft hung in the air for the longest minute of Leah's life; then the whale slowly, with the utmost control, lowered its flukes and deliberately set them back on the water unscathed.

Leah released a sigh of relief and tasted the blood in her mouth, unaware that all the while she'd been viciously biting her own lip.

For the first time Leah spotted two young calves who loafed nearby. Cain saw them at precisely the same moment as Leah, and again she heard a long series of clicks. More pictures.

The gargantuan creature circled the raft twice more before rejoining her young and swimming away.

"That had to be the most fantastic adventure of my life," Cain called, his voice heavy with excitement. "You won't believe the shots I got."

Leah couldn't believe that he could be that unaffected. She had faced a watery grave with Cain at her side and worried about his safety. All he'd thought about were his precious pictures.

Leah was silent until they reached the shore. Doing her best to restrain the growing dismay, she wordlessly helped him secure the raft. His eyes burned over her questioningly, but Leah paid no attention. Her only desire was to be away from him as soon as possible.

"Leah," Cain called to her as she raced up the wooden stairs, but again she ignored him.

When he arrived at the hut, Leah was pacing the floor, her arms crossed, her knuckles clenched. She stopped and glared at him with all the fury of her pounding heart.

Standing just inside the door, Cain regarded her grimly. "All right, let's have it. What's wrong?"

Her arm swung out as she pointed toward the ocean. "We could have been killed out there." Even speaking was difficult as the words crowded on her tongue and escaped on a giant rush of anger.

"Come on, Leah, that mama was just protecting her young. She gave us a warning, that's all."

His calm only served to fuel her fury. "And you loved it."

"You're this angry because I wasn't scared?"

"Are you so incredibly stupid that you don't know the destruction those whales are capable of? Our lives were in jeopardy."

"I wasn't unconcerned," he flared.

"You could have fooled me."

What really angered Leah was that her thoughts had been on Cain. Her fears had been more for him than for herself. Whirling, she stormed into the kitchen area and made herself lunch. Taking the sandwich with her, Leah picked up her gear and headed toward her observation point on the cliff top.

Cain looked stunned for a minute. "Where's my lunch?"

"Take a picture of mine and eat that," she shouted.

Leah didn't make it out the door. Cain's hand snaked out and gripped her arm, hauling her against him. "Leah, for the love of heaven, you're not making any sense."

Her shoulders heaved as she forcefully pushed herself free. "I should have known that you'd be more concerned about your stomach. That fits right in with your character."

"Would you be serious!"

"It's difficult to talk to a man whose hair is practically as long as my own."

Cain regarded her sharply, his eyes narrowed and confused. "My hair? We're arguing about my hair? For heaven's sake, woman, be real."

"You know what your problem is, Cain Hawkins? You don't care. Nothing in this world or the next is more important than those pictures you take. Not relationships. Not family. Nothing." Her sarcastic gaze blazed across his face. "The irony of it all is that you hide behind a lens and reveal your soul."

Cain clamped his mouth shut, but his eyes glinted dangerously.

"But once the camera is gone, there's only this… this…immature idiot. A man who takes pride at shouting to the world that he doesn't care."

"Who gave you the right to dictate how I should live?"

"No one," Leah admitted dryly. Cain was incapable of understanding what had upset her. Care and consideration were beyond a man like Cain Hawkins. Everything today had been her fault. She'd allowed herself to get too close to Cain emotionally, allowed herself to care. Well, no more. He could rot and she wouldn't lift a finger to aid him.

He smiled, but his expression was decidedly unpleasant. "Go sit on your perch, Queen Leah, and when you've worked everything out in that twisted, irrational mind of yours, then maybe we can talk."

She scooted past him, but not before she was gifted with a hard, taunting smile and a verbal jab of his own.

"If you want to bring up the subject of hair, then maybe you should consider cutting your own."

Leah usually wore her long blond hair tied back at the base of her neck. But today, her hair had somehow worked itself free during their ordeal with the whale. The long stringy strands hung limp and lifeless across her cheek.

"You're right," she muttered, dumping her lunch and binoculars in his arms. "You're absolutely right." Charging across the room, she flung open a drawer and took out a large pair of scissors.

"Leah?" Cain gasped. "I didn't mean—"

"Maybe not, but I did." Tilting her head to the side, she grabbed a handful of her hair and chopped away. Six inches fell to the floor. She quirked her head in the opposite direction and lopped off another handful, letting it fall heedlessly away. Her bangs followed next.

"Leah, stop," Cain shouted, and the horror in his voice made her look at the cold, hard floor now covered with a thick layer of golden hair. Shaken, Leah cupped her mouth as tears burned her eyes. The first drops scalded her cheeks as she recognized what she had done.

"Cain, oh, Cain." She raised stricken eyes to him and lifted a tentative hand to the side of her head. The clump her fingers investigated prompted a sob.

At her side, Cain removed the scissors from her numb fingers.

In her anger, she'd lashed out at him and ended up hurting herself even more. Her hair, her lovely golden hair, was the only beautiful asset she possessed. And now that, too, was ruined. Gently, Cain put his arms around her and held her as if he would never let her go. At first she shrugged, resisting his touch, but he would have none of it, holding her fast in his strong arms.

She cried then in earnest for caring so much and for hurting just as much because he didn't.

His kiss was at her temple, offering her the comfort she craved. Of their own volition, her arms slid around his waist, molding her slight frame to him, seeking his warmth.

Cain's healing lips found her eyes as he kissed aside each fresh tear. Unable to bear another moment of this torture, Leah tilted back her head so that her lips sought his first. Trembling, her mouth stroked his in a caress so light that it was tantalizing torment.

With a muted groan, Cain ravaged her lips as if he were starving for the taste of them. Leah met his urgent hunger with her own, winding her arms around his neck, her head thrown back under the force of his kiss.

Again and again he kissed her until he shuddered and left her lips to slide his mouth across one cheek. "Leah…"

"I was so scared," she wept. "I thought the whale would kill us, and all you cared about were your pictures."

"I'm sorry, love," he breathed into her ear. "So sorry."

"Hold me," she pleaded. "Just hold me." Her whole body trembled.

"Always," he promised. "Always."

Chapter 6

Taking a step backward, Cain cocked his head to study his handiwork. A pair of scissors dangled from his index finger as he positioned Leah's head first one way and then another before nodding slowly and smiling. "It doesn't look half bad, even if I do say so myself."

Tentatively, her fingers investigated the blunt cut, expecting to find gouges and nicks. Instead, her fingertips brushed against her exposed ear. With a rising sense of dread, she let her hand fall lifelessly to her lap. "It's horrible."

"The least you can do is look," Cain chastised, and gave her a small hand mirror.

Her reflection revealed incredibly sad eyes, red and glistening from recently shed tears. Her full lips were slightly swollen and tender from the heat of Cain's kisses. And her hair, her once-lovely long hair, was gone, replaced with short choppy curls. The sides were styled above her ears and then neatly tapered to the base of her neck. Leah couldn't remember the last time her hair had been this short—probably grade school. To his credit, Cain had done an admirable job of softening the butchered effect resulting from her craziness.

He was right; her hair didn't look bad, but it wasn't her. The stranger whose face flashed back from the mirror was someone else. Siggy wouldn't know this woman, and upon her return she'd be forced to deal with his disapproval. Siggy had always loved her long hair.

"Well?" Cain waited for her approval.

"You did the best you could."

"Leah, you look fine. I mean it."

Standing, she brushed the blond hair from her shoulders and lap. The ache in her heart was heavy as she reached for the broom and swept up the remnants of what once had been her greatest asset. Never had she done anything so foolhardy. She'd behaved like a crazy woman, lashing out at Cain, and then destroying the one part of herself that was lovely.

Replacing the broom, she gave him a feeble smile. "I'd better get back outside." She retrieved the equipment, then paused in the doorway. "Thank you, Cain."

"Anytime." He let her go without an argument, for which she was grateful.

To Leah's surprise, the afternoon passed quickly as she charted her finds and recorded the various sounds of the whales on the battery-powered recorder. The sun was settling from an azure sky into a pink horizon when Cain reappeared. Usually he spent part of the afternoon with her, but today he'd granted her some badly needed privacy and she was grateful.

"How'd it go?" He stood at her side on the cliff top, gazing over the long stretch of rolling waves that crashed onto the virgin shore below. Silently he slipped his arm around her shoulders.

"I saw my first southern blue." Despite the despair that had wrapped itself around her only hours earlier, Leah's voice rose with enthusiasm. "It was magnificent."

"You say that every time," he teased.

"This time it's different. Blue whales are the largest creatures ever to inhabit the earth."

Cain's gaze was skeptical. "Larger than the dinosaurs?"

"Yup."

"You're kidding?" He looked genuinely surprised.

Laughing, she shook her head and slipped her arm around his waist. "I'm not. The largest whale ever recorded was a female blue that measured over a hundred and thirteen feet and weighed about a hundred and seventy tons."

"Wow." The hand that cupped her shoulder tightened, bringing her even closer to his side.

"To put that into perspective, that one blue whale weighed the equivalent of thirty-five elephants or more than two thousand humans." Having him hold her like this, linking herself to him, was flirting with danger, and Leah knew it. But his arm helped ease the ache in her heart, and she couldn't resist this small comfort.

"If you're trying to impress me, you just did."

"Good." Their eyes met, and by unspoken agreement they turned and sauntered lazily toward the hut.

"Now it's my turn to impress you," Cain murmured, his voice an intimate caress against the sensitive skin of her neck.

"Oh?" Quivers of awareness raced down her arms. It cost her the earth to remain stoic. "And just how do you plan to do that?"

"Wait and see."

Leah didn't have to wonder long. When they reached the hut, Cain swung open the door, allowing Leah to step inside first. A flash of unexpected color captured her attention, and Leah gave a small cry of pleasure. In the center of the small wooden table was a handful of wildflowers. White, blue and yellow blossoms stood proudly in an empty beer bottle that served as a vase.

"Oh, Cain, they're lovely." No man had ever given her flowers before, and happiness surged through her. These simple wildflowers were more precious to her than exotic orchids.

His eyes crinkled with a smile at her obvious pleasure. "I read somewhere once that flowers are supposed to lift a woman's spirits."

"Thank you." Impulsively her lips brushed his cheek. "They're beautiful."

"There's a method to my madness." He straightened

and held out the chair for her. A half smile touched his hard mouth. "After dinner I want you to cut my hair. And when you do, I want to make sure you're in a happy mood."

Leah raised stricken eyes to him. "I can't cut your hair. Good grief, look what I did to my own."

"I took that into consideration."

Shock receded into astonishment. "You're serious, aren't you?"

"As far as I'm concerned, we have a deal. I cut your hair—now it's my turn."

"But—"

"It should have been trimmed weeks ago."

Leah opened her mouth to argue, but his look discouraged further discussion. She wasn't sure she could do as he asked, but clearly Cain wasn't going to let her out of it.

The meal, succulent white fish sautéed in a delicate wine sauce, was another surprise. Cain had spent the entire afternoon doing little things to lift her spirits. Not only had he hiked across the island in search of wildflowers, but he'd gone fishing. Leah loved him for it because she knew he'd much rather have been out with his camera.

When the table was cleared, Leah dried her damp palms on her thighs as Cain held out the scissors.

"You're sure?" she questioned for the tenth time in as many minutes.

"Leah!"

"All right, all right." He sat in the chair, and Leah

draped a towel over his shoulders, using a clothespin to hold it together. Stepping back, she tilted her head to one side and bit into her bottom lip, unsure where she should begin. She chose the back of his head so he wouldn't see how badly her hands were shaking.

The comb brought the disobedient locks to order, and she ran her hand over his crown and down to his nape. The first snip would be the worst. His dark, silky hair curled over her finger. Holding her breath, she cut. She didn't take much, just enough to keep the length above his shirt collar. The dark strands fell to his shoulders and littered the floor. More confident now, Leah moved from his left side to his right, trying to keep the lengths evenly matched.

Content with her progress, Leah moved to stand in front of him as she considered the best way to trim the crown of his head and the loose hair that fell haphazardly across his forehead. Cain seemed constantly to be brushing it aside.

"Well?" he teased. "You're looking at me as if you've seen my picture in the post office. Let me assure you, I'm not on the FBI's most-wanted list."

Not the FBI's list, but certainly on hers. The thought struck her dumb. She did want Cain. Siggy seemed a million miles away, and the necklace she wore felt like an albatross around her neck.

"Leah?" His hand reached for her waist. "Are you okay?"

"I'm fine." She forced a smile and ran her fingers through the hair at the top of his head, pretending she

knew what she was doing. The gesture gave her time to
align her wandering thoughts. Cain had made his position clear; giving him her heart would only complicate
an already complex situation.

"Are you going to finish this or not?" he demanded
irritably, beginning to squirm like a five-year-old. "I
hate sitting still."

"All right, all right." She used the comb to lift the
first locks and snipped carefully, fearful of cutting too
much. As she worked, she inched closer and closer. Not
until Cain's labored breathing disturbed her concentration did she realize that her breasts were directly in his
line of vision. Abruptly, she stopped cutting as the color
blossomed in her cheeks. She tried to ignore the obvious and concentrate on cutting his hair, but every move
made her all the more aware of how intimate it was to
stand so close to him. When she lifted her arms higher,
her breasts brushed Cain's cheek, and he breathed in
harshly and shifted to pull back from her.

Leah felt her face go ten shades of pink, but as hard
as she tried she couldn't tame her body's response to
him. Leah closed her eyes to the onslaught of foreign
sensations that rushed over her with an intensity that
made her knees go weak.

"That's enough." Abruptly Cain gripped her waist
and pushed her back so he could stand. They faced one
another, Cain unnaturally pale, the grooves bracket-
ing his mouth white with barely restrained frustration.

Leah knew that her reddened cheeks were as bright

as a lighthouse lamp. Surely Cain didn't think she'd purposely tried to seduce him.

Impatiently, he jerked the towel from his shoulders and tossed it on the table. "I'm going out for a while," he mumbled gruffly, and was gone before Leah could reorient herself.

She was reading when Cain returned an hour later. Or at least she made a pretense of being caught up in the book, hiding her face behind the large volume to disguise her uneasiness. Cain apparently didn't feel all that comfortable either, and ten minutes after his return he made an excuse and went to bed.

Leah waited until she was certain he was asleep before joining him. His body was turned away from hers, his back rigid. The mattress dipped as she slid under the blankets. Feeling more self-conscious than ever about their sleeping arrangements, Leah rolled onto her side and forced her eyes closed. It was a long time before she slid into peaceful slumber.

The early-morning light stirred her awake, and unconsciously she turned over, automatically seeking the comforting warmth of Cain's back. When she realized what she was doing, she jerked back. With a small gasp, she sat upright, surprised to find Cain's side of the bed empty.

The coffeepot on the stove was full, and a note propped up on the wooden table told her that he was going to the other side of the island and not to expect him back before late afternoon.

She crumpled up his brief message and tossed it inside the wrought-iron stove to burn. The coward! What did he think she was going to do, play Salome and entice him to her bed? In case he hadn't figured it out he already was in her bed.

Dressing in washed-out jeans and an old sweatshirt, Leah was determined to make herself as unattractive as possible. To her deepest regret, that didn't take much doing.

By the time she'd positioned herself at the lookout perch, her temper had cooled. Within minutes, she was once again content with her world. Placing the earphones over her head, Leah recorded what she was sure was the courting ritual between two whales. The squeaky, high-pitched vibrations grew fainter and fainter as the whales headed south, but the simple message stirred a breath of excitement. A brief smile touched her eyes as she imagined Cain's look if she were to sing such a blatant song for him.

Later, she decided with a chuckle, she'd play back the tape for Cain and see what he thought. No! If she suggested that these sounds were a courting ritual, he could misinterpret her motives.

At noon, Leah spotted the largest pod she'd seen since the first whales arrived. She was so busy documenting their numbers and route that she didn't break for lunch. When she glanced at her watch again it was past four. It didn't make sense to break for lunch now when dinner was only a few hours away.

Cain reappeared sometime after six. Not wanting to appear overanxious for his company, Leah did little more than acknowledge his wave. Mud caked his shoes and pants, and she wondered what adventures he'd gotten himself into today.

"I'm going in to wash up," he shouted as he threw open the door of the hut.

In other words, she was to give him a few minutes of privacy. Not that she minded. There were several things she wanted to do yet this afternoon. It went without saying that she'd missed him! As much as she hated admitting it, Cain's active involvement with her work had cemented a bond between them. The hours they had spent together in the sun were her most pleasant times on the island.

Leah was kneeling down, collecting her equipment, when the gentle breeze carried the sharp sound of the hut door slamming closed. She tossed a look over her shoulder and was shocked to see Cain's angry strides devouring the distance separating them. His fists were knotted at his sides, his hard features twisted with disdain. Leah couldn't imagine what she'd done to displease him.

Not allowing his anger to intimidate her, she rolled to her feet and brushed the sand and grit from her jeans. Squaring her shoulders, she met his fiery gaze with an outward calm.

"When was the last time you ate?" he demanded.

Leah cringed inwardly. Not that again! From the moment they'd arrived on the island, Cain had appointed himself her nutritionist. He cooked breakfast every morning and sat at the table with her until she'd finished eating. Although they divided the lunch duties, Cain insisted that she eat whether she was hungry or not. Rather than argue, Leah complied.

Her shrug of indifference only flamed his fury. "I am sick to death of having to babysit you."

The facade of indifference evaporated, and Leah flashed him a look as cold and brittle as an Arctic wind. Anger swelled up inside her. From the moment they'd stepped foot on this island, Leah had more than carried her share. "Babysit me!"

"What else do you call it when I'm forced to spoon-feed you three times a day?"

"I don't need a guardian," she snapped.

His face turned to hard, cold stone and filled with such intense anger that it frightened her. There was no reasoning with him, she told herself, and she wouldn't try again. He'd twist her words to suit his anger. It wouldn't do any good to provoke him. And, admittedly, part of her couldn't help cowering from the savage fury in his eyes.

He stormed away, descending the stairs to the beach far below, leaving Leah stunned and shaking. Her legs felt like rubber, and she sank to her knees in the sand. Although she made an effort to refocus her attention on her duties, she discovered she couldn't. Her hands shook, and she pressed her cool palms against her hot cheeks.

Cain didn't reappear until dinner was on the table. Without a word, he pulled out his chair and started eating, attacking his meat with a savagery that really was directed at her.

"The beef's already dead. There's no need to rekill it," Leah chided him.

Cain's jaw tightened ominously, and he shoved his plate aside and stalked into the bedroom. It struck Leah how ludicrous this whole situation was. If Cain weren't so serious, she'd have laughed.

Days stretched into weeks, and Cain acted as if he were on the island alone. It was as though he couldn't tolerate being around her. Leah didn't know what she'd done that was so terrible, but after a while she gave up trying to guess. When she spoke to him, he snapped one-word replies. What he did with his time, she could only guess. He disappeared in the morning and returned late in the afternoon.

At night they would lie side by side, not speaking, barely moving, the sound of their breathing filling the strained silence. She was convinced that if Cain edged any closer to the side of the bed, he'd fall off.

Leah felt trapped in a maze with no exit. She was thoroughly confused and bewildered by his actions. The afternoon she'd cut his hair, Cain had seemed profoundly affected by what had happened. He'd wanted her. She wasn't so naive and inexperienced that she didn't recognize that. Yet, he had rejected her and hadn't treated her the same since. Whatever it was that was troubling Cain had destroyed their friendship.

Leah's fingers toyed idly with the gold heart hanging from her neck. She missed Cain's friendship, missed sharing her findings about the whales. She'd been lonely and hurt these past weeks. Part of her longed to reach out and touch him, yet she couldn't, and a sadness seemed to press heavily on her chest.

Her dreams that night were heavy and dark. She was on the rubber raft alone, pulling up the sonar equipment while Cain stood watching from the beach. Out of nowhere came the blue whale. Its huge flukes rose out of the sea and slammed into the ocean surface, flooding the small raft. Leah clung for her life. Frantically she cried out for Cain to help her, but he was intent on taking her picture and ignored her pleas. Trapped on the surging waves, Leah was tossed into the dark depths of the ocean. Water closed over her, but she clawed her way to the surface. Salt water filled her mouth and eyes, and she gagged as she fought for every breath. She was drowning while Cain emotionlessly documented her demise.

"Leah...Leah." Cain's voice was a soothing purr in her ear.

He'd come! He wasn't going to let her drown.

"Leah." A hand on each shoulder shook her gently. "Wake up."

Her heart pounded as her chest rose and fell dramatically with every hoarse breath. Panic-stricken, Leah clenched his shirt, still trying to save herself from the terrifying depths.

"Leah," Cain's voice rasped close to her ear. "It's only a dream."

A dream. Dazed, she stared at him with eyes that

refused to focus. She was going to live. The raft, the whale, the frantic fight for her life had all been a figment of some horrible nightmare. Relief coursed through her as she sagged against the bed and relaxed her death grip on Cain's shirt.

"Are you all right?" he asked in a rough whisper.

She lifted her gaze to his and nodded. The constricting muscles in her throat made speech impossible. Tears shimmered in her eyes and spilled down the side of her face.

Gently, Cain wiped them aside, his calloused thumb slightly abrasive against the softness of her cheek. "None of it was real," he murmured.

She nodded, still unable to formulate words. Cain parted his lips as though he wanted to say more, then reconsidered. His mouth hovered above hers, their breaths merging, and she knew he was going to kiss her. His hands roved from her cheeks to cup her ears, tilting her head to receive his kiss. But neither moved. A soft, choppy breath shuddered through her as she flattened her palms against his chest, feeling the wild hammering of his heart. Cain groaned and rolled onto his back.

Together they lay side by side, not speaking, not moving, hardly breathing.

"Would it help if I apologized?" she whispered, not chancing a glance at him.

"For a dream?" he scoffed, and some of the old anger crept into his voice.

"No," she murmured, and her lashes fluttered closed

as she swallowed her pride. "I want to apologize for whatever I did that made you so angry."

"Leah," he groaned, and rolled onto his side, propping his head up with the palm of one hand. Tenderly, he brushed the short blond curls from her temple. "You didn't do anything."

"Then why?" She turned her head so that she could read the answer in his eyes.

In response, Cain lifted the delicate gold chain from the hollow of her throat, winding it around his index finger until Leah feared it would snap. His brow knit as his grip relaxed. "I made a promise to you in Perth, and with God as my witness, I mean to keep it."

"But?"

"But being with you twenty-four hours a day is making it more than difficult."

Using her elbow as leverage, Leah raised herself, wishing she wasn't so affected by his nearness. "I didn't mean…for that to happen…when I was cutting your hair." Embarrassment caused her voice to quiver, and she lowered her gaze, not wanting him to see how much the incident had stirred her as well.

Cain chuckled lightly and her heart melted. "Do you think I don't know that?"

Leah lowered her head to the feather pillow and released a deep sigh. "I've missed you."

"Me, too, lady."

He seldom called her that anymore. In the beginning it had been a minor source of irritation to Leah. But tonight, in the distant light of the moon, it sounded very much like a lover's caress.

"Friends?" she whispered.

For a moment, a furrow of concentration darkened his brow. "Friends," he finally agreed.

The reluctance in his voice dimmed the brilliant light of joy that had shone so brightly just seconds before. "Good night," Leah mumbled, rolling onto her side so that her back was to him.

"Good night," he repeated a moment later, drawing his words out slowly.

The tense silence was back, and Leah forced her eyes closed, wondering if things could ever be the same between them again.

Leah felt the weight on the bed shift as Cain turned toward her, slipping his arm around her middle. His hold was firm but gentle.

"We'll talk in the morning," he promised.

"Yes," she breathed, and a tremulous smile touched her mouth.

Again Cain was gone when Leah woke in the morning, and she wanted to cry with frustration. Hadn't last night meant anything to him? He'd promised they'd talk this morning, and instead he'd run like a rabbit bent on escape. Well, he couldn't avoid her forever.

She quickly donned her mauve cords and a thick cable-knit sweater. The leaden gray skies promised a storm, and the room was cold. She was further surprised that the stove hadn't been lit and the coffee wasn't made.

After tucking her feet into tennis shoes, Leah moved outside to investigate.

"Cain."

Her call went unanswered.

Wandering to the edge of the cliff, she buried her hands in her pockets and looked out over the crashing surf. The sight below made her knees go weak and trapped the breath in her lungs.

Cain was in the rubber raft, the angry seas tossing it about like a toy boat. Without warning, a humpback hurled itself from the water and slammed back onto the surface with a thunderous roar.

Leah gave a cry of alarm and covered her mouth in horror. The tiny raft rocked with the impact.

Soon Leah realized it wasn't just one humpback, but a pod of eight feeding from a rich underwater pasture of krill. Like graceful dolphins, they leaped from the ocean bed, their cavernous maws open and spanning thirteen feet.

Amid the humpbacks, oblivious to any danger, was Cain, snapping pictures as fast as his fingers would allow.

Chapter 7

Leah was pacing the beach when Cain landed the craft. His face was flushed with exhilaration as he pulled the raft onto the shore and hurried toward her, his feet kicking up sand.

"You idiot," she stormed, her eyes burning with a smoldering light. "You unmitigated idiot. What did you think you were doing?"

"Did you see them? Eight humpbacks feeding cooperatively. It was like a riotous pack of school kids." Oblivious to her fear and anger, he continued to describe what he'd managed to document with his camera. "They launched themselves out of the water like they were bouncing off trampolines. Those pictures were the opportunity of a lifetime."

"Is your life worth so little? Are your pictures that important?" Leah was so frustrated that her voice throbbed. She was shaken to the core of her being, frightened out of her mind for him. And he hadn't even acknowledged the danger.

"Leah," he pleaded, gripping her by the shoulders. "Don't be angry. These pictures are going to impress the world."

"But you could have been killed." She stuffed her trembling hands into her pants pockets and hung her head, reluctant to reveal the tears that clouded her vision. "But I wasn't," he cried exultantly. "Don't you understand? I can't wait to show these shots to my editor."

Once again he had taken his life in his hands with nary a thought. What would she do if anything happened to Cain? Her life wouldn't be worth living.

Draping an arm over her shoulders, Cain led her to the rickety weatherworn stairs built against the cliff wall. "Let's have coffee and I'll tell you all about it."

Leah raised the angle of her chin several degrees, not wanting him to know how much his adventure had terrified her, nor the reasons for her deep-seated fear. With a wry twist of her mouth, she decided that it would serve no useful purpose for Cain to know she loved him.

Back at the hut, hugging a steaming cup of coffee in her hands, Leah listened to Cain talk nonstop for an hour. He'd awakened early, before first light and wandered outside. The thunderous commotion coming from the ocean was what had drawn him to the cliff. The sight of the humpbacks had caused him to run for his camera, and there hadn't been time to wake her. Or at least that was what he said. Leah knew better. Cain must have realized an argument would have ensued had he told her his plans, so he'd left her behind to discover his absence later.

As if he wanted to make it up to her, Cain spent the day at her side, using the telescope while she documented migration patterns and routes.

They chatted about inconsequential details, afraid to speak of the matters that were prominent in their minds.

"Once we're back, how long will it take you to develop the film?" Leah wanted to know, sitting beside him in the grassy brush at the cliff's edge. What she was really asking was how long he'd stay in California before moving on.

"Not long."

Leah blanched. That answered it: Cain wouldn't stay a moment longer than necessary. "I suppose you'll be anxious to get these pictures to your editor."

He hesitated for a moment. "He'll be anxious to see them."

"Of course."

He didn't mention the divorce, although it was paramount in both their minds. Three weeks was all the time that they had left together. A sad smile touched her troubled eyes. Three weeks. It seemed decades too long and a lifetime too short.

The morning air was cool and scented by the fresh breeze coming off the ocean. A shiver danced up her arm, and Leah didn't know if the chill came from without, or within. She'd never forget this moment: Cain was at her side, his look tender, his smile so warm it seemed capable of melting her heart. Her spirit soared like a kite racing toward the heavens. Yet as free as she felt this moment, she knew the reality, the string that controlled her flight.

To distract herself from bewildered thoughts, she plugged in the recorder and slipped the earphones over her head. The faint sounds being transmitted were ones she didn't recognize: deep, mournful sounds unlike the high-pitched squeaks she normally cataloged. Leah thought they sounded like a funeral dirge.

Lifting her binoculars, Leah studied the ocean to see if she could identify the source of the distress signal she'd overheard.

Two humpbacks, possibly from the same pod that Cain had seen in the morning, were lagging behind the rest of the pod. A mother and her young calf swam side by side. Although it was difficult to determine its age, the calf didn't look more than a few months old.

"Cain," she murmured, slipping off the headphones, "listen to this and tell me what you think."

He eyed her curiously, and then did as she'd requested. His brow creased into thick folds of concentration. Slowly he shook his head. "A mother and her calf?" He arched his brows in question.

Leah nodded, handing him the binoculars as well.

"I don't know," Cain admitted soberly a few moments later. "What do you think's wrong?"

"I'm not exactly sure." All her textbook knowledge

wasn't a help to her now. "I'd say it has something to do with that calf of hers." A dark glow of uncertainty entered her hazel eyes.

Turning off the recorder, Leah stood, preparing to deliver her equipment to the hut and pick up what she'd need from inside. "I'm going to take the raft out and investigate."

"Oh no, you're not." Cain bounded to his feet like a rocket, his eyes shooting hot sparks. "You can't go out there. The humpback's first instinct will be to protect her calf."

"But I want to help her," Leah argued.

"You get within ten feet of that calf and the mother will come right for you. You wouldn't have a chance."

"I'm not going near the calf."

"The calf's by the mother." His piercing gaze and sarcastic tone shredded her faulty reasoning.

Leah's fingers tightened into a fist. "In other words, it's perfectly fine for you to take a risk, but not me."

"You're exactly right. I'm the man."

Seething, Leah closed her eyes to the rising surge of anger. How any man could be so unreasonable, she didn't know. "I'm going out there to help that whale," she stated flatly, brooking no argument.

Cain mockingly inclined his head toward the beach. "And I'd like to see you try." An unnatural smile curved his mouth, and his dark eyes glittered with challenge.

Undeterred, Leah squared her shoulders and with long, purpose-filled strides headed back to the hut.

Cain was blocking the doorway when she reappeared, her rain gear draped over her forearm. "If you think I'm letting you out of here, then you can think again." There were overtones of mocking laughter in his voice that provoked her all the more.

Crossing her arms over her chest, Leah unflinchingly met his gaze. "I'm the scientist here."

"And I'm the one with common sense."

"Ha!" Leah scoffed. "This morning your life was hanging by a thread because you wanted a fistful of snapshots. So don't think you can dictate to me." Not two inches separated them as she came to the doorway of the hut. His outstretched arms prevented her from proceeding.

"Cain, please." Leah's words were filled with anxiety and urgency. Her fists were clenched at her sides. "I'm losing precious time."

A muscle leaped along the line of his jaw and captured her attention. Her gaze strayed down the tanned column of his throat to the unbuttoned front of his shirt. The smooth muscles of his chest gleamed like those of a statue. Leah scolded herself for being affected by his virility. This wasn't the time to notice these things about Cain. Not when she had a mission to accomplish.

Cain hesitated, seeming to measure his words. "I'm asking you as your husband not to go."

Leah's jaw sagged with surprise. The fact that they were married had never been mentioned, never discussed. Yes, they were bound to each other, but not in the normal sense. That he would use that form of persuasion with her now was unscrupulous and unfair.

The flash of resentment from her narrowed eyes must have convinced him of that.

"Leah," he whispered enticingly. His hands gripped her shoulders, keeping her at arm's length. "If you're so concerned, I'll contact Hugh by radio and have him send someone out."

"Whoever came wouldn't be able to do anything more than I could."

Cain held her gaze for a long moment, looking deep into her hazel eyes. What he saw there, she didn't know.

"I'm sorry," he muttered, tightening his grip on her shoulders, his gaze narrow and menacing. "I won't let you go."

"Cain." The breathless tremor in her voice betrayed her frustration. "Please." Her eyes were shimmering with the powerful desire to aid the distressed whale.

Leah felt Cain's resolve weaken as he slowly shook his head. "Can't you see what you're sailing into?" His face turned grim, and white lines formed around his tight mouth. "If you're going out, then I'm going with you."

Leah's pulse leaped wildly. He was conceding even when he felt she was wrong, but he wasn't letting her go alone. Her lips curved into a faint smile. "Thank you," she whispered, knowing what it had cost him to bow to her wishes.

He dropped his arms and moved across the room to where his rain gear was stored in the corner of the hut.

"Hurry," she pleaded, "they may have already moved on."

Together they ran to the edge of the cliff to descend the wobbly stairs. The rubber raft was high on the beach, where Cain had left it earlier that morning.

Abruptly, Cain stopped running. His hand gripped Leah's elbow as he pointed toward the spot where the two humpbacks had been sighted.

"What's wrong?"

"They're swimming closer to the shore."

Leah's heart sank, and she felt an oppressive weight settle onto her chest. The humpbacks' direction meant only one thing. "She's dying," Leah whispered.

The fifty-foot humpback came within a stone's throw of the beach. The calf remained close by his mother's side, swimming around her in tight circles. It was apparent that whatever had caused the mother's illness was not afflicting the child. Leah and Cain stood by helplessly; all they could do was watch.

By evening the mother was dead and the mewling sound of her son could be heard up and down the beach. Two days later, the calf was so weak that he didn't protest when Leah got into the water with him. Swimming at his side, using a snorkel and goggles, she could do little more than let him become accustomed to her presence.

With Hugh Kimo's assistance, Leah attempted to feed the young calf enriched milk using a hot water bottle, rubber tubing and a five-gallon drum. Hugh made the trip to the island daily, bringing in large quantities of the formula, but it all ended up in the sea. Leah spent hours coaxing the calf to eat. Cain did what he could to help, holding her makeshift device.

"Leah," he groaned, standing in the surf. "It's not going to work. Give it up before you collapse."

"No," she refused stubbornly. "Come on, Jonah, eat. Please eat."

A half hour later, shaking with cold, miserable in body and spirit, Leah abandoned the effort and walked out of the ocean.

Cain draped a thick towel over her shoulders and set her down in front of a warm fire he'd built on the sand. He sat behind her so that she could lean her back against him and be comforted by his warmth. With his arms wrapped around her, he brushed the wet strands of hair from her face. Numb with cold, and utterly discouraged, she battled back tears of exhaustion.

"I want him to live so much," she whispered.

"I know, love."

The affectionate term barely registered. "He's just a baby. He needs his mother."

"I know."

Completely drained of energy, Leah closed her eyes and fell into a deep, dreamless sleep. Lying side by side in front of the fire, Cain and Leah slept on the beach. Leah woke at dawn, her arms and legs entwined with Cain's. Her first thought was of Jonah, and she rushed to the water's edge. Jonah was alive, but for how much longer she couldn't know.

That morning, using the rubber raft, Cain hauled the decaying mother out to another part of the island.

On close inspection, Leah was amazed at how heavily encrusted with seaweed, worms and crustaceans, especially barnacles, the humpback was, but she doubted that any of this had contributed to her demise.

When Hugh arrived later that same morning, he brought another specialist with him from the Diamantinas to aid Leah with the autopsy. The postmortem revealed that a liver ailment had caused the mother's death. Antibiotics were administered to the three-month-old Jonah, although the calf showed no signs of the mother's sickness. After an hour's struggle, the four managed to get the young whale to accept the rich, creamy formula, but the young calf was nervous and objected strenuously to all these humans fussing over him. Only Leah would the young mammal accept at his side.

Five days later, Jonah gave up eating, and Leah realized it would only be a few days before he joined his mother.

Death was just a matter of time, but Leah refused to allow her friend to die without her at his side. She spent several hours every day in the water, swimming at the calf's side, stroking the top and sides of his head, doing what little she could to encourage him.

Other humpbacks passed, and Leah came to enjoy their sporty nature. She smiled at their antics and was amazed to see that they sometimes scratched themselves against the rocks. When Cain asked her about two whales that he saw smacking each other with their flippers, she explained that this was part of their mating ritual. The sounds could be heard up to a mile away.

In the evenings, Cain built a fire on the beach so that Leah could warm herself when she came out of the water. The flames flickered invitingly as he stood ready with a towel to dry her.

Miserably cold and defeated in spirit, Leah welcomed the iron band of his arms as he draped a thick towel over her shoulders.

"How much longer can he hold on?" Cain whispered, leading her to a blanket spread out in front of the warm fire that crackled with dry wood.

"Soon. Not more than a couple of days," she answered, holding back the tears.

No one would have guessed that Jonah would hold on to life as long as he had. For two weeks, Leah had expected him to die, and for two weeks he had held on, growing weaker, less and less responsive.

Leah was at Jonah's side the following morning when he died. She shed tears, grateful that she had been there with him, and continued patting his head long after he'd stopped breathing. Only when all her tears of sadness had been shed did she come out from the water. Cain met her on the shore and held her tight in his arms. Willingly Leah accepted his comfort.

Once she was warm and dry and sitting at the kitchen table with a hot cup of soup in front of her, Cain radioed the news to Hugh, who promised to return the following day.

For the second time in as many weeks, Cain hauled the corpse of a humpback whale out to sea.

An incredible sadness filled Leah as she watched Jonah being towed away. She stood on the beach, holding back the tears until Hugh, Cain and Jonah were out of sight. Her arms cuddled her stomach as she tried to beat down the emotion. Staring sightlessly ahead, she closed her eyes and fought back a sob, but still tears flowed from the corners of her eyes and down the sides of her face.

By the time Cain returned, Leah had composed herself and was busy at the duties she had neglected while working with Jonah. Cain had kept a log of the passing whales, and she spent the afternoon reviewing his brief notes.

When dusk arrived to purple the sky, Leah paused from her position at the lookout over the Indian Ocean and sighed sadly. In a few days, less than a week now, they would be leaving the island, and this magical adventure would be at an end. Once in California, she and Cain would separate and there would be only her memories to remind her of this enchanted time.

Even Cain noted her mood that evening as they readied for bed. The entire time Leah was working with the young calf, she had slept on the beach, Cain at her side. He had cuddled her close, spoon fashion, his arm draped protectively over her waist. He'd warmed her with his body and comforted her with his quiet concern. He'd brought her meals, but didn't force her to eat. He'd spoken soothingly to her when she was too cold and weak to answer. He'd held her, encouraged her and cared for her. Leah never stopped to question

Cain's gentleness during that time. He was there. She needed him and she didn't analyze his motives. If the situation had been reversed, she would have done the same for him. There wasn't any reason to read something more into his actions.

"You've been quiet tonight," he murmured as they lay side by side in the darkened room.

Leah's fingers gripped the sheet. "I haven't been good company lately. I apologize for that."

His hand reached for hers and squeezed it gently. "There's no need to feel sorry. You were busy." His thumb made lazy, circling motions at the inside of her wrist. A warm, tingling sensation was creeping up her arm. He was so close, she could smell the fresh scent of the sea mingled with the faint smell of hard work and the spicy aftershave he'd used that morning.

"After the past two weeks, I'm willing to promise never to take the raft out in a pod of humpbacks if you promise not to risk your health by nursing a sick whale."

Leah bit into her lower lip and nodded. She'd so desperately wanted Jonah to live. She'd have done anything to help him. Fresh tears burned for release, and she inhaled a shuddering breath. "Okay," was all she could manage.

Cain rolled to face her and wiped the tear that had started down her cheek. "Don't cry." The words were filled with a warm tenderness that she'd never thought to hear from this man who cared only for his work.

"I'm sorry," she sniffled, rolling away from him. It

was bad enough that he was witness to this display of weakness and emotion. She couldn't stand to face him.

"Leah." He moaned her name, and tugged gently at her shoulder, easing her onto her back. "Don't block me out. Let me hold you."

With a weak cry, she did as he asked, reaching for him in the dark. Her arms went around his neck as she buried her tear-streaked face in his throat.

Half sitting, half lying, Cain tightened his arms around her. One arm was draped across the small of her back while the other hand stroked her head.

"I wanted him to live," she moaned.

"I know. I wanted him to live, too." The words were so soft, so tender that Leah lifted her red, blotchy face to him and smiled tentatively. She didn't speak, although her heart was bursting with a thousand things she realized she could never say. Her eyes filled again, but these tears weren't for the loss of the young whale. They were the tears of a virgin wife who would never know her husband's love.

Cain shifted their positions so that she was lying flat on the mattress and he was bending over her. His finger wiped the moisture from her face and paused to skim her tear-moistened lips. His gaze locked with hers in the golden rays of a disinterested moon.

Leah felt the small shudder that went all the way through him. She knew before he dipped his head that he was going to kiss her. This was a time predestined, a kiss ordained, and her heart pounded erratically in eager anticipation.

At first his mouth merely touched hers, as if he expected her to push him away. Leah didn't move. He retreated, bringing his head back so that he could gaze into her eyes. Willingly she met his look and gave him a weak, trembling smile of encouragement.

He groaned her name, and his mouth moved closer to hers until their breaths mingled. He was a scant half inch from her when he paused. Her mind reeled crazily, demanding that he give her what she craved. How could he come so close and deny her? Deny them both? A weak cry of protest slipped from her parted lips. Cain ignored her pleas. Her hands tightened their grasp at the nape of his neck to force his head down. He resisted. Timidly she arched her back and he groaned as she pressed herself intimately closer. Yet he wouldn't yield and grant her the kiss.

No longer demure, no longer shy, Leah brought her mouth to his and outlined his bottom lip with the tip of her tongue.

Cain went rigid. Every hard muscle in his body grew taut, and reaction rippled over him as if his world had exploded. Yet he didn't move to gather her more fully into his arms. Nor did he kiss her with the passion she knew was simmering just below the surface.

Dazed with these strange, unrelenting waves of longing, Leah kissed him with a lifetime of suppressed womanhood stored in her heart.

His mouth played over hers, tasting and nibbling, taking and giving. Giving so much that Leah's world spiraled crazily.

Her arms moved possessively over the hard muscles of his back, glorying as his bronze muscles rippled under her fingers. Pressed together as they were, Cain pushed the covers down from her waist so that his hard thighs molded her against him.

After what seemed like forever, he lifted his mouth from hers and took in deep, shuddering breaths as he cradled her face between his hands. Leah covered his hands with her own, turning her head so that she could kiss the inside of his palm. Cain's reaction was immediate as he slowly, languorously buried his mouth in hers until a need, a desire she had never known, sent flames shooting through her. Straining to be closer to him, her hips rocked, seeking more.

His hand lowered to her flat stomach, and it was Cain who groaned. The sound throbbed in Leah's ears, and she tightened her grip on him, teasing him with her tongue, giving him biting little kisses over his face and ears until his mouth branded hers in burning, searing possession.

Without warning, Cain tore his mouth from hers and raised himself. He took in deep, measured breaths as if he were holding on to the last vestige of his control.

"Cain," she whispered, not knowing what had stopped him.

"Leah," he murmured, and gathered her in his arms. "Dear, sweet Leah, shall I go on?"

The air felt trapped in her lungs.

"You know what I want?" he asked slowly.

"Yes." Her whispered voice trembled. "Oh, yes. I want you."

He hesitated for only a moment. His hand reached for her neck, locating the delicate chain that held the gold heart. With a vicious jerk, he broke the chain and tossed it aside. The sound of it hitting the wall barely registered in Leah's passion.

When dawn came to lighten the room, Leah gave a soft sigh of satisfaction. Cain was cuddling her, his hand around her middle. He had made love to her last night until she thought she would die from the pure joy of it.

"Morning," he whispered near her ear.

"Morning." Maybe she should feel shy and awkward, but she didn't. Rolling onto her back, she looped her arms around his neck. "I had the most wonderful dream last night."

He nuzzled her throat, fiercely holding her to him. "That wasn't a dream."

"It had to have been," she teased lovingly. "Nothing in my life has ever been that good."

"Maybe we should have a repeat performance so you'll know," he said, his voice hoarse with tenderness.

"I think we should," she breathed. "Oh, Cain, I think we should."

The island became their personal paradise. With less than a week left of the expedition, they spent long hours with each other, never speaking of the morrow or life back in San Diego. At night, Cain would reach for her, loving her with a tenderness that managed to steal her breath.

During the day he was often at her side, taking her picture. Leah was uncomfortable with that, but didn't want anything to ruin this idyllic happiness.

With a deep sense of regret, Leah packed for their return trip to San Diego. They had found this complete sharing of themselves so late, Leah feared it would all be ruined once they returned to civilization.

On their last morning together, Leah lay in Cain's arms, dreading the time Hugh would arrive. Their luggage was packed, their gear lined up in the outer room ready to be delivered to the boat.

Almost shyly, Leah dressed, pulling the jeans over her slim, narrow hips. Not until she was finished did she realize that Cain had been watching her. There seemed little need for modesty now, and yet she blushed when she discovered he'd been studying her so intently.

"Hugh will be here anytime now," she murmured, glancing away.

"Yes," Cain answered awkwardly.

She was headed for the door when Cain stopped her. "Leah."

She turned, uncertain.

"I thought you might want this." The gold necklace Siggy had given her was dangling from his hand.

Leah couldn't have been more shocked if he'd slapped her face. She stared at it, and the color drained from her motionless features.

Then she understood as clearly as if he were shouting it at her. Their time together was over. When they arrived back in San Diego, he would go about his life, and she should do the same.

Her chin trembled, and she bit into her bottom lip as she reached across the short distance and snapped the gold heart from his grasp.

Chapter 8

"Leah!" Surprise and delight lit up the aged face as Dr. Brewster stood and moved to the front of his desk. "My dear, you look absolutely radiant." He gave her a brief hug and, shaking his round face with wonder, took a step back. "How tan you are. You remind me more of a golden goddess than a capable scientist."

Leah's thick lashes lowered with the praise, not knowing how to deal with such wholehearted approval. "Thank you."

"Where's Cain?"

Leah's heart constricted painfully. She didn't know where he was. Not exactly. Somewhere in San Diego, she assumed. He'd dropped her off at her apartment, his face a tight mask, wiped clean of expression. His last words were that he'd contact her when the film had been developed. With her heart crying out to stop him, Leah had given a perfunctory nod and told him that would be fine. Neither one mentioned the divorce, although according to their written agreement it was to take place within a week of their return.

"Leah?" Dr. Brewster prompted. "I was asking you about Cain."

"He'll be contacting you soon." Her answering smile was weak and a little wobbly. Being without Cain was still so new. She had tried to sound reassuring and happy but knew that she had failed miserably.

"Sit down," he ordered, his voice laced with concern. "You look like you're dead on your feet. I'm so anxious to hear of your findings. Tell me everything."

Leah did as he bid, sitting on the chair opposite her mentor's huge desk. She didn't know where to begin. "Cain was a wonderful help," she murmured, lacing her fingers together tightly in her lap. "He helped me in every aspect of the expedition and still managed to obtain some fantastic photographs."

"I knew he would." Walking to the other side of the small office, Dr. Brewster poured Leah a cup of tea, adding two lumps of sugar to the steaming liquid.

Dr. Brewster was well aware that Leah drank her tea straight, and the action brought a sad smile to her face. Like Cain, Dr. Brewster seemed intent on fattening her up.

"I personally chose Cain Hawkins," he explained, and handed Leah the cup and saucer. "Of all the peo-

ple I know in this world, Cain seemed the best man
for the job."

"Yes, of course." Leah's gaze refused to meet his.

"I can't tell you how pleased I am that you two re-
solved your differences."

A bubble of laughter nearly escaped from her throat.
She wondered what Dr. Brewster would think if he
knew to what extent they had settled their "differences."

Facing such eager enthusiasm, Leah began to tell him
about her adventures on the island. They talked nonstop
for an hour, until Dr. Brewster was reluctantly forced
to leave for class. He hugged her again as she rose, a
gesture Leah found strangely comforting.

"I'll be bringing the documents in to you at the end
of the week," she assured him as they stepped out of
his office. Together they headed across the lush rolling hills of lawn that comprised the university campus.

Two young men dressed in tattered cutoffs, probably freshmen, were throwing a Frisbee. With a gentle
smile, Leah watched the red disk float through space.
Once she would have found this sight disconcerting.
The university was an institution of higher learning,
not a playground.

When Leah returned her attention to Dr. Brewster,
his brow was knit in thick lines of concentration. "Bring
Cain with you the next time you come."

Leah dropped her gaze and nodded miserably. "I'll
do that."

Back at her apartment, Leah examined the luxury
that surrounded her. She would gladly have traded it

all for another day with Cain in the stark island hut that had been their home. She hadn't thought she'd miss him so terribly, but this ache was far worse than anything she'd ever known. The pain in her heart was a thousand times heavier than any hurt she'd ever suffered.

They'd only been back three days, and it felt more like three years. The nights were the worst. A hundred times she'd rolled over, unconsciously searching for the warm, loving body beside her. Her thoughts were shameless. It wasn't only his warmth she missed, but his touch, slow and infinitely gentle. His lovemaking had never been hurried or urgent. He'd loved her as if they'd had all the time in the world.

Without thinking, she moved her fingers to her throat as she recalled in vivid detail the way Cain would slide his hand over her throat and body as if every inch of her was a treasure. Leah had shivered with delight, teasing him with her own fingers. She had thrilled with unexpected pleasure at how responsive his body was to the mere brush of her fingertips as they lightly grazed his chest. In the darkened room, Leah could refuse him nothing, completely entrusting herself into his gentle, skilled hands. He'd whispered the most wonderful things to her, his voice hoarse and tender, and not once had she doubted him. For those few, all-too-short days, the world had been theirs. Little had she realized their utopian happiness was to be so short-lived. From the moment Hugh arrived to deliver them to Ruaehu, Cain had been like a polite stranger.

Leah drew in a long steady breath as her gaze fixed

on the telephone. He'd promised to call; with everything that was in her, Leah demanded that the phone
ring. She was dying to hear from him, though she had
no idea what she'd say once he did. Nonetheless, her
whole concentration was focused on the telephone that
stood tauntingly silent.

When the doorbell rang later that afternoon, Leah's
heart raced until she was forced to stretch out a hand
and grip the kitchen counter to steady herself. If it was
Cain, she was determined to meet his gaze with the
same lack of emotion that he had shown toward her.
With her head held high, she would greet him coolly
and invite him inside. Then, with complete indifference,
she would ask him to sit down. She was determined to
do nothing to ease his discomfort when he told her that
the past three days had taught him he couldn't live without her. Only when he'd revealed the depth of his love
and humbly come to her would she disclose that she,
too, had come to love him. Against her will, of course.

The doorbell chimed impatiently a second time before Leah moved. She forced a plastic smile on her tight
lips and opened the door.

The disappointment that surged through her was so
strong that she was forced to swallow back a cry. Siggy,
dressed impeccably in a pale-blue suit and navy-blue
bow tie, stood on the opposite side of the threshold.

"Leah…darling." He took her by the shoulders and
kissed her lightly on the forehead. "My heavens, what
have you done to yourself?"

"Hello, Siggy." The happiness she should have felt

at seeing her fiancé simply wasn't there. Only an aching heart for the man she loved, the man who hadn't come. Cain.

Siggy slid an arm around her narrow waist and impetuously closed the door with his foot. Thinking himself devilishly suave, he chuckled and swung her around to embrace her tightly. Leah gave him all the response of a rag doll. She purposely hadn't contacted Siggy. She didn't want him to know she was in town until she knew what was going to happen between her and Cain.

"Let me look at you," Siggy said, stepping back and frowning. "Your hair," he moaned, shaking his head. "Is that hippie photographer responsible for destroying your lovely golden tresses?" His mouth tightened, and with a display of anger he smashed his clenched fist into the open palm of his other hand. "That Hawkins man did this to you, didn't he? Now don't bother to defend him, Leah. It's just the kind of stupid stunt I'd expect of someone like Hawkins."

She managed to contain the laughter that welled in her throat. "I'm the one responsible," she explained.

"One can only wonder what else he forced you to submit to."

"Siggy," Leah groaned with a decided lack of patience. "Cain didn't force me to submit to anything."

Stroking his chin, Siggy nodded thoughtfully. "That's what he said."

"*He* said?" Desperately, Leah's gaze cornered Siggy's. "He's talked to you?" Her mind whirled in fury.

Cain had no right to contact Siggy. Heaven only knew what he'd said to him.

With a snort, Siggy crossed the room, sat on the leather sofa and crossed his legs. Leah sat across from him, studying his tight features.

"Threatened me is more like it," Siggy continued indignantly. "He said if I didn't make you happy then I'd be answering to him personally." A finger edged the shirt collar from his neck as he cleared his throat. "I do care for you, Leah." As he spoke, a flushed color crept up from his neck. "Deeply. Enough to remember that your hair will grow back and that eventually…you'll be my same lovely Leah once again."

"Oh, Siggy." How could she explain that she would never be the same again? Never wanted to be. Now that she was back from Kahu, she realized that what she'd shared with him was only a pale imitation of what love was supposed to be between a man and a woman.

"Yes…darling?" He leaned forward, bracing his elbows on his knees as he looked adoringly into Leah's deep, hazel eyes.

Straightening, Leah offered him a tight smile. "I…I think that I should be completely honest with you."

"Yes?" He stiffened, his action mirroring Leah's.

"While we…Cain and I…were on the island…" Leah paused and sucked in a troubled breath. This was a thousand times more difficult than she'd ever dreamed. She didn't feel ashamed over what had happened. Never ashamed.

"What are you trying to say?" Siggy prompted, moving closer to the edge of the cushion.

"There was only one bed on the island."

"And so you slept together?" His words were low and shocked.

"We had to," she returned forcefully. "There was only the one bed."

"And..." Siggy paused and cleared his throat. "And did you do...anything else?"

Closing her eyes, Leah nodded.

"I...see," Siggy said with infinite sadness as he pushed himself upright. "I guess it's only to be expected. The two of you alone on the island like that." The hurt-little-boy look was back again. Squaring his shoulders, Siggy met her gaze. "I think you should know that I forgive you, Leah."

It was on the tip of her tongue to scream at him that she didn't want his forgiveness. She had no regrets. Instead, she nodded and smiled, knowing what it must have cost him to say that. "Thank you," she murmured gently.

He wiped a hand across his face and dramatically pinched the bridge of his nose. "I need time to think."

"Of course you do."

"I love you, don't misunderstand me, but in the light of what happened between you and this Hawkins fellow, maybe we shouldn't see each other for a few days. We both need time to think things through."

"I understand." She stood and clasped her hands in front of her.

"There isn't a possibility...?" he mumbled, and gave a small cough. "You wouldn't be pregnant, would you?"

Pregnant? The word hit Leah's mind with the impact of a hand grenade. Of course there was that possibility, but crazily it hadn't occurred to her.

"Leah?"

"I don't know," she answered honestly.

"I see." Siggy edged his way toward the front door. "Let's say the first of next week?"

Leah looked at him blankly. "Pardon?"

"I'll call you the first of the week. We can have dinner."

The offer flabbergasted her even more than the possibility she could be bearing the fruit of those last days on the island with Cain. "Fine."

"I'll call you." His hand was on the doorknob. "I do care for you, Leah."

"Thank you, Siggy."

The door closed after him, and Leah leaned against it and placed a hand on her flat abdomen. A smile touched her features and grew and grew until she was on the verge of breaking into great, gulping laughter. A baby. Emotion welled in her heart as she raised her head, lifting her eyes to the heavens, and offered a silent prayer.

Heaven answered her three days later. A visit to a local gynecologist confirmed that she was indeed in the early stages of pregnancy. Happiness flowed through her until she wanted to dance and sing and laugh. Maybe she should be experiencing bitter regrets. Instead she felt like stopping strangers on the street to announce her wonderful news.

The gold band around her finger that had once felt awkward and heavy now seemed right, almost a part of her. Once home, she opened the refrigerator and poured herself a glass of milk. With a baby to consider she wouldn't be skipping any more meals. Cain had finally gotten his wish and was responsible for fattening her up. The thought produced a happy laugh.

Cain. She'd have to tell him. That was when the niggling apprehensions started to mount. How would her news alter their relationship? Would Cain insist on delaying the divorce? With his lifestyle, Leah was confident he wouldn't try to take the baby from her. A child would only complicate his life, and he wouldn't want complications. That was fine, because she wanted this baby very much.

Ironically, the first person she thought to call was Siggy. Her heart was burning to contact her mother, but her family didn't even know she was married. There would be plenty of time later to talk to her mother. In fact, she would probably have to move back to the farm later in the pregnancy. She'd want to be with people who loved her.

Her finger shook as she punched out Siggy's office number.

The line rang three times, and when he answered, Siggy sounded slightly flustered. "Harcharik here."

"Siggy, it's Leah."

"Leah." His voice filled with pleasure and surprise. "How are you?"

"Wonderful." Curtailing her happiness was impossible; even with Siggy. "I went to the doctor today."

A stark silence followed her announcement. "And?"

"And I'm going to be a mother."

Another shocked silence followed. "I see."

"Listen, Siggy," Leah murmured gravely. "I can understand if you decide you don't ever want to see me again. I realize that this is a shock to you."

"How are you feeling?" he interrupted her sharply. "You aren't ill or anything?"

"No, no, I've never felt better." Her spirits were soaring to the highest heavens because her love for Cain was bearing a precious fruit. How could she have believed for even a moment that what they shared wouldn't produce a child? It had been so beautiful, so right.

"You sound happy about it," he whispered accusingly.

"Oh, I am. Very, very happy."

"I see."

Leah wondered if he really understood any of this. "I apologize for hurting you, Siggy," she whispered contritely. "That was never my intention."

"Yes, well, the best intentions aren't going to change the facts, are they?"

"Not in this case."

"Goodbye, Leah," he said, his soft voice cracking, and almost immediately the line was disconnected.

For the first time since hearing the test results, Leah

experienced regret. She hadn't meant to hurt Siggy, but clearly she had.

Replacing the telephone receiver, Leah curled up on the couch and reached for a book the doctor had given her. She read it straight through, so engrossed that Siggy was soon driven from her mind.

When the doorbell chimed, Leah glanced up with surprise. If it was Cain, she wouldn't know how to tell him about the baby. Maybe it would be best not to say anything.

But when she opened the door, it wasn't Cain who stared back at her. Siggy, white-faced and obviously flustered, met her gaze.

"I've been thinking," he said as he strolled into the room. "The baby doesn't matter."

"What?" Leah looked at him with openmouthed disbelief.

"You heard me. We can raise it as our own."

Her jaw remained open and refused to close.

"Of course, we couldn't tell Mother that the baby isn't mine. That would shock her into an early grave."

"Siggy." His name was all she could manage.

"I love you, Leah. I've always wanted you to be my wife. I refuse to allow this unfortunate experience with Hawkins to ruin our lives."

Chapter 9

Cain phoned Leah the first part of the next week. She'd been awaiting his call for so long, but she made herself answer calmly.

"Hello, Leah."

"Cain." Her hand tightened around the receiver as she forced her voice to remain level and devoid of emotion. He sounded tired, and his voice dipped with a trace of impatience.

"How have you been?"

Miserable. Lonely. Afraid. Excited. "Fine," she murmured finally.

"Would it be inconvenient for me to stop by for a few minutes?" he inquired with starched politeness.

How could they talk to each other like this? Leah's

heart cried. It was as if he had never held her in his arms or whispered that he ached all the way to his bones with wanting her. Apparently, he'd blocked out the love they'd shared on Kahu as effectively as if he were changing rolls of film in his camera. Leah wanted to cry out at the injustice of it. Instead, she found her voice and assured him he was welcome anytime.

"I'll be there in fifteen minutes."

"Good," she said, her voice as flat as his had been.

Pacing the living room carpet, Leah tried desperately to decide what she should tell him. She found the irony of the situation highly amusing. She had been the least attractive girl in her high school. The brain. The girl most likely to succeed outside the bedroom. And here she was pregnant by one man, with another eagerly waiting for her to divorce Cain so they could be married. Leah didn't doubt Siggy's sincerity. He would be a good father to her child. And he certainly must love her to be willing to accept these unusual circumstances.

With the minutes ticking away, Leah made her decision. If Cain sauntered in and asked that they make the arrangements for the divorce, then she wouldn't let him know she was going to have a baby. It was important that they not stay married simply because of the new life they had created. She didn't want to trap him.

On the other hand, if he came and told her he was miserable and had missed her dreadfully, that would change everything. Then Leah would tell him she was pregnant. From there a reconciliation would come naturally. Leah yearned with all her heart to tell Cain how much she loved him, but after the way he'd so heartlessly handed her Siggy's necklace, pride wouldn't allow her to speak first.

The doorbell chimed, and inhaling a steadying breath, Leah strode across the apartment and opened the door.

"Hello, Cain," she greeted, even before looking to see who it was.

"Leah." He marched into the apartment, carrying a briefcase. His hair was mussed as if he'd raked his hand through it several times. Finely etched lines fanned out from his eyes, giving the impression he hadn't slept well in several nights. Yet when her gaze met his, she saw the sparks of anger igniting. He looked as if he couldn't decide whether to haul her into his arms and kiss her senseless or berate her.

She smiled uncertainly, hesitated, and then gestured toward the sofa. "Would you care to sit down? I've got a beer, if you want one."

His hot gaze shot to her. "When did you start drinking beer?"

"I...I didn't."

"You bought it for me?"

It had been an insane thing to do. From the morning Cain had dropped her off at the apartment, Leah had known he was coming back. Ever since that day, she'd been doing little things to prepare for their meeting. Buying a six-pack of his favorite beer had seemed the natural thing to do.

"Yes, I picked up a six-pack at the store this week,"

she answered thoughtfully, lowering her gaze so he couldn't read her eyes.

"Why?"

Because I've thought of you every minute since we left the island. Because doing a wifely thing like buying you beer made the ache inside me lessen just a little. Because your child is growing in my womb and I'm so happy I want to shout it from the hilltops. "I...I knew you'd probably want one," she supplied lamely, still centering her gaze on the carpet. "Do you want one or not?" she asked with a trace of defiance, more angry with herself for buying it than with him for making an issue of it.

"Have you got anything stronger?"

"No."

"Then a beer is fine."

At least getting it for him gave her a few moments to compose herself. Cain was sitting on the edge of the sofa when she reappeared, his face hard and unreadable. He accepted the open bottle mechanically and, without looking, set it aside.

Stiffly, Leah sat opposite him, waiting.

Slowly, gently, his gaze moved over her, and in his eyes Leah witnessed uncertainty, indecision and a multitude of doubts. She longed to reach out and reassure him, but they both remained as they were—silent, intimate strangers. A lump of desolation swelled in her throat, and Leah swallowed back the tears that threatened to spill at the least provocation.

She spoke first, needing to break the horrible silence. "Have you developed the film?"

Cain shook himself lightly and nodded. "Some of my best work is in those photographs."

"I knew it would be," she said.

He set the briefcase on the coffee table and pushed back the lock. The clicking sound vibrated across the room. Without a word, he removed the first one and handed it to her. It was one of her, taken when she hadn't expected it that night in Perth when they were meeting Hugh for dinner. Leah recalled how upset she'd been at the time and how she had attempted to look away. It was that night that they'd walked on the beach and Cain had kissed her for the first time.

"Well?"

Speechless, Leah stared at it and shook her head. He'd caught her with the element of surprise lighting up her face. Her eyes glowed, and a soft smile turned up the edges of her mouth appealingly. "It's very nice." Probably the most flattering photo ever taken of her.

"Now look at this." He handed her the second photo.

This time Leah gave a small gasp of surprise. This one had been taken while she was sitting at the cliff's edge. She was wearing white shorts and a red pin-striped cotton top that accentuated her deep tan. Her hair had been cut, the short style wind-tossed and ruffled about her face. She was laughing into the lens, waving her hand, yelling at Cain to take his camera away. She didn't want her picture taken. Again, Leah was shocked at how attractive the photo made her look.

Cain had captured her image in such a way that she looked stunningly attractive. No, beautiful.

Speechless, Leah stared at him, shaking her head. Numbly, she accepted the third and last photo from his outstretched hand. This one had been taken the day before they left. She was walking along the beach, her arms reaching to him, imploring Cain to put the camera down and come to her so she could kiss him. Her eyes were sparkling with warmth and laughter and so full of love that she wondered how Cain could ever look at it and not realize her feelings for him.

"Well," Cain demanded harshly. "Do you see it?"

Leah set the photo aside. Unwanted, embarrassing tears brimmed in her eyes, threatening to spill. "How'd you make me so beautiful?" she whispered.

Cain cocked his head and gave her a fiery glare. "Are you fishing for compliments?"

Leah stood and walked to the other end of the room; her arms hugged her waist. "Of course not," she answered softly. "But in each one of those pictures, you made me something I will never be."

Cain rose to his feet and tiredly wiped his eyes. "What do you mean?"

"My eyes." She walked back to the coffee table and picked up the first picture. "Look. You made my murky brown-green eyes look radiant."

"Murky eyes?" Cain repeated, and slowly shook his head. "They've never been that. You have an unusual eye color that reminds me of aged brandy."

"Me?" Leah flattened her hand across her breast.

"Come on, Leah, I didn't bring these photos to discuss the color of your eyes."

"But…but you made me look so pretty," she argued. "How did you do it?"

Cain jerked his hands inside his pants pockets, then angrily pulled them out again as if he weren't sure if he could refrain from shaking her. "Do you or do you not see anything different in these photos?"

So he was back to that again. "Yes," she barked, "you made me…pretty."

"And that's all you see?"

"Yes." What else could he possibly mean? Magnetically Leah's gaze was drawn back to the three pictures. Once, a long time ago, Cain had told her that he took pictures exactly the way he viewed the subject. She couldn't keep her gaze from the three images. Cain saw her like this? Beautiful, warm, full of life? Her heart swelled with appreciation. No one had ever thought she was beautiful. Not even Siggy. But if Cain could see all the love in her eyes that shone only for him, then why had he given her back Siggy's necklace?

"Leah." Cain murmured her name, pacing the floor. "Look at me." He stopped and turned to her, his face twisted with anguish and some unspeakable torment. "Are you pregnant?"

Automatically her hand flew to her flat stomach. Cain knew, but how?

"Are you?" he demanded with a wealth of emotion, his fists clenched at his side.

Words refused to come. Nodding seemed a monumental feat.

"You've seen a doctor?"

Again all she could do was answer him with a brief nod of her head. "How did you know?"

A crooked smile slashed across his face. "The picture," he said cryptically. "It's in your eyes in the last photo, the one taken on the beach."

Sinking into the chair, Leah picked up the one he'd mentioned and studied it again. Heavens, she'd only been a few days along. As far as she could see there wasn't anything different about that picture.

Silence reigned in the confined quarters as Cain continued pacing. He stopped and regarded her with narrow eyes. "Are you going to marry lover boy?" Cain demanded next, revealing none of his thoughts.

"I…I don't know yet," she answered honestly.

"Does he know you're pregnant?"

"Yes."

Cain looked furious enough to shake her senseless. "You told him, but not me."

"I was going to let you know."

"When? After the baby was born?"

"No," she answered weakly. "I've been waiting for you to get in touch with me."

"Don't give me that," he tore out angrily. "You could have found me if you really wanted to tell me the news. Were you waiting until after we were divorced and you were married to Sidney? Which brings me to another point." He paused and leaned forward, his hands gripping the back of the sofa. "Is that spineless idiot prepared to marry you while you're carrying my child?"

"Don't call Siggy that," she protested.

"Just answer the question," he barked.

"Yes…Siggy said it didn't matter to him. He wants children. He'll be a good father."

"And I won't?"

Leah didn't know it was possible for anyone to look so angry. "I didn't mean to imply that."

"Then just exactly what did you mean to imply?" His question held blazing animosity.

Leah dropped her gaze, suddenly feeling weak and a little shaky. "Nothing," she mumbled, her weakness reflected in her voice.

Instantly, Cain was kneeling at her side, his look contrite. "Are you feeling sick?"

"Just a little," she murmured, fighting to keep her voice level. All this anger and bitterness was taking its toll. "I'm sorry," she gulped miserably. "I didn't mean for any of this to happen. The consequences never occurred to me. I suppose it was stupid of me."

His eyes cut into hers as if he were penetrating her soul. "Are you sorry?"

"No." She wanted to tell him so much more but found she couldn't. If he couldn't tell that she loved him by looking at those pictures, then explaining the joy she felt at discovering she was pregnant wouldn't help.

"You're going to keep the baby?"

Her eyes flew to him in horror. How could he imagine anything else? "Of course."

"And you and…Sidney are going to go ahead with your wedding plans?"

"I told you I don't know yet," she cried.

"When will you know?"

Forcing herself to her feet, Leah lifted one shoulder in a shrug. "In a few days, I imagine." She longed to scream at Cain that everything depended on him. But it wouldn't do any good.

"You'll let me know right away?"

"Yes, yes, of course." The muscles of her throat were constricting painfully, and Leah knew she was just seconds away from bursting into tears. As it was, her legs felt like rubber and her heart was pounding so loud it was a miracle Cain didn't hear it. Sick with defeat and failure, she walked to the door and held it open for him. "I'll call you by the end of the week."

Carelessly, Cain stuffed the photos inside the briefcase. Leah knew by the furious way he was handling the pictures that he wished his hands were around her neck. Straightening, he stalked to the front door. "I'll be waiting."

The apartment was as silent as death after Cain left. Feeling exhausted, Leah lay down and was shocked to wake up two and a half hours later. She felt she could sleep her life away. Whether that was because of the baby or a desire to escape the dilemma that faced her, Leah didn't know.

At dinnertime her appetite was nonexistent, but she forced down scrambled eggs, toast and a tall glass of milk. Cain would be pleased to know she was at least eating properly.

After her extended afternoon nap, Leah had trouble sleeping that night. With her hands tucked under her head, she stared at the ceiling of the darkened room. Her mind whirled with ideas. The spare room she now used as her office could easily be transformed into a nursery. And although her skill was limited, she was capable of sewing what clothes the baby would need. As for the blankets and such, she'd always wanted to know how to knit. There was no better time to learn than the present.

Someone pounding against the front door startled her, and she bolted upright. Had she imagined the commotion? A repeat of the pounding assured her she hadn't. Dragging the robe from the bottom of the bed with her, Leah turned on the hallway light and moved into the living room.

"Who is it?" she called without opening the door.

"Cain," he answered, and continued beating on the door. "Let me in. I want to talk to you. I demand to talk to you." His voice was slurred and angry.

Concerned more that he'd do himself harm than with any fear for herself, Leah unlatched the lock and opened the front door.

Cain staggered into the room and made a three-hundred-sixty-degree turn attempting to find her. With his index finger pointing to the ceiling, he laughed loudly. "There you are."

"You're drunk," she announced accusingly, smelling the offensive odor of whiskey. In all the time they'd worked together, Leah had never known Cain to over-indulge. Not in alcohol.

"So you noticed."

"For heaven's sake, sit down before you hurt yourself." Convinced he'd never make it to the sofa without help, Leah slipped an arm around his muscular waist.

As if he found her touch painful, Cain froze and gave a small cry. He pulled her into his arms, crushing her against his chest until Leah was unable to move. He buried his face in the silken curve of her neck and breathed in a deep, shuddering sigh. "Oh, Leah, my sweet Leah," he muttered unevenly; then, stiffening, he pushed her away. "Before you tell me your decision, I want you to know I've made one of my own."

Leah's blood was pounding in her ears. "Yes?" she murmured meekly. Even if he admitted that he loved her in a drunken stupor, it wouldn't matter.

"You can have your stupid divorce," he shouted with a harsh edge, cutting through her meager defenses. "But you aren't marrying your Sidney creep while you're carrying my child. Understand?"

Tears stung the back of her eyes, and Leah boldly met his fierce gaze. She held herself stiff, her whole body tensing into a rigid line. So he was going to give her a divorce. What difference did it make if it was before or after the baby arrived?

"I see," she said quietly.

"I don't want that stuffed shirt raising my child," he

declared, collapsing onto the sofa as if his legs would no longer support him.

So that was his reasoning. Not that he loved her. Not that he cared about the baby. Not that he couldn't bear to live his life without her. No, he didn't want Siggy raising his son. "You're drunk," she said, her eyes limpid pools of misery.

"That I am. Does it please you to know you have the power to drive me to the bottle?"

Hands on her hips, Leah glared down at him and shook her head. "At this moment," she confessed, "it thrills me."

Suddenly she stormed into the other room, then returned with a blanket and pillow. "Look, right now I don't want to hear a thing from you. But I can't let you drive home like this. You're staying here."

"Good," he said, groping for the sofa arm to help him stand upright. His face fell when he saw the blanket and pillow in her arms. "You don't honestly expect me to sleep in here? This sofa is as hard as a rock. I'll toss and turn the entire night." His gaze slid longingly down the hall to her bedroom.

"Good. A miserable night on a hard, cold surface is exactly what you need to sober you up." She tossed the pillow at his face, then whirled around. "And don't you think of leaving. The minute you walk out that door, I'm phoning the police. You have no business endangering your life or anyone else's by driving."

"Yes, Your Honor." He saluted her mockingly. The action caused him to lose his balance, and he teetered awkwardly before falling onto the sofa, his head hitting the arm. He let out a muffled curse.

A smile curved Leah's soft mouth as she left him alone, Cain rubbing the side of his head.

The smell of fresh coffee woke her the following morning. After donning her clothes as quickly as possible, Leah hurried into the kitchen. Cain was sitting at the table, his head cushioned between his palms, his elbows propped on the tabletop.

"Morning."

His response was little more than a grumble.

Leah took a mug down from the cupboard and poured herself some coffee. The aspirin was tucked in the back of a drawer; she slid it out and set the plastic bottle in front of Cain. The slight sound made him grimace.

Without speaking, he flipped off the lid and shook two tablets into the palm of his hand, then downed them without water.

"Thanks," he mumbled, still not glancing her way.

"You're welcome."

"Do you have to sound so cheerful?" Again he scowled at the pain his own voice caused him.

"No." Carefully she slid out the chair and sat across from him.

"Good. Now..." He paused and sucked in a breath. "Quietly, please, tell me what I said last night."

Her palms cupped the mug, seeking its warmth. "Not

much." Her voice was barely above a whisper. "You said you'd give me the divorce after the baby was born."

He lowered his hands for the first time. "Well?" His gaze sought hers. "Do you agree?"

"No." She gave an uncompromising shake of her head. What difference did it make when they were divorced? The only thing Cain wanted to do was ruin any chance of happiness she'd have with Siggy.

"Why not?" he barked, and widened his eyes at the pain that shot through his head.

"Because our agreement states that you're to give me the divorce one week after our departure from Kahu. That time limit is long past."

"That was before—"

"We didn't list any extenuating circumstances that would prolong our affiliation."

"You call our marriage an affiliation?" Cain emitted a harsh laugh.

"Why?" Leah ventured timidly.

"Why what?"

"Why do you want to wait…you know…for the divorce?"

His mouth went rigid. "I told you I didn't want that pompous stuffed shirt delivering my kid."

What he'd said was that he didn't want Siggy *raising* their child. Cain didn't expect her to notice the difference, but she had.

Lowering her gaze, Leah traced her finger in lazy circles around the rim of the coffee mug. "Is…is that the only reason?"

"Should there be another one?" he challenged.

"No," she whispered soberly. "No reason that I know."

"And?"

"And I say no. The divorce will proceed according to the agreement."

Abruptly he stood up, knocking the kitchen chair to the floor with a horrible crash. "Fine. Have it your way. Can you be ready by ten tomorrow morning?"

"Ready?" So soon? her heart cried in anguish.

"Yes, we'll fly to Reno and be done with it. You can have your freedom and you precious Sidney."

It took a full minute for her to compose herself enough to raise her head and meet his rigid gaze. "I'll be ready."

Chapter 10

The front door clicked shut behind Cain. Slowly, with excruciating effort, Leah lowered her lashes to accept the pain that she'd gambled and lost. Cain would grant her the divorce and be done with her.

Her fingers tightened around the ceramic handle of the mug, and she forced down her first sip. The hot coffee burned her throat, but Leah welcomed the pain. She marveled at her composure. How could she sit and drink coffee when her whole world had just shattered into a thousand pieces? Tears burned for release, and her throat grew thick with the effort to suppress their flow.

Her gaze dropped to her hand and the gold band that adorned her ring finger. This plain gold band had been Cain's mother's, and she had given it up freely. Tomorrow Leah would be forced to relinquish it, too. But Leah knew she would face a lifetime of doubts without this gold ring. It seemed so much a part of her now that she couldn't imagine life without it.

Her melancholy persisted for the remainder of the day. Siggy arrived for their dinner date at precisely six o'clock and studied her covertly as she opened the door.

Leah let him in and nervously clasped her hands in front of her. She didn't feel up to an evening in Siggy's favorite restaurant, watching him down another plate of zucchini quiche.

Briefly, he placed his hands on her shoulders and kissed her cheek. Not for the first time, Leah noted that he treated her as if he were an affectionate older brother rather than a fiancé.

"Sit down." She motioned toward the sofa. For a half second she toyed with telling Siggy that Cain had spent the night. She couldn't; it would be too cruel. But something in her wanted to know if he'd forgive her for that, too. Somehow she suspected he would.

"How are you feeling...darling?" The endearment almost stuck on his tongue, and Leah hid a sad smile. Siggy didn't love her any more than Cain did. She was the prize in a battle of fierce male pride. Cain couldn't tolerate the bespectacled, nonathletic Siggy, and Siggy was determined to prove that what he lacked in the he-man department he could overcome with brains and persistence. He was the preferable of the two, and Leah would prove it to the egotistical Cain Hawkins.

Though by this time, she was thoroughly disgusted with them both.

Sinking into the deep, cushioned chair opposite Siggy, Leah guiltily lowered her gaze. "I'm not feeling all that well tonight," she murmured tightly. The ache in her heart had made this the worst day of her life. Putting on a cheerful facade for Siggy tonight was beyond her.

"I can order something and bring it back here," Siggy offered eagerly.

Even that was more than she could bear. All she wanted was a few hours alone to prepare herself for the ordeal in the morning.

"Cain and I are flying to Reno tomorrow," she supplied reluctantly.

Siggy slid closer to the edge of the leather sofa. "For the divorce?"

Her fingernails cut unmercifully into her palms as she nodded her head.

"But, darling, that's wonderful. Now you'll be free for us to marry." He sounded so eager, so pleased. "I'll make you a good husband, Leah," he said almost reverently. "Making you my wife will be one of my life's greatest accomplishments."

"Siggy..." Leah swallowed, profoundly touched that this man was willing to overlook so much to marry her, no matter what his reasons.

"Yes?" He gave her a nervous glance.

"I can't marry you."

"Leah." His hurt response was immediate. "But you must for...for the baby's sake. I've already explained that as long as Mother doesn't know, I'm perfectly happy to be its surrogate father."

Standing, Leah walked around the coffee table and sat beside a flustered and unhappy Siggy. Taking his hand in her own, Leah offered him a genuine smile and tentatively touched the side of his face, wanting to ease some of the hurt and disappointment.

Siggy's cheeks flowered with color. Clearing his throat, he pushed up his glasses from the bridge of his nose. "I'm hoping you'll reconsider, Leah."

"I want you to know I'll always treasure you as one of my closest and dearest friends."

"But…but I want to be so much more," he entreated on a faint pleading note.

"Don't you understand that I'm a married woman? I'm going to have a child by my husband."

"But…but you said it wasn't a real marriage. You said that you and this Hawkins fellow were getting a divorce in the morning. You said that everything was going to work out fine and that nothing was going to happen between you on the island."

"But it did," she countered softly. "I'll have my baby by myself, and someday, God willing, Cain and I will be together again. I love him, Siggy." It was the first time Leah had openly admitted her feelings. Ironically, it was Siggy who heard her admission, and not Cain.

For a full minute Siggy didn't speak. Hoping to reassure him, Leah squeezed his hand. She was convinced he was about to burst into tears, and she couldn't bear that.

"Nothing I can say will change your mind, will it?"

he asked again stiffly, and tugged his hand free from her light grasp.

"I'm afraid not," she answered honestly.

"Just as I thought." Proudly he rose to his feet, holding his back rigid. His mouth was compressed so tight that his lips were an unnatural shade of white. "In that case, I must ask for the necklace I gave you. I can't see wasting good money on a...on a vixen like you."

Leah managed to restrain a gasp. She forgave Siggy without his ever asking her pardon. He was hurt and angry, and in his pain he was lashing back at her. Leah understood and granted him that much pride.

She did as he asked, retreating into her bedroom and returning a few moments later with the necklace.

Siggy gave her a long, penetrating look, and his mouth twisted with open disdain.

Awash with regrets, Leah held her trembling chin high and watched him go. No matter why they'd parted, or Siggy's feelings toward her, Leah would always have a special place in her heart for him. Before Cain arrived in her life, Siggy had been the only man to care about her, genuinely care.

The next morning Leah packed an overnight case. Cain hadn't mentioned spending the night, but Leah assumed it would be necessary. A heaviness pressed against her heart as she folded her nightgown and placed it inside the small suitcase. Twice she stopped and took in deep, calming breaths in a desperate effort not to cry. Only heaven knew how she would manage to stand before a judge and not make an idiot of herself by bursting into tears.

Ten minutes before Cain was due to arrive, the doorbell chimed. A sad smile touched Leah's tired expression. Cain was eager to get this over and be done with her. Emotions were warring so fiercely inside her that for one crazy moment she considered throwing herself into his arms, admitting her love and pleading with Cain that they stay married. The insanity passed as quickly as it came.

But it wasn't Cain who was at her door.

"Siggy!" Taken unaware, Leah hadn't time to disguise her surprise. Although he was impeccably dressed in a suit and his ever-present bow tie, Leah could see that he was distressed.

"I didn't mean it, darling. Not a word." He moved past her into the apartment, turned and fiercely hauled her into his arms.

Totally taken by surprise, Leah let out a small cry. "Siggy." Her breath came in a giant gulp. "It's all right. Don't worry about last night." Not knowing exactly what to do with her arms, Leah patted him gently on the back. Siggy buried his face in her neck, his words muffled and incoherent.

A movement behind Leah shocked her into utter stillness.

"I suggest you take your hands off my wife, Harcharik."

Never had Leah heard anything so chilling. Her

breath was stopped in her lungs, and she felt the accusing eyes that bored into her shoulder blades.

Immediately Siggy dropped his arms, freeing her, and Leah turned to face the icy rage that contorted Cain's features.

He said nothing, his face as hard as granite and his eyes as cold as ice chips. Speechless, he stood, feet braced, waiting for the slightest opportunity to crush Siggy.

Knowing he had lost, knowing his health was in imminent danger if he proceeded, Siggy cleared his throat and straightened his glasses. "Goodbye, Leah." His voice was low and wavering as he stepped around her, taking short, sliding steps.

"Goodbye, Siggy," she whispered.

Still Cain didn't move. Even after Siggy had left the apartment and closed the door, Cain didn't budge. The controlled fury exuded from him at every pore. His fists clenched and unclenched at his sides as if he remained eager for a fight.

She stepped into her bedroom and returned with the suitcase. Slipping her arms into a light jacket, she met him at the front door. "I'm…I'm ready now," she whispered, her eyes downcast.

"I'll just bet you are," he said with a snarl.

When Leah locked the front door, Cain took the overnight case from her hand and headed to his car, leaving her to follow. It was as if he couldn't get away from her fast enough.

They drove for an hour, and Leah was tempted to

demand just where they were headed. The airport, any airport, was miles in the opposite direction. But she was too angry to speak up. When Cain pulled into a huge parking lot, Leah understood. They were at a lake, the name of which she missed. Several floatplanes were moored along the dock. Neither of them uttered a word as Cain helped her out of the car and carried her suitcase. Perilously close to tears, Leah followed him down the long, narrow dock to the plane moored at the end.

Two men were waiting for them, and Cain paused to talk for a few minutes. Leah stood back, not wanting to be forced into light conversation with people she didn't know and would never see again. Like Cain, all she wanted was to get this divorce over with, she decided miserably.

Cain returned and helped her into the passenger side of the two-seat Cessna. It became immediately obvious that he was to be their pilot. Leah didn't know he could fly; but then, she doubted that she really knew this man at all.

Like a robot programmed for servitude, she did everything he instructed. Even when he handed her a cup of light decaffeinated tea, she drank it. Why argue? What good would it do now?

Leah kept her face averted as they sped over the glassy surface of the lake.

"Don't…don't you have to contact an air traffic controller?"

"No," he answered crisply, not glancing her way. "Visual flight rules apply here." His words were clear and precise. The way their relationship should have been. Where did they go wrong? Leah wondered wretchedly. In her mind's eye, she tried to pinpoint the exact minute that they had made their first mistake. An unbearably sad smile touched her eyes. The turning point for them had been the last time they stood before a judge. Now it was just as much of a mistake, and she was helpless to prevent it.

Without a glance in her direction, Cain accelerated the little plane. Leah emitted a soundless gasp as they left the glass-surfaced lake and were cast into the blue heavens. Her tense fingers bit into one another, then gradually relaxed.

Her gaze fell to her clasped hands in her lap. The ring felt heavy and awkward again. Briefly, desperately, she toyed with the idea of telling him that because of her pregnancy her fingers had swollen and she couldn't take the ring off. The thought produced a silent sob that heaved her shoulders.

"You sick?"

"No." She continued looking out the side window, oblivious to the beautiful scenery of the world below. All that stretched before her was boundless blue sky, empty of anything but a few scattered clouds. Leah felt that her life was as empty as the sky, while not nearly as beautiful.

Unconsciously her fingers continued to toy with the wedding band, moving it up and over her knuckle, then sliding it into its rightful position over her long, tapered finger.

"Don't be so anxious to take that ring off," he snapped.

Leah froze and dragged her eyes from her hands to stare out the window again. She was utterly desolate and so very tired. The hum of the engine lulled her into a light sleep. With her head propped against the side of the plane, she felt reality slip away as she surrendered to the welcome oblivion. Even in her hazy dreams, though, tears burned the back of her eyes. One must have slipped past the shield of her thick lashes, because Cain gently brushed his finger over the curve of her cheek, waking her. Leah's throat constricted painfully at the tenderness she felt. How unbearably sad it was that she had to be half-asleep for him to demonstrate his gentle nature.

Later, much later, Leah again felt Cain's touch. Only this time it was his whole hand as he ever so carefully laid it over her stomach. A brief smile touched her mouth. She never knew how Cain felt about the baby. When he'd come to her with the pictures, after first discovering her condition, he'd been shocked and concerned. But he'd never said what his feelings were. Would Cain want a hand in their child's upbringing? Holding on to the beautiful thought of Cain with their child in his arms, Leah stirred and sat upright. Her neck ached, and she rubbed some of the soreness away, rotating her head as she massaged the tired muscles. Confident that their baby would have his love—even if she didn't—Leah spoke for the first time.

"How much farther?"

"We're almost there now."

A scan of the area revealed only dense forest below.

"Where's Reno?" Certainly she should be able to see it by now.

"A ways," he answered noncommittally.

"But shouldn't we be within sight of it?"

"No."

Cain began his descent, and Leah searched around her, looking for a place for them to land. As Cain made his sweeping approach, a large lake came into view.

Concerned now, Leah swiveled her gaze to him. "Where are we?"

"A lake."

"I can see that. What are we doing here?"

"Nothing." The plane glided effortlessly onto the smooth surface of the deep blue water. Cain's concentration was centered on controlling their landing.

"We…we aren't going to Reno, are we?" she whispered.

Cain turned and stared at her with eyes that looked into her soul.

"No."

Chapter 11

The Cessna coasted to a stop at the large private dock that extended from the shore. A log cabin stood back from the land, its wide porch facing the lake, a rock-hewn chimney jutting out from the shake roof. Overhead, a hawk, its wings spread wide, made a lazy circle above them. Its cry could be heard for miles. Leah sighed at the beauty of the scene. But then she remembered and she stiffened. They were supposed to be in Reno.

"I demand to know where we are." A chill raced up her spine, reminding her she was no longer in the warm desert air of San Diego, but in the mountains.

Cain didn't answer her. Instead he swung open the door of the cockpit and leaped down onto the wooden dock that rocked with the force of his weight. "Are you coming or not?" Hands on his hips, Cain regarded her idly, giving the impression that it didn't matter to him if she sat in the plane all day.

"Tell me where we are first."

He hesitated as if debating with himself. "My home."

The curiosity to know what awaited her prompted Leah to move. Cain gave her his hand and helped her onto the dock so that she was by his side once again.

"Why are we here? Did you need to pick up something?"

His mouth remained tightly closed as he ignored both Leah and her question. He turned aside, leaving her to follow if she chose.

Leah did. Her gaze fell on the house. This was no simple log cabin, but one of polished pine built by a master craftsman. The wide porch and open door of the two-story structure beckoned her inside.

Timidly, Leah climbed the steps to the porch and came into a huge central room. Sunlight spilled into the room from the open door, setting the interior to glowing.

Cain was kneeling in front of a huge fireplace, whittling off slivers of wood, preparing to start a fire. Briefly, Leah wondered what was wrong with igniting paper, but she didn't ask.

Her thin cotton jacket was no longer sufficient to warm her, and she rubbed her hands over her arms and closed the door. The central room led off to a quaint kitchen with all the modern conveniences.

"You might look around for something to eat," he said without turning around, intent on his task. The sound of a match being struck was followed by the first faint flickerings of the fire.

Leah's gaze wandered to the stairs at the end of the room. Four steps led to a landing and then angled to the left. Cain's photographs covered the cabin walls— if she could call this spacious home a cabin. The landing held his awards. Leah walked up the first series of stairs, and with hands in her pockets to keep her fingers warm, she paused to read the framed certificates. Her heart swelled with pride as she scanned them.

"I thought you were fixing us some lunch." Cain stood and crossed his arms over his broad chest, regarding her curiously.

"I...will." Her fingertips ran over one oak frame. "You never told me you won a Pulitzer."

He shrugged carelessly. "I wasn't aware it would impress you."

A lazy smile crinkled the lines about her eyes. "In other words, you'd rather eat than overwhelm me with your credits."

His returning grin was his first smile of the day. "Exactly."

The fire added a cozy warmth to the cabin in quick order. Shortly Leah served them hot tomato soup and turkey sandwiches. They both ate ravenously.

Dabbing the corner of her mouth with the paper napkin, Leah pushed her empty bowl aside. "Are you going to tell me why we're here?"

He regarded her coolly. "I could."

"Then please do. Good heavens, I don't even know where we are."

"That's the way I wanted it."

Leah forced out a light laugh. "You make it sound like you've kidnapped me."

"I have." He inclined his head toward the front door and the plane just outside. "No one knows you're here. Certainly not your precious Sidney, and I have every intention of keeping it that way."

"And just how long do you plan to hold me here?" she inquired stiffly.

"Until the baby comes."

Leah choked out a gasp. "Why, that's months...that's crazy." She couldn't believe what she was hearing. Had the pressures of the Kahu expedition caused Cain to lose his sanity?

"The desperate plan of a desperate man," Cain said in a clipped manner, and stood to pour himself a cup of coffee. He handed her a glass of milk. Twisting the chair around, he straddled it and regarded her as though they'd been discussing football scores.

"You're serious, aren't you?" His declaration was just beginning to sink into her bemused brain.

"Dead serious."

"But why?"

"I told you I didn't want Sidney around my child."

Leah gritted her teeth. "His name is Siggy. Why... why do you insist on calling him that?" Tears blurred her vision. Cain was so full of insane pride and jealous anger that he couldn't see what was right in front of his own two eyes.

Standing, Leah delivered their dirty dishes to the sink. Her arms cradled her stomach as she walked back to the table. "What if I promised not to see Siggy again? Would that convince you to let me go?"

"No."

"Why not?" she cried.

"Because if you have your freedom, you might run away from me. I couldn't take that, Leah. Not with my baby growing inside you." He caught her by the waist, bringing her close to his chair so that she had to drop her eyes to meet his gaze. "You once told me my problem was that I didn't care about anything."

A chill that had nothing to do with the room temperature raced up her spine. She recalled the conversation well. They had been planting the sonar equipment when their rubber raft was lifted from the ocean by a playful whale, threatening their lives.

"You were wrong," Cain continued. "I care. I care very deeply for our baby and for you." His hand slipped inside her sweater. He lifted it up at the waist and very gently kissed her smooth, ivory stomach.

Leah's fingers slid through his hair, holding him to her. Tears rolled unheeded down her pale face. "Are you saying—" she whispered with a harsh breath "—that you love me?"

"How can you even ask such a question? I care about you more than anything in my life," Cain breathed.

"Then why...why did you give me back the necklace?" Tears streaked her face and fell onto his shoulders.

Stunned, Cain lifted his head. A myriad of emotions passed over his face as he slowly stood. Taking a clean handkerchief from the back pocket of his jeans, he tenderly wiped the tears from her face.

"Why did you give me back the necklace?" she repeated, almost angry. How could he stand there with his eyes full of love when he'd practically shoved her into Siggy's arms?

"Why did you take it? I was asking you to make your choice between Harcharik and me."

"Choice?" Leah echoed in disbelief. "I...I thought you were telling me that...that what we shared was over. That the time had come to go back to our lives and that Siggy was part of my life...and you weren't."

"Are you crazy?" His eyes narrowed with a dark frown.

"Yes," she shouted, breaking free of his embrace. "Crazy enough to have married you and even crazier to have fallen in love with you."

Cain stiffened and raked a hand through his hair. "You love me?" he asked in a low, wondrous voice as if he couldn't believe what she'd said.

"Oh, Cain," she sobbed. "How could you have known me so intimately and not know me at all?"

He looked so stunned, so utterly taken aback, that Leah had to laugh.

"Could I have given myself to you so freely without involving my heart?" Leah asked softly.

"But…" he stammered.

"Do you love me?" He'd said he cared, but caring and loving were two different things.

Cain's features hardened until they were sharp and intense. "Are you crazy?"

Leah smiled. "I believe I already answered that question."

Reaching for her, Cain held her so close she could barely breathe. "I love you, Leah Talmadge Hawkins. I think I'd rather live the life of a hermit than be without you."

"How could we have been so stupid?" she asked, winding her arms around his neck. "Oh, Cain, hold me. Promise me that you'll never let me go. Not for any reason."

Swinging her into his arms, he looked adoringly into her eyes. "Are you crazy?"

Laughing, crying, Leah looped her arms around his neck and spread kisses over his face. Her lips found his jaw, his temple, his eyes and nose, lingering every place but his lips.

A low growl escaped from his throat as he paused on the landing. "I'm hoping that by the time we reach the bedroom your aim will improve, Mrs. Hawkins."

"I may require more practice," she teased, bringing her mouth a scant inch from his.

"A lifetime, my love, a lifetime."

Sometime later, Leah propped her head on her hand and basked in the lambent glow of love coming from her husband's eyes.

"I love you," he whispered, kissing the tips of her fingers. "I plan to spend the rest of my life proving it to you again and again."

"You just did." Ever so gently she pressed a kiss to his lips.

"Would you be angry if I got out my camera and took your picture? I swear I've never seen a woman more beautiful than you are at this moment."

A soft, radiant smile lit up her hazel eyes. "I think I could get to be very jealous of that camera of yours."

Surprise flickered from the depths of his dark eyes. "You needn't worry, love. Ever. Nothing will stand between us again, and certainly not my camera."

Not for a moment did Leah doubt him. At one time in his life, Cain had needed the camera because pictures revealed the emotions that he couldn't. Love had changed that.

Twisting around so that he was braced above her, he gently brushed the hair from her face. "We've never talked about the baby," he said on a sober note. "Are you unhappy?"

Her eyes widened with incandescent wonder. "I don't think I've ever been more delighted about anything in my life. I wanted to shout it from the highest mountain." She wound her arms around his neck and planted a lingering kiss on his parted lips. Averting her eyes, she tenderly brushed the hair from his temple. "What about you? How did you feel about…the baby?"

He chuckled. "You mean after I got over being furious that you hadn't told me?"

She nodded, still not meeting his gaze.

He paused and grew so still that Leah's heart lurched. "You want the truth, I suppose."

"Yes," she whispered.

"I got down on my knees and thanked God. I've never been more grateful for anything. I knew that if you were pregnant, then you might be willing to give our marriage a second chance. And if worse came to worst and you didn't, then I would still have a tangible part of you through our child."

"Oh, Cain, I do love you so." Now, finally, with his arms wrapped securely around her, Leah could believe that this wonderful, loving man was hers. Completely, totally, utterly hers.

* * * * *

#1 *New York Times* Bestselling Author

ROBYN CARR

Love comes unexpectedly in Thunder Point, Oregon...

Grace Dillon was a champion figure skater before she moved to Thunder Point to escape the ruthless world of fame and competition. And though she loves her quiet life running a flower shop, she knows something is missing. She could use a little excitement.

High school teacher Troy Headly appoints himself Grace's *fun coach*. When he suggests a little companionship with no strings attached, Grace is eager to take him up on his offer, and the two enjoy... getting to know each other.

But things get complicated when Grace's past catches up with her, and she knows it's not what Troy signed up for. But Troy is determined to help her fight for the life—and love—she always wished for but never believed she could have.

Available now, wherever books are sold!

Be sure to connect with us at:

Harlequin.com/Newsletters

Facebook.com/HarlequinBooks

Twitter.com/HarlequinBooks

www.MIRABooks.com

MRC1772

New York Times bestselling author

LINDA GOODNIGHT

**welcomes you to Honey Ridge, Tennessee,
and a house that's rich with secrets and brimming
with sweet possibilities.**

Memories of motherhood
and marriage are fresh for
Julia Presley—though tragedy
took away both years ago. Finding
comfort in the routine of running
the Peach Orchard Inn, she lets
the historic, mysterious place
fill the voids of love and family.
Life is calm, unchanging…until a
stranger with a young boy and
soul-deep secrets shows up in
her Tennessee town.

Julia suspects there's more to
Eli Donovan's past than his
motherless son, Alex. But with
the chance discovery of a
dusty stack of love letters, the
long-dead ghosts of a Civil War romance envelop Julia and Eli,
connecting them to the inn's violent history and challenging them
both to risk facing yesterday's darkness for a future bright with
hope and healing.

Pick up your copy March 31, 2015.

Be sure to connect with us at:
Harlequin.com/Newsletters
Facebook.com/HarlequinBooks
Twitter.com/HQNBooks

www.HQNBooks.com

PHLG964

CLASSIC ROMANCES IN COLLECTIBLE VOLUMES

#1 *New York Times* Bestselling Author

DEBBIE MACOMBER

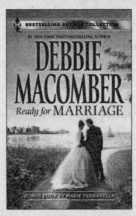

HE'S READY FOR LOVE—AND EVERYTHING IT MEANS. IS SHE?

Three years ago, Mary Jo Summerhill fell completely and utterly in love
with Evan Dryden. But she was a kindergarten teacher, and he was a Boston
blue blood with political ambitions. His family said she wasn't the "right
kind of wife" for Evan. Mary Jo agreed—she didn't belong in his world.

READY FOR MARRIAGE

"Debbie Macomber's name on a book is a guarantee
of delightful, warmhearted romance."
—*New York Times* bestselling author Jayne Ann Krentz

Available March 31, 2015 wherever books are sold!

**Plus, ENJOY the bonus story *Finding Happily-Ever-After*
by Marie Ferrarella, included in this 2-in-1 volume!**

www.Harlequin.com

DEBBIE MACOMBER

32988	OUT OF THE RAIN	___ $7.99 U.S.	___ $9.99 CAN.
32918	AN ENGAGEMENT IN SEATTLE	___ $7.99 U.S.	___ $9.99 CAN.
32858	HOME FOR THE HOLIDAYS	___ $7.99 U.S.	___ $9.99 CAN.
32828	ORCHARD VALLEY BRIDES	___ $7.99 U.S.	___ $9.99 CAN.
32798	ORCHARD VALLEY GROOMS	___ $7.99 U.S.	___ $9.99 CAN.
32783	THE MAN YOU'LL MARRY	___ $7.99 U.S.	___ $9.99 CAN.
32743	THE SOONER THE BETTER	___ $7.99 U.S.	___ $9.99 CAN.
32702	FAIRY TALE WEDDINGS	___ $7.99 U.S.	___ $9.99 CAN.
32569	ALWAYS DAKOTA	___ $7.99 U.S.	___ $7.99 CAN.
31741	THE RELUCTANT GROOM	___ $7.99 U.S.	___ $8.99 CAN.
31624	ON A CLEAR DAY	___ $7.99 U.S.	___ $8.99 CAN.
31598	NORTH TO ALASKA	___ $7.99 U.S.	___ $8.99 CAN.
31587	A MAN'S HEART	___ $7.99 U.S.	___ $8.99 CAN.
31580	MARRIAGE BETWEEN FRIENDS	___ $7.99 U.S.	___ $8.99 CAN.
31535	PROMISE, TEXAS	___ $7.99 U.S.	___ $8.99 CAN.
31514	TOGETHER AGAIN	___ $7.99 U.S.	___ $8.99 CAN.
31457	HEART OF TEXAS VOLUME 3	___ $7.99 U.S.	___ $8.99 CAN.
31441	HEART OF TEXAS VOLUME 2	___ $7.99 U.S.	___ $8.99 CAN.
31426	HEART OF TEXAS VOLUME 1	___ $7.99 U.S.	___ $9.99 CAN.
31413	LOVE IN PLAIN SIGHT	___ $7.99 U.S.	___ $9.99 CAN.
31395	GLAD TIDINGS	___ $7.99 U.S.	___ $9.99 CAN.
31357	I LEFT MY HEART	___ $7.99 U.S.	___ $9.99 CAN.

(limited quantities available)

TOTAL AMOUNT	$ _____
POSTAGE & HANDLING	$ _____
($1.00 for 1 book, 50¢ for each additional)	
APPLICABLE TAXES*	$ _____
TOTAL PAYABLE	$ _____

(check or money order—please do not send cash)

To order, complete this form and send it, along with a check or money order for the total above, payable to MIRA Books, to: **In the U.S.:** 3010 Walden Avenue, P.O. Box 9077, Buffalo, NY 14269-9077; **In Canada:** P.O. Box 636, Fort Erie, Ontario, L2A 5X3.

Name: _____
Address: _____ City: _____
State/Prov.: _____ Zip/Postal Code: _____
Account Number (if applicable): _____

075 CSAS

*New York residents remit applicable sales taxes.
*Canadian residents remit applicable GST and provincial taxes.

MIRA®

MDM0315BL

www.MIRABooks.com